CH004461026

THE SUMMER OF DISCONTENT

HISTORICAL MYSTERIES COLLECTION

BARBARA GASKELL DENVIL

Copyright © 2020 by Gaskell Publishing
All Rights Reserved, no part of this book may be
Reproduced without prior permission of the author
except in the case of brief quotations and reviews

Cover design by
It's A Wrap

ALSO BY BARBARA GASKELL DENVIL

HISTORICAL FOREWORD

While I am an ardent follower of accuracy when writing of history, my own beliefs, based on documentation and strict logic, do not always coincide with others' chosen opinions. These facts, however, cannot be disproved, and instead I hope they will be proved correct one day.

My insistence on accuracy, however, is contradicted by one other small point, for I purposefully do not use the vocabulary of the time. If I did so, very few today would be able to understand it, and even those who could wrestle out the meaning, would be infuriated by the difficulty. I therefore use modern English, and this includes many words which were not known at all during that time.

I do not use words which rely on scientific breakthrough, such as 'sadism' or 'graphic' nor 'gravity', but I do not stick only to medieval terminology. Apologies. But everything else in the storyline follows the natural life of those living in the year 1483.

Regards

Barbara Gaskell Denvil

Anne C
for all your wonderful encouragement

CHAPTER ONE

The tiles shone like marble beneath his feet, but a tiny scurrying black beetle was spoiling the perfection. Without bending, he tipped it onto its back with the toe of his shoe and watched as it lay there attempting frantically to right itself. Lord Hylton then stamped down his heel and crushed it into the flagstones.

Looking up, his gaze returned to the Royal Crowning and Anointing now taking place at the Abbey of Westminster. He wished he could grind the new king underfoot as easily, but that plan would have to wait. He coughed loudly, then sniffed, wiping his nose on his long velvet sleeve, but avoiding the gold embroidered cuff which bore his own coat of arms. The smeared velvet showed remarkably well in the shimmering candlelight.

This continuous disruption was embarrassing to most, although clearly not to the man making all the noise. Lord Wetheral, standing to his left, nudged, but Lord Charles, Earl of Hylton, scowled back and continued to splutter. For a moment it seemed he might heave up his breakfast ale. Some wondered if the poor man was about to faint or die from a heart attack. Anyone dropping dead at the new king's coronation would hardly be seen as a good omen.Gradually it became obvious that the suffering, the cold and the cough, were entirely

1

unnecessary, being simply the most flamboyantly disruptive manner in which Sir Charles hoped he might interrupt the grandest coronation of the century. Bourchier, Archbishop of Canterbury, heard nothing and continued the ceremony as their majesties sat peacefully and breathed in the almost unbelievable magnificence. More than a thousand candles glittered, each flame illuminating the huge vaulted roof, the rich colours of the glass in the many windows, the swirling silks, damasks and velvets, and the gleaming polish of the trumpets.

Sunday, 6th day of July, and the weather was glorious. In the great Abbey of Westminster and seated on the traditional marble chair, royal seat of justice, surrounded by the greatest lords of the land and by the massed officials of the Law, in front of the crammed body of London's people and flanked by clerics, Richard, Lord Protector and Duke of Gloucester, took the oath of allegiance to England as rightful King and Liege Lord, unto death. And then, being who he was and had always been, he extended the public ceremony, beginning his rule with a statement of intention, declaring that henceforth all men, for the first time in history, would be considered equal in the sight of Law and that bribery and corruption of Justice would cease henceforth. He then called for the presence of one of his past Woodville enemies, a man who had been working against him and was hiding in the sanctuary. The man was brought. Richard took his hand and promised friendship, offering the same to any who would promise loyalty. He then swore to rule with impartiality and without malice, trusting to God to guide him and lead him in justice in all things.

And so the new King Richard III left the grand hall of Westminster and went directly to the shrine of Edward the Confessor in the Abbey, where he knelt and prayed, and accepted, before God, his destiny as long as he might be blessed to live.

The new king was crowned and anointed beside his queen. A double coronation was rare enough, but one so colourfully beautiful had rarely been seen before. Velvet and ermine swished as the great flowing robes clustered beneath the swinging banners. The procession from the Tower, the walk from the Abbey to Westminster

Hall, the cheering of the people in their thousands and the sunbeams gleaming on the golden crown were all magnificently celebrated.

The following feast was a much proclaimed success with a multitude of dishes over two courses, and lavish gallons of excellent Burgundy which had half the lords rushing behind the screens to piss out the excess and rush back to their benches to drink some more. Those who, after several hours of festivity, fell from their seats in alcoholic unconsciousness had to be kicked under the tables since otherwise they spoiled the aristocratic elegance of the evening.

Richard, who drank very little, and Anne, who only sipped from her cup, smiled gently at each other as though in sweet approval of all they saw spread before them. It was Richard, however, who whispered quietly to his queen, "Is that Buckingham I saw sliding beneath his bench, cup still in hand?"

And Anne, suppressing the laugh, replied, "I expect so, my dear. Although I am very carefully not watching. My crown is so heavy, I can't move, or it will topple. So, I'm simply concentrating on staring straight ahead."

Which is when Richard passed her a slice of roast venison and asked if she'd like him to feed her by spoon, or by fingers. She told him to behave himself, giggled, but took the venison anyway.

Lord Hylton complained that the third course had been shamefully inadequate, comprising only the sugar sculpture which no one could eat anyway, but since his platter was still covered by pork chunks and walnuts with herbs and spices, he could not claim to be on the brink of starvation. He burped as he stood, and admitted to the Lord Sunderland, who was also rising from the table, that he had enjoyed every crumb. Yet this did not stop Lord Charles from riding back to his three storey home in The Strand, cursing the stable boys, glaring at the head steward who opened the door to him, swearing at his little brother, and slapping his sister extremely hard across her face before stamping upstairs, half pissed, to his bedchamber. There he kicked open the door, roared for his valet and the page to light the candles, then sank back on the heaped pillows and smiled to himself. The palm of his right hand stung a little, but that was something he enjoyed. It meant that Louisa's cheek would be stinging far, far worse.

In her own bedchamber nearly an hour later, she stood in the garderobe with a malevolent grunt and considered her reflection in the small framed mirror, inspecting the bright red flush over one cheek. "I'll hammer him one day," Louisa mumbled to the glowering face opposite.

"I'll do it one day, big bullying hypocrite," Francis told his own bedchamber, unsheathing an imaginary sword. At fourteen years, however, when his elder brother Charles, lord and earl, was just turned twenty-five, this was optimistic, and he knew he would have to wait. Patience, his tutor had told him, was a virtue, even if murder wasn't.

With a new king on the English throne, the country individually decided on approval or disapproval regarding the unexpected change, and generally agreed it would make little difference in the end. Kings often promised a lot and then managed none of it. This king had promised some excellent improvements such as fighting corruption and not demanding loans which would never be paid back. Most of the people, however, would be convinced only when they saw it. Some, and the lords in particular, were at least relieved that the monarch would no longer be a child, since children on the throne were invariably controlled by some ungracious family member. This time it would have been a Woodville, most of them grasping and defiant without scruples or any right to rule.

Richard wasn't as impressive as his older brother had been, but he was known to be hard working, often humorous and charming, passionate concerning loyalty and justice, and was highly religious. He had, however, long avoided court gossip and the endless conspiracies by living with his wife in the north, and so his friends were either country bumpkins or those who knew little of him in spite of claiming otherwise.

Summer and not quite dark, the trees were silhouetted against a vivid blue as the gloaming oozed between the branches. A late blackbird trilled his territory as the first owl of the twilight called to the sunset. At the back of the house the Thames surged downstream, high tide as the pike, trout, tench and roach swam amongst the silt, feeding on the muck thrown out by London's citizens.

Louisa watched the moon slip up from the horizon. As a young unmarried sister, she had been too unimportant to attend the coronation and now she was neither tired nor content. She wore only her bedrobe, had dismissed the two maids, and stood quietly at the window, fists clenched and her thoughts running ahead into the future. As the moon's halo silvered, she heard singing, and knew this could be neither of her brothers. The voice was mature, masculine and unusually beautiful. One of the young eunuchs from the Abbey choir perhaps, repeating his melodies from the coronation. She listened and it distracted her, but when she climbed into bed, she could not sleep, yet still dreamed. It was the dream of escape.

Married once, almost, the memory of that introduction haunted her nights. It had been the previous winter, when she was still eighteen, that Charles had arranged the union and proudly brought the great man to meet his intended. Baron Newport, wealthy, willing and seventy-three years old, he was bald, limped with a gout riddled leg, and leered above the short grey beard. Although disgusted with the idea of this creature in her bed, she had felt more pity than revulsion. Holding out her hand, she curtsied and smiled.

"My lord."

"My sweet little lady." And he had wrapped one eager arm around her, his large hand squeezing her breast while his other hand rubbed down her back.

"I won't marry him," Louisa told Charles afterwards.

"You'll do as you're told, my girl," and her brother slammed his fist into her belly, throwing her backwards to the rug and perilously close to the fire blazing behind the grate.

"I won't. I'll run away. You saw what he did. You shouldn't want that vile creature in our family."

He locked her in her bedchamber for five days, but she did not relent on her release, and Charles reluctantly halted the marital arrangements. His own wife had died after only two years of marriage. It seemed that the curse of the Hyltons would not loosen its clutch.

Not having forgiven her, Charles spoke to his sister less since the cancellation of the engagement and slapped her more. When furious with mother, wife, servants or brother, he had always punched Louisa. Now the habit multiplied. She had not yet risked further violence by punching him back.

The door clicked open although Louisa had already climbed into bed and snuggled beneath the soft fluff filled eiderdown. Few would disobey her orders and creep into her chamber after she had sent all servants away. Even Francis, even Charles, would not care to enter a female's private chamber without first knocking. Then, peering up and discovering who it was, Louisa smiled. Even though it was a servant, this woman was always welcome.

"Bella, come in. But hush."

Isabella slid silently through the open crack of the door and closed it behind her. Sitting on the side of the mattress, she leaned over and kissed Louisa's cheek. "My lovely child, the bruise will soon fade."

"I shall run away," Louisa insisted.

Having heard these words before, the old nurse patted Louisa's hand. "You turned down your one opportunity to escape," she said softly. "Marriage would have brought you freedom from your brother, my love. And once your husband left you a widow, for he was elderly after all, your freedom would have been complete."

"After sharing that vile old monster's bed for goodness knows how many years."

"A fate most of us have to accept," the nurse said calmly.

"You were never wedded," Louisa objected. "And you had me as a baby without even having to give birth. Perhaps I'll run away and pretend I'm a nurse and work for some lady looking after her children."

Pulling a face, Nurse Isabella said, "But I promise you, my dearest, not every moment was a joy. Oh, with you, yes indeed." She sighed. "But other problems arose. Some extremely unpleasant problems."

"Like changing nether cloths and getting baby pee on your fingers and baby puke on your apron?"

Isabella didn't laugh as had been expected. She lowered her eyes. "I will not break the promises I once made," she murmured. "Nor speak of past history. Nor," and she lowered her voice even further, saying, "can I explain those matters which once you asked me."

Thinking quickly through her own flurry, Louisa tried to remember what never answered questions she had once asked, and finally remembered a few. "So why didn't you ever marry? And why is my brother Charles such a pig? And what did my parents die of so young? And what was my mother like?"

She had, it seemed, hovered close to the relevant questions. "Your mother was a poor abused saint," Isabella said, "and your father was not. And that's all I can tell you."

After another kiss on forehead and burning cheek, Nurse Isabella stood, stretched her back, and trotted silently from the room.

Left to wonder what on earth had been hinted, Louisa planned to ambush her nurse one morning. Not that this had ever served her in the past, but it seemed that Isabella was longing to tell her story after such a long obedient silence. Having protested promises of secrecy, the woman had promptly hinted at revealing the hidden truth, with a clear indication that whatever dreadful secrets concerning her parents remained concealed, there were interesting facts which just might soon come to light. Louisa curled quite cheerfully between the covers, entirely forgetting the remaining discomfort from the marks on her cheek.

CHAPTER TWO

Doric flung the small paper arrow so high, the sun permitted no scrutiny. His aim had seemed unimportant, since gazing into that golden blindness seemed as magical as the young man had claimed. And when the little dart, fashioned from something so fragile and yet so expensive as paper, somehow returned festooned in leaves, three types, all firmly attached, the crowd was utterly converted. Oak leaves spread over the dart's tip, three of them, though one a touch dead and dried up at the edges. Along one folded side, the twitches of fir leaf were attached, and on the other side were three dropping willow fronds. The crowd stared in wonder at the spectacular change and gasped in chorus.

While the girl climbed carefully from the tree, unnoticed by an eager and clustering crowd, the young man collected the money which had been wagered against him, now having proved to all that he was a magician of the highest grade.

"I never thought," one old woman said. "them magic stories were true before. Only the Lord God and His Son on Earth can do aught like that. But you is surely a warlock, my lad, and I's mighty pleased to know you. Can you tell me what's coming for me, then?"

"Telling fortunes costs too, I'm afraid," the young man said. "But just a penny for you, mistress."

She struggled with an empty purse and dragged out two half pennies, handing them over without hesitation. It was Doric who then hesitated, returned one half penny, and said softly that he'd accept no more. Then, gazing at her open, grubby and very wrinkled palm, he said, "I believe your husband died recently, and left you destitute."

The woman started, open mouthed. A front tooth wobbled. "'Tis true, lad. How'd you know that? You bin talking to me neighbours?"

Doric shook his head but smiled. "I can tell you something else, mistress, which none of your neighbours would know." And he dropped his voice, almost whispering. "I doubt you know it yourself, but before his stroke, he hid money outside the back window. There's a gap there, I think, perhaps between the cobbles, or maybe where the walls have shrunk inwards. He's left you no fortune, mistress, but there's a few shillings, and that will help you while you go looking for your son. Your son lives in Sparrint, two villages east. His wife will welcome you. No value in living alone."

Having turned away, he didn't see the wash of flushed excitement which turned the woman's face scarlet. She grabbed at his departing sleeve. "I reckons you's a magician right and proper, lad," she mumbled at him.

'Bless you, warlock, bless you indeed."

Now down from the tree where she had caught the paper dart and exchanged it for the other, Lizzie pouted. "That's mean," she told him under her breath. "Taking the old crone's last coin and filling her head with hopeful rubbish. She'll probably drop dead on the road home."

"You'll never know." He laughed at her.

The sunshine was fervent, and the larks were singing. Lizzie turned away, shrugging., walked back to the wide branched tree and its clinging ivy, and waited for the final bedraggled remains of the crowd to disperse.

Two more came to confront Doric, whispering their own questions. "Me name's Casper," the small man croaked. "And reckon

I's interested in political treason more 'n anyfink about meself. Wot can you tell us, wizard?"

Doric smiled at the woman. Although simply dressed, her gown was richly dyed, and her outer sleeves were well trimmed with silk embroidery. Her hair was pinned up beneath a gossamer net, so signifying a married woman, yet Doric could not imagine that such a woman could be wedded to such a man. He smiled at her. "And you, mistress? Do politics interest you, or do you want to know of the children to come?"

"That might be interesting too," the young woman said. "But it's the political conspiracies we need to know first."

Doric shook his head. "I dislike politics, mistress. But two children, both boys, yet not for two years from now."

It was Casper who grinned and shook his own head rather wildly. "This ain't me wife," he told Doric. "This be Lady Tyballis, wed to the fellow as employs me. So if you ain't got more to say – "

It wasn't a subject he wished to delve, but Doric recognised the need for next week's bread and board. "Cost you a shilling," he warned.

And quite absurdly, the woman Tyballis handed over the handful, twelve silver pennies, and without a hiccup. Doric wished he'd asked for more. Instead he breathed deeply, shut his eyes and muttered whatever came into his head. "It's a bishop. Does that sound ridiculous. Perhaps an archbishop. Him, and a lord. Rebellion, perhaps, but it'll come to nothing. Our king has barely claimed his crown, and he's a popular sovereign."

"What bishop? What lord?" asked Tyballis at once.

"Harder to pinpoint. Names don't come easily." Doric risked once more holding out his hand. The little man snorted and stamped one short leg, blinked his only eye, and told Doric to piss off.

The woman, however, handed over another three pennies, counting them out while saying, "No more will be coming, sir. I expect a fair exchange."

Impressed and grateful, he answered her at once. "I can't swear accuracy, my lady." but he kept a tight clutch on the money. "The name Morton springs to mind." Doric added after some silent moments. "And Ellie. Perhaps Bucks." Then his thoughts swirled, and he seemed to hear other details. "Not my usual predictions, mistress, but I believe there's disruption to come, in both the west and the south, Bishop Morton is the name that sticks, but there's also a lord. of power and high title. Yet the threat is a small one and quickly overcome."

Tyballis regarded him with considerable suspicion. "Morton is the Bishop of Ely. At present he's in the custody of the Duke of Buckingham. No doubt you know all that already? Has that coloured your prediction by any chance?"

Without any noticeable sign of guilt, Doric waved an innocent hand. "I can only tell you what my head tells me. Besides, I have no desire to know anything of the church. Bishops do not interest me, and if this one is planning a conspiracy, I'm hardly surprised. I can only add that whatever seems to be brewing, is quickly dealt with. His majesty clicks his fingers and the problem subsides."

"Mighty clever fingers, then?"

"Names don't come easily," Doric shrugged. "What someone calls us means little enough. I can see the people I speak of, but they don't carry names on their foreheads. Now the bishop is already known as an enemy while the lord is not. Yet they combine, since the lord is a brainless fool. But his rebellion is quickly over, and his death follows."

"Don't sound mighty likely," Casper muttered.

Again, Doric shrugged and walked away to Lizzie, who was leaning against the oak tree, half covered in leaves herself. It was only moments later when another elderly man sidled over, cupped one hand, and hissed in Doric's ear. "T'weren't the same bit o' paper," he said.

Doric blinked. "What makes you think such a thing, old man?"

And the old man sniggered. "I seen both them arrowhead things," he said. "That first 'un, t'was folded up tight at them sides. Then wot come fluttering down all covered in leaves, that weren't folded the same way. Tis a fraud, young fellow. And reckon the fraud be you."

"Ah, but," Doric said brightly, moving quickly from his accuser, "if it was truly another dart, then that's even more of a miracle. Some angel from the heavens must have taken the first, and then sent me the second."

Taking Lizzie's hand, Doric walked off and sat at some distance on the banks of the Wytham Stream. He kicked off his boots and dangled his feet in the cool of the water. Lizzie sat beside him and asked, "So I'm a heavenly angel, then?"

"Of course, my dearest," Doric told her. "My own little angel. Now wash your heavenly feet, my dear. They smell of bat shit."

"This place is covered in bat shit," Lizzie protested. "All sorts of shit. Pigs, dogs, and likely folks too."

"All the more reason, my dear, to splash your feet in this nice clean water. It won't be clean anymore by the time we've finished, but we don't intend drinking it, so no problem. Clean up, sweetling, if I'm supposed to swive you tonight."

"Makes no difference to me," she snapped, sitting heavily on the damp grass of the bank next to him. "You bugger off if you wants, and I'll see who else I fancy swiving, and earn as much and more than you, show off. Telling them poor folks a load o' rubbish. T'isn't nice."

He watched her flounce off, but knew she'd be back. Stretching out, he enjoyed staring up into the rich blue of the sky, feeling the perfumes of the grass beneath his head, and hearing the tiny splashes of the fish jumping and the voles slipping from their muddy tunnels into the water's ripples.

Then, rolling over to the hessian sack he carried with him as they wandered the countryside, he hoisted out the small lute, tucked it beneath one arm, checked the tightness of the strings, and began to play, very softly and only to himself. Then he hummed, gradually murmuring the words to the melody. He did not raise his voice, but soon realised that someone stood behind him. Muddy boots tapped, so not Lizzie then.

Turning, he saw the old man who had accused him of cheating, swindling, and therefore stealing the money he charged for his magic. But the man was smiling. "No, dina worry, I won't interrupt. But reckon you ortta stop them magic swindles and get yer monies from the music. It's proper beautiful, lad. You plays right well, and sings well too."

Doric continued playing. He said softly, "I'm a minstrel by trade, old man. A wandering minstrel. And wandering means nights in the rain and no dinner. So I earn where and how I can." He looked back down at the lute and changed the tune. His fingers on the strings sped suddenly, dancing to the complicated festivity of Rondell's spring, as Doric smiled, and began to sing the most crudely erotic lyrics fitting the melody.

The old man cackled and threw down two pennies on the grass. "Reckon you ortta give them back to the folk you done cheated," he said without rancour. "But you sings mighty fine, lad, and deserves a sovereign fer that, if only I had one." And he strode off, still grinning.

Grabbing up the money, Doric also grinned, slowed the melody, and sang softly, again to himself.

CHAPTER THREE

With Charles out, Francis and Louisa spoke with hopeful privacy. Charles was not at court. He would not attend court, nor in any manner converse with the new king. Invited to attend the coronation, he had cheerfully accepted. Otherwise the rest of the gossiping nobility might suppose he had been ignored and insulted without invitation. So he attended where he wished to make an impression, but rarely in any other place. Where he had gone this day was unknown to his family. They were simply delighted to see him leave.

July galloped onwards and his majesty clearly retained, possibly increased, his popularity. Yet there were rumours. Rumour was invariably more enjoyable than the dull truth, but this time the whispers were harder to ignore.

"Alright, so Gloucester proved his right to the throne. I won't deny that. And the boys are little bastards, so the fool Edward's sons can't even be called princes. But that don't mean they should disappear."

"Still housed in the Tower. Out of the royal quarters, since after all, his majesty needed that to prepare for the coronation. The lads are settled with their staff in another of the better apartments there. I saw them the other day at target practise out in the grounds."

But gossip continued. Since Hastings treachery before the coronation, conspiracies were all the fashion.

It was a very different conspiracy that Francis was cuddling. "I've known her for months. Three – no – I think four. That's a long time. And I know my own mind."

"Francis, you're fourteen. No fourteen year old knows he's even got a mind."

"Maybe not girls. But boys do."

Louisa frowned. "I think it's the other way around. But that doesn't matter, who is this girl?"

"Joletta," Francis sighed, his eyes softening at her name. "She's the Brewster's daughter in the ale shop by the Fleet. And she's so beautiful, I just dream of her all the time."

Swallowing back the grunt of shock, Louisa nodded, and asked quietly, "And does this girl know you, Francis? I mean, is this wonderful love affair reciprocated?"

"Of course it is," Francis said with a look of scorn. "You think I'm a baby to imagine important stuff like this? I've asked Joletta to marry me if I can ever get Charles' approval. But she didn't think that very likely."

Louisa thought she was quite right, "And does she say she loves you too? Have you spoken to her parents? Four months isn't long, you know, to decide you can spend the rest of your lives together."

"If it was an arranged marriage – which is what I'll end up with if Charles has his way, then I wouldn't know the girl for more than five minutes before meeting on the church porch. You sound just like Charles."

"No I don't," she objected, since the thought of being remotely like her elder brother, made her feel quite sick. "Charles would just punch your nose and lock you in your room."

"Which is why I'm running away now," said Francis with a sniff.

"Oh, don't do that." Louisa flung her arms around her little brother. "Let me meet this girl. I won't be horrid, I promise, I just want to know her. I might even be able to help. What do her parents think? And is she the same age as you, dearest?"

"Same age? Oh no," Francis said with cheerful candour. "I never liked to ask her. I mean, it's a bit rude, isn't it. But I'd guess maybe twenty-two or something. She hasn't got a father, but her mother thought it was a great idea except now they've gone. That is, they've moved back to the grandpa's family in the Tanneries. It was that mean sheriff's assistant who accused the mother of theft and put her in the stocks for a day. And now one of the wherrymen on the Fleet accused her of giving him half full kegs to deliver. So now they want her in gaol."

Listening in dismayed silence, Louisa hiccupped. "And you think that's a lie? The wherryman is lying?"

Naturally Francis nodded and raised his voice. "That nice little woman wouldn't insult a snail, let alone cheat the customers. She'd get no more trade, would she, if she sold half kegs at full price? I'd swear it was the ferryman who stole what he could. But it's always the criminal trial that gets stuff the wrong way round."

"Then take me to meet these people. Maybe I could help."

But Francis stared at his shoes. "They went so quick. I don't know exactly where. But Joletta promised she'd get back and tell me all about it."

Louisa smiled. "So you can't run away. You have to wait until Joletta tells you where to run to."

She watched her brother as he turned, about to speak, but then changed his mind. Having thought several times of running away herself, yet without a place to aim for, she sympathised even though she thought her brother out of his mind. Louisa sat up again and blinked as Francis mumbled, "You could come with me."

"Of course I couldn't." Then, "Well, perhaps I could."

Jumping up in eager excitement, Francis hugged her and added, "How about this weekend? Saturday. Or Sunday? That gives us two days to pack."

That evening she trotted downstairs to find Bella. Knowing that her old nurse was usually either busy in the laundry or basking, feet up, in the kitchens, Louisa searched both, and finally saw her emerging from the pantry with an overbaked codling in her hand.

Bustling up, Bella smiled at the young woman who had nestled in her arms almost since birth. "Louisa my dearest, I'm sure you have more questions."

Louisa led her outside to sit in the slanting shade beneath the bower of hanging vines and roses. The garden bench rested in the perfume. She sat there and pulled Isabella down beside her. "Lots of questions, but not the ones you think."

"I'm pleased to hear it, since my sworn promises are as sacred as the holy book."

"Which is exactly pertinent," Louisa said in a rush, "because I want you to swear secrecy again. I'm going to tell you someone else's secret and you have to promise six times over and over never to tell a soul, Especially Charles."

The sun's heat was ebbing below the treetops and a sheen of pink sweeter than the roses, hung as a wrestling echo. The shadows dipped Isabella in grey. She clasped her hands in her lap but watched the skylarks flying home on the breeze. "I rarely speak to your brother, my lady. And I never break my promises."

With careful avoidance of names and places, Louisa repeated Francis' story. "And I am thinking," she finished softly, "of going with him."

Bella dropped her codling. "Louisa dearest, you cannot," she said at once while retrieving the codling, wiping it free of ants and wisps of grass, and took a small bite.

"Then," Louisa demanded. "Tell me why not. My brother treats me like a half-witted target for punching practise. He doesn't care for me, you know, not even one teeny weeny toenail clipping's worth. I think he thinks I'm not worth the food he has to buy for me."

"To leave this house, my dear," her nurse told her, "would be a great mistake, for you may resent your brother, but you have all the care you need, as you know. You live in luxury, my girl, and even your bed is made for you each night. Your clothes are washed, your food prepared, your bath filled each week. If you run, you lose your good name, and any chance of marrying into wealth and title. My dear girl,

17

think on this, and stay here, out of your brother's way whenever you can."

Louisa sniffed. "You're right." She felt stupid, taking on the idiocy of a fourteen-year-old when she should know better at eighteen. "But I hate it here. I'm miserable and I'm cross and I'm surely old enough to do something about it."

Nodding, "Find a good man to marry, my dear. But someone who can afford to look after you properly, and not a brewster's son or a wherryman wanting to steal the ale he's supposed to deliver."

"I can't marry without falling in love," Louisa insisted. "Even though that's what the rest of the world seem to do. Living with another brute as bad, if not worse than Charles? Not very clever!"

The silence kept pace with the sunset but as the darkness silhouetted the trees against the last faint light of the sky, Bella drew one deep breath and tightened the clasp of her fingers. "The Tanneries, my dear, are not a pleasant place to live."

Looking up, Louisa said, "You mean it's a good idea after all?"

"For an extremely different reason," Isabella said. "I could take you there, perhaps, since my brother-in-law lived there half his life and has his own home. It's a vile place for its stinks and as noisy as a cow shed. There's only poverty and the folk are all more interested in squabbling than in work. But," and she paused, her hand reaching out for Louisa's, "we might go together, for a very short escape, but more to rescue poor little Francis. He cannot be abandoned there. And you, my dear, would be counted a heroine and not a miscreant run-away, for you'd be going to find your brother, meet the bride-to-be, and rescue one from the other. In the meantime," and now she clutched Louisa's hand, "you might discover, my love, what makes your life, whatever its difficulties, so much better than many."

"Is it excitement or fear?" She jumped up, almost dancing. "They feel the same most of the time, don't they! That sneaky sick feeling deep inside, with your belly turning circles. One minute you want to sing and cheer. And then suddenly you're scared stiff."

"I doubt the experience would be worth either,' her nurse told her.

"I shall certainly protect you, both of you of course. But the tanneries are a vile place and you'll not be dancing."

"Just getting away from here for a few weeks will be worth dancing for."

"There is one more thing," Isabella decided slowly. "I promised, and swore on my life, oh so long ago, that I'd never reveal the secrets I had discovered. But, and I said it clearly at the time and afterwards too, this was as long as I was employed in this house, and would feel secure as I grew older." Now, should I leave this house, I shall be free to speak as I wish."

"That's exciting too," Louisa sat down and hugged her. "But you won't get sacked, I can promise that myself. You'll still be employed here – even when you aren't here."

"Most unlikely," the nurse said. "Your brother will try to have me whipped once he knows I've spoken." She shook her head. "From the moment I shut the doors here, I will consider myself unemployed."

"Then I'll employ you myself," and Louisa hugged her again. "I may not have any money, but you can sleep in my bedchamber and share my food."

Too late to tell Francis, Louisa stood at her own window before climbing into bed, watching the first white feathered owl fly soundlessly from the old pear tree and into the thicker foliage beyond. She slept well, dreamed of hope, and woke to a dazzle of sunshine creeping through the cracks in the shutters. Hopping out of bed, she shrugged on her bedrobe and hurried down the corridor to the smaller bedchamber where Francis nestled each night. Knocking lightly, she then flung open the door and ran to the bed.

But, staring down, she stopped suddenly. The heaped pile beneath the eiderdown was only the pillow and her brother was neither in bed nor in the room at all. Nor was there a page sleeping on the pallet nor a valet dozing on the truckle bed. It was too early for everyone to be up, especially dopey Francis and Louise half tripped downstairs to find him.

She did not find him. Back in her bedchamber, she discovered a note attached to one of the pegs in the garderobe.

'Dearest Lou, I'm doing it. I may come back with my wife one day. With five little brats – who knows? Don't follow me, Lou. There's no danger and I'm not going to Newgate. Just to a working place outside the city where people need help. Look after yourself, Lou Lou, I'll send someone with another letter when I can.'

She cried. But when her pillow-slip was soggy and creased, she sat up and pulled out the horse-baggage case at the back of the same garderobe, and wondered what on earth she should pack in it. Isabella had suggested Saturday. This was Friday and Louisa saw no reason to wait.

Charles had returned late in the night but had risen early and now sat morose and alone in the breakfast room annex. spooning his ale into a stomach well stuffed with manchet, cheese and sliced apple. He looked up as Louisa appeared somewhat flustered. "Humph," said her brother. "Where's Francis?"

"I think," Louisa said at once, "he went riding really early. To enjoy the weather I suppose, since it's glorious."

"I've an early appointment," Charles mumbled into his ale. "I'll see him later. I imagine I'll be back by supper time."

"I'll tell him," Louisa said, "when I see him." She sat, sitting one place away from her brother on the table's opposite side.

He regarded her with the usual dislike. "I'll need to talk to you too at some point I suppose. I've been arranging suitable marriage companions for you both." He didn't manage a smile, but finished his second cup of ale.

Excessively glad that he was about to leave the house, Louisa swallowed this unexpected news, and so knew that her plans to leave would be perfectly timed. Hiding the scowl, she asked, "May I know – who? and how old?"

"For goodness sake, girl, what does his age matter?" Charles demanded. "Young enough, I believe. But the best suitors have all long been snapped up by the wretched Woodvilles. There's few decent catches left. I know some boy was eaten alive, squirming beside some ancient Woodville woman with a squint. No choice offered to either.

Arranged, and that was that. He was about fifteen. She was well-nigh ninety. No doubt amusing, but of little benefit to either."

"You wanted me to marry an ancient lecher when I was eighteen and he was about eighty." Louis no longer hid the glare.

"That's an entirely different matter," her brother told her. "arranging for a girl is quite acceptable. Arranging such an unsuitable match for a boy is far more absurd. Besides, you and Francis will be marrying a brother and sister, both of noble family and both with an adequate allowance and more to come on their parents' deaths. You should be suitably pleased, and I expect both obedience and considerable gratitude."

"But you can't remember their names?"

"Behave yourself brat. I shall tell you later." He chewed the last slice of apple. "And if there's any bad temper or selfish refusals, I shall have you thrashed."

CHAPTER FOUR

Making love beneath the moonshine with the soft perfumes of grass, clover and daisies, and the rippled gurgle of the stream whispering in your car, Doric found as soothing and as delightfully enticing as real love might be.

He held Lizzie, kissing her neck and down to her breasts as they lay together in the night's long shadows with moon glow a soft silver sheen against her nipples. Her gown of frayed linen, and the straps of her shift below, were now lying around her waist. He kissed the moon glow, lifting her breasts to his lips as he would a goblet of the finest wine, and then bit, very very gently, teasing his own erection.

Then thrusting his hand beneath her skirts, whispering. She jerked, her pulse racing, as he pinched there, rubbing as his fingers pushed inside.

It was later when they both lay on their backs, a little apart, staring at the stars as the invisible clouds dissolved, exposing the heavens waiting behind. Doric murmured goodnight to Lizzie and the stars, turned in the opposite direction and closed his eyes. Lizzie said nothing. Her pulse was still racing. When she whispered her own goodnight, Doric was already asleep. The night was a balmy drift of warmth and they needed no cape or blanket, but the breezes played amongst the daisies and ruffled Lizzie's hair. She smelled the sweet intoxication of their love making before she fell deeply asleep.

Doric woke her at dawn. The clouds had formed again and just a wisp of rose-pink flushed along the treetops. "We need to move on," he said, stretching and breathing in the new day. "We've out played this village and grabbed every penny they have. It's time to move east."

She didn't want to leave. "I like it here. I like the stream and the meadow and the folk too. If we do something different, the same folk will surely come back."

"Something different? Stand on our heads?"

"Play the lute, Doric, and sing. You know you do that best of all. And I can beat the rhythm on the upturned bucket. Or dance. I dance well enough."

"With your sleeves rolled up and one shoulder bare." He was laughing.

"Piss off, idiot," Lizzie told him. "It's good advice. You play well and you sing well and folk like that better than your silly tricks. Why do you avoid it so often? You got some silly problem singing to folks for coin?"

"We walk on this morning," he told her, "and follow the stream over to the next town. Then I'll play. You can lead the company in a spring reel up the banks. But not here. There was a fellow last night accused me of cheating with the paper darts and I don't want him spreading the word."

"But if you're singing -?"

"We move on," Doric said again. "Start packing up."

She sighed, and stuck out her tongue at him, but then packed their bags and smiled and remembered how that same tongue had tasted all of him the previous night.

The sun slid higher, blazing on the water so it glittered with floating jewels. Rain frosted the grass mid-morning, and the stream's waters splashed and sparkled while the swans upended, fishing amongst the bubbles. He was singing as he strode, practising for the evening, avoiding the minor key in which all the melodies he loved laid their hearts. Instead he would sing the dancing songs and the happy tunes which brought in more money and cheered the customers after their long dismal days at work.

'Simmer the ale pot,
and stammer her name,
Savour what you got,
lad, for tis always the same.

Show her a clean sheet,
and puff up the straw.
Step out on bare feet,
And show her much more.

Unlace your codpiece,
Pour the ale in her cup,
Tell her you want her
And pull her skirts up.
But remember one problem,
For the future will tell,
There'll be no clean sheet
For the next lass you fill.

"You would think of that one," Lizzie complained.

"It brings in twice the money," Doric interrupted his singing and hung the lute back around his neck.

Bannertow, overlooked by the Sheep Hills, was built on both sides of the stream and had grown over the years as prosperity grew alongside. Wool was first sheered, collected, boiled to clean, stretched with two metal combs and finally spun into the threads of yarn, ready to be sold. The sheered sheep, no longer sweltering under the sun, scampered back on the hills while their owners sat smug, counting their money.

Doric and Lizzie camped down by the stream where one bank

remained solid beneath long grass, rain damp and alight with sun scorched glitter. Overlooked on the other side of the water by the covered market square, at least All Saint's church spire seemed far off over the rooftops, and no reminders of gospel confession echoed from the pulpit.

They lit a fire before the sunset moved them into darkness, and although the grass and fallen twigs were wet, the flames lit and sparked and Doric roasted their bread and cheese, just as though he was roasting chicken. They had managed to steal a chicken once, but that had been months ago. Now in the heat, the cheese slipped into a melted squash, tasting both sweet and sharp over the hot cheat bread, with a crust as deliciously crunchy as the skin of roast pork.

It was when he plucked at the lute that the crowd began to gather. There was clapping and the chink of coins thrown to the grass. Then folk requested their favourites, most of which Doric knew well, and Lizzie reached out a hand and began the dance. Each hand joined another hand, and skipping to the beat, twenty or more townsfolk stretched in the ever growing line, twisting around the fire's splatter, and back again, intermingling before winding away along the banks with a splash from a swan's nest as she hissed and stretched out her feathers.

"You sing well, lad," the voice boomed behind him, interrupting both fingers and song. "But you should take that voice off to church where I'd say it belongs."

The sudden reminder of monastery, choir and priest roared from ear to belly and Doric stopped playing. This was no priest, yet Doric stuttered, as though forgetting his age. "Yes. But no, master, I sing for the people. This is what they like."

"And the people come regularly to church, young man, and love that too." He was smiling, seemingly affable, but stood tall as a bishop. Yet the middle of his body, which faced Doric as he sat the sloping bank, was a curdled toll of belly fat proving good appetite and a love of good ale. "And let me introduce myself, being the Mayor of Salisbury, north of here, and I'm Master Vanuss, Thomas by name, and I've no desire to stop your pretty singing, lad. I simply bring a reminder to keep the words clean, and not encourage the common folk in such a fashion."

"I sing what is asked for." Defensive, Doric lowered his eyes, fingertips to the strings.

The mayor, turning away, waved a genial plump hand. "Just remember the Lord on high, lad. Keep those words where they belong."

Lizzie stood behind Doric, protective, with hands on hips. "It ain't no Sunday, Mister."

"The Lord God does not wake only on a Sunday and sleep the rest of the week," smiled the mayor. "There's some shocking behaviour we must not encourage, knowing what happens at night behind closed doors. But you'll do as you wish, no doubt, as do all the common folk."

He was gone when Lizzie smiled down at Doric, and Doric looked up, grinning. "We'll not travel as far north west as Salisbury this time I think."

Lizzie giggled and Doric returned to the tune which Thomas Vannes had disliked. *'When the bare stripping of the wench is done and over ---'*

Doric was singing and so were half a dozen others, joining in with the wrong words, and daring to fling out the inuendo into blatant description, the alternative version which the minstrels never sang, but a pissed congregation loved to indulge.

Their money pile grew, and the coins rattled into the fire's ashes as the moon escaped the clouds and the night passed every man's time for bed. Now while the night was deepening so the dancers flung themselves down, caught their breath, threw their last coins, wished a hurried goodnight and disappeared into the town's dark and winding lanes. One by one they shrank away, returning home and left only a trail of shadow, the trudge of feet on cobbles and the faint hum of those who repeated the tunes they'd enjoyed.

Briefly, Doric noticed Casper, his shape easily recognisable, scurrying in another direction, heading further north. The woman who had been with him earlier did not now seem to be around and

Doric supposed she would have taken a bed at some inn along the way.

Finally alone and unwatched, Doric sang the songs he loved, no coarse hints or vulgar rambles, but the minor key of long lost love and the soft voice of heart break. It was after some slow and introspective hours that Doric stopped singing, quickly built up the fire, and lay back, as tired as those now snoring in bed. Lizzie bent over him.

"Let's do it quick. Then cuddle down together in the warm."

Doric yawned. "A pathetic minstrel you have here, my dear. I have no energy even to take off my boots, and my tongue longs for wine, not kisses. Leave me sleep tonight, Lizzie. We've made good money. That should sizzle better than a candle. You'll dream sweet, and so shall I."

"And I can't state my own wishes?" she demanded. "Only you get what you want? Her hand, stubby fingered and forceful, crept from his ankles up to his groin and she pulled back his shirt, thrusting inside his codpiece. Doric grunted and rolled away.

"Leave be Lizzie." He gripped her thumb and hauled her hand backwards. "You've said no at times, and I'd never insist."

"I never say no."

"Hmph. Apologies," was a mumble of sorts, his eyes already tight shut.

Lizzie stood with a flounce. "Then I'll go find some willing fellow with a hard on who will pay·as well as satisfy. I could earn as much as you, you know, bloody weakling. Indeed, I used to before we met. With the music and the dancing I'm fired up, so snore your guts out if you wish. I'm off."

Yawning, he mumbled agreement, and rolled back to smile at her. "See you in the morning, Lizzie." She'd done this before. Doric didn't care.

He lay on his back as she grunted and marched off towards the town square. The clouds bustled to the east but had dissolved from the west and he stared at the hugeness, blinking at the moon and the scattered wonder of a million stars. He didn't notice falling asleep until he woke at dawn with a stiff neck and dew damp hose.

The fire's embers still glowed in tiny specks, but the morning was already warming, and still in his boots, Doric stood and stamped out the last of the red ashes. Lizzie had not yet returned, so, with no breakfast but a heavy purse, he brushed down his clothes, rebuttoned and tied where everything had come undone, stamped the mud from his boots, and packed up the bag, hessian and corded, which he flung over his shoulder.

He found the nearest inn with no trouble since the first street he walked had three, and ordered ale and oat cakes, enough for Lizzie as well. The barman was still sweeping out last night's spills, but he dropped his broom and fetched Doric's order. "You're the lad that stole all me business last night," the barman grinned. "I come out fer a bit to hear. You were good, I'll give you that. And you can have the ale on the house, though pay for the oats."

Since it was free, Doric had a second cup, then stuffed the extra oat cakes in his doublet and wandered back to the stream. When Lizzie still did not return, he ate one of the saved cakes and sat down to dabble his feet in the water, avoid the swans, and dream of a very different future. The past often entered his dreams when asleep but was never permitted into his day-dreams nor his hopes that one day he'd have the courage to play the music he had written himself.

As the sun tiptoed directly over his head, Doric was reminded that this was midday, dinner time, and he had nothing to cook, and secondly that he might as well eat the last two oat cakes since Lizzie had still not come back.

He ate as he walked. Troubled, although not over much, he could not imagine the market for whores stretching into daylight, and even further into the afternoon. Lizzie was pretty in spite of the eyebrows and had made good money on the game before they had met, when she had chosen instead to follow him. It was possible then, that she had finally decided he was too irritating for any prolonged friendship and had no further desire to return. Perhaps one of the night's customers had offered more and she'd chosen the change, without even bothering to tell Doric she was leaving.

But she'd been a good friend, and Doric found it hard to believe the worst of her. He judged no whore and thought his own wandering lifestyle no better. But, munching the last oat crumbs, he began to walk upstream, dodging buildings, storage sheds and warehouses, until the township faded out and the banks of the Wytham were clean again and dancing with the breeze amongst the daisies.

There was a small pier for the flat wherries to stop and gather the wool for shipping down river where the Wytham joined the Thames, and here Doric strolled over the loose wooden slats and stood silently, looking down into the water.

He was moving on when he saw it and hurried again to the end of the pier.

The half-naked body of a young woman had caught on the pier's pillars, but the current pulled her free and she swirled onwards and downstream towards the town of Barretown where someone would surely see her.

Neither wide nor deep, the Wytham's force was stronger than expected and when Doric kicked off his boots and waded into the water, he was able to grab at the hair and pull the body back, but found he held a wisp of dark curls and the girl had gone. Although her face had been split with a knife across her eyes and her skull half open, Doric had known it was Lizzie, He knew her breasts, though now the nipples were missing, he knew her little bare feet and the bottom half of the gown she'd been wearing although now it was hitched high above her knees. Splashing back to shore, he then started to run back to the town, with his heavy bag bump its weight against his back and his heart racing.

Then he stood by the last ashes of his own fire and stared at the crowd. A bigger crowd than his own happy customers, and all now scowling at him, some women crying, and a burly man standing there with the dripping body in his arms.

"Grab that bastard," he roared. "That's the bastard as did it."

He tried to shake his head, but it was pointless.

Doric turned, and slipped silently between high walls, making the path back towards the earlier village, and although it was a bright day, the shadows covered him.

CHAPTER FIVE

The night's trudge from The Strand's great palaces to the filth of
the tanneries on the other side of the city, was a long one. The
city gates were locked, so they could not cut through from the
Ludgate to Aldgate and skirting the city wall to the north was even
longer. But they stopped halfway at a small tavern with rooms to rent
and Isabella paid for them to share a bed, with bread and ale supplied
in the morning.

"We could rest here another night if you wish, my dear," Isabella
said as they woke to the sunshine through the cracks in the shutters.
"No one would think to look here. and I believe a rest would do you
good."

"I look haggard?" She supposed she did. The endless trudge
through the night had been exhausting but it was her bleak
incoherent thoughts that tired her more. "We must have slept six
hours. That will be enough."

"Five hours, Lou dear," her nurse told her. "But if you insist, we can
make good progress today with the sunshine and no one chasing us to
worry about."

"Will he even bother to chase?" Louisa wondered. "He dislikes

Francis. He dislikes me twice as much. He might be delighted to see the last of us."

But Bella shook her head. "You forget his pride, my dear," she said, clicking her tongue. "And his horror of any gossip against him. He can't keep the disappearance of his entire family quiet for long. I imagine he spent the first day in drunken fury beside that wretched empty fireplace with its old crinkled thorn bush in the pot, which should have been thrown out to burn two years back. But today he will rise with sober fury, which is far more dangerous. He will call for his destrier to be saddled, and ride through the city like a hurricane to find you both. But he will not suspect the tanneries, for why would his respectable siblings run to the worst place around?"

"That's so true," Louisa said. "Which is why we have to get there fast." She wore her oldest travelling clothes, but they were fine cloth and had cost more than a year's lodgings, vulnerable, then, to theft and attack. But she carried a knife beneath her cloak, and Isabella was a stout woman in cheap but serviceable clothes, who carried three knives from penknife to carving knife, each one hidden.

The Ditch had been cleaned a year back and was not yet as overflowing as it had been before the ban on discarding waste and using it for direct access from the privy. The old Roman wall was kept in good repair, since it protected the city and the Ditch outside was of less importance. Yet any stench from there quickly travelled as if hurdling the old stone, since chamber pots were still sometimes emptied where no one would see. Yet the rubbish had decreased when large fines were introduced. Louisa and Bella followed the Wall and its outer Ditch up to the long road leading from Bishopsgate, unlocked now for passing traffic, leading to Bedlam, the home for the insane, with the dogs barking incessantly from the kennels outside.

With no further need to follow the old wall, they crossed directly towards the tanneries, and arrived close to nightfall. The stench of the tanning, involving lime and urine in the huge pits reeked out for almost a mile around, the skinned and discarded corpses of animals now ready for the cook pot, the piles of hooves thrown, and the almost equal stink of the old tumbling buildings, tenements half in ruins, but still holding together for the tannery workers and their families. Accustomed to the smells, no doubt, they lived where it was convenient, for no tannery was permitted in townships or cities, since the smell could kill off half the inhabitants. Banned as though criminal, the tanners, having no clothes free of the stink, remained within the space mapped out for them and kept to their own taverns and markets. The dead cattle, goats and pigs, once their hides were removed, could be sold to the butchers, but the faeces and the brains were kept for the huge basins since the tanning process was not either simple, or clean.

Louisa smelt it as they walked closer, stopped and quickly backed off. "It's a graveyard," she whispered. "Can we go a different way?"

"Tis the only way, my dear," Isabella said, "since we're here, lass. The stench dies away after a few days, becoming accustomed. But here we are, and it's here we hope to find your young brother. If after a day or two you feel the same, I'm happy to leave and take you home. But your other brother won't be too welcoming."

"He'd probably try and kill me."

The nurse frowned. "He'd stop before that, I think, but you'd be in bed for a month at least, and would need to lock your door."

"I'd set the house on fire."

Isabella took Louisa's hand. "Courageous words, my love. But you'd never accomplish such a thing, and I doubt you'd do anything but plead for mercy once he confronted you. But I have other ideas, my dear, and if you hold your nose for a few more steps, I'll take you to my brother. My sister's husband in fact, so brother-in-law, but she died soon after the wedding, poor lass, so there's no children nor good memories. Yet as far as I remember, he's a good man and will take us both in if we can pay for our food and maybe do the cooking and cleaning." She smiled to herself, then explained. "Yes, a good man. We were always rather attracted."

"I – I can't cook," Louisa whispered.

"He'd not notice the difference," her nurse assured her. "But I shall do the cooking and cleaning, lass, if you search for young Francis."

The tenements rose five storeys and never having seen a building this high before except the great churches and cathedrals with their mighty spires, while deciding that not even the Palace of Westminster could top this ramshackle building, Louisa stood quietly, staring upwards.

"Only the first floor up," Isabella told her. "His name's Robert, and he lives a quiet life, far as I remember. We were friends while my sister lived. He'll surely remember me." And once again she held out her hand to lead Louisa up the steep and narrow but never-ending staircase.

Both stepped back, waiting a moment as the tall man thumped down the stairs and out into the murk of the sultry sunshine blurred with smoke and stench. Seemingly too well dressed for the slums, he did not, however, appear as an aristocrat in spite of the silks, for his face was badly scarred and his nose told the story of past fights and beatings. He nodded to them and moved out of their way. Louisa hurried into the shadows, but Isabella, intrigued, turned and asked, "My good sir, I'm looking for Master Robert Rudge who lives somewhere on the first floor. Do you know the man, perhaps?"

"I don't live here, mistress, so cannot be sure," the man replied, one foot straining to move on. "But I've an idea I've heard of him from a friend. I would say he lives behind the second curtain on your left after the first flight of stairs, but I cannot be sure. If you call there and it's not the right man, no doubt he'll tell you where better than I can."

Peeping back around the shadows, Louisa looked at the unexpected figure, and when he caught her glance, she smiled. He also smiled, removing his hat. Immediately she asked, "Even more important, sir, do you know of a brewster recently arrived here, and her daughter called Joletta. And a young man, son and brother of a lord, who has come to find her."

The large man paused in his turn and nodded. "The wine shop," he said, frowning slightly, "has reopened and could perhaps have been taken up by a brewster. It's a woman and her daughter but I know of no names. The son of a lord has not yet passed my way. Is this a problem, mistress, since it's an unusual story. Perhaps I could help?"

"I would love someone to help," Louisa said at once. "My brother has run away, you see, because of reasons I don't want to tell. He's Francis, Lord Hylton's brother, and I'm Louisa, and this is my great friend Isabella. I'd be most grateful, but how do you think you might help, sir?"

"I haven't the slightest idea," said the unknown lord, putting his hat back on, the brim covering his eyes. "And as a matter of possible interest, is this first floor tenant Robert a part of the problem?" He raised an eyebrow. "Incidentally, my name is Andrew, Lord Leys. Andrew will do. I can take you to the alc house with the wine shop at the back, but I cannot promise you'll find your brother there."

With nervous repetition, Bella said, "Oh, my lord, we don't wish – and I mean – I would never have asked – but if you wish to help. That is, he's my brother-in-law but I've not seen him for years. Not the brewster of course, but the tenant here on the first floor. We, my young friend and I, intended to ask if we might stay. Not really a friend of course if she'll forgive me, sir, and I used to be her nurse as a baby. She was the baby, but we have become friends of a sort over the years. Please forgive me, I am getting a little confused, my lord."

"Of no consequence," said Andrew. "I own a large but somewhat ill-kept property a little west of here, and you are both more than welcome to take up temporary residence there. Although it is in a shameful state of ill repair, it will suit you better than this tenement building, I assure you. If you have any interest in this, I will gladly lead you there. The place is not empty, but many rooms are, and you're welcome to stay as long as you like. Then during the days you can search for your brother, and meanwhile," he turned to Bella, "visit your brother-in-law."

Louisa wondered who such a person could be visiting in the tanneries. Blushing without knowing it she thanked him five times. "This will help so very, very much. Can you tell me where this ale shop sits?"

"Follow me now," Andrew said, "and I shall take you to the house for the night. Tomorrow I shall ask someone to take you to the wine shop and ale house. If your brother is there indeed, I might be able to help further."

"We might even get a real bed," Isabella whispered to Louisa. "Otherwise with Robert we'd have been given only the floor and perhaps a blanket."

The old house was larger than either had expected, and when they were led through a battered iron gate broken on its hinges and followed an overgrown pathway towards the building, both women were somewhat awed. The manor seemed even larger than the palace where they lived in the Strand. Yet it was, seemingly very old and chimneys, windows and outbuildings were tumbling.

"A home, of sorts," His lordship nodded, and unlocked the door.

They were met by shadows, but through an archway stretched the main hall, serviced by a hearth so huge it might have offered seating to half a dozen people. The fire, however, was not lit since the weather basked in summer swelter. Large chairs faced the empty hearth, and other furniture glimmered through the darkness. A staircase led upwards and Lord Andrew pointed.

"I am never quite sure," he said without expression, "how many of the bedchambers might be occupied on any evening. One perhaps. Or ten. But ten is unlikely although there are indeed ten rooms. At the back other rooms rise over the kitchens but the largest are at the top of these steps. You are welcome to move in wherever seems most spacious and most comfortable. None, I fear, will be luxurious, nor tidy. In this house tidiness is a matter of ridicule. Yet space is better filled. There are too many folk in this age who cannot find – or afford – shelter even for the night."

"My lord," Isabella breathed, "this is so wondrously kind."

"Andrew," Andrew corrected. "And hardly kind since most of the house stands empty. Those you may meet here will not always be the best company, but I leave you to decide for yourselves." He had turned towards the door and was leaving when he turned back, having thought of something else. "The door is easily opened from inside, but once shut, it locks automatically. Since you have no key, walk around to the back. Entry comes at the end of a corridor through the kitchens. You might even find something to eat."

He left and Louisa stood shocked and delighted. "I cannot say it's as inviting as a nice clean polished manor house, but it is so intriguing and must tell a hundred stories."

But Isabella, half way up the broken steps and trailing their two luggage bags, called, "My dear Louisa, first we must settle into a room of choice, and meet our neighbours."

No neighbours rushed to greet them yet several rooms, once they opened the doors, revealed lumps in the bed, groaning, moaning, snoring or swearing. At the end of the passage, however, a larger bedchamber in a semblance of cleanliness and order, seemed to be waiting for them. Only one bed, but large enough for two people, stood central and all around it were stacked buckets, bowls, tubs and basins, each washed and empty. The bed itself was unmade and the feather mattress had been left well shaken, fluffed to capacity. At the end was clean folded linen, a bolster already linen covered, and two somewhat limp pillows, flock filled.

"This will do nicely," Isabella said, unpacking both bags of luggage, then stretching over the bed itself to lay the sheets.

But Louisa was watching from the window and could see the great darkness of the tanneries beyond the garden. Even in the semi-black she could see the fumes rising over the roof tops, the flicker of fires where tin basins of water were set to boil and wash the partially tanned skins. At least, with the window closed and the frame tight, no smells entered and she decided she was going to sleep very well indeed, even while dreaming of her Luna-crazed brother and his capacity to live in such a place of stench and sordid poverty.

The tester was complete and would protect them from whatever might fall from the ceiling beams in the night, but the bed curtains, pulled back, were in rags. "An unusual man, that lord," Louisa mumbled as she closed her eyes.

"Men," murmured Isabella, "are all quite absurd, my dear."

Yet, once in bed and although warmly comfortable, it was not her brother who haunted Louisa's rambling thoughts, but the man Andrew, lord as he was, who offered his home to strangers and allowed what could have been a palace of sorts become a ruin of rust and dirt, broken stone and tumbling frames, holes in the grand staircase, and with the real glass remaining broken in some of the windows.

In her mind, listing such absurdities, she began to wonder if this was some secret assassin, not a lord perhaps, in spite of his claim, instead someone who would threaten and cheat them once he found the errant brother. For why else would such a gentleman help in this manner, and why could any lord look as he did? With a shiver of abrupt fear and doubt, she sat up to ask Isabella, but the snores vibrated, and Bella was fast asleep and smiling in her dreams, seemingly without any doubts at all.

CHAPTER SIX

L ying on his back, he could look up at the sky without the sun masking his view or bringing the squint of water to his eyes, for now it was westering, and the treetops stood black against the blue. The starlings were swooping high in great flocks like fluttering specks of ash blowing in the wind, until they turned in perfect formation, swooping downwards and turning again to spin and twist, the flock growing as it flew, and then in silence to rest, roosting amongst the trees' branches for the night.

Doric watched the birds and the falling light, the rising shadows and the rustle of the grasses and reeds around him, but he also saw the memory of the woman he'd lived with for a year or more, whose company he had enjoyed, who had invariably stayed affectionate and who had kept away the bitter loneliness and more bitter still, the memories of his early life.

Continuously at the back of his eyes he saw Lizzie's tortured body, the ripped flesh and the smashed skull, as she floated downstream through every flicker of his mind as if his head itself was the stream that carried her on. Seeing her so clearly, he was drifting with the current as though eager to reach the sea.

Never having cried since he left the monastery, Doric did not cry now but the lurch in his stomach was of fear and misery, loss and anger. There was also a sense of guilt for had he taken the girl into his arms last night as usual, this could not have happened to her. A customer, perhaps, had killed her. Or some hater of whores, despising the slut but enjoying the evil he could do to her.

The sheriff would have been called, but he had no knowledge of being followed until a voice behind him dragged him back to the possible danger and he sat up abruptly, turning to face whatever threatened. But it was a middle-aged woman, poorly dressed but excited, and he recognised her vaguely although without remembering who she was.

"Three days ago, young sir," the woman gabbled, too happy to speak slowly. She was holding out a shining unclipped penny. "You told me of what were to happen, and so it did, just like you said. I went home and in the morning, I dug by the wall where there be a little ditch tween wall and cobbles. I laid there, true magic, lad, you being a wizard and all that. A purse as full as could be. Pulling it up I knowed at once it were heavy, and the purse were me husband's poor fellow, what died not long past. There be well-nigh two whole sovereigns, since one were proper gold like a crown, smiling at me like me old man used to do alive. Then the rest were in pennies, great clumps o' them, and might be more'n a sovereign's worth when I count them." She thrust the silver penny into Doric's hand. "You gived me that magic predeliction half price, and now I wants to pay the rest. For I's off to see me son, like you said, lad. I feels as rich as a queen, and tis thanks to you. I'd never have dug there had you not told me. So bless you, young sir, and may you find as much luck as I done."

He had taken the penny since it had been thrust into his hand, and now watched as the delighted widow ran back into the village. Lizzie had criticised him for that prediction and he wished he could tell her it had finished well.

Lying back on the short grass again, Doric now closed his eyes. The plop of some animal, a beaver perhaps or a vole, splashed while scampering into the water, and eyes still shut, he heard the night calls of the frogs amongst the reeds. He had not expected to sleep but he dozed, and this time Lizzie's face, unspoiled, drifted above. And then he woke to something very different for six men, angry and shouting, had marched the banks of the stream. One ran forwards, waving a builder's hammer, another, taller, behind him with a scalding iron. Four more, trudging close, were cursing and shaking their fists.

It was because of Lizzie, Doric knew, although it could have been for some inaccurate prediction made some time ago. He sat quickly again and faced them, raising innocent arms. "I did nothing," he called loudly. "Lizzie was my friend and I'll miss her more than any."

With the hammer brandished in one hand, the first man stretched out his other, grabbing at Doric's sleeve. "You'll come with us, lad," he growled. "We reckon on taking you to the sheriff and you can make your excuses to him cos I ain't interested."

Doric shuffled backwards, still sitting. "Why would I do any such thing? She was a friend and helped me in my work. Danced to the lute. Why would I ruin my own future by killing a friend?"

"I dunno, mate," the taller man said, poking his branding iron into Doric's face. "Mayhaps you wanted her 'tween her legs and she would'na have it." But you listen ter Wilham cos we's here ter take you in."

He thought it pointless to claim the problem had been the other way around and Doric rushed into the man's fat body, head to stomach, leaving the other winded, the tall man fell back, dropping his makeshift weapon. Doric grabbed it, swung it full length and smashed the next man in the face. Slipping on damp grass as he tried to dodge, the other tumbled, yelling, into the stream. He had lost his hammer but scrambled out and yelled his head off. Now Doric had the hammer in one hand and a branding iron in the other, but the four remaining men approached, furious and prepared to fight. Kicking and twisting, flinging out both weapons, Doric downed the first, but the three others were surrounding him. The scuffle had barely started when Doric knew he had no possibility of saving himself against all five, so he darted, twisting free and running. Dodging back between the old cottages and the narrow lanes, he doubled back to the stream and without options, waded in, both hammer and branding iron now slotted through his belt. Briefly, he saw the man Casper once again, but there was no time to stop, exchange greetings or ask for help.

The water was shallow, but Doric dipped downwards and began to swim. The sack hanging over his shoulder was soaked immediately, and he hated the thought of ruining his lute, but he swam quickly, making himself invisible from the village streets. Soon he was beyond the last shadows of thatch and the uneven whitewash and continued to swim until he was tired. Downstream, the current was faster and the watery bed deeper. He felt the touch of fins and soft silky scales against his hands and saw the sudden green leap of frogs. Then, with the sweet warmth assuring him of silence, he turned on his back and allowed himself to float.

The cool wet ripples carried him and he heard music in his head, perhaps the swish of the stream in his ears, but perhaps the music he had not yet written, which waited, impatient to spring alive. Doric did not confess to his head that now his lute was ruined he could not afford another. He was not even sure whether his purse still remained safely tucked inside his shirt.

But the drifting, swirling current was a friendly mattress, and as he travelled, Doric waved up to the falcon in the sycamore tree, and the two tiny marsh warblers amongst the reeds. The tunes in his mind spun a gentle background to his thoughts, which were not always so gentle, mixing childhood memories with his own vague guilt, his sense of loss, his confusion concerning the future with fear, then with pleasure, and then laughter at himself for his puzzled meanderings.

The wandering minstrel, and a minstrel no more if he owned no lute! A vagabond without coin or skills to earn it, would mean starvation or trudging the local farms asking for a few days cleaning, picking, raking or cutting hedges. Thorns in your hands, dust in your eyes and spiders down your shirt. He'd done it before. Before Lizzie. Because now without her, much of his magic would sink and only his predictions, sometimes gloriously right and sometimes savagely wrong, would earn him the occasional penny. And perhaps the occasional punch. His purse was full, if it still sat safe against his heart, but that would not last forever. He even thought fleetingly of his two

41

elder brothers and what they might now be doing. Married perhaps, with children of their own. Involved in the usual conspiracies, or simply snug at home with Papa snarling his orders. Pointless thoughts that blew with the wind like the aspen leaves fluttering over his head.

And so finally, entirely soaked and dripping from clothes, fingers, hair and nose, Doric found his feet and climbed back to the bank. Bare toes, since his boots, complete with mud, had been squeezed into his shoulder bag and were now surely too wet to wear. Yet he felt free with his feet bare and walking on grass felt as soft as fur.

His first duty was to his lute. He hauled it from its bag and examined the soaked wood and sheep gut strings. They could still be plucked. Wiping the wood as dry as feasible on his doublet and shirt, he left the instrument in the shade, but where the heat of the sun might hopefully work wonders.

"Reborn, little one," he begged it, his fingers rubbing at the back of the neck. But since he had no intention of playing to any audience, large or small, over the next weeks, he later hung it on its cord across his back and cradled it close at night.

He had coin for the purse had also survived, heavy with promises. Yet if he wished to draw no attention to himself then it would be sometime before he earned more.

Well accustomed to sleeping in the open, with or without a fire, with or without a tree above to shelter him, Doric wandered the countryside as he wished, entering no towns or villages except to buy dark cheat bread, cheese directly from the cattle farms, and eggs from the outlying cottages where a few hens, protected from foxes in their tight little houses with the front door locked at night. There were always too many eggs laid for the old couples usually living there, sharing their beds with the rooster or discovering the new laid eggs on their pillows, on the empty hearth, or in the pot where bacon had last been fried.

So Doric ate eggs, rye bread, cheese and sometimes bacon, thinking himself lucky as he cooked over the tiny fire most evenings, drank from the local well or stream, and sometimes bought ale from the local inn.

Eventually he cut across country, leaving Oxfordshire for Wiltshire, then Wiltshire for Dorset, Dorset for Hampshire and finally into Surrey. He moved north. Signposts were rare, but he wished to avoid London and took a lodging in Kent. With the money he still had left, and as a consequence of the rain crashing down onto his head, he paid for two nights in a decent sized room, bought the first mug of decent wine he'd drunk in more than a month, and added a large beef pie to his list.

He would, he told himself, probably have served himself better had he bought a horse or even a donkey, but he had no coin sufficient for a healthy beast and didn't want the misery of such an animal dying beneath him. So he carried both pie and wine up to his room, enjoyed eating and drinking very slowly to savour every mouthful, dropped pastry crumbs all over the bed and later gathered them up to eat, lit the only candle, and returned to the endless roll of drifting irrelevance which had passed backwards and forwards through his mind for so very long. And he slept.

The rain still pounded against the thin horn window when he woke, so he plodded downstairs for breakfast, and sat on a stool amongst the locals at the small breakfast table, enjoying bread, ham, ale and two roasted chicken legs which seemed the greatest luxury of all.

None spoke, too busy eating fast, then rushing off to work, most starting at sextet or even before. Only one other still sat at the table when Doric had finished and scraped back his stool. But the inn keeper, stomping to the table, asked him, "I done forgot yer name, young fellow. But what I needs to know, since this storm ain't stopped fer nigh on two days, whether you might be wanting a third. Same room. Cheaper price."

Nodding, Doric said, "I may, master. But as yet, I can't be sure. I'll see if the rain's still ours this afternoon. In the meantime, I'll be comfortable here, and will be back for midday dinner. And the name's Doric. Doric Fleet."

It was only half an hour later when someone knocked on his door.

He hadn't locked it and called for the visitor to come in. He expected the landlord.

It was someone else, a shorter and wider man who Doric had never seen before. This stump of a man, his short russet beard quivering, stood beside the bed, facing Doric, his hands clasped behind his back.

"As it happens," said the man, "I was at the table with you this morning, young fellow. A few stools along, but not being deaf, I heard the landlord and I heard what you answered. Now, like I told you, I heard every word that you said, but just to be sure, I'd appreciate it, lad, if you were to once more give your name."

They stared at each other and gradually Doric swung his legs from the bed and stood. The other man came just to his shoulder but did not seem in any manner intimidated. It was Doric who guessed the worst, and said quietly, "Doric Fleet is my name. And you, I'd guess, are the local sheriff."

The sheriff nodded. "And as the news flies faster than the pigeons, young lad, I'm arresting you in the name of the king, for murder and the wicked wounding of a girl name of Elizabeth Bantham. You'll come with me now, lad, and don't think to fight or run, for outside this door there's a dozen men waiting to grab your miserable hide."

It was bound to have happened one day. Doric grabbed up his lute, put his boots on, slung his bag across his shoulder, and nodded. "No desire to fight and I've run long enough," he said. "I never hurt the girl, but it'll be hard to prove. At least I don't have to pay for shelter in one of your cells."

Over his square shoulder, the sheriff said, "True, lad. But if you want feeding, then you'll pay like everyone else."

Soaked again from the walk to gaol, Doric eyed the whitewashed wall, and the double locked doorway, hinged in massive iron blocks as though each inmate was suspected of planning his escape. He would certainly try planning his own, but Doric ducked his head as the doors were pulled open and stood in the entrance. Although it was not yet midday, the cell seemed lightless. Black corners leaked into a shadowed centre, floored in misshapen planks and ceilinged in spiders' webs. He grunted and walked further inside. With a small crowd outside shouting at him, this was not the time to turn and run.

There was no window, but his eyes became accustomed, and he saw four others, slumped on the boards, leaning back and half asleep, against the walls.

"You'll get ale and bread for dinner," the sheriff said, and he slammed the door closed. "Pay up, and you'll get wine and a pie."

Doric paid. "For three days," he said, handing over sixpence. "And something for supper too. But do trials take place here, or in London?"

"You'll be told when the time is right," said the sheriff, swapping his scowl for a beaming smile and clutching the sixpence. "But you've no talent at arithmetic, young fellow, if you think this will cover three meals for three days. Today will be covered, and perhaps tomorrow too. No more. But the guard will bring your dinner soon and give you a reckoning of how long you'll be here, and how much that will cost."

Slumping down on the filthy floorboards, Doric moved both lute and sack to his lap, gripped it with both hands, did not bother staring through the darkness at his fellow prisoners, and closed his eyes while the anger with both himself and the sheriff bubbled at the back of his mind.

At first, he didn't hear the words from the man opposite. Doric was aware only of his own fury and the blankness of his own thoughts as regards escape. The smell of the place was bleak, contrasting so sadly with the clean wide openness of sky and trees, river and flowers that he had breathed for more than a year past. The smell was now of urine, old dirt, new dirt, unwashed sweat, and destitute misery.

If he had once met some unpleasant criminal in the past, it was of no interest and no consequence now. But the other prisoner spoke again. "Reckons I knows you, my friend. Met you way back, I did. Was wiv me master's lady wife, and we done talked 'bout political whatsits. "

"Sorry, friend." Doric didn't bother peering through the blackness. "I don't remember you. Did my predictions come true?"

"Not yet," said the small man. "But tis early days. There ain't no rush when it comes to rebellion, I reckon. But I's Casper Wallop, a right proper one-eyed genius, I is. So clever that I's bin in every single dungeon in this bloody country. I could tell ye all 'bout every one. But I recommend, best not to go visiting them Limboes at Newgate. Bloody horrible, they is, wiv folks dead afore they even gets to trial."

So Doric remembered, leaning over to see more closely. "Casper, yes indeed. One eye, and a lady as pretty as the sunrise. But I'm sorry my prediction didn't come true. They don't always work, I'm afraid."

"Well," Casper nodded, his cackle echoing in the stony black, "reckon I can make a predilicton meself. I'd say tis mighty certain, me friend, fer you'll be hung on the gibbet fer murder afore this month be over."

CHAPTER SEVEN

At court for the first time since the coronation, and with an inner fury fostered daily since he had sworn never to grace the court of this new king, Charles, Lord Hylton, marched the corridor, pushing through any crowd daring to walk in the opposite direction. The myriad of candles in the chandeliers had not yet been lit as the golden sun blasted through every long window and it would be some hours before supper, and the first glimpse of twilight.

The sunshine on the back of his neck was giving Charles a headache. He thumped on the door along a side passage and thumped again until finally the steward opened it. Charles then pushed in and glared at his friend.

"Is it true?"

Sir Alfred Bray sighed as usual when Charles marched in on his dreams. "Probably," he said, blinking hard. "But possibly not. Rather depends on what the hell you're talking about, Charles."

Having sat heavily on the chair, hard wooden backed, Charles now thumped both fists on his knees. He wore one of the fashionable short doublets, but his heavily muscled legs, now hosed in vivid turquoise, really did not reveal the right shape for such exposure. "You know well, it's that undeserving king again. Claims he's going to bring in a law next January against criminals having their property forfeited before conviction. Now that's absurd. Means the little buggers keep their goods and could be forever. We have until January to block such a law."

Calling the steward to pour the wine, Sir Alfred rearranged himself on his own chair, first snatching up a cushion from the bench. "Charlie, my dear friend, slow down and remember your tendency for headaches when you get irate. Firstly, this won't come in to force until next January when the next parliament sits. So, if you've a mind to snatch up some poor man's life savings, then there's five months still open. Secondly, I uphold the justice of it. I know you were a friend of old Edward, and supported the Woodvilles, whether you liked them or not, but the Woodville queen grabbed a fortune from that poor fellow, who was never convicted since he was innocent and we knew it. Yet he never managed to claim back his property. How can you say that was right and fair?"

"I never supported the bloody Woodvilles," Charles grumbled. "Edward yes. Hastings, yes. Both now dead. As for the wretch who lost his goods to the queen, he was under suspicion, and so was Harold Harcourt when I claimed his manor." Charles fisted both hands once more and shook them at the window. "The permission and paperwork has taken some time, but I've been assured that the claim is valid, and I'll get the place in my name before autumn. What if they slow it all down, waiting for the new law next year?"

"Having never heard of this Harold Harcourt," Alfred sniffed, "I have to ask – is the fellow innocent? What did his trial say of him?"

"They found him not guilty," Charles grumbled, eyes to his lap. "But I believe he bribed the jury. The fellow is as guilty as I can be sure."

"Because he did something to you?"

"Of course not." Charles looked up, eyes fierce. "But he swindled any way he could to get that damned manor. And I'd swear my father was one of the many he cheated."

"So already found innocent, and you're still claiming his property?

Crazy, my friend, crazy. Is this Harcourt fellow living in the house you're trying to get your hands on?"

Charles had no idea. "It's bloody well my house now."

"I can't judge." Alfred leaned back in his chair. "You've five months to sort your claim, my friend, and I won't be involved." He yawned but disguised it. "I understand our new king is planning many new laws against corruption. He's even cancelling the tax on books. That'll bring the price down. I'm planning on buying half a dozen of the new printings." Charles stared back, blank faced. So Alfred said, "And what about your more pressing problem, my friend? Have you found your little brother? Has your sister returned home?"

"She hasn't. And nor has he. I'm better off without either." Charles gulped the last of the wine in his cup. "But it's a wretched scandal and I have to find the pair of them. I've a good group of men searching high and low. It's costing me a fortune."

"Have you any idea where or why, Charlie?" He didn't offer a refill from the jug. "For instance, did they run off together? Or did the boy run first, and the sister go after him to bring him home? Or on the other hand, did the girl run off after some improper romantic nonsense, and the brother go after to drag her back?"

"Anything's possible." He did not particularly care. "They're both idiots. And they'll both get a good thrashing. I'll lock them in their bedchambers for a month or more."

"I wish you luck," Alfred sighed again. "But remember one important thing, my friend. You don't want folk to say you take after your father."

"At least," Charles shook his head, "he got what he wanted. A bully no doubt, arrogant by today's standards, but a man who knew his own mind."

"Charlie, do you really admire a man like that? But it's no matter." Alfred paused, and Charles stood, as he'd hoped.

"I'm off, Alfred, and may not be back for some time. I hate this bloody court and the damned king with it. But I warn you, I'll oppose this law when parliament sits next year." And then, at the doorway, "I never loved the wretch, but my father knew how to get his way and lived comfortably because of it. He beat me well-nigh every week, which was just about the only time I ever saw him. But he was no fool."

"I never knew him, which is as well, but I knew his reputation, Charles. Don't let folks say you take after him. And as for claiming the property of an innocent man, well, I'll stand against you without rancour." Alfred called back the steward to get his friend's cape and hat and opened the door. His sigh was one of relief as Charles disappeared into the wide passageway outside. A friend was a friend and as boys they'd shared a tutor, practised at the lists and played at rivalry when shooting targets. But childhood friends were often unrecognisable once adult.

Charles, returning home, called for quill, parchment and ink, sealing wax and his seal bearing his coat of arms. Then he called for wine. And finally, he called for a page.

"You take this to the Sudbury House, the two storey, just twelve houses from here towards the Fleet. This goes into Sudbury's hand, neither steward, the son Bryan, wife or any other servant. Should you be stopped, this message gets hidden inside your livery. Do you understand?"

The page assured his master that he did. He was, however, somewhat wobbly kneed when he set off, and prayed he would not be stopped. The letter clearly contained heresy, treason or something else wildly wicked. He took a deep breath and ran as fast as he could.

Charles waited for the reply, sitting comfortably with his fingers interlocked over his stomach. He was interrupted, not by anyone from the Sudbury family and nor by the return of his page.

"My lord," the steward said with lofty importance., first clearing his throat, "your lordship's groom Jason has returned. He wishes to report personally to yourself, sir, regarding whatever he found on the expedition you ordered."

It was an interesting return, and Charles stood, striding out to the main corridor. He signalled to the rough looking man on the doorstep and led him into a private Annexe.

"Well?"

"We ain't found nothing, m'lord," said the man, removing his cap. "We knows where they ain't, and we knows where they never went, as you might say. But tis nigh on a month, m'lord, and we ain't got no idea where to go next, as it were. So I come fer new orders. There be James and Jonny waiting by the stables, but they doesn't know more 'n me, m'lord."

"Shit," exclaimed his lordship.

"We done the whole o' the city, sir, and Southwark too," the groom complained. "And then we done north up through the Norfolk fens and then over to Oxford after Cambridge and all the way down far as Dorset. Then up agin. T'were a mighty long trip, m'lord and we done questioned every mayor and every sheriff, and at the markets an' more. In every blasted place, sir, till we was total exhausted."

"There are clearly places you've not been," Charles frowned. "Go East and start again in Kent. And even Westminster and the western villages. They have to be somewhere, and they were on foot so going as far as York or the Midlands seems impossible. Here," and he flung a handful of pennies. "I want those two brats found, dead or alive, and I want them dragged back here. I'll give you another month, but that'll bring you to the end of August, which is absurd. I'll pay you all handsomely when you bring my brother and sister home with you, but otherwise you'll simply go back to your old jobs in the stables."

He turned away as the steward showed the man out. Jason plodded back to the stables to reclaim his horse and his companions. Charles, meanwhile, continued to wait for the answer to his letter.

CHAPTER EIGHT

"So what did you do to get yourself into this luxury wayside inn?" Doric asked. "Or are you as Innocent as I am?"

"Me?" Casper snorted. "I's always innocent. I reckons I gonna be out soon."

Food had been brought. The pie Doric had paid for was cold, but intact. The ale was sour, the bread and cheese cheap and tasteless. He didn't complain, and ate with his fingers. Casper watched him. He'd drunk a good deal but eaten very little. So Doric had looked up. "Do you need food? I have bread and cheese to spare."

Casper sniggered. "'Tis a kingly offer, lad. But I's no need of a fat belly. Me master has surely spoke to the sheriff by now. I reckon I'll be out in an hour or less."

"Then you have a very powerful master," Doric sighed. "What do you do for him?"

"What I's told," Casper said with vague dismissal.

One other man sprawled and half slept, while two played cards, quarrelling and laughing together. The sleeping almost faceless recumbent was possibly badly injured, but when Doric bent over and asked him if this was true, the man simply grunted and wiped the blood from the back of his calf. Even Casper lapsed into apathetic silence. The cell walls, without window or pallets, were cut with the curses of past inmates but it was too dark to read them, and the floor, even though much had trickled out between the boards, was a slop of piss and spit.

Muttering to himself, Doric retired to the corner nearest the door. He breathed through his mouth, avoiding the stench as far as was possible, and again began to plan his escape. It seemed essential. Otherwise he would descend into misery before being dragged off to a trial without hope of justice, accept his conviction and await the hanging. Escape seemed the only alternative.

And then after some hours, the door finally burst open. Doric, disguised by darkness, jumped up and edged towards the open door. Expecting the guard, he'd not glanced at the large arrival, while tentatively approaching the slit of light. Instead he heard Casper. "Right good timin', m'lord. And I reckon take this 'un too. Right useful he'll be."

The tall man blocking the doorway now stared, eyes deep with shadowed curiosity. "Your name?" And Doric realised the man was talking to him.

"The name's Doric." He looked back. This was no guard, fine in fur and silk, but the face of a fighter, nose broken at least once, and a scar almost splitting the expression in two. "And you, sir?"

From the shadows, Casper stood and trotted over. He snorted and pushed Doric even closer to the open doorway. "Tis me master, Lord Leys," Casper said, now halfway to freedom.

Andrew, Lord Leys, was studying Doric. Then he turned back to the shadows. "I've come for my man Casper," he said, indicating the disappearing figure. "I shall also take this young man with me, if he is interested in working instead of slow starvation." With a slight pause, the large man looked once more at Doric. "My friend Casper suggests I bring you with us, Master Doric. What have you been arrested for?"

What point in exclaiming his innocence when every guilty man did the same. "Murder," he said.

Doric stared at the open doorway, hopeful. Lord Leys paused again, "Come with me. We shall see what you are prepared to do." And he turned marching out into the flickering light. Now the last three in the cell was standing but the guards blocked the doorway and shoved them back. Doric, however, was permitted to follow Andrew into freedom. He had no idea of what had happened, but the release seemed as unlikely as the arrival of a lord in scars and furs who did little but point, and so set criminals free.

Long legs disappeared into blinding sunlight as Doric scurried after. He breathed fresh air, stood a moment stretching out his arms, lungs and smiling delight. No more stench and no more absolute hopelessness. Yet he had not the slightest idea what this unusual lord might want of him. A supposed murderer might be required to murder again.

Catching up with Casper, Doric muttered, "Well, friend. You've more or less saved my life and that's a miracle, so I thank you. But what does he do, this master of yours? I doubt I'd make a great assassin."

Casper sniggered. "You reckon? Well, I doesn't know does I? Best wait fer me master to have a chat."

"As unlikely as it may sound, I was innocent of that foul murder. You were nearby at the time. Did you know the girl was killed?" But Casper, scuttling after his lord, was disinterested. Doric eventually caught him up.

The inn was a long planked cottage beneath an untrimmed thatch, the noise of a song thrush which was either nesting or simply lost, and the straggles of moss and weed decorating the deteriorating long straw, water reeds and sedge that drooped its weave over the gables. Andrew strode through the main doorway, open to the scent of stale beer, and arranged his accommodation. When he wandered back to the men waiting outside, he smiled. "What pleasant and convenient benefits come with a title," he smiled. "I am sleeping here tonight, my friends. You two, on the other hand, sleep in the straw over the stables. But, and his smile grew, "the ale is on my tally. Drink as you wish, but do not drip blood on the horses below."

Casper and Doric grinned as their lord marched off

The weather remained kind, with late sunshine merging into the blue hour and the last melodies of black birds. Once the stars replaced the shadows and the first dew began to glitter like raindrops along the grass and hedges, Doric submerged himself in the depth of the straw's warmth and slept far better than he had expected for his first night after the rough arrest. He missed the girl in his arms, but he was asleep before the puzzle of who had killed her kept him awake. The whiffle and snort, shifting and nudging of the sleeping horses beneath did not intrude his dreams. His dreams swelled only with music.

It was the following midday when Lord Leys sat them down on the benches outside the tavern, ordered bread, pies and cold roast chicken, and with the obvious solitude apart from the wood pigeons, began to explain what he wanted of them. "I am," he said, "an earl of moderate experience and have little interest in regalia or parade. I have, however, a considerable interest in the safety of our country and of our new King Richard." He raised his tankard of ale, as though toasting the monarch. "He has long been an acquaintance of mine. Almost a friend. And I intend to protect both the man and his title as far as my life and my position are able. But I am not a guard who thrusts his sword at every passing stranger. I work quietly. I work secretly. And this is what you will do alongside me."

"A spy?" breathed Doric. The idea appealed. "Spent half my life on the road." He turned to Andrew. "I'm a minstrel, my lord. My lute is water-logged but still plays. It's years I've lived as a wanderer, doing magic tricks along the way. And that must be a fine way of finding out what's going on."

"What's going on amongst the shepherds, mothers and their children, the weavers, perhaps, and even the charcoal burners. No. I intend putting you in Westminster, young man, where you may play for the king. As a man who loves and understands music, his majesty will enjoy your lute, but not your magic tricks. I've heard of your talents, and that's why you are here."

His smile spread throughout his body down to his toes. Doric said, "Not only a new life, my lord, but a salvation from the old one. I thank you, my lord."

"Thank me by proving loyal, and by bringing me information.

There is an old building," Andrew continued, "outside the city's eastern wall and banking the tanneries. We stay there one night. Afterwards, Doric, you will accompany me to court, and I shall find you a lodging nearby. You will stay there quietly until I arrange the next stage. But," and he smiled faintly at the two who sat, chicken wedges in one hand and cups of ale in the other, staring at the lord, "remember one thing, my friends. I treat my men well, and I shall treat you well. But I am also adept at seeing what occurs beneath the surface of any situation, and if I discover disloyalty, you are likely to die for it. However, and he drained his own cup of ale, the old manor where we'll spend this first night is a ruin, belonging to me for many years, and you are free to stay there at any time should you have need of a hiding place."

Doric, nodded vigorously, raised his cup and thanked his lord. He felt the tingle in his groin in the same manner he'd once felt the desire for Lizzie's breasts against his bare chest and knew that he was excited.

Casper looked at Doric. "You heard of the Hastings affair?"

He had. "And was it loyalty to the old king, or a scheme of his own?"

"Conspiracy, as usual." Andrew discovered his cup was empty, and set it back on the table, then stood, stretching. "Others across the city were arrested at the same time, although only Hastings executed. Morton was part of the rumour, naturally, and should also have been executed, yet as a bishop was safe from a pedestrian death. Lady Beaufort too. Now, why would such a woman be involved in unpleasant plots, if not for her son?"

Such matters appealed. Never fascinated by politics, and only ever by music, Doric realised that a minor key could exist in many situations, and felt virtually reborn, eager for a change in his life.

The following afternoon beneath a blistering sun, they smelled the encroaching stench of the tanneries, but by-passed them, walking directly towards the old house. It soared in long broken elegance, a draught of cracked and smashed windows and a door lopsided but still clinging to its hinges. The pathway passed a twisted iron gate, and then suddenly smelled of everything sweet enough to overpower the tannery's reek, a blur of lavender, meadowsweet and lilac blossom. Finally, Andrew unlocked the door.

"Casper," he said, "you know this place well enough. Set yourself up somewhere you'll be comfortable." But then he spoke to Doric. "You'll come with me, young man. This will not be your home."

As the door and its double barricade stood widely open, two women appeared from the shadows within and were leaving. One was older and well wrapped against the storm that not there, she turned to Lord Leys. "Oh, my lord, we've spent nights of such unexpected comfort. I thank you most sincerely."

Andrew nodded. But the other woman was young, hair golden tinged amongst the light brown curls, lying loose across her shoulders. Her chin was a little pointed and her nose less pointed than was normal, but her eyes were amethyst and glowed as though alight. Doric turned without interest, but turned back, curious, and was immediately alert.

The girl said, "My lord, I thank you too, for both your kindness and your hospitality. Four days now we've benefitted and have scoured the tanneries for what we need. Five days past, you mentioned taking us to the ale shop to meet the new brewster. Will that still be possible?"

He had forgotten. Now Andrew nodded towards Casper. "I apologise, my lady," he said with the clipped sentences of impatience. "I cannot spare the time now. But Casper will take you." He turned back to Doric. "No longer mounted," he said, "we must walk the mile across the city and that may take some time, and then find you a suitable place to stay." He threw the keys to Casper and started to walk back down the overgrown pathway.

Doric followed. But he turned several times, having bowed to the younger of the women, smiling, before leaving. At the broken gateway he turned again. The girl was also on the pathway, but her head was down, and she was speaking to the older woman. At Andrew's side, Doric asked, "The girl? The young lady? She's staying here, and has no home of her own? Do you know her name?"

Andrew's pace was deliberately fast, and his stride was long as he shook his head without turning. "I cannot remember," he said softly. "But she is looking for a runaway brother. Now, through Aldgate and take the quickest road to Westminster."

For a last time, Doric turned, the temptation too strong to resist, staring back across his shoulder. It was then unsurprising when he saw the girl had also turned, peeping back, and smiling before hurrying away.

CHAPTER NINE

Displeased, Lord Sudbury glanced only briefly at the handwritten summons, and marched upstairs. Banging on his daughter's door, he called her to appear immediately in his private solar adjoining his bedchamber, then proceeded along the corridor to his son's bedchamber where he repeated his orders.

Obedient as always, the unalike twins trotted to the solar and stood before their father.

"I need it done," he said. "The wretched man is calling for action. As soon as he finds his damned siblings, I shall announce the engagements"

With silent fury, Beatrice lowered her eyes. Bryan, on the other hand, accepted loudly. "And about time, father. I've wanted that experience for two years now, and without opportunity. And you're a man. You know what I mean."

"Your sordid appetites," said Lord Sudbury, "do not interest me in the least, boy. I care only for the politics as you damn well know. Sit down, both of you. Bryan, the girl you'll get is a proper little nuisance, far as I can tell. Not that Charles gave me much of a description. Louisa. Pretty but not beautiful. About to turn nineteen years, so two years older than you, boy, but that's of no account. Probably virgin but now the brat has run away, who knows! Not that it matters. You'll enjoy taming her, and be wed by autumn. Buckingham is planning the rebellion for September."

"And it's a wealthy family?"

Bryan's father frowned. "The wealth is there, but sits with Charles, lord of the family. You don't marry for gold, my boy. You marry for politics and to get this wretched man off the throne."

"Fine," the boy said. "You sort the politics. I'm marrying for a naked tart in my bed."

"I doubt she's a tart. Charles would never have allowed it."

It was Beatrice who scowled at both her brother and her father. "But Francis is a baby. I don't want him in my bed. I'm seventeen, for goodness sake, father. How old is he? Ten?"

"Fourteen, approaching fifteen," Lord Sudbury spat back. "Old enough to fight if there's a battle, and I promise you, there'll be one. And you'll wed him, my girl, whether he's a baby or not."

"Yes, father." Although she had certainly no intention of doing so.

Beatrice discovered her mother in the kitchen garden, pottering cheerfully amongst the herbs and plucking dead leaves from the parsley. Hearing the disgruntled breathing behind her and without bothering to turn, Lady Sudbury murmured, "What is it now, my dear? Him? Or the younger him?"

"Both of them," grumbled Beatrice, swirling her skirts from the parsley.

Her mother popped one of the leaves in her mouth. "Beety dear, you know I can't control either of them. Is it the marriage plans again?"

"It certainly is," complained her daughter. "I have to wed a silly little boy three years younger than me, who probably still wears nether cloths, and has now run away from home. Perhaps because he doesn't want to marry me either."

Lady Sudbury shook her head. "He doesn't know about you yet. Charles plans to tell him when he finds him, Well, he can't tell him much until he brings him home again, can he!" She ate some more parsley.

"I don't care. I don't want a baby husband," Beatrice told her. "I want a tall romantic companion, dark and beautiful, who can sing to me, and beg for me in marriage. And in bed. I want a friend and not a fishing expedition."

"Oh dear," sighed her mother. "Romance again. Those knights on silver horses don't come around too often, Beety my love. And that's a foreign language to your Papa. It would be utterly pointless trying to disobey him, you know, and I can't stop a single thing he sets his mind on. Besides," she sighed again, "I'm not talking to him anymore."

"Again?"

"Permanently," said Lady Sudbury. "I may claim an annulment."

"With two children?"

"Only one, really," the lady complained, "since you're twins. That shouldn't count as two. Here, Beety, have some parsley. It's very pleasant."

It tasted of sunshine. Beatrice took it and returned to the house.

Lord Sudbury ordered his favourite horse saddled and, cuddling tightly to his stomach as he rode twelve palaces west, dismounted and strode to the grand doorway of Hylton House. The brass bell hung to the side and his lordship shook it with considerable vehemence. He was still ringing as the steward opened the door. Sudbury marched in.

He glared at his friend and demanded to know why he was being officially summoned instead of getting a friendly visit.

"Simply because," Charles muttered between clenched teeth, "there's no one here to spy on us or hear a damned word we say, whereas you have a son, a daughter, a wife and sometimes an extremely interfering valet."

"Nothing wrong with Jackson," objected Sudbury under his breath. But he sat, crossed his legs, and waited. In the following silence he asked, "Have you found the brats?"

Charles shook his head. "No, damned them. But they can't be that far, since none of them took horses or any other means of transport. I doubt Louisa knows how to walk further than your house from here. She's been a miserable lazy brat since birth."

"My Bryan will wake her up," Sudbury grinned. "Has a few ideas of his own. But more to the point, how is our own business progressing?"

Charles was not a man of generous smiles, but now his face turned from the grey of frown, crinkled up and turned to grin. "It is done," he said. "Mortimer has succeeded, and Buckingham is hooked as neatly as a salmon to the bait. The fool thinks he'll end up as king, or if the boy Edward takes it, then the idiot duke imagines himself the guardian, ruling in the child's stead. Between them Buckingham and Mortimer are collecting backers. They know we're with them, and Baron Northcroft as well. None are backing Buckingham, but no one will tell him that. The boy Edward will be king in spite of the title of bastard. And each of us will have a place as advisor. I shall take back Harrcroft House and all the wretched man's worldly goods, and this so-called King Richard can run off to join that other miserable exile in Brittany, if he manages to stay alive long enough."

"It'll work well enough," Sudbury said. "And the illegitimacy can perhaps be over-ruled."

Surprised, Charles called for wine and looked back to his friend. "Tell me how, John, after all that elaborate theatre from the entire family and a hundred other cohorts, all proclaiming the secret marriage of the king to their Lady Eleanor. It could hardly be denied. Dear Edward was a bigamist and since he wed both women in absolute secrecy, it's clear his intention was to leave them both. So he left the first one even though she went on considering herself wedded, and why he finally announced Elizabeth Woodville after months of secrecy, we have no idea. No doubt she blackmailed him when she discovered his motive. They'll stick to their story and have witnesses enough, so how do we contradict an accepted fact?"

"Simple." Sudbury looked pleased with himself. "We find a usefully needy priest who will state that the king's first marriage to Eleanor was later annulled, and shortly before he married the Woodville bitch, he was a single man again."

"The Vatican won't uphold that. No papers, no documents."

"By the time they sort that out, it'll be too late. The young prince will have been crowned."

"You've spoken to Buckingham or Mortimer about this? Mortimer can use his bishop's title to support the statement, but no one would believe him. He's too obviously against the king.:

"We don't need Mortimer," Sudbury said at once. "I have two priests who will swear by it."

"And then disappear?"

Sir John Sudbury put the palms of his hands together in mock prayer. "Oh believe me, they won't last long. No need to worry about them."

"And Mortimer knows this?" But Sudbury shook his head.

"Tell him yourself, there's no one will miss you since you appear to have lost your family."

Charles snorted into his wine cup. "They'll be found soon enough. And after I've given them both a beating - bare arsed, I think, since it's a long time since I saw my little sister naked – lock them in their rooms for a week or more –bring them out to meet their intended husband and wife. I think," he added with delight, "this is all going to work extremely well."

CHAPTER TEN

Louisa watched him go, striding long-legged down the tumble-down pathway beside Lord Leys. But the young man turned back twice and although she lowered her eyes, she saw the flicker of his third turn before disappearing through the remains of the gate.

With a hesitant whisper, Louisa told Isabella, "He was rather gorgeous. Don't you think so?"

"Lord Leys," answered her nurse, "is a most unusual and amazingly clever gentleman. I'm not so sure about gorgeous, my dear, but most assuredly impressive. If only you had a brother like that, instead of poor Charles."

"*Poor* Charles?"

"Well." She hesitated. "He had a terrible childhood, you know. And I daresay many of his present attitudes reflect back to that."

"Anyway," Louisa said, dismissing both her brother and Lord Leys," I was talking about the young man. I don't even know his name – but there was something about him. Those eyes!"

"I expect he had some, dear. Most people do."

Casper, having overheard, had kept a discreet ignorance, but could no longer resist saying, "The lad's name's Doric, m'lady. Met him in the slammer. He were there fer murdering his girlfriend." He didn't look back to see the girl's expression but heard her gulp. "But if you ladies wait just a titchy nose-pick, I shall be wiv yer fer showing wot you wants."

"The ale shop?"

They had searched for it already. Over past days, Louisa and Isabella had explored the spread of the tanneries and considered it a place of terrible wretchedness. The smell of urine from animals and the inhabitants of the tenements began a welter of stinks so vile, accumulated in a stench almost impossible to breathe. The first day of exploration had ended after only moments when Louisa heaved and vomited, adding to the smell herself. Horrified and embarrassed, she begged to return immediately to the house where she lay down, breathed fresh air and the perfumes of mint and sweet thyme, rose petals and greenery, long grass sprigged with daisies and buttercups, and the crisp breeze through the broken edge of the window.

The following day she had forced herself further and they risked the tenement building, visiting finally the owner of a tiny apartment where they had once meant to stay. The door was a dirty and partially torn curtain of hessian sacking and inside this was one room only, a bed of straw heaped in one corner, a slab of old paving in the centre of the wooden floor boards, no fire lit and no hole in the roof for smoke to escape. A clutter of other belongings were pushed into the shadows around the walls, and a window, not much larger than an arrow slit, was covered by oilcloth scrubbed into virtual translucence. Some light entered, but little reached the shadows from ceiling beams to doorway.

Her brother-in-law was surprised to see her after so many years, and Louisa was delighted that the necessity for sharing this tenement apartment had been so suddenly overcome. She had never yet slept on straw and quickly decided that she never would. Yet Robert Rudge welcomed them all and insisted they must come to share his one room should they ever need to. As for the ale shop, he was not sure since he worked in the opposite direction as a guard at the Tower, a part-time cleaner, and a repair man when needed, which wasn't often. London Tower was not a building at the point of collapse, in spite of its age.

"Tis a good job," he told them, "and I gets me bread and ale in the kitchens there, and sometimes me bed too. Well looked after, we is. When I gets promoted, which is what I aims to do, I gets a room in the guard's quarters outside the Ditch. That will be free. But meantime this be cheap and often I ain't even here. It does me well. But I avoid the tannery and don't go east, not for a year or more. No ale shop in that stinking mess would pull me in."

The following day, with headaches and other excuses, they did not continue their search, but after that they were obliged to spend their day deep in the tannery pits, determined to discover Francis, the ale-shop and the new brrewster. When the locals avoided speaking and looked away as they approached and muttered ignorance when asked for directions, Louisa decided she was too well dressed, and changed her clothes. Having no suitable gown herself, she borrowed one.

"Mistress Dawson, I is," the woman said, standing straight which accentuated her breasts. "Eva Dawson. And I lives here proper legal, for it ain't no brothel but I got permission of the lord wot owns it."

Meeting a whore for the first time in her life was a delightful curiosity for Louisa and although Isabella blushed scarlet and turned quickly away, Louisa clasped the woman's hand and wished her well. "And do you," she asked, "know the popular places in the Tanneries?" Somewhat surprised and pleased at this friendly greeting from such a lady, Eva supposed she did and nodded rather vaguely.

"I knows the ordinaries, my lady."

"Louisa," Louisa corrected her, "since we are neighbours. And it's the ale shop I want. Is there more than one? And do you know of a newly arrived brrewster?"

But she shook her head. "There were a tavern I still goes to, plenty o' beer and ale and wine too. Tis a good place fer customers, if you knows wot I means, ma'am. But no respectable shop would let me in. Frighted o' losing their own custom, and since I doesn't need ale in me room, Them fellows brings it, and if not, I doesn't care. I ain't interested."

Louisa smiled. "I understand." Although she didn't. "But I wonder, if you wouldn't mind and if you have any to spare – and I would pay, I assure you." Eva waited for some complicated erotic request, but Louisa said in a tumble, "Old clothes. Something that might fit and make me look – well – like you. Not that I could ever look like you," she added, "since you're much prettier, but so I can stop wearing silks and stuff. They make me stand out and people here don't help me. They seem to think I've just come to complain about them, and that's not what I want at all."

The following morning Louisa set off in a plain linen shift, tied at the waist with her own belt, worn loose, with a neckline she found uncomfortably low since she lacked Eva's inches, her own petticoat shift below. The gown was dyed light blue but much of the colour had faded and the original linen showed beneath.

"It ain't proper clean," Eva had admitted. Louisa tried not to notice and Isabella, marching beside, sniffed only once, and smiled with approval.

There was a stall selling ale beneath an oilcloth awning, but the trader insisted he knew of no other. Clearly, he did not intend to publicise the competition.

Beneath the canopy of reeking cacophony, the tanners were busy. Slouching from their pallets at dawn, both men and women, helped by their children from the age of seven years, prepared the leather needed for so many uses.

From cattle, aged horses no longer suitable for either battle or farm, goats, sometimes donkeys, and pigs were brought in already dead, often from age or accident, or were killed in the long troughs which stank of blood, death and shit. Meat was hung and sold to locals, the guts preserved, hooves thrown into piles for disposal, sometimes into the river downstream, and the carcasses were skinned carefully, keeping just a little fat attached.

The huge pits dug for boiling the skins could be avoided, but their stench could not.

Dragging through the wastes, the lanes of wet cobbles and past the pits, Louisa and Isabella arrived home in bleak and bewildered disgust. It was late and they were exhausted. With the weight of failure, and the guilt of not persisting, they spent the following day in the old house, speaking to Eva and to an old man who lived in the smallest bedchamber downstairs, close to the little outside privy, and without the need to climb stairs. Lame and slow witted, he was unable to speak clearly so lived unused to company although he craved it. Louisa and her nurse, sometimes dragging Eva with them, went to join him, talking and laughing, and so gathering excuses not to venture again into the tanneries.

It was another day when Lord Leys brought Casper and Doric back to the house. He had been gone far longer than Louisa expected, but now Casper was going to show them whatever ale-shops existed in the area, and meanwhile she had Doric the murderer to dream of.

Francis had known where the tanneries lay. Every Londoner knew, when the east wind carried the reminder, and so avoided the whole area unless working as a cobbler or a glover who either braved the much polluted air or sent a messenger boy with a written or memorised list.

"There be three ale shops and twenny-nine taverns," Casper told them, marching out with them in tow. "Hold yer lickle noses if you doesn't wanna puke, cos them ale houses be all over."

It was as usual a beaming day of sun sheen, which exacerbated the stink. Yet in spite of the heat, Louisa wished she had a scarf to wrap up around her nose. Acceptable during a freeze. Rude, unfortunately during the height of summer.

It was the first day of August and a bright Wednesday. Finally, Louisa expected to see her absurd little brother. She wore the old clothes she'd purchased for two pennies from the whore next door, and smiled into the buckets of collected lime, urine, oak bark, willow leaf, and faeces.

They found the first clues at the second ale-shop.

Francis had left home at night.

The night was stunted in summer, but still dragged far enough to cover an escape. No servants saw or heard him, and his sister was fast asleep in her own chamber. Brother Charles was lying half doped with wine in his office annex.

Every groom and every horse slept in or above the stables, but in any case, taking a horse would have alerted the entire household and made it easier for them to find him later. He walked. With the city gates locked, he walked around the outside ditch of the old stone wall as later Louisa would do. Longer, of course, but quiet. Not even the Watch would see him. He crossed the Fleet over the narrow bridge and moved north east. He had never walked alone in his life before. There was always a friend, an entourage, his tutor or at the very least a page at his side. Now alone in the middle of the black pitch, Francis hurried, making his way as far as possible before daybreak.

The stars watched him but there was no moon, so he was careful not to slip into the ditch where he would no doubt sink into the contents of a hundred chamber pots, a few dead dogs and drowned cats, and the general rubbish of half the city. Long before reaching the street into Bishopsgate, he heard screaming from the inmates of Bedlam Hospital for the insane. Francis ran past. At such speed he was already outside Aldgate when it opened.

The scrummage delayed him but the pause allowed him breath and thought while a small flock of sheep were filling the space, well Shawn and ready for the butchers and to end their sunny days as mutton on the bone. The shepherd looked up and saw a small kestrel sitting atop the gate posts, and he threw a stone at it. His aim was poor, but the kestrel flew east where meat lay fresh in the gutters. Robert Rudge was one in the crush of those entering the city for work, but neither he nor Francis had reason to recognise each other.

Pushing through, Francis continued walking south east until too tired, when he discovered a grassy hedge without thorns, and lay sheltered from sun and wind, closing his eyes to rest.

He had been warned against the smell but had never expected anything quite as disgusting. He wondered how anyone, especially Joletta, could accustom themselves to anything quite this sickening, but he kept walking and since the rest had brought back his energy, he walked into the tanneries. He watched, fascinated, as one tanner scrubbed a piece of boiled leather with handfuls of sheep's brains, another stench to add to those already thick.

Francis asked, "Are they brains? What for? More importantly, I'm looking for a – friend, lives at an ale shop here, her mothers the brewster?"

Not having removed his gaze from his work, the man said, "Taking the hair from the hide. You wants hair over yer boots? And the ale shop I knows is a half mile direct south from here. The lane starts past the two pits." And he continued scrubbing.

Thanking him, Francis moved on, hurried past the reek of the pits, and kept walking. It was just after the setting sun spilled its goodbyes in pastel pinks, and orange across the Thames, that he discovered the ale-shop, tall and dark, and firmly shut for the evening. At the back, pushing through the tangle of discarded rubbish and weeds, was the slide where empty kegs could be rolled to the basement ready for refilling. A tiny thatched cottage sat alongside, its windows covered in sacking and its door wedged shut with rocks.

Dark now, Francis was unsure, but he was hungry for food and desperate for soft arms around his neck, a soft warm cheek to kiss, and a gentle voice to wish him welcome. So he knocked. The door nearly fell inwards, but as it was shuddering with a groan of the hinges, someone thrust it wide and stared out. She was not elderly, but older than Charles. With his voice shaking as insecure as the door, Francis asked, "Madam, I apologise for the hour, but does Mistress Annie Smithson live here? And – her – daughter. Joletta, that is."

The woman said, "That's me and she's me daughter, and I reckon you be Francis. We met once, but now tis dark and you ain't the grand gennelman you was then."

Admitting "It's me," Francis stumbled in the doorway, ducking his head below the lintel, and peered inside. The relief was enormous, but the tiny dark room was neither welcoming nor comfortable. He saw shifting shapes and felt the clogging sweat of unrelenting heat. Then two arms were flung around his neck and he felt wondrously welcome and as comfortable as ever in his life. The second space up the tiny crooked steps was the bedchamber, but since there was space for only one palliase, the strings piled with a mattress of straw and rags shared by Joletta and her mother, Francis cheerfully spread himself on the bare floorboards downstairs, covered himself with the thrill of having arrived and the enclosed heat of the room itself, and slept without difficulty.

By morning and fully awake, Annie squatted on one of only two stools and told him, "I hopes you slept well, lad, but I got little enough time fer talking afore I starts work. Tis a long day for a brewster, and my Joletta must help. But first, since you come all this way which be mighty impressive fer a grand lad like you, I gotta say you done made my lass mighty happy. Nigh on jumping the stairs, she is. But there be problems. Will you answer me honest, lad?"

Not having expected interrogation, Francis nodded at once, but clenched his teeth. "I've told no one where you are," he promised, "nor does anyone know why I ran out in the night. Well, my sister knows a little, but not all. And my loathsome elder brother has no idea of anything to do with me."

Annie smiled. "How old is you, lad?"

He told her. "Nearly fifteen. And I know Joletta is a little older, but that doesn't bother me in the slightest. Nor should it. King Edward always liked older women."

"My Joletta be turned twenty-three," Annie said, "and tis right if you doesn't care. You is of the legal age, so I doesn't care neither. As it happens I ain't much older n' Jolly meself since I were thirteen when I had her. But one day your brother gotta find out, don't he! Is he gonna set out to slay us for feeding his hounds? And since your Charles be a good deal the older, will you ever benefits from the family coin ?"

He had never considered it. "I suppose not," Francis mumbled. "I don't know if either my mother or father made any separate consideration – perhaps when I come of age. No one has ever told me. My mother died when I was born. I've no grandparents either. There's an uncle somewhere but I think he lives in Flanders. So no inheritance, I think. But I'll learn the trade and work as a brewster. Or perhaps we could open a tavern, an inn or our own shop."

"With wot?" demanded his hoped-for mother-in-law. "Costs a right heavy sack o' pennies to start any business wiv premises, lad. That ain't gonna happen. So's you wanna wed me daughter wivout the slightest idea of how you gonna keep the lass fed. That's the way she's gonna end up on the streets."

"Never." Horrified.

"I can teach yer the skill o' the brewster. But tis hard work fer a lad wot never done harder than gettin' outta bed afore."

"I – I'm willing," Francis assured her. He was not sitting on the other stool, but standing at the window, elbow to the stone. Joletta had gone to collect water from the well. He wondered when she'd be back and hoped it was soon. "You teach me, I'll learn." He hesitated. So Joletta was almost as old as Charles. He brightened as the door opened.

Joletta slopped water as she entered. "You coming, Ma? You start and let me talk to my Francis for a bit."

Sighing, Annie hoisted up both buckets and kicked open the door, marching off to the brewing shed behind the shop. Joletta took the ready-warmed stool and Francis sat on the other opposite, smiling, eyes alight again. "Your mother's going to teach me the trade. I'll live with my wife and mother-in-law and we'll make a handsome living, my love."

Staring back but also smiling, Joletta said, "Or learn the trade as a tanner. Them good 'uns make a good wage."

Francis froze and waited until the heat returned and thee sweat down his back trickled once more. He shook his head. "Never," he stuttered. "That place is terrible. They work with piss and shit and brains. Rubbing it, scrubbing with it. How could I do that and then come home to make love to you?"

"Some do. Not with me, o'course." She did not mention that some had. "But with you to protect us, dearest, mayhaps we could go back to the brewery on the Fleet. Mighty fine customers we had back then. But reckon your brother would see you if you worked so close."

Again, Francis felt the ice down his back.

CHAPTER ELEVEN

The house that Doric saw first was a little north of the abbey, with the open square of sanctuary behind, leading to the royal palace in all its glory. Yet from court, it was only a short walk north to a home that seemed as large and as beautiful as the palace itself.

"My home," said Lord Leys, "tonight you will stay here."

Staring in silent delight, Doric nodded, then managed to ask, "Truly as a guest? I'm honoured, my lord, but I'd gladly sleep in the attic with the staff."

"Unnecessary," Andrew said. "But I cannot have you stay here beyond the one night. A little too strange, I think, for a wandering minstrel supposedly looking for work. Tonight you may stay. And tomorrow I'll find you a nearby lodging."

It had been a long stretch of years since he had seen his own home, having been sent to the monastery at the age of eight. But this, he thought, was a grander home than the one he vaguely remembered. At a young age, everything seemed larger and grander and if he ever saw his ancestral home again, which seemed unlikely, he imagined it might appear small and dull.

Andrew marched the steps, the steward opened the door without being called, and as his lordship entered his own home, a young woman with pleasure in her eyes, ran up the passage and flung both her arms around his lordship's neck.

He kissed her fondly and introduced her to Doric. Doric bowed. Then Tyballis said, smiling, "I've met you already young man. I was travelling with my husband's friend, and you offered an interesting prediction."

He remembered her immediately. "Interesting, my lady? I confess to many truths but many mistakes."

He was shown to a bedchamber and stood for some time gazing around him. One wall was painted with a mural of sunshine and flowers overlooking a scene of a great green valley and reminded him of the past twelve years of his wandering life. There was a bed which could have slept another dozen perhaps. The hearth was huge but bare, the rugs glowed from both floor and wall, and an eiderdown covered the bed in a blaze of embroidery. The bed curtains were dark silk, but Doric decided he could never pull these closed, and instead could spend the night staring around him.

He told his hostess, "A bedchamber I would love to copy in my own home."

Tyballis was pleased, "Because," she said, "I designed that myself. We haven't been long in this house and when we moved in, it was dark and musty. After being accustomed to very small quarters, I adored decorating such a huge space."

But Doric spent the evening with Andrew, a large cup of Burgundy wine, a platter of sugared oat biscuits, and a detailed explanation of what was expected of him. Andrew said, "I have long worked as what you may call an officer of security. This country despises conspiracy and yet it is that which fires the ovens and pumps the wells. But conspiracy destroys as much as it enlivens and discovering the rivers which run continuously underground turns the danger stagnant before the boiling water may rise up and bubble, overtaking this country's prosperity. After years of skirmish, we need peace, Peace is not born of conspiracies."

Doric leaned forwards. "I know of the Hastings affair. One of the others arrested lived in the town where I stayed three months back."

"I had the pleasure of uncovering the plots seething in that creature's ambitions, to kidnap the elder of Edward's boys and become the power behind the throne. I've worked for his majesty for several years."

Nodding vigorously, Doric sat back. "And me now? I'll do that with enthusiasm, my lord."

"You'll be paid from my purse," Andrew said, "but you must remember that in public you do not know me. You do not know my wife and you do not know my servants. Nor have you spent time in gaol accused of murder. I've no interest in your guilt or innocence, but others might feel differently. You have never before met my man Casper, not even others I've hired. You receive orders and payment from me and beyond that you do not exist."

"It brings purpose," Doric said. "I've had absolute freedom since I found my own way at the age of twelve. I've taken orders from no one. But I've promised loyalty, and if I should ever change my mind, I'll inform you before leaving your employ."

Andrew grinned. "I might have something to say about that, should it happen. But for now, I need to explain our situation. As a beggarly minstrel, you arrive seeking an audience. I find you work amongst the king's men. His majesty is a great lover of music. Once at court you will hear every word, follow every lead, listen to every whisper, and make your own judgements when needed. Live with suspicion and doubt. Play your lute, but while you play you must also watch and listen far beyond."

"I'll live at court?" It was a dream, except for the risk of being seen by his father.

"No. I'll find you lodgings." Andrew frowned. "You need to be a wanderer during the day. Hastings' treachery was first suspected because of meetings with those already suspect for other actions."

"And I never come to you for orders. So how do I send you my discoveries, if I get any?"

"I shall contact you in my own manner and choice," Andrew told him. "At present there are two situations which concern me, though neither centre at court, nor even in London. One is the influence of

Mortimer, Bishop of Ely, who has already been proved disloyal to our king. I believe that he is both capable and surely inclined, to compromise the man who has been, wrongly I think, set to guard him. Buckingham has neither brain nor resilience. You spoke to my wife concerning this, and predicted conspiracy and rebellion. Was this knowledge? Simply guesswork? Or perhaps a genuine insight?"

He wondered if he was blushing. "My lord," Doric said, "when asked, answers appear behind my eyes. I call them predictions but perhaps it really is just a guess. Sometimes I'm right. Sometimes I'm wrong."

Andrew crossed his arms and smiled as if travelling great distances. Finally he said, "A fair answer, perhaps. So, tell me what you see for the second conspiracy which now interests me." He watched his new accomplice with interest. "Do you see names? Do you see anything?"

Although he immediately saw the shooting colours of many roads without names, Doric was apologetic. It was not the best moment to make a fool of himself. "I warned you, my lord," he mumbled, then raised his voice. "I'm easily as wrong as right. I might tell you something more appropriate for your barber. But what I see is a small boat. A ship, perhaps, since it has a sail the size of a kerchief. You take the gangplank into pouring rain. But there's a castle on the horizon. That's where you're going. And I think – stupid perhaps, that I'm walking beside you. The man you want to see is in the castle. But there's a woman in England. Maybe his wife. The situation is urgent. But," and he looked away, "I see failure. Someone is crying."

"That," Andrew said after a pause, "is a prediction I might call both intensely close to probability, yet deeply disappointing. I will not imagine failure before I even begin. I can only contemplate success, and in this matter, it is more important than usual. Yet you have come close. So very close. I shall ask questions again, perhaps. But in the meantime, I suggest you watch the Lady Margaret Beaufort. An unusual and interesting woman, but with a less unusual and less interesting son. The son does not reside in England, but his mother does. She is not often at court, but Lord Stanley is her present husband, and since he owns Derby House in the city, he uses court as a useful stage."

Knowing names but neither faces nor loyalties, Doric winced. The last he'd heard of the nobility was when he was permitted only to study the Bible. He blinked. "You accept we might travel abroad together?" It seemed unlikely.

"Perhaps. I have no plans yet for myself, let alone for a boy I've known only four or five days. But everything in life is possible. I have proved that many times." Andrew stood. "Take yourself to bed, young friend. Practise your most useful talents. We'll meet to break fast in the morning, and then I'll take you to your new lodgings."

It was a night of strange dreams but the small pointed face of a girl he'd seem so briefly, and who should now be forgotten, insisted on reappearance.

He woke to what was most certainly a new life, to a long table set with platters of cheese, porridge made with cream, apple codlings and two jugs, one of ale and one of light wine. But he also woke to the same sweet face drifting at the back of his eyes as his predictions for the future tended to do. Though the amethyst eyes had now banished the floating predictions.

CHAPTER TWELVE

The temptation to throw the bucket of water she'd just humped all the way from the well, was a serious attraction. Joletta, however, said, "Yes, m'lady," and passed the bucket to her mother. She then left and returned to the brewery.

Staring out of the tiny window, Francis stood with his back to the women, and Isabella stood on the bottom step of the rickety staircase while Annie Smithson and Lady Louisa hunched on the two stools and compared opinions.

"He hasn't any money," Louisa said. "And nor have I. I'm not sure we even have a future since I'm quite positive our eldest brother wants to murder us both. And Francis hasn't the slightest idea how to earn anything because he's only been taught to read and write and be polite to the nobility. That's not an insult, by the way. It's all I know too. But at least I'm nineteen. He's fourteen. Honestly, I remember being that young. You do silly things even when you secretly know it's wrong."

"You speaks a lot o' good sense, lass," Joletta's mother nodded in cheerful agreement. "The lad's too young for my daughter. I reckon my Jolly needs a husband wiv more experience wot can give her a better life – not a bloody worse one."

Francis muttered from the shadows. "Love makes everything better."

"Well, it don't," said Annie. "It don't replace bread and cheese fer a start, lad. And that love stuff fades quick when you's bloody starvin'. Besides, you be wanting little brats no doubt. More wailing and whinin' and mouths to feed. Or is you gonna sleep downstairs whilst me lass locks herself in bed alone? I ain't gonna stop you nor my Jolly. But she ain't got the sense she were born wiv, and you, lad, is a baby just born yesterday anyhow. No coin, no work, no home and no bloody hope, that's wot you got."

The silence echoed and no one answered. Then the first to open her mouth was a surprise.

"I have," said Isabella softly, "a few suggestions, should you permit me a moment or two." Everyone turned to look, and Francis sighed.

"You just think me an idiot," Francis muttered.

"I think you young," Isabella said. "But there are ways and means beyond simple surrender, and simple banishment. There might also be a most improper way of gaining some coin, or even some premises."

Everyone was staring. The room, being small and dark, created its own sinister secrets. Louisa asked, "Bella, you know so much. Can we kill Charles off? Then Francis would inherit the lot."

"As it happens," the nurse answered, "I remain in your home, my dear, in spite of my age and frankly useless existence, simply because I know so much of the past, and have promised to tell not one word of this to anyone within the family, or anyone else, just as long as I remain in the house, bed and board paid. It is possible, perhaps, that the same arrangement might be made for Francis. Not to live at home, of course, which would be extremely uncomfortable once married. But to gain something of his parents' wealth."

Still staring, Francis gulped, Louisa hiccupped, and Annie clapped her hands, smiling widely.

Francis said, half whispering, "So what's the secret you can't tell? Is it so terrible? What did my father do? Or my mother?"

"Your dear mother," said Isabella with determination, "was a beautiful little angel. However, I shall tell no tales until I believe I must."

"You must," sniffed Louisa.

The nurse sat straight, knees crunched beneath her skirts. "Not yet, my dear. They call it blackmail, I believe, and is a shocking way to behave. But it has kept me alive and goes some way towards balancing the facts I find so upsetting." Having refused the home brewed ale, Bella now retrieved her cup of well water from the step above and drank the lot. She patted her mouth dry and said, "Yet that would only help for a temporary year or so. I cannot believe you could enjoy living there with your wife, living on your brother's supposed charity, with very little to look forward to. Perhaps you could buy a brewery or a tiny tavern, but nor is that a charming prospect. Personally, I would suggest you live here, perhaps with a donation from your sister, and learn the business before you commit yourself to marriage. You sleep downstairs on a pallet and work hard. After some months or even less, you will know if you are suited to such a life, and Joletta will decide whether or not the wedding should be planned."

"I've nothing to donate," Louisa mumbled in surprise, "except a puppet doll my mother gave me when I was four, and a few old clothes. I do have one of the new printed books by Chaucer, but I don't think that would help either of you."

Isabella regarded her with faint impatience. "You will soon have plenty to share around, my dear, if I have my way."

With a slow gathering of wits and ideas accompanied by disappointment, Francis leaned back against the window and spoke softly. I could do that. I mean, I wouldn't mind. I could be a brewer. Actually, I could be anything I want because I'm not an idiot and I like learning. I can do what I wish. I'm fourteen but that's not a crime and I can legally wed whoever I want to. Well, maybe not that, but you know what I mean. Away from Charles, I'm free and it's up to me and Joletta. If she likes the idea, then I'll do what you say. And if I can get some sort of dower, well, all the better. Jolly and I could get a bigger house or build another room out back, just for us. And have fun. You know what I mean. Or we wait while I learn the trade. It's up to Joletta."

"I reckon she'll listen to me," Annie said. "You ask her, lad. and I'll arrange a nice cosy pallet fer you downstairs. Four months, I reckon. We might even get a bit more dosh wiv three of us workin'. So go ahead and ask me daughter."

Which is when Louisa nodded, and stood up. "Can I have a quick word outside, Francis dear? And then we'll have to go. Casper said he'd be back to take us home and without him I'm quite sure we'd be lost in moments." She turned to Isabella. "Wait for Casper outside, Bella. I have to talk to my brother. Just a few quick words."

Outside where the stench of the tanning pits reintroduced itself, Louisa smiled at her reluctant brother. "I'm not just a bossy sister. Running away from Charles is a wonderful idea. But honestly, Francis darling, I'm just thinking of your happiness."

"Patronising! Condescending! None of your business."

She supposed he was right. "I'm coming back tomorrow if I can remember the way," she said, forcing the smile. "Then I should be able to tell you about Bella's secrets and how I'm going to find you some money."

"Hold a nice sharp carving knife to our dear brother's throat."

"Tempting. But blackmail is a safer plan. And besides, I'm longing to hear this dreadful family secret. I wonder if father never married mother illegally or something. We could all be sad little bastards. Or was he a pig like Charles. I don't remember him much, I was so young when he died, and mother even younger. Did she have an affair with someone else and we're not Papa's children? Goodness knows. "

"I don't even care," Francis sulked. "I just want Joletta and I don't care what father did. I'm sorry I killed off Mamma being born but I couldn't help it, could I. And besides, knowing Bella, I bet it's just something daft that no one else would care about."

"But Charles," Louisa pointed out, "wouldn't have kept her on without anything to do if he didn't care about the secret getting out."

"Well," Francis turned sulk to pout, "I'm off to find Joletta and talk to her about this. That's the only thing that matters. You wouldn't know. You don't know anything about love."

She thought about that as she followed Casper home, and as he was about to leave her at the broken gate, she gathered courage, refused embarrassment, and asked, "Master Casper, you told me that young man's been accused of murder. The young man who was here. You said his name was Doric. Is the law still after him? And do you know – if he did it?"

"Liked the look of the lad, did you, mistress?" Casper sniggered. "Well, the lad reckons he didn't do nuffing, but they all says that. Me – I wouldn't call no fellow guilty. Tis all the same to me. But I don't reckon his lordship woulda took him on if he reckoned he were a nasty bastard."

"How would he know?" Louisa asked softly.

"Ah, well then," said Casper, one finger to the side of his nose. "We doesn't know, does we! But I reckons his lordship knows bloody everyfink. He'd have done a bit of lookin' under the sheets, if you knows wot I means." Casper's laugh was a cackled of considerable enjoyment, but not usually understood by others. He cackled now. "Fing is," he continued, "I's worked a fair time fer me lord Andrew, and tis all done under them shadows, as it were. So I doesn't like t say this be it or this ain't nuffing. I shall say just one itsy bitsy lickle clue, being as I knows, the lad never walloped his mistress."

"And," casually, walking away as if she did not really care, "where is he now?"

"Wiv his lordship. Most likely at court." And Casper strolled back into the tanneries.

Louisa sighed. She decided that Casper was teasing for how a penniless minstrel would accused of murder be accepted at court, and come to think of it, that was, in any case, irrelevant. He would now be beyond her reach and since he was simply a stranger and possibly a killer, there was no common sense to her attraction. It was common sense she had preached to Francis and now she needed to preach it to herself.

She was interrupted by Isabella halfway up the stairs.

"I have just one question," she said, "before we settle in the bedchamber. I just need to know, my dear, if you are thinking of returning home sometime soon."

"I keep thinking about it, but I don't know. Why does it matter?"

"Because, my dear," answered her nurse, "if you do, I have two options. I could stay here with my brother-in-law, although there is so little space I doubt if I could do so without deep regrets. Or I could return home with you. In the latter case, naturally, I could not break my promise concerning your brother's secrets."

With muffled guilt, Louisa said, "Or you could stay here. It's big and fine."

"Utterly penniless with no protector? What little money I had saved has now been spent getting here. And I am a little too aged to go working the streets. As for brewing, I cannot imagine even lifting the bucket."

"Anyway," said Louisa at once, "I don't ever want to go home." She paused. "But I don't want to starve either. As for working the streets ---"

"No, no," Isabella was flustered. "But perhaps, until it is necessary, I will keep those secrets to myself."

It started to rain in the night with a pattering of light drops against the window which woke Louisa from her drifting dreams. Isabella beside her was cuddled beneath the covers so her snores were muffled. Nor did Isabella wake as Louisa rolled from her side of the bed and tiptoed to the large cracked window. The shutters missed more than half their slats, leaving a fair view of the garden. A small throng of bats were flying through the damp mist, their little dark bird-like shapes blurring together as they massed upwards towards the house attic, disappearing just beneath the roof.

Then silence except for the drip and patter of the rain against the glass. Then Louisa saw another dark shape, this time a small man pushing through the undergrowth below and entering the house around the back. Then she heard his footsteps on the stairs. So Caspar was not a daytime wanderer. This was, Louisa guessed, around four in the morning, still black but approaching dawn. Casper was alone, but clearly, he had been up to something he wished hidden by the night.

CHAPTER THIRTEEN

The new lute seemed so utterly beautiful to Doric, he not only adored it as the new path to richer music but saw it as feminine. A woman he loved, and who, once he had mastered its wealth, would adore him in return.

Of spruce, and as long necked as a swan, with the central rose carved as the wood curled and wound around the circular edge. Veneered in dark polished mahogany, the pegs sturdy for tuning, and the strings of sheep gut lay like sleeping angels over the frets, a thirteen courser with its twenty-four strings tightly pegged.

Doric was a fingertip lutist and had never used a quill. With naked fingers, he made love to his instrument and invented his own melodies as he played.

The third lute he had ever owned, this was the queen. His first lute was the baby, and he'd loved it but given it no name. The second, after owning it for a few years, he had called Lizzie, and laughed as his new companion Elizabeth smiled and kissed him. As yet, this lute had no name.

Lord Leys had presented it to him as he settled into his new lodgings, and had then left quickly, promising to return that evening. Doric sat, placed the lute on his knee, the neck resting across his left arm, hand curled around to the frets, and began to play. He played for many hours and was still playing when Lord Leys returned.

"You have changed," Andrew told him. "Your face is clean and shining. Yet I cannot think this is the miracle of water. It is surely the miracle of music."

Doric beamed. "I thank you with all my heart. The lute, my lord, is the most beautiful I've ever seen."

"A superior instrument," Andrew agreed. "But not the best available. A minstrel belonging to neither troop nor manor, is a poor man however good his fingers. No wandering beggar boy can own anything of the highest quality. Now I shall tell you how to integrate yourself into the palace. I have informed his majesty and Richard will adopt you on a temporary basis. You must earn permanent employment yourself."

With lodgings tight yet not only adequate but extremely comfortable, Doric was prepared to earn his keep by playing the music he adored until he had enchanted every member of court, their wives, their children and even the staff. He spent one day closeted in the lodgings he now called home, practising both the music and the speech required. Addressing royalty and those who considered their titles almost as valid, was neither as simple as calling to back street villagers, nor even explaining his art to the craftsmen who knew more than he did.

The bedchamber upstairs had no garderobe, but the bed was wide and feather rich, as comfortable as a swan's nest, while one wall held as many pegs as he could ever need. The window, well shuttered, looked out both to the Abbey and to the palace. Downstairs was a genuine hearth, a low table, five stools and shelves for platters and other objects he had never owned. A trivet over the fireplace would allow cooking once the flames were lit, and there was space enough for barrels of ale beneath the wide window. A sweet home then, for remembering any aptitude he had since forgotten and playing music into the early hours without consideration for the neighbours.

His royal highness, King Richard, regarded this new minstrel, recommended for secret work by his own investigating friend

Andrew. Yet even a necessary spy within the court's walls, would of necessity be talented enough to explain his new elevated employment. And so Doric played and Richard listened in delight.

"Clever," Charles, the young Earl of Hylton, said loudly on one of his rare visits to court. "I'm no lover of music, boy, but I appreciate skill." He turned as Andrew, Lord Leys, passed him in the great hall.

"I find music inspirational" said the taller man, walking in the opposite direction and so meeting Charles face to face. Neither knew the other.

With polite indifference, Charles nodded but added, "Inspiration, I feel, comes not from music but from determination."

"Indeed," Andrew answered, moving on as he spoke. "Yet invariably determination saves a life or kills another. "A common necessity. I find inspiration sings to me in my sleep."

"No wife, then?" Charles laughed.

"My wife often sings to me in my sleep," Andrew lied. "She is, naturally my most vivid source of inspiration." And that, perhaps, was true. Smiling, Andrew walked on, slowly approaching the king's seat. He had never before been acquainted with Charles of Hylton, had neither spoken to him before nor spoken of him to others, but he had overheard sufficient gossip, and this was why he had walked in that direction. Gossip was frequently slander, and once overheard it would be repeated by many and believed until proved otherwise. Yet the gossip Andrew had heard had been secretive, always more dangerous, and more likely to be true. Tyballis had also overheard the occasional mumble and had told him of it.

"I would now," she had informed her husband, "be quite sure that the strident Lord Hylton is plotting treason and will unite himself with Morton." But it would not be so easy to prove.

Now Andrew's wandering direction took him to the king's side, where he bowed low, staying on one knee until his highness ordered him to rise, and come close. "Your minstrel is a blessed discovery," Richard told him. "Whether or not his underground work will prove useful to you, my friend, his music is most certainly pure enchantment. Find me a group of that quality and I'll thank you at every sunrise and every sunset."

"I knew him as excellent," Andrew said, "but did not know his power until yesterday. I believe he also sings, but with less confidence."

"Then I shall crown the boy with newfound confidence," the king smiled. "By tossing coins, perhaps? Kingly praise? Or a request to accompany me next time I travel north."

But Andrew blinked, an unnoticeable shake of the head. "I mean to take him over to Brittany," he murmured. "The Tudor son has lately been often in touch with his mother and that strikes me as dangerous. But the closest danger comes from Morton."

"As a bishop, my friend, I can neither arrest nor execute the man."

"He will run," Andrew said, "when the time comes. I would sanction that. His principal danger is here and his long talks with Buckingham."

"We shall see." Richard smiled and Andrew bowed again, backing off.

The king had spent long weeks travelling to introduce himself to his people. His young son Edward, small and shy, was now Prince of Wales, so delighting the Welsh. Yet Wales remained a bubbling simmer of anger while supporting no one, or sometimes the boy Tudor who claimed to be Welsh himself, son of Welsh myths, Welsh princes, and Welsh pastures.

Richard had persisted. Now late August, he dreamed of placid justice and time alone with his queen.

And as the court mused and gossiped, considered and plotted, spread truths and untruths while inventing others, flirted and then marched to chapel, milling through hall, corridor, courtyards and bedchambers, Doric continued to play, seated high and alone on the minstrel's gallery over the hall, and was both amazed and dismayed to hear his royal majesty's request that he sing.

He did, once, and that evening again practised until his head ached.

The diamonds glitter in her eyes

And bring a musical surprise.
But she loves another, and tells him so,
Though he's a creature I despise.
Her love bleeds everlasting hope,
But for me tis agony, and sighs
So forlorn I cannot cope.

"It's the melody, isn't it, not the words," Doric told his lute. "It's you, my love, who brings magic alive and tears to the women who listen."

Since he found Andrew a man of considerable and clear explanation who somehow made his instructions sound more like an admittance into adventure, he enjoyed their meetings. But when he heard the key in the lock of his front door several days later, it was Casper who entered, and Doric was disappointed

"You?"

"I ain't that bad," Casper said. "And I come 'cos his lordship is too bloody busy. Tis all or nuffin in this game."

'But I have the 'nuffin' to report," Doric said. "I need to come down from the minstrel's gallery and mix amongst the courtiers. With my own music in my ears and a quarter mile of space below me, I hear neither news nor slander."

Casper sat on the table rather than a stool. "His lordship knows and done said it. You ain't in no gallery tomorrow. it gotta be like this, fer it looks less susspecting if you goes separate first. But tis more afoot. Me lord is gone orff. So if you hear ought from them Welsh Marshes and Brecon where them buggers is living, then you tell me, right? Tis proper important. Don't expecting ter be long gone he don't and has took Nobb wiv him to leave out there an'all."

"Buckingham?" Doric asked.

"Got it right on," declared Casper. "Tis wot you says to me when I met yer very first off. Ellie, you says. Well, tis Ely fer Mortimer done it all, I reckon. Buckingham's just a podgy twit."

Nodding obediently, Doric promised to be ready, and meanwhile to keep entertaining the court and overhearing gossip. "And his lordship's taken the Lady Tyballis? I'd have been ready and willing to go myself.'

"You doesn't like bein' proper polite at court, eh?" Casper sniggered. "But mayhaps you un his lordship will be orff even further if there be time. Fer tis that Tudor bugger next, wot be in Brittany fer now."

Andrew's explanations were considerably more eloquent, but Doric understood, and once Casper had left, he leaned back, closing his eyes and dreaming. He began in the Welsh Marshes and moved on to Brittany. But then the dream changed into mist and fog, dark clouds obscured direction, and when the pictures leaked back, they were more nightmare than dream. He saw Lizzie floating past, her throat slit open, her skull crushed, her nakedness protected by the modesty of water weed, clumps of moss and the silvery flicker of tiny fish across her breasts. Her mouth gaped open as though her desperate screaming had been silenced by the water's current carrying her downstream until halted by thorn and the curve of the banks.

And Doric began to realise that it could have been Casper who had murdered Lizzie. He had been there – exactly there – at the time of her murder. He must have been on horseback since the Lady Tyballis could never have been expected to walk that far, and so Casper could have also heard him play at some time along the route, and known his music was of quality enough. And even been arrested, perhaps, for the same crime, until rescued by his master. Explaining why, which until now had seemed so strange, he had asked Lord Leys to rescue him too. To save a virtual stranger from being hanged for the murder he himself had committed.

Andrew might know, or he might not. Whether Casper would confess, and if so whether Lord Leys would overlook such a thing, Doric could not even guess. But the brutal murder of a pretty young girl was an indication of a mind sick with proving its own power, and capable of evil.

He remembered their first meeting. Lizzie was a hard-working whore and Doric had never loved her, but she was sweet natured, eager to help, and was the friend he'd never had before.

Within the silken clamour of court, he spent the day slipping between the crowds, smiling at those who gossiped and sang of laughter while wanting to cry. A song of loss and misery sank without atmosphere while the buzz of chatter was louder than the swish of heavy robes and dancing petticoats, almost drowning the music of the lute.

That evening his majesty dismissed him early and Doric returned to his lodgings without appetite. The evening was still bright as the summer sun sank late, and while the gates remained open, he knew he might walk to the tower within an hour, or a little more.

It was Casper he hoped to see at the old house, but there was another reason too, and gradually, as he walked, it was the second reason which grew to fill his mind. He blinked at the amethyst eyes staring back at him from the misted indecision he felt, the little pointed chin, the small nose, and the sweep of long sun-bleached curls. He saw small hands, slim fingered, small breasts peeping beneath the gown, and a smile which lit the dark more surely than any candle.

It was Casper, he muttered to himself, that he was going to see after all. And he remembered her name even though he was sure she wouldn't know his. It was not Lizzie who drifted into his thoughts as he marched on through the city lanes towards the stone walls of the Tower.

Dusk dipped past the rooftops as he left the city through the Aldgate and approached the old Leys house and its dilapidated grounds. The front door was locked and he saw no one so wandered to the back of the building to find some opening or some tenant to let him in.

Wading through parsley, thyme and rosemary, Doric gazed at the partial stone wall which had once been the stables. To the side were the kitchens, a series of small thatched huts now in ruins, but what had once been the dairy still stood with walls intact and a doorway that stood open. Doric walked through into a dark corridor and passages led both left and right. He then walked into light and stood in the great hall, a hearth covering one whole wall, and chairs so comfortable he felt himself back at court.

Louisa sat in shadows beside the empty hearth, staring at nothing. Alone in one of the cushioned chairs, she seemed to be dreaming. To speak aloud and interrupt sweet silent dreams seemed too much of an intrusion, but Doric walked carefully across the floorboards and that was enough, for the squeak and groan of the wood brought Louisa back into the present. She sat straight, staring, and did not tell this most unexpected visitor that it was him she had been dreaming of.

"Oh dear," Louisa hiccupped, "Are you looking for Lord Leys? I'm afraid he isn't here."

"No." He stood in front of her and she jumped up from the chair as though stabbed. "It was Casper," he said, then wondered how he might confess the truth. "Actually," he began slowly, "I thought, remembering seeing you, my lady, and your elderly nurse at the doorway as I left -," and now was interrupted himself.

It was another woman who entered, young but clearly older than Louisa, with a thump of wooden soled shoes and the hoarse breathing of someone who had been running. She stopped beside Louisa, stared at Doric, and waved both arms before collapsing on a stool, legs stretched out and skirts pulled up to her knees. "I had to run," she blurted. "There were some bastard wiv a bloody big knife. Says he were using it ter chase some burglar he seen, but he bloody waved it at me, and I reckon he looked eager, so I run fast and come home."

Louisa was sympathetic. 'Shall I fetch you some ale, Evie dear? What a horrid experience." Both then turned to gaze at Doric, who did not move. Louisa said, "Um, this is a gentleman I believe is named Doric something, but we are virtual strangers. Perhaps I should get us all a cup of ale. Or maybe – if I can find some – even wine."

"Wine," smiled Eva, "sounds bloody good ter me, lass." She looked at Doric. "You too, I reckon?"

He grinned. The meeting was not what he had expected. "A cup of wine would be more than – welcome," he said, "if there is any. Otherwise, if there's a tavern open nearby, I could buy a jug.?"

"I think," Louisa said, hurrying out of sight, "there's some in the pantry." Her disappearance permitted not only the discovery of the wine, but an opportunity to brush down her skirts and tidy her hair. Returning with the full jug and three cups, she found the guests already in conversation.

No candles were lit but the sunlight had slipped below the surrounding buildings and shadows had crept in through the unshuttered windows.

Doric interrupted his conversation to bring another stool, and Louisa rested her jug and cups on the flat wooden surface.

"So, you knows I's a whore," Eve was saying. "So, I reckon you doesn't approve. Well, let me tell you lad, I doesn't care."

Smiling into the shadows, Doric accepted the cup offered. "Every career has its advantages," he answered, "and I object to very little. My best friend was once the same – a job she took because nothing else was possible."

Luisa started. "Is that the girl you murdered? she asked abruptly. "Or is there some other poor girl you pimp for?"

Eyes now heavy lidded, Doric stood, finished the wine and replaced his empty cup on the stool. He felt his heartbeat quicken and had no idea whether this was from anger or attraction. More confused than ever, he relied on impulse and turned, walking back towards the doorway. "Naturally," he said, half choking. "I run a brothel full, and only murder those who are rude to me for no reason."

She watched him leave, gazed back at the empty cup on the stool and then at her own cup, still full, and suddenly burst into tears.

"I only meant to sound worldly," Louisa wept as Eva rushed to embrace her. Louisa buried her head against the other girl's ample breasts. "I didn't want to sound timid or prissy and all ladylike. I thought it was a knowing sort of thing to say. Half joke, half sophisticated."

"Reckon not so wise," Eve told her, "not if you reckons to like the lad."

"I've been dreaming of him for a week," Louisa sobbed.

CHAPTER FOURTEEN

Confessing to Isabella had several advantages. Her criticisms were generally constructive, and she rarely pointed out how the original motive was entirely at fault.

"It's done now, my dear," she told Louisa. "Plan the next move, not the one you can't change."

"But," moaned Louisa over what now pretended to be the breakfast table, "I've been awake half the night working out what I should have said. Perhaps I should have said nothing at all. Or at least I could have laughed when I said that rubbish, to show I wasn't serious. Or maybe I could have said, '*Well, Doric, you were in a difficult position and I admire your –courage.*' On the other hand, I should have talked about living in the countryside and absolutely ignored all the stuff about trollops and murders. But I couldn't laugh at the trollop thing because Evie was sitting right there."

"My dearest Louisa, we cannot journey back to alter what was said and done. Shall we perhaps seek out your young man and plan what you should say next?"

"I don't know where to find him. Besides," Louisa mumbled, almost choking on her cup of cold ale, "he already doesn't want to see me and he's angry and that's all my fault." She wiped her mouth and drank again, swallowing hard. "And I was such a pathetic idiot. I just wanted to sound interesting and sort of grown-up and not a silly little girl who gets shocked at everything."

Sweeping the soft cheese over her wedge of dark bread, Isabella kept her eyes on her platter. "We had a plan, my dear, which I believe to be a good deal more important."

"I expect it was. But I was awake all night thinking on what I shouldn't have said." She sniffed and drank again.

"Eat up dear," her nurse told her. "Now, I think we've decided. Yes? We wait a little while for young Francis to decide whether he's fit for trade and can conquer the details of brewing – or not. Then, with or without him, you return home to practise your new courage with Charles."

"Which means you can't tell me all these delicious secrets because you'll still be employed at home and have to stick by what you promised. Which is a shame because you sort of hinted you'd tell me anyway. We've been away from home for nearly two weeks."

"Telling you that, my dear," Isabella replied while chewing her break-fast and re-establishing her balance on the little kitchen stool, "would not help either of us. On my death bed I shall reveal it all."

"You're never going to die. You know that, don't you, Bella?" But it was Doric she was thinking of.

Walking slowly towards the small distant brewery, they smelled the brilliance and sweet scent of the sunshine, as delicious as frying onions or pulling the new baked pie from the oven. Yet soon enough the reek of the pits and the many preparations of leather were all anyone could smell, and even though they were becoming accustomed, both heaved and clamped fingers over their noses.

Staggering with her usual two buckets of water, Joletta kicked open the brewery door and dumped the double weight beside the cauldrons. Francis sat beside the door, staring at his notes. '*Oats and yeast with added water. Specific amounts must be judged by the brewer.*'

"But," Francis muttered to himself, "how can I judge that? It could be a handful to every quart. Or it could be a quart to every handful."

"Oh, pooh," said Louisa loudly as she followed Joletta into the barn. "At least you could carry those heavy buckets for Joletta."

"Jolly said not to," Francis looked up, abruptly startled. "I did offer. But I'm not quite sure how to pump a well."

"Time to learn."

Louisa followed Joletta from the room.

"Are you quite sure you actually want him?" she asked. "I mean he's sweet and passionate and well-intentioned but he's a baby and thinks like one."

Turning, blush pink, Joletta wiped her hands on her skirts. "Of course I does. He's such a sweet darlin' and I wouldn't find anyone else wantin' me, would I now? And if we has little 'uns, which is wot we both wants, stead o' growing up in the gutter, the poor little mites will have a grand Papa and maybe a little coin too."

"You love and pity your children before you even have them?" Louisa had never considered her own future offspring. "That's so kind and unselfish. But I'm afraid Francis isn't being any help at all."

"Tis early," Joletta shook her head. "Poor lad only started learnin' this morning. Can't learn this trade in a day, can he now? No bugger could. And sides, I can learn him most of it meself, but he gotta get the idea fer hisself first."

"Perhaps." Louisa stared over her shoulder at the open door to the brewery shed. "But if he doesn't know how to collect water from the well, and even I know that, then it's a poor start."

"We got time."

A gloom coloured cloud sank over the sun and seemed to warn of problems to come. Yet quickly it broke into melted wisps and sunshine blazed once more. As Louisa turned back towards Isabella, she spoke only to herself. "Dear Doric, you do know I was teasing, I hope. My apologies and I hope to see you again soon. No, too much like begging. I'm so sorry if I misled you, Doric. I am looking forward to seeing you again. No – almost as bad. Perhaps this is better, well now, Doric. Your turn to insult me. And I hope you weren't offended by my joke. Stupid. I know well he was."

But having entered the shed and once more breathing in the

doubtful scent of yeast, Louisa flopped onto the tiny stool and rested her head in her hands. Isabella bent and kissed her cheek. "My dear, Francis will improve, you know he will. There's time."

"I think I want to go home," Louisa whispered.

⛫

"Reckon I found your young run-aways, my lord," the chief groom announced. "Fairly sure, I is. But I didn't bring em in right away, since there be other folk there, and it'll end up a fight. Them fisticuffs in them tanneries ain't easy ta beat, and I reckon I need a couple more at me side afore I goes in. There ain't no bugger messes wiv them lads. Makes great leather, they does, but they fights bloody well an' all."

"The tanneries?" Charles did not believe it. "That is the most loathsome place south of York and east of Wales. Anyone who can smell that stench for a day and not collapse, is a rare creature indeed."

"Rare maybe, my lord. But I hung around and reckon I'm as sure as an arrow from a long bow. The lad, your brother, my lord, seems to be living in a right nasty little slum and is learnin' the ale-making business. Do he like it that much?" A moment's pause, and the head groom shook his head. "Pardon, my lord, but that be what's afoot. And far as I can see your lordship's little sister, she be living just outside the wall in an old house, strange as a horse plaiting his own mane. Wiv her female, and they be visiting this brewery place behind the Falcon's Nest inn. Actually, they done changed the name and tis now The White Boar. For the new king, that is, my lord."

"I know why they'd have changed the name, fool," Charles growled from the depths of his cushioned chair. "And is entirely irrelevant, But I see no reason on this troubled Earth why my brother and sister would conceivably leave their comfortable home and take up the trade of the brewery in the most vile place I've heard of."

"You knows them tanneries well, does you my lord?" asked the groom with slight curiosity.

"Of course not, idiot," shouted Charles, emerging from the

shadows. "Now take the five other grooms with you and go there and drag back my two wilful siblings."

"Three of them other grooms is already out searchin' out further east, sir," the groom explained. "Maybe won't be back fer a week or more."

"Then take a couple of scullery boys,' Charles ordered. "And hurry. Now – out of my sight."

As the groom marched around to the Stables and remounted his master's horse, calling to the other two remaining grooms to hurry and join him for the day, leaving The Strand for a three mile ride east, Francis was learning where the well lay and how to fill the buckets. Louisa had returned to the house. Eve, meanwhile, was watching Louisa pack her bag.

She was sorry. "I'll miss you, lass."

"I'll invite you to my wedding one day," Louisa said as she stuffed a grimy shift into the side of the bag. "But that probably won't happen for another ten years. I certainly don't think Francis is doing the right thing, but at least he's found all about being in love. And she loves him right back. That's not going to happen to me."

"Ain't never happened to me neither," Eve said. "Me Ma were a whore too. Dead now, o' the pox four years back. I never knew what else to do. I mean, fer a lass like me, I weren't gonna be wed any time soon, were I? And I ain't got no skills except the moanin' and groanin' at the proper moments. I were pretty enough as a young lass, so I got on and copied me Ma's trade."

"And you have a nice home to live in," Louisa nodded, "instead of the usual slum tenement. Finding this place was good luck."

Nodding, she agreed. "Amazin' luck. No, his lordship weren't no customer. I met the lady Tyballis one day when she dropped the nice fresh bread she were carrying. Dropped in the gutter, it was, so she couldn't eat it. I says can I have it, 'cos I ain't got naught and I can wash the crust easy enough. *'Come home wiv me, '*she says. *"No pretty lass should be that hungry.'* Buy I's a whore, I says, and she says, *"And I be Tyballis,'* she says. *'How does ye do?"* I lived here free ever since. Not that I sees her ladyship often, but tis a right nice place to live."

The following morning, their bags bulging, Louisa and Isabella first returned to the brewery said goodbye to Francis, Joletta and Annie, and said they hoped to see Francis again soon. Louisa wished him luck with the brewing business and promised to keep an eye for possible new premises, and the possibility of getting enough money to pay for them.

The long walk home was sweet at first, with the call of soft beds and luxurious meals, but as they entered the Aldgate they were utterly exhausted and sat on the bank of the river, leaning against their bags and hoping for the evening to cool the heat against their backs.

"Doric slept in the open under the trees for years," Louisa whispered. "But I don't think I can. Do we have even a penny left for a straw bed in the tavern stables?'

"Three pennies," Isabella sighed. "Enough for a room and a small break-fast. But," she stared out towards the calm tide as the Thames flowed downstream, "only one night, and the very poorest inn we can find. Then on the morrow, my dear, we must reach home or sleep by the Fleet."

It was the following day when they arrived home and Isabella returned meekly to her quarters within the servant's attic chambers, while Louisa lay flat on her warmly tucked bed, utterly exhausted, and wondered what in the name of madness and fury, Charles might do when he discovered her within his property once more.

But Charles was not at home. He was, said the steward, carefully showing neither surprise nor disapproval at the young mistress's return, visiting with Lord Sudbury and family at a short distance down the Strand nearer the Fleet, and would no doubt be home for supper.

Louisa decided she did not want supper. Exhaustion had killed her appetite, and facing Charles so soon after her miserable return seemed far too sudden and unnecessary. He would spend the night thinking of interesting punishments. Whereas if she appeared well rested, washed and decently dressed, she might have the courage to make her own excuses and inform him that it was her life, and she could go where she wished.

Meanwhile she was free to dream of Doric, hoping that somehow, she might see him again one day.

Indeed, having begged the steward not to inform Charles on his return of her creeping back with her hair in her face, her hair pins lost or askew, her shoes thick with gutter muck and her back as bent as an old woman's, she could only hope that the promise would be kept, and she could sleep uninterrupted.

She slept, and as expected, she dreamed of Doric.

CHAPTER FIFTEEN

W aking to the chitter of the sparrows and the sharp call of the crows, Louisa woke and wondered how soon she might risk approaching the optimistic sunbeams across the breakfast table where no doubt Charles would already be enjoying his first cup of ale.

Both delighted but somewhat surprised that the steward had clearly kept his promise, Louisa then lay on her bed a little longer, pleased to hear any bird song and not the expected roar of fury from her brother. Yet those moments of summoning courage were a shameful admittance that Charles still loomed his everlasting disdain across her shoulders. But her recent escape had indeed taught her how to be herself, and shown that far worse than brotherly bad temper could rain down from even a sunny blue sky.

The maid's truckle bed was empty, since young Mary had supposed her mistress to be still away from home. Louisa was therefore able to dream uninterrupted. Although there was no one there to help her dress, she was quite able to shrug herself into the thick crimson bed robe hanging on the garderobe peg, and this was sufficient as a cover while trotting downstairs to the breakfast table, pretending that she felt invincible.

Arriving, however, in her first moment of confidence, Louisa quickly saw that Charles was not even present and the only person who sat there facing her was Isabella, and as Louisa sat hurriedly and stared, she asked in a mumble, "So where is he? What has happened?"

"Where he is my dear," Isabella told her, "remains unknown. I have no idea. And even questioning some of the staff has not brought up an answer. Evidently your brother left home yesterday afternoon with his horse and two more mounted grooms, and rode off in what seems to have been a furious hurry. No doubt he's argued with the King again, or something along those lines."

Louisa stared, shook her head, and waited for Isabella to pour her a cup of ale. "Charles is always angry. But he doesn't ride off with a couple of grooms, no baggage and no reason."

Later, once Isabella had helped her dress, Louisa sat in the gardens leading down to the river beneath a blaze of late summer sunshine. With her eyes closed her mind became a jungle of interwoven pathways, some leading to the motives of her brother, others to the gentle promises of love from Doric, and also to the desperation and talentless problems of her brother.

Charles had already arrived at the tanneries and rode the stench lined streets to the Smithson brewery. The ale shop which stood close beside, yet larger than its partner, was bustling with custom, being a Friday afternoon. Charles pushed aside the queue, strode to the table counter at the back of the shop, and demanded to know where the brewery stood with its new kidnapped idiot boy who would no doubt mix sugar with the ale, and ale with the wine.

"We doesn't make no wine here Mister," the proprietor told him. Mistress Wran was neither accustomed to such rudeness nor to grand gentleman customers of any kind. Not that he appeared to be a customer. "But our brewery, what is a mighty fine place, and supplies the very best ale in London, is just outback. If you wants mistress Annie Smithson, then you go off there and don't go pushing my customers off their feet."

Marching from the small shop and its floating smells, Charles resisted the temptation to punch the woman, stamped back to the brewery behind and before even opening the door, called for Annie Smithson. Kicking opened the door with one impatient riding boot, Charles immediately came face-to-face with an astonished and quickly terrified younger brother. Francis dropped the handful of crumbling yeast which he had been holding and abruptly sat on the stool behind him.

"You have the unbelievable stupidity," Charles glared at Francis, "to hide yourself in a squalid slum purely in order to escape my orders? "

Eyes already darting forwards and then back over his shoulder towards the quickest possible escape, Francis clenched both fists and suddenly ran for the back door. With just two strides, Charles caught his brother by the ear. As Francis squealed, so Charles dragged him back into the room and began his threats with malicious explanation.

"I'm sorry. I'm truly sorry." Francis called, his fingers poking between his ear and the furious grip of his brother. "I wasn't doing anything bad. I wanted to be a Brewer. I'm learning, really I am. I know the beginnings. And Joletta and Annie are teaching me so well, it's inspiring." He gulped, then hurried on, "I can earn my own living. I won't be a drain on you any longer. It's not a crime."

"Who the devil are Joletta and Annie?" Charles demanded, yet seemed uninterested in any answer. Indeed, both Joletta and Annie stood staring, amazed at this sudden and terrifying interruption.

But never intimidated for more than a few moments, Joletta neither curtsied nor introduced herself. "Francis," she said, "is a very close friend of mine. He came to help. And I intend to help him. I presume you're his brother. Of course you must be head of the family. But that doesn't mean you can terrorise him all the time. He may be young but he's old enough to ride off to war, if there was one, and lose his life for his King and country. So he's old enough to make up his own mind."

Charles had not released his hold on Francis, and the sting of his ear, half torn from his face, was adding to the fright, making it impossible for Francis to add a single word. Instead it was Annie who rushed forwards. "Let go of that poor lad," she said with her own echoing screen. "Our Francis ain't done nothing to hurt you, so don't you go hurting him."

"Let me inform you, madam, that I am this boys' legal guardian. And since the death of his father some years ago, I am solely responsible for his behaviour. He will therefore obey me at all times whatever those orders may be. My orders are now that he immediately accompanies me home and will not on any occasion be returning to this slum. I bid you goodbye, madam."

Joletta rushed them both.

With no clear idea of what she could possibly do to protect the boy she wanted as her husband, Joletta kicked first and thumped afterwards. The kick at the back of the calf did not make Charles loosen his grip but simply annoyed him beyond measure. Hauling Francis around with him, still in his grip, Charles lashed out at Joletta with his other hand. The fist crashed down on the side of her cheek. She flew backwards, directly into her mother's arms. Annie stumbled but managed to stay upright. Dropping Joletta, she then ran at Charles, tugging at his hair with a grip as strong as that which Charles already had on Francis. The three of them bounced kicking, stumbling, punching without any clear idea of where that punch might land, and finally, each tripping over the other, they landed in a heap on the wet floor boards, already encrusted with the yeast crumbs which Francis had previously dropped. Annie flung away the thin strings of hair from Charles, while Joletta, now back on her feet, stared in horror at the disaster before her. She began to yell and opened the door further to shout for help. The screech was alarmingly loud, and her voice was familiar to those working nearby

Two of the local men, both previously in the queue to buy ale, came running. Both workers at the tanneries, they wore the usual stained aprons over stained smocks, and stank of the tannery stench from hair to clogs. Not knowing who was at fault, nor who might be threatening who, they yanked at both Charles and Francis, leaving Annie safe and free in the middle. It was the men they attacked, with growls of anger, the men dragged Francis and Charles outside.

Francis was wriggling trying hard not to cry and allowed himself to be punched to the ground. But Charles bubbled with increasing fury and fought back, reaching for his long knife hidden within his doublet. Some of Francis's hair was still clumped between his fingers, but now his hand was bloody and covered in both yeast and dirt. The blood came from one of the men, as Charles had punched him in the nose.

Within the brewery shed, Joletta and Annie listened to the noise without seeing more than sunlight and shadows, but Francis was crouching beside them, trying to explain exactly what had happened. He was not entirely sure himself and his explanations explained nothing. Joletta, finally peeping from the half-closed door, saw only flying feet and heard the curses and grunts. She ran back inside, slammed the door behind her and clung to Francis. "You're safe, my dearest," she whispered in his ear. "Why should I care what happens to the others?"

Charles stabbed out, his knife point found flesh. But he was immediately outnumbered and overpowered. Following six hard knuckled punches, three from each man, arriving in various parts of the head and face, Charles finally collapsed unconscious. The collapse did not last long, but when consciousness returned and he blinked open his eyes, Charles believed he was dying. Amongst the floating skins of a dozen cattle, complete with guts, thirty thickly skinned remains and their bleeding threads of flesh, Charles sat in a deep pit of hot liquid filth to his chin. With a yelp of absolute horror and disgust, he stood and was quickly able to climb from the pit, half slipping, but able to fall out on to fresh earth. First retching, he bent over and vomited. Half boiled beside the uncleaned skin of dead animals, the stench now seemed his own. His lace, silk and damask reeked of the filth that stuck to his clothes. Charles was remembering what had happened, although with vague confusion and the loss of all detail, and in spite of the burning pain across his entire body, he scrambled to his feet and ran again towards the brewery. The two men who had already attacked him, stood solid now blocking the door. Charles screamed for them to move, and ignoring his own recent danger and present pain, he punched out with both fists.

The men laughed at him, not moving. Charles managed, with difficulty, to hold his temper. He approached both men slowly and with a semblance of dignity. But he spoke with menace, though his tone was soft. "That man is my brother," he said, "and I have every right to punish the boy for his appalling and dangerous behaviour. Indeed, he is engaged to be wed to the daughter of a Lord, a Lord of this country who stands as a friend to his Majesty the King. My brother has instead run to this brewery, to be drunk on ale instead of being true to his future wife. I understand you were trying to protect two women, but these women attempted to restrain me when all I wished to do was bring my brother home where he belongs. Would you condone his behaviour? Would you protect a boy who escaped the protection of his own family on the eve of his wedding to a virtuous young daughter of a high Lord, when all he wishes to do is both intoxicate himself and take a strumpet to bed before facing his future wife."

Listening closely to this explanation, both men chewed their lips, nodded to each other and gradually moved aside.

Charles entered the brewery unhindered, and stood facing Joletta, Annie, and his brother Francis. Francis bowed his aching head. "All right," he said. "I'll come with you. I suppose I have no choice. But you'll not attack me, nor Joletta, nor Annie. Both of these women have been so kind to me, and don't deserve your brutal anger." He turned again to Joletta and stroked the bruised side of her face, then leaned forwards and kissed the bruise and then her lips. 'This isn't the end," he whispered. "I love you too much. Bless you and your mother for trying to help but let me go now. I'll come back as soon as I'm able."

In total silence, Charles nodded, and led the way from the brewery. He did not bother to turn or see whether Francis was following. He assumed his own authority. Francis was indeed following behind.

Joletta, though seething, remained silent as Charles led Francis towards the river, distant but glittering like a thin blue line past the tenements and tannery pits. Here, the two grooms waited, three horses snorting and impatient to leave. Charles turned to Francis, his eyes narrowed and shining in cold venom. "You will ride the horse with John holding the reins walking in front," Charles said without expression. "You will speak to nobody. You will not move. You will not take the reins. You will not attempt to do anything but sit astride that horse and hold your peace."

As ordered, Francis mounted. The groom led the horse as arranged, while the other groom and Charles himself were mounted and rode forwards, leading the way back to the London wall. Unable to gallop through the crowded city roads, they trotted, then walked along the Cheapside, through Goldsmith's Row, down to St. Paul's and finally rode slowly through the city to Ludgate, and out of London again towards the Strand. The sun continued to shine, sparkling like the gold and silver in the smith's glittering shops, but also on the tears sliding down Francis's cheeks.

Within a little more than an hour, they were home.

Louisa was watching from the window of her bedchamber. Isabella sat beside the bed, darning a pair of outworn stockings. When Louisa saw the approach of both her brother's, the obvious temper of one, and the obvious misery of the other, she felt sick, and started to cry.

And as they entered, Charles pushed Francis into the great hall, Louisa could see that her little brother was also sobbing openly, with no attempt to control his misery. The steward stepped back, accepted an order to bring hypocrass and disappeared towards the pantries. Louisa, half falling as she raced the stairs and tripped on her hems, ran to her younger brother and flung out her arms.

Francis stepped back and avoided her embrace. He scowled, still weeping, and pointed one angry and trembling finger at her. "You told him," he accused between sobs. "No one else knew. It was you. Perhaps you hate Joletta but I never knew you hated me."

CHAPTER SIXTEEN

With no other choice, Louisa spoke to her brother through the keyhole of the locked door.

"Bloody Charles."

"You do believe me, don't you, Francis dear?" Crouching in the corridor unseen by her brother, Louisa clasped her hands as though praying in church, and begged for recognition. "Dearest, you must know I'd never ever dream of sneaking to Charles and telling him where to find you. Have I ever sneaked to Charles about anything? Ever? I know I'm not very encouraging about you and Joletta, I mean, this wedding isn't perfect, is it dear. But tell Charles? Never, ever."

He believed her, although had not at first. "I mean, who else knew? No one. Just Joletta and Annie of course. Do you think Annie might have come here to tell Charles? She might just have thought it would be the best way to stop me."

"I think he had spies out," Louisa said. "Your arrival in the tanneries and the ale shop wasn't exactly secret, was it. Very few noble young gentlemen suddenly appear and start working as a penniless brewer. People must have been talking about it.

"I never thought," Francis sounded muffled through the small keyhole, "I could be so interesting."

He had been whipped. Charles had used his own belt, a thin leather strap with a silver buckle, but the buckle was usually kept safe within the clasp of the hand. This time, however, feeding on the frenzied fury he had nursed since waking in the utter filth of the tannery pit, his level of determination had changed. Charles thrashed his little brother with twenty strokes, both the first and the last lashing out with buckle as well as leather. The screams had echoed through the entire house and one scullery boy was still hiding under the kitchen table twenty minutes later, and three maids had sobbed through their work, on their knees, scrubbing while weeping. One page had quickly disappeared outside, another hid in the pantry, and all of the hounds raced downstairs and back to their kennels, ears flat and tails between their legs.

Francis could no longer lie on his back, which was bleeding beneath the bandages, and was a far worse agony than the sting to his ear and the missing twist of hair. Now he knelt inside the door, the tears drying on his cheeks but still luminous in his eyes.

Speaking to his sister this way, as though he was a prisoner at Newgate Gaol, seemed not only humiliating but so grossly unfair that Francis was gruff voiced and could stop crying only when concentrating. Yet now, knees to the floorboards and his thrashed back bent low, concentration was most difficult. He spoke, but grunted when he moved and the pain increased.

"And the bastard mumbled and hissed at me as he thrashed great stripes out of my flesh," Francis mumbled. " He kept calling me a common tramp like my mother. First, I heard the words through his teeth, like *'Our mother was a fool who deserved none of our family riches.'* Then the bastard told me about some girl he wants me to marry. That's not the way he put it, of course, he said, I *have* to marry. It's not like I'm going to get any choice. But perhaps he was just being nasty. The nasty stuff came out like spitting. Wanting to flay me and donate my hide to the tannery. But then said I'd be married and off his hands soon, but never to a whore stinking of piss. He didn't give any names. Though, come to think of it, he said something about you being married too."

Listening with tears in her own eyes, Louisa wasn't yet concerned about vague threats that surely could not be serious. Louisa sat with a plop and wondered how on earth she could help Francis with a solid door between them. "Listen, Francis dearest, I'll do whatever I can. But to be honest, I don't know what I can do. You are getting enough food, aren't you, dear?"

All she could hear back, was a series of sniffs and gulps. Francis was still crying, and she wasn't surprised. She could not imagine the pain, since thank the Lord, she had never been whipped herself. She had been slapped, she had been punched, her arms had been twisted up behind her back, she had been kicked, pushed away and thrown down, her hair had been pulled and a spiteful pinching grip on her ear was a common enough experience. But she was thankful that she had never been punished in such a brutal and unforgivable manner.

There had been once, she remembered it clearly, when she had thrown a bowl of custard at her older brother, he had ordered her stripped to the waist and caned. She had been eleven years, and hadn't dared run, but after one slap Charles had stared, turned, walked away and left her to dress herself again. He had called their mother a strumpet, inspiring her initial temper, but both she and Charles had abruptly abandoned the anger and such a situation was never repeated.

"Darling, Francis. I'm going to go and try to get you some strong brandy and perhaps some lovely lemon tart with lots of cream. Would you like that?"

Again, there were only sniffs and gulps. Finally, Francis managed to mumble a hopeful yes. "Especially the brandy. I just want to sleep and sleep and sleep." But it was as she was turning away to fulfil those promises, she heard the last call. "And go to Joletta. She must be frightened. She must be told I'm alright. And I'll be back to see her as soon as I can."

Doric walked from his lodgings towards the Ludgate, and Charles walked towards Westminster from the strand, they passed on the street leading to the Abbey. Neither knew the other, and neither had any reason to gaze at the insignificant shadows they passed. Charles continued on towards Westminster Palace where he had an appointment to meet with Lord Sudbury to discuss the marriages already arranged, now that both his brother and sister were back under his control.

His brotherly fury had also wrapped around his little sister, but Louisa, glaring back at him as he threatened her with everything he could possibly think of, explained loudly that although she apologised for not leaving any written note, she had gone in search of her lost brother, knowing that poor Francis was in great trouble and needed her sympathy and help. She had then returned of her own accord and could hardly be blamed for a single thing. "You really must not be so wicked towards poor Francis," she yelled at Charles, purposefully speaking in front of the steward, the chief valet, and several lower members of the staff.

Having, therefore, resisted the temptation to thrash his sister as well, Charles permitted her to remain unpunished, although with narrowed eyes and a lowered voice, he warned her never to shout at him again.

Doric, meanwhile, made his way towards the old house where Louisa and her nurse Isabella had been staying. He was unsure, thinking perhaps he was making a fool of himself. But however foolish, no man gained even a flame's last ashes of what he wanted, unless he tried. Days had passed in shadowed doubt. He had felt a form of misery unknown to him since leaving the monastery. Not agony, perhaps. But a creeping shadow which dampened any enthusiasm for any action he might try. He was positive that his music was suddenly without feeling for his feeling had moved elsewhere. Instead of the great love it had always been, his lute was now a quiet friend, unable to help him in the way he so desired to be helped. His head ached. He could not eat, and rarely spoke. Twisting his way amongst the courtiers as he played, he heard several mutterings of interest and he remembered these carefully in order to repeat them to his employer, Andrew. But the fervent enthusiasm with which he had started, had faded. And he doubted whether any of these whispered secrets would prove importance.

He walked fast, but without particular haste, for he expected no satisfaction on this self-motivated errant, yet enjoyed the pace with the sunshine on his back. Once through the Aldgate, leading out from the city, he strode towards the old house where he hoped still to find Louisa, and, if he deserved such luck, her sweet forgiveness regarding his previous behaviour.

The iron gate, loose on its hinges, lay open as always. But this time, which was unusual, the front door to the house was also wide. It was Eva, the girl he had met before, who sat on the front doorstep with tears in her eyes, reflecting the sun.

"Who? Tis a shame, and I miss her, but Lou ain't here no more. Went home, she did. Don't know why. Got all upset after you was here last time. Then went to see her stupid brovver, got even more upset, and buggered off home. I doesn't know where her home is, but summint grand, I reckon. Surely hope she comes back one day, because I likes her. She were like a proper friend. And I ain't got no others." Eva wiped her eyes on the strap of her shift which she pulled up from her shoulder.

"And you're crying, because of Louisa?" said Doric.

"No." Sniff. "Got bashed in the chest by some john what I done with last night." Eva was no longer crying, but the sun glinted in the tearful reflections. "Still hurts a bit. But ain't no damage. You goes off and finds Lou. That sweet little lass, you tells her that I misses her. She got a come and visit some time."

"So we'll make a bargain, both ways," Doric smiled moving backwards to the garden path and its overgrown weeds. "For if you find her before I do, you can tell her I miss her as well."

King Richard was not present at court as was usual, since he travelled frequently, fulfilling the responsibilities of a monarch asked to speak on important matters, to attend some special ceremony, to announce, to close, to add to a sermon or to hear the pleas at a distant Guildhall.

This facilitated Sudbury's private speech with his friend. Outside in one of the small open courtyards, although overlooked by many windows, Sudbury and Charles were able to speak for the few minutes necessary, and without being overheard. Sudbury muttered, "Beatrice is a bitch of a bitch. She's going to cause trouble if forced to marry Francis. Your Francis. But the fault is with my Beatrice. On the other hand, Bryan is as happy as a boy with his boots in a puddle. He's waiting for some girl's arse to settle on his sheet, and although she is just a little older, he thinks your Louisa is as pretty as a pork pie and wants her as soon as he can get her."

Nodding without the slightest care for either his brother all his sister, Charles spoke quickly and softly. "It'll be done. Seems my idiot brother lusts after a slut in the tanneries. Louisa doesn't know yet about Bryan, but I know damn sure she'll complain. She has before and has some stupid idea about falling in love before the wedding. Sentimental puke, but females grow up with this disgusting rubbish in their heads and need to be tamed by their elders. She'll swear to not marry anyone I choose, no doubt, simply because I said so. And I don't want a screening match at the church porch, but perhaps I can slap them both into shape before we arrive in front of the priest."

Frowning, Sudbury shook his head. "Is it so important, my friend? I agree that binding our houses together in such a double union might help, should we ever be discovered. But I doubt it would be such a desperate matter, nor such a vital one. Nor do I expect to be discovered. We are neither of us such fools to be discovered by this fool of a king."

"I shall do as I see fit," Charles told his friend. "Whether the result proves the necessity, frankly I now find that virtually irrelevant. My sibling brats will not disobey my orders and I shall teach them exactly that."

"I consider Morton more important than our incompetent children. I need to speak to Morton, and Buckingham too. I've had a word with the only two trembling Woodvilles, including

Buckingham's wife. But, and it's a bothersome but, they seem more interested in sitting that pathetic little squint-eyed exile Tudor on the English throne."

"Tudor is claiming the Lancastrian inheritance?"

"Yes," Sudbury raised his voice. "Although he's no right to it. Fifteenth in line, perhaps. Sixteenth?"

"Even to those who claim the Lancastrian right," Charles was impatient, "Tudor is near twentieth in line, so has no right at all. It's Edward's young prince who must be crowned, and Buckingham supports that, even if he fancies the crown himself."

Whispering again, Sudbury muttered, "If we find the elder prince dead, then perhaps Buckingham stands some chance."

"Don't tell the fool that. He'll kill off the young prince himself."

"Some think him dead. He's not been seen in the Tower for some days."

Charles grabbed his friend's arm. "Foolish and dangerous talk, Thomas. I'll sort this damned marriage of the brats. You take yourself off to Brecon and prepare Buckingham."

CHAPTER SEVENTEEN

"I t will be Brittany," Andrew informed the young man standing before him. "You and I alone, young Doric. Nobb is neither discreet or presentable and Casper is in Breccon."

"The information I brought you concerning Margret Beaufort seemed reliable?"

At roughly the same height, Andrew and his interesting new apprentice smiled each at the other. The meeting was momentary for they spoke only briefly of the time when the journey would start.

"Interesting indeed, my friend," Andrew answered. "It is some weeks that our Lord King has been forewarned of Buckingham's disloyalty. But what you brought is the confirmation, the timing and the details. And so now we know with absurdity of the Lancastrian plots, with Morton and Buckingham, but also backed by the wretched Henry Tudor who plans to sail from Brittany. Until now the Lady Margaret has financed her son, but since the Hastings plots, the Beaufort money was confiscated and handed over to her husband. Stanley has never said no to additional riches, whatever the scandal. We guess that it's the Breton duke who is lending the funds to his less than illustrious guest. But we know too little. So now it's Brittany. Be assured, their plans are advancing. And our plans, my young friend, are advancing at the same pace, or perhaps even faster."

Doric was grinning, eyes bright. "You returned from Brecon – when? And left Casper there?"

Nodding, Andrew remounted the great gleaming black stallion, turning to say the last words. "I discovered all I thought necessary, even details of the plans already in progress, and those not yet begun. That covers the Tudor invasion he plans for mid-October. He'll sail on or around the twelfth, depending on weather. Meanwhile they expect Buckingham and his followers to be triumphantly striding towards London, leading an entourage containing our king under arrest, manacled and on his way to the Tower dungeons. This won't happen, of course, nor any thread of such nonsense shall be spun. But that's the rattle of optimism at Brecon. Casper stays in case changes are adopted. But you and I, young Doric, sail to the Breton coast, to study the ambitious Tudor's secret plots."

"We have a month?" Doric called as Andrew took up the reins and turned towards home.

"I've no intention of staying so long," Andrew called back. "Ten days. Two weeks if I must, and no more. So this day, my friend, at your own lodgings, pack a bag, as light as you can, and cross into Southwark before the Bridge closes. I shall bring the horses at midnight or a moment before. Be ready."

It was sweet moonlit night when they set off. Doric had grown up on horseback and was quickly in love with the mare brought to him. She was a grey, a little shaggy perhaps, her tail rough and active, her eyes huge and trusting. "My advice would be never to trust those trusting eyes. If I were you," Andrew said. "But she's ready saddled. Our time is limited, so we'll leave at once."

They had met in Southwark having crossed by the bridge some time before, each attending to his own business until the gates were locked and no one either crossed the Bridge, or swarmed the roads except to run for the inns, the taverns, and the brothels. It was the Rabbits Ear where they met, ate, wined, and murmured of the route already planned.

"I've trailed this countryside half my life," Doric said. "So I'm guessing we travel south through Sussex into Hampshire. And we leave through the Portsmouth docks?"

Eyes steady over the lip of his cup, Andrew agreed. "That's exactly the way it will be, Doric. And it will be a long ride and no stopping for a further bed at any wayside Inn. Once at Portsmouth, we break fast and we rest. We sail at five as the afternoon wanes. I expect, depending on whether, to be in Brittany by the morning."

"The weather promises sublime cooperation," Doric smiled. "What is it? The third of September? And we'll be in Brittany in two more days. That's remarkable."

"That's the way it'll be."

Through the back alleys, the tenements and slums of Southwark, where the thatched roofs bowed low, almost hiding the tiny windows with their shedding moss and windblown straw, they rode south, avoiding the homeless crouching in the alleys, and the street girls leaning against the rickety walls and the tavern stables.

But soon they were out in the countryside, heading south into a black night as deep as the Cheapside gutters. To their right the stars blinked out through the rich midnight sky, but to their left, the ink was uninterrupted, and clouds were forming.

They talked little, as Andrew planned his route across the open countryside, the glimpses of forest, across shrinking streams, and on through the open grasslands of Sussex. With an early gallop, refreshing the horses after their long day in the stables, they raced the laneway's and did not stop for browsing, drinking, nor talking. But as they rode further into the rich rolling pastures, they ambled, resting the horses and allowing them to stop on the banks of the stream's to drink, and on the grasslands and verges to graze at the long and uncut grass plaited with wild flowers and bush, sedge, and lichen.

So from walk to gallop, gallop to browse, and browse to trot, they cut through the borders of Sussex, heading towards the ever closer sunrise of Hampshire.

The stars were losing their sparkle and shimmer when Doric and Andrew still within the lush peace of Sussex, looked up, on a ridge to their right, two gibbets were outlined against the diamond-studded night. Both swung their heavily burdened ropes in the night's breezes, but the winds were not strong, and no gales whistled through the outlines of those criminals hung for whatever crimes they had committed. One had been there for days, perhaps four weeks, since the body was little more than bones within its clothes. A skull beneath the wide brimmed hat displayed only shreds of flesh around lipless teeth and empty eye sockets, the eyes perhaps taken first by the ravens, before the scrawny neck disappeared into a filthy coat, doublet and the piteous rags of leg bones, twisting a little from beneath the doublet's pablum, bones alone, down to its toes.

The other corpse had once been a woman and was not as long hung as her companion. But the winged scavengers had found her and already in a day or two, perhaps no more, she had neither eyes nor flesh plump enough to tell her story and save whether or not she had ever been pretty.

Doric stared, but Andrew called him onwards. "No time to stop for either sympathy or condemnation, my friend. We have a long way still ahead and limited time to finish it. The dead won't worry us, cannot hinder us, until we die ourselves. And this is definitely not the time to contemplate that."

"It would have been sympathy," Doric muttered, but looked away and rode on.

The sheep were still out in pasture, but the farmhouses were closed, and no candlelight flickered in their windows. The cattle were quiet in their sheds, the pigs in their sty's and the horses in their stables. The birds, heads beneath their wings, would be sleeping a while yet, till a sweet treetop trickle of lilac light would call them to the dawn chorus.

And so the two riders continued through the night's silence, peering ahead, avoiding the sudden dash of a badger and the tiny hedges with the scamper of field mice or the sudden golden blink of fox eyes.

It was many hours riding before Andrew and Doric arrived at the old port. The sea was calm, and no icy wind blew across from the narrow sea. Andrew had already prepared for their arrival. Their exhausted mounts were immediately taken to a warm stable, soft with piled hay and straw. Their own food was waiting, and so was a large, comfortable room for them to share. Up a tiny steep staircase, with a creek at every step, both staggered towards the wide mattressed bed and grabbing a pillow each, were both asleep within minutes.

They woke not in the morning but close to the following afternoon as the sun streaked in between the shutter's slats, promising that the tide was in and the Narrow Sea was a snuggled blue with barely a wave. Splashing hot water from bowl to face and hands, both men dressed and took the stairs down to the parlour, then to the thin pebbled beach outside. The inn's windows looked away from the sea, unprepared to cave inwards from the icy winds blowing in during autumn, winter, and springtime storms. But this was summer, and the rippled blue was a welcome.

With a sail as small as might brave the wind, the little boat waited at the quay. Four men sat at the oars, waiting to take turns at rowing once their passengers were seated. There was neither cabin nor any comfort supplied. No wine jugs nor sacs of bread, and the privy was a straight shot over the side directly into the water. No women, therefore, could travel a boat such as this. But as Andrew climbed in and seated himself, one of the oarsmen reached out a hand to steady Doric and wished his guests welcome.

"Can't promise no quick journey," he told them. "For there ain't not a gulp nor a sneeze o' wind. But, if that wind comes a-visiting and blows us hard, then reckon tis worse, fer we needs to hold tight and don't reckon on no chance o' sleeping."

Andrew grinned. "And if the wind blows against us in the wrong direction?"

"Then I recons we comes a'flying back home fer a late dinner or an early supper."

"I can row if need be," Doric added.

But the man who had already spoken, shook his head. "We needs the right rhythm and that rhythm gotta be same fer us all, when we needs four pair arms together. And we ain't got place fer any other to row, lest you wanna take a spot at the prow."

Andrew added, "Your decisions are those we'll follow." He shifted a little on the long bench but seemed as settled as anyone facing perhaps forty hours crossing. He continued, "I chose a small boat with the intention of arriving at St. Malo without arousing curiosity. Preferably without notice of any kind. But you speak of a quick or a long crossing. Yet I believe the quickest we can expect will take more than a day and a night."

"If the luck be aginst us," the sailor relied, "could be two long days. If you brings the luck wiv you, then yes, one day with a night hard rowing and blowing. I hopes fer tomorrow maybe six or eight in the evening. Wiv this channel, you ain't gonna guess. You just gets on wiv it."

There were old fishing nets beneath the benches, the smell of scales and the crunch of salt water. Doric avoided the nets, disliking the smell. The first hours carried them over the sun-glazed sapphire, with the rhythmic splash of wood to water and the glitter so strong in their eyes that it was easier to doze. Then as evening tumbled across the water's reflections, the wind sped in cold and swift from the south-west. The rowers paused, tucking there oars down beside them.

"Tis the wind we was wanting," yelled one man, and the captain nodded.

There was no further chance to doze, and the small keel picked up speed. It was a cold crossing, but the wind was at their backs and the tiny ship cut through the waves with its sail ballooning out before its small teak mast.

Exhaustion again was on the attack, for it was many hours, once blown off route, and continuously battling the mid-stream currents which pulled like sea serpents at the keel. Morning brought the first sighting of the Breton coast, Doric held his breath. Although having absolutely no desire to stay in a foreign country, he had no desire ever to travel in such a manner again. Yet the Breton coast, so hopeful and calling of solid ground, dry grass and dry cobbles, real food and a real bed, it was as distant as the clouds above, just a long flat streak of grey across the horizon.

That evening they were rowing carefully within the St. Malo port, avoiding the docks where the larger ships anchored, two men jumped out into the shallows and waded to shore. With a scratching of keel to gravel, the boat was hauled onto land, and they had arrived.

Doric fell from the boat to the rough narrow beach and stayed on his knees.

"Not an eager sailor, then?" Andrew helped him up. "But I'll not make you suffer too much until it's time for sailing home. First, we're expected in the Jour e Nuit tavern not far from here. We dine, we sleep, and we have two horses for the morning's ride onwards."

Stretching, hands to his back, Doric stared around. It did not seem so different to any English coastline, and he wondered what vague exoticism he had been expecting.

"Bed," he breathed.

"It will be perfectly obvious that we are both English," Andrew said very softly, "there's no way to disguise it. But the country is full of English, some of them loyal to the Tudor exile and disloyal to King Richard. We'll be accepted easily enough. But make no mention of our recent arrival, nor any specific attempt to join Henry Tudor's followers. We are perhaps a little lost."

"True enough." Doric was still gazing around. The wind had increased, and it battled with the lowering sun, turning heat to shiver. "But I feel as though I'm falling with each step I take."

"The delight of land after ocean," Andrew smiled. "We climb this slope and by the time we reach the top, you'll be a man of the solid ground again. Up there the tavern is waiting, with the sweet smell of roasting spices, the promise of a feather mattress, and a jug of Malmsey."

The sun had slipped low and the setting streaks of pink and gold drifted over the peaks of scrub and stone. Doric followed Andrew up the slope and once again found his feet. He found the rest of himself once sitting, even though half asleep, at the tavern's long rough table, several Bretons banging with their spoons, and the scent of roast lamb and garlic floating through his brain. He could, he thought, almost dine on that alone.

Yet, so far away and so exhausted, once he curled beneath the light counterpane and buried his head in the pillow, it was still Louisa he dreamed about as she bent over, one cool hand to his forehead, and kissed him lightly on the mouth.

"But you're in England," he whispered to her. *"and I'm in a Breton bed. How can you kiss me?"*

With faint disdain at his distrust, she shook her head and her long tumble of soft brown curls caressed his cheek. *"I can do anything,"* she told him. Her eyes seemed fashioned from the water and gazing at her with adoring simplicity, he saw the ripples and waves, and even the seagull which had hovered, braced against the wind. *"You have no idea of the woman you've fallen in love with. I'm more than you'll ever guess."*

"Loving doesn't have reasons," he said, mystified. *"Loving is just there because it is. And do you love me too?"*

But he woke, found only Andrew sleeping gently beside him, and heard no whispers of love, only the sounds of the sea lapping on the shoreline down from the tavern bedchamber.

Rolling over as carefully as possible without waking his bed partner, he discovered he had lost his side of the counterpane. Now entirely uncovered, he hoped the chill would not keep him awake. Within two breaths he was deeply asleep once more, but this time Louisa did not visit.

Instead he dreamed of Lizzie's fish eaten remains floating downstream, and of the gruby cheeks and stubby fingers belonging to Father Balcrest, and the monastery he had escaped more than ten years past.

CHAPTER EIGHTEEN

"Really and truly, I just yearn to be loved." Louisa, her expression merged between self-shame and self-pity, stared down at her lap, where her fingers were twisting and turning together like ribbons in the wind.

But Francis could not see her for his bedchamber door still stood between them. "You are loved Lou," he said. "You know you are. I love you so much. And I bet mama loved you to, very very, very much."

"I just can't really remember her," Louisa said, small voiced. "I only have two memories. I was just turned five, and I wanted to play, and I wanted to dance and I wanted to kiss my puppets. But I heard Papa's voice roaring from the great hall, ordering me to bed. I had to pack away my three little toys and Mama led me up to my bedchamber. And I remember her kissing me goodnight and reassuring me that I hadn't been naughty, and it wasn't my fault that I had to go to bed so early. It was just because Papa had a lot of work to do. Then I can remember Mama kissing me, once on each cheek, and me looking up and then seeing those beautiful eyes. Suddenly seeing a tiny reflection of myself in her eyes, I thought that meant she was magic. That she had me in her head, just as I had been born out of her tummy." Louisa sighed, sitting back onto the low foot stool which she had brought with her. Not so comfortable, but easier than grovelling on the floorboards. "My other memory is when she was in bed and I crept in to say good night to her. Her face was so wet that it shone in the candlelight, and again, I thought it was magic to have such gleaming skin. It was only later, remembering back, that I realised she had been crying. It wasn't long after that she died. I didn't understand for years. Because she was magical, I believed she must have chosen to go away, and left me a baby to play with. But she didn't want me anymore."

Francis was on his knees at the keyhole. "My beautiful big sister with big smiles and arms to hug me with. I loved you with my first breath," he insisted.

"You remember that?"

"Well, no, not exactly. But I do understand." He gulped the words. "Papa sounds brutal, though I don't remember him much. Just his voice shouting his head off from somewhere. And Charles – well we both know about Charles. But you had Bella too."

"And I still love her," Louisa said. "And I think she loves me. But that early stuff about Mamma and Papa and Charles, I think it's left me sort of empty and longing for something without even really knowing what that is."

"You make me want to cry too." Francis muttered into the keyhole. "And I feel so horrible as well now, not only because my back still hurts and I'm sick of being locked up like a rabid dog, but because I can't remember what it was like loving Joletta. This is horrid, and I'll never tell her. I'll keep my promises. But," and he paused, exhaling with a grunt, "I've realised I don't love her. Not properly. I mean – it was all excitement and her kissing me and feeling all tingly and wanting to touch her. And I thought I'd feel like that forever."

"But you don't?"

He shook his head, although Louisa couldn't see him. "No. I think of desperately trying to find her and then, even more desperate, trying to learn about brewing. I served in that shop for a little while and the people were so impatient, and I didn't understand half of what they were saying. And then Annie came in and told me off. I went to explain to Joletta, and she went sort of pale and asked me if I understood everything she said or not. Well, of course I did. But everything went grey and gloomy."

"Might that be a good thing, Francis dear?"

"It's horrible. When they ran the ale shop down by the Fleet, I felt so tingly about her. She was gorgeous and alluring. I'd never really seen a girl that way before, just snooty ladies and a few servants running here and there. It was exciting to pass her in the shop window. Then she called me in and smiled and fluttered her eyelashes at me and I was smitten. But afterwards she told me they had to leave, and how unjust it was, and I felt so sorry for Joletta. On the last day as they were packing up and putting their things in the wheelbarrow, Joletta smiled and she sort of tripped, and her skirt went up. I saw her ankles. Oh, my heart raced. I dreamed of her for ages. It was half wonderful and half a nightmare."

"And what now?" The story sounded familiar and Louisa felt suddenly sick, wondering if she was so childishly smitten with Doric, and if that would end the same way.

"But now," Francis croaked, "I just don't care about Joletta anymore. Nor brewing. That stink and that miserable job and the thought of living there and carrying dirty buckets all day. It's just about put me off ale."

Without seeing his face Louisa was unaware of just how miserable Francis was looking. "Be honest darling," she said. "Tell Joletta. She deserves to know. She has Annie, and she has lots of friends, and she will get over the loss. You cannot possibly spend the of the rest of your life being married to someone in that manner. If you really don't feel you can care for her anymore, there is nothing else that could be right about your relationship. You don't understand her life and she could never understand yours. Charles would make everybody even more miserable than we are already, you might not ever get the money you would need to make a decent business, and you probably wouldn't have learnt brewing well enough to sell what you've made. So be honest and tell Joletta. And," she added very cautiously, "I have an idea Joletta isn't in love with you either. She was just dreaming of a grand house and lots of money and living with the son of a lord."

And then, clutching her knees, she realised that she could hear Francis crying. His next words were muttered so softly that she could barely make out what he was saying. "I can't bear to make her as unhappy as I feel myself."

"So you really just feel sorry for her and you don't want her anymore?"

"True. Isn't that a shocking thing to say? Looking back now I think I was just being a baby, passionate about the first really pretty girl, who was smiling at me, and I was flattered and she sort of – made me feel really manly instead of being a little boy. But after all the fuss and bother at the tanneries and their place being so horrible, and then Charles and coming back here and him being violent and me being locked up – well, I just feel sick. And feeling sick is all mixed up with thinking about Joletta."

Two days later Charles unlocked the bedchamber door, opened it, stuck his head around the gap, inserted the key back into the keyhole but on the inside of the door, and told Francis that he was free. "But if you ever run off again," he scowled, "I shall personally throw you down the well, or in some other manner ensure that you die in agony. You will never see that tannery slut again nor will you ever associate with her mother. You will not ever return to the tanneries and if I ever catch you coming home with that foul stink in your hair, I shall have you thrashed once more."

Life did not return to normal. Although free to leave when he wished, Francis rarely left his room except to wander the garden, walk the banks of the river, or curl up in his sister's bedchamber. Even when Charles was out on some business of his own, Francis remained quietly desolate.

Finally, it was Louisa who returned to the tanneries. Francis had asked her, and she felt obliged to help. But she also went with her own vague hopes, and left early one morning. It took her quite some hours to cross the busy streets of London and by the time she reached the old house where she and Isabella had stayed, she was tired and ready for dinner. The door was swinging open and Louisa stumbled directly into the great hall. No one knew where Doric had gone, he had not returned to find her, and it seemed he had disappeared. Eva was not there to tell her story, and had already left to find the night's work, which is how she had always described it, while the old bent man living on the ground floor in the room no larger than a privy, informed her in his usual genial gabble, that Lord Andrew was off in foreign lands far, far away..

With wilting stamina, Louisa trudged onwards through the tanneries, gulping at the renewed introduction to those thundering smells. But eventually she managed to arrive at the brewery. It had taken her so long, originally, to find the place, that now she remembered the way quite easily. The only problem was the stench.

So she knocked on the door of the brewery shed behind the shop and waited for Annie to answer. She took a little time but eventually the door was pulled open and Louisa stared at Joletta's small stout mother.

"Oh, my dear Mistress Smithson," Louisa said walking in to the shed where the huge cauldron was bubbling fiercely on its trivet and the flames beneath were blazing and sparking. Louisa kept well away from the sparks and turned to Annie. "I do hope you and Joletta are well and were not too disturbed by the horrible interruption from my wretched brother. Charles is a very difficult man and he likes to control us with an iron fist. Poor Francis is never able to get his own way, and both of us are treated as disobedient little children. Once Charles dragged Francis home, Francis was whipped and locked in his bedchamber for days. At least dear Joletta did not have that sort of punishment. But the trouble is, Francis will not find it easy to return. Personally, I think the relationship he wanted so badly, would never have worked. Clearly, he is never going to be an efficient Brewer. And I know you were not in favour of their marriage either. But Francis feels very guilty not being able to come and explain to Joletta, so he asked me to come instead. May I speak to her?"

Then Annie stared back. The little woman seemed more fragile than Louisa remembered her. Her shoulders were slumped, her eyes seemed blank, and her tight smiling mouth was no longer smiling at all.

"Joletta?" She said, "then she isn't with young Francis?"

"You mean she isn't here?" Asked Louisa.

And she shook her grey curls beneath her cap, still staring. "She ain't here. She ain't nowhere. I doesn't know where my lass is. I bin worried fer days now, and it ain't getting no better. I heard no word. All I dun saw, were a gennleman, looking a bit elderly, mayhap the same as me. He come for Joletta, and told her there was exciting plans for my lass with young Francis. He reckoned Joletta should go with him and see what were going on. That were days past. And I ain't seen no one since, nor got no word, nor got no message. That fellow ain't come back, and I got no one to ask. I was gonna come to your house my lady, in a few days, once I gunned me courage in me mouth. Now I knows what your brother Charles is likes, I knows it were gonna be a proper fight and I might get me comeuppance. But I has to know where Joletta is. And I never thought as how she'd stay away, for my lass knows I can't do the brewing all alone."

Louisa and Annie stared at each other without any full understanding. Knowing that Francis had certainly not sent any elderly gentleman to speak with Annie nor to take Joletta to meet him, Louisa had a sickening feeling like a huge stone in her stomach, and thought perhaps Charles had set up a trap.

But without genuine proof, how could she know? He could have arranged to lock her away somewhere, or even have her beaten. But there had been no clue, no hint and no obvious action. Louisa murmured, "That's very strange and very upsetting. All I know is that Francis sent nobody to get her and has no idea that anything like this happened. It wasn't his design so I can't imagine what has been going on. But I'll try and find out as soon as I can."

"Oh please do," Annie begged her. "Because if I doesn't work, I doesn't get paid. Then money be ever so tight. Already it ain't every day I can eat, but I'd gladly stop work and go off looking if need be. I won't be happy for the rest of me life, wivout my lass. But if I takes time off to go and search for my baby, where does I go? I got no idea."

Wondering if she could ever again face a cup of ale, Louisa slumped down on the stool and risked the sparks from the fire and the hiss of the boiling water smelling of yeast. Unwilling to say more, she sat thinking silently that although without Joletta, Annie would have only one mouth to feed instead of two, there would only be one person working and the single worker was the elder, the least energetic, and one slowed by misery and hunger.

"I'll do my best," she said as brightly as she could. "In the meantime, this is from Francis, hoping it will help compensate just a little for all the trouble that brother Charles caused you." She tugged out her small purse and tipped it to Annie's lap. The few coins jingled, and Annie was clearly delighted.

"I's ever so grateful," she mumbled, "really I is. Tis gonna help a lot, my lady. And thank you from the bottom o' me heart. But tis my lass I wants back more an' anything else."

Louisa nodded and stood, trying to smile. This had been her own money and not from Francis at all, but she didn't mind the loss of it. But how she would find Joletta, she had no idea.

It was late that evening before she arrived home, having only just manage to squeeze through the Ludgate before it was locked for the night. Having hurried upstairs she ran directly to see Francis, who was, as usual, in his bedchamber, half dozing.

The disappearance of Joletta frightened him as it had her. "Charles," he said immediately. "Charles has done something horrible. But who was the fellow sent to get Joletta?"

"A servant or a hired thug, I don't care. It's Joletta and where she is that bothers me. Only one way to find out," Louisa answered. "Tomorrow I start looking."

"I'll be coming with you," Francis told her immediately. "But where do we start? There's just no place that comes into my head. No place that makes any sense."

"The sheriff," Louisa suggested. "And if we run out of places to look, and she isn't anywhere, then there's only one thing left. Unfortunately. But it means facing Charles and asking him directly."

CHAPTER NINETEEN

Sunbeams had always fascinated Doric, he stood beneath the brilliance, directly under the slanting rays of the sun as it sprang through the clouds above. He was holding up the palm of his hand, speaking loudly to the small group of people around him.

"Now look, my friends. What can you see on the palm of my hand?"

Chattering to each other, confused, particularly since some of them spoke only Breton and needed a translation from their friends. But, whatever the puzzle, it was quite obvious that this young man's hand was unmarked. He held nothing, his fingers were straight, and no stains showed anywhere on the palm he held up.

"Nothing, lad. Nothing at all. We can all see that."

Doric laughed. In his other hand, he held a small sprinkle of Ashes, hidden between finger and thumb. Now he stretched out bringing both hands together and dusted one palm with the Ashes from the other. He held up the hand which he had shown before as clean and unmarked. Yet now everybody could see clearly, there were dark words written across his skin. Those words were, '*Bon jour,, mes ami.*'

The small crowd gasped audibly, turned in astonishment to their friends, and muttered how this was magic. Doric grinned at his own success, although this was a trick he'd often used in the past. "And shall I do more magic for you, mes ami?" Somehow, when his own laughter was joined by others, he delighted in it.

There was a unanimous and joyous, 'Yes, yes,' in two languages, muttered, mumbled, shouted, shrieked, and generally welcomed with applause. Many began to clap and cheer while others threw coins. Yet for the first time while doing such tricks, Doric did not care about the money. Indeed, he had been living in luxurious lodgings that he did not have to pay for, a good deal of free food, and a large handful of money chucked at him on a regular basis.

Now in Brittany, he was on his own. With careful agreements for when and where to meet, they had separated. Andrew, although arriving with him, now needed to be alone. Their tasks and intentions were quite different. As a known Lord of England and the close friend of the new king, Andrew, was travelling Brittany as if for pleasure, staying at the best inns, visiting the castle's, listening to every bit of gossip that could be heard in the taverns, but principally and more than anything else, spending time in the docks to see whether ships were being prepared to sail across the narrow sea carrying men at arms. On the other hand, Doric looked exactly like the wandering minstrel he was. As such he could play his part and infiltrate wherever possible. He might even proclaim himself a faithful Lancastrian and slip in to meet the ambitious Henry Tudor himself.

That had not yet been achieved. However, Doric was on the road exactly as he enjoyed, the lute in a sack across his back, and sufficient coin to sleep and eat at the local inns. Not only was his purse well filled by Andrew, but he was paid along the way by the crowds impressed by his music, his magical tricks, and his occasional predictions.

Doric knew tricks enough. He knew a hundred or more that would excite and even terrify any crowd. He knew how to crush incense so that a candle flame would appear to light the hand holding it. He knew how to toss apples in the air, so they seemed to be dancing entirely on their own, but this needed a thread of horse hair and a dull day. Instead now under the sun Doric turned water to wine in a cup where he had laid crumbs of bread previously soaked in wine, but afterwards dried into hard specs impossible to recognise by any peering group of eager spectators. He held out the bowl and even in the dazzle of sunshine, the colourless crumbs seemed impossible to notice. Then, taking a jug of water, he poured this into the bowl, and then presented the miracle to the crowd. For the water had turned to wine, not only taking the rich colour, but also some of the taste. Having made a considerable amount of money from his tricks Doric settled on an outcrop of stones and began to play the lute and sing. He knew no Breton songs, but the melodies were sweet enough to attract the rewards, as the crowds grew and called him a wonderful musician and a sublime Lord of magic.

One bright afternoon as the trees fluttered their red and golden leaves in the sunshine, Doric knew that he was gaining fame as he wandered, as the local people would point and shout. "That's him. Our Merlin. But if you have a coin to spare, we can get him to sing and that's even better."

Beneath the gracious stretch of a willow, Doric sat and grinned and sang to his own music, words of a tree bereft after losing its leaves in the autumn, but then of the joy as spring comes and the buds reawaken. *Life*, his words promised, *is always more beautiful reborn, blossom replaces tired leaf, and after the night comes the dawn.*

Then, looking up with a grin as wicked as his magic tricks, Doric placed his well-used pack of cards on the grass, and flushed them, sending them dancing in the air, and using his wide embroidered cuffs as a hiding place. But when someone called out that he must have the missing card up his sleeve, Doric tugged his sleeve open, and instead pulled out a tiny kitten, as white as eiderdown and as soft as velvet. It curled, opened huge blue eyes, and mewled for lost comfort as the crowd whooped and cheered. So Doric tucked it down the front of his doublet where it settled in peace. It was later that afternoon when he returned it to its mother, that he received the message he had been waiting for. An invitation, and a request for paid entertainment.

That night Doric slept well. He had fulfilled his intention, the hope that some would carry news of his name and talent to the castle nearby for that was where Henry Tudor was living. Exiled, but thanks to the Breton Duke, it was an exile of luxury and comfort. Attempting to keep England as a friend, whoever was in power, the Duke had offered Henry every possible pleasure including a financial allowance. However, now that Richard of Gloucester was King of England, the duke had been told he must cease to pay the Lancastrian claimant, and indeed even Henry's mother could no longer send him coin, her fortune was under the control of her husband, confiscated when she had been found encouraging rebellion.

Any English newcomer was immediately a suspicious arrival to Tudor's following. But, to the local villagers, this was a man of great magical talent. The inevitable invitation therefore came from two directions.

The Chateau L'Hermine was both acting as gaol and a huge house of magnificence and impressive comfort. Although his freedom was limited, this not only served to keep Henry Tudor as a supposed prisoner, but also kept him safe from possible English abduction.

Neither short nor tall, neither thickset nor wiry, but narrow shouldered, sallow and frowning with a slightly disfiguring distortion in his left eye, the young man appeared considerably older than his twenty-six years. Doric the minstrel and swindler, just three years younger, felt he was looking at a man near decrepit enough to be his father.

Henry Tudor looked up only briefly as Doric was shown in, and then returned to the letter he was writing. Doric regarded him for some moments, waiting either for acknowledgement or dismissal, and then, receiving neither, abruptly turned to leave. But he was interrupted. "You are the young lutist and singer the locals have mentioned?" Henry Tudor put down his quill. His voice was heavily accented, as if his language had been influenced by others and after many years it was Breton which had become his native tongue.

Doric bowed. Once, as Margaret Beaufort's son, Henry had been the Earl of Richmond. In exile, this title had been withdrawn but Henry used it still. "My lord, yes indeed. I'm honoured by your interest." He paused, then shook his head. "No doubt you've heard both the best and the worst of me, my lord."

"Perhaps not so incorrectly, as it happens." Henry Tudor remained forward hunched in his chair, put the tips of his fingers together, elbows on the desk, and squinted into the morning's dreary cloud. "But you do not know me, although no doubt you know something of me." His mouth remained prim and there was no smile in his eyes. "You have been invited here to perform for my friends, yet a visitor from England who comes so close to my home, is of more than musical interest. So tell me without subterfuge, young man, why are you here?"

Doric remained standing. The tiny oriel window at his back allowed little light and he stood in gloom. "I am simply a wanderer, my lord, and so I'm interested in hearing the cause of your interest." He smiled. "After many years in the sweet countryside where I was born, I met a fisherman who sails the Narrow Sea. This man offered me a voyage to another shore. I have never refused opportunity or excitement, since I have the freedom to do as I wish."

"We are all prisoners of a sort, boy."

"Freedom," Doric replied, "can be described, granted, and curtailed in many ways, sir."

Henry still peered over the tips of his fingers. "Personally, I do not have the freedom to search excitement." He paused, almost smiling. "At least, not yet."

"I am sorry to hear it." Doric clasped his hands behind his back, looking around the grandeur of the room. "But if lack of freedom brings such blissful comfort, I cannot see it as so terrible a disadvantage."

"You have an unusual vision of the world around you," Henry said, his Breton accent increasing, as though annoyed, while his defect in one eye made Henry squint, and only one eye gazed directly as he spoke. "Perhaps music brings alternative lights to the mundane."

"A virtue I doubt I have." Doric laughed suddenly, "Although I accept the title of mundane." Outside, the pelter of rain was abrupt and the clouds lowered. It was a day that demanded candles, but

Henry was not the man to waste his small allowance or use the funds his mother had previously sent him on unnecessary extravagance. The lack of light probably explained the several blots of gall ink on the paper at his elbow, and the fact that the quill was cross-nibbed.

Doric had expected to be interrogated and suspected as a spy, but now it occurred to him that Henry Tudor might have hoped he brought secret funds from his English friends. His thoughts were interrupted.

Tudor asked, "You leave what you call sweet green, and choose to walk here beneath the rain. Do you regret your choice, boy?"

"Nostalgia, my lord? Do you hold your homeland in such affection?" Tudor frowned, and Doric laughed again, changing his own expression. "I came on a rowing boat with my feet entwined in netting and the smell of sardines my only dinner, sir. So now I miss my homeland and will return when I can afford it and find a ship to take me. In the meantime, my lord, may I play for you? I should prove my value, I think."

"It is why I permitted your entrance here." said Henry Tudor at once. "I have no need of a minstrel, but music often brings peace. Yet there can be many motives for every man's choices." The slow smile did not warm Henry Tudor's face. "I trust no one," he said simply. "No man has ever entirely earned my trust. Nor am I gullible by nature. Therefore, I withhold all opinions until assured of the facts. And even facts lie. I shall listen to your talents, boy, and judge them. If I like your playing, then you shall bring that same pleasure to myself and my friends this evening."

Pulling his lute gently from its sacking, Doric smoothed three fingers across its polish as though touching the woman he loved, and strummed briefly, checking the strings. Very softly, he began the gentle melody of one of his own creations and murmured the words. Henry Tudor listened without comment and finally, as Doric finished, he said, low voiced, "Music has been my saviour, my lord. Perhaps it could save others."

The other man tapped his fingertips, proving the lie to the claim of endless patience. "God does not send us frequent saviours, boy, nor do

I expect one. But in some matters, especially when uncommon, the Lord's intentions are made remarkably clear. We must simply be grateful for what comes."

Doric smiled at the clear suspicion. His music had, perhaps, not been good enough to convince this man he was not a spy. "Can I play something of your own choice, my lord? A family favourite, maybe? A tune of the church, although I cannot be compared to a choir. Or does your mother love particular music of any kind to bring you a reminder of home?"

Tudor jerked, as though waking from a dream. "My mother," Henry Tudor nodded, "was just thirteen years old and already a widow when I was born. She also nearly died, myself with her. I believe her suffering was terrible and she has never been able to bear more children. But we both survived. It is a sign, you see, of what our Lord God intends for us. Clearly there has been no time for music or frivolity, boy. Play what you will, but expect no accolades from me."

"Yet I'm not entirely sure," Doric said after a pause, "what is being asked of me. What exactly is it I'm being required to – fulfil? To please you, my lord? Yet if music cannot please you? To entertain your friends, which I shall do gladly? Or to convince you that I am not sent to spy on your intentions, with orders from England to see what may happen next?"

Once more Tudor seemed to jerk awake and this time the table trembled. Henry stared, narrow eyed. "You are impertinent, boy. You'll not speak to me in such a manner, nor question or judge me. But you may return tonight. Come to the chateau this evening. You can sing for your supper." And he turned away, waving one dismissive hand. Doric took his time repacking the lute, then bowed briefly, thanked his lordship, turned and left the room.

He clattered down the winding stairs and strode back outside for a grateful gulp of fresh air. Soon his hair was soaked, hanging lank to his nose and dripping from hat to shoulders. But Doric was laughing as he hurried back to the tavern.

Having no idea whether they would feed him at the castle, and presuming not, he ate at the inn, each mouthful a pleasure. His freedom, which he had loved, had also included weeks of great hunger and the forced acceptance of stale crumbs, mildewed pastry thrown in the rubbish heap, and the fatty rind of bacon. When there was nothing at all to eat, he had laughed at himself, denigrated the savage pains, drunk fresh water from the streams, and waved at the birds as they pecked at worms and insects, leaf and seed. Other wanderers begged at the back doors of cottages where the perfumes of cooking floated with the smoke from the chimneys. Doric had never done this, though cursed his own pride. Now he ate the food of kings and laughed at his luck.

The evening was less jovial than he had expected, but as forty or more of the English traitors sat almost silently at their meal, Doric played dancing tunes, fast sunshine music, and finally the tunes he loved himself, including many he had written. In the past he had wondered why sadness brought him happiness and puzzled over the absurdity. Memories were miserable enough but that brought no pleasure at all. Yet as he played on, often singing, many of the men looked up as though noticing him for the first time, and cheered, threw coins, invited him to join them at the lower table, and asked for the songs they remembered themselves. At the centre of the high table, Henry Tudor watched with little interest. His frown brought additional years to his face.

Some others were vaguely familiar faces, Woodvilles, relatives of the queen dowager, wife of the late king, and in particular Doric noticed Bishop Morton, lately left in the custody of the Duke of Buckingham, a supposed supporter of the king. But Buckingham was not present, and Doric had been too long from nobility and on his return as a minstrel, such lords had long left both court and country. He recognised few.

As many diners left, scraping back their chairs as the pages ran to help, Doric bowed again to Henry Tudor. "My lord, I thank you for such an honour. Playing to your lordship's friends has been a great pleasure. May I return at some time?"

Tudor blinked. His eyes still appeared bruised with suspicion. "This chateau is the property of the Lord of Rieux, a gentleman I respect," he said, "but who at present is absent, in company with Duke Francis. I therefore invite you just once more before the lord returns, to play here tomorrow evening. You will pretend no magical nonsense and you will perform no acts of swindle or wickedness as I have heard you have done in these streets below. You will play and you will sing but you will speak to no man except myself, and you will not eat at our tables."

The dark wet night meant candles flickering in the breezes whining down the chimneys, men huddled over their platters, food cold before it could be eaten, and candle smoke in twisting threads mixing with the rising perfumes. Doric was glad to be gone and had only a short stride back to the tavern and the bed which waited.

"Wine, brought to my room, and none of your sickly-sweet Malmsey," Doric called on his way up the stairs. The Gascon was served before he managed to pull his boots off, and the tavern boy helped with that too, though he got mud splashed up his smock for his pain, yet quickly compensated with two bright coins. Lying back on the bolster, cup in hand, Doric closed his eyes and smiled to himself. He had heard very little, but some of the whispers he had found extremely important and would remember each word until he saw Andrew once more. Opening his eyes again, careful not to spill the wine he was enjoying, he saw the angel of luck smiling at him from the rumpled eiderdown. He raised his cup and drank.

The rain pattered against the gleaming cropped horn of the tavern windows and that rhythm entered Doric's dreams, almost a lullaby for a tired man.

But as he dreamed on, he found himself clutching his lute, caressing the neck, tightening the pegs, and listening to the music in his ears. Then he looked down and saw neither shining wood nor the sheep gut strings he loved. Instead a woman lay in his arms, her head in his lap, and his fingers in the flowing silk of her long brown hair. Her breath was soft, her eyes closed, and the thick black eyelashes rested like a crown of jet across her cheeks.

He knew who she was and caressed her as he had his lute. But she did not wake, and he was sure she had no idea who he was.

CHAPTER TWENTY

Thomas Tewkesbury grinned. "So you've met our handsome Earl of Richmond, I believe?"

Looking up, surprised, over his break-fast platter, Doric nodded. "Indeed, sir. Did I meet you last evening at the chateau?"

The other man sat opposite, his cup now on the table. "You play well, lad."

Doric thanked him. "So you follow Henry Tudor?"

"We all serve ourselves in whatever manner we think will bring us the greatest benefit."

"As I have every intention of doing," Doric laughed. "A man without title or wealth must make his living in whatever way he can." Having eaten and drunk, he clasped his hands behind his head, leaning back on the stool, and regarded the newcomer with a small sigh. He spoke softly, but the pounding rain outside seemed to give rhythm to his words. "I wonder if my own loyalties. are under question, sir. I assume you are here, instead of breaking fast at the chateau, in order to question me regarding my motives. So ask away, and I'll answer cheerfully. Or have you come to cancel my performance at the chateau this evening?" His toes steamed a little in their damp wool since he had no spare dry shoes. "I'll take my fate as it comes, and neither complain nor rejoice."

"I'm Thomas Tewkesbury," the man smiled, "and I've no single question to ask. I presume you're loyal to your king, as any young man should be who knows nothing of politics and can't tell a Lancastrian from a Yorkist any more than he can tell a Christian from a Muslin. I didn't come here for you at all, lad. I came for the sausages."

'I've never mct a Muslim," Doric said, "Nor the king I support. But I've eaten the sausages they serve here, and they deserve their reputation, sir."

"Then be my guest, lad," Thomas said as five sausages were delivered steaming hot to the table. "Should the rain ever stop, since otherwise it's pointless, come to the chateau grounds, and get someone to point you to the mews. It's there you'll find me. Don't bother to bring your lute."

'By order of the Earl of Richmond, or for your own curiosity, sir? Or havc you some alternative interest, perhaps, such as cadging a lift when returning to our mother-land?"

"None of those," The other man frowned, straightening his back. "I've no interest in whether you spy or simply write music."

"Perhaps I am a spy." Doric once more closed his eyes. "Has that occurred to you, sir? It certainly has to the Earl of Richmond."

Thomas ate the second sausage. "You spoke the word *'cadge'*, lad. As it happens, falconry is my passion. And I find you very different to some ordinary wastrel wandering the country lanes. You play too well. You know fine music and not simply the repetitive songs of the village folk. You speak as a man who knows far more than he should, and you have the confidence of a lord, not that of a hopeful beggar. And you laugh. Laughter to me is a form of music, and we indulge it very rarely as exiles and men whose hope is greater than their purses. Your laughter is infectious." He raised the third sausage between his fingers, but before stuffing it in his mouth, he smiled, asking, "Now I wonder, young man, if you also know something of the art of falconry."

It seemed more than a hundred years gone since a yearling hawk had clasped his glove, its sharp face close to his own. Doric shook his head. "They fascinate me, sir, and I watch them flying high. But I know nothing else."

"Then come to me at the mews this afternoon," Thomas said, "and discover a pleasure as magical as music."

When Thomas left, the rain had eased to a drab desultory drizzle. It was midday when the sunbeams etched their doorway through the grey clouds, and broke into wide smiles across the Breton fields and the lanes of Vannes.

Stamping the mud from the soles of his boots, Doric set off for the chateau grounds, and the long dark building which housed the mews. Thomas stood already in the doorway. The bird's claws grasped his gauntlet, her eyes reflecting the sunbeams slanting between the trees.

Awaiting a quiet falconer's contemplation and his bird's swift pleasure, the great Breton forests stretched down from the base of the chateau's tower in one direction, the open fields and spreading valleys to the other. The sunlight pooled in dappled gold between the marching greens, blues and grisaille. The low mews stood between hushed stone and black beams where the falcons sat plume-hooded and quiet within their shadows, jesses stilled, tiny brass bells silent in the gloom, pounces gripped to perch one legged, varvels stamped in silver with the Lord of Rieux's crest.

But quickly unhooded, no longer sleeping, the rows of feathers roused and lifted. Outside the men were standing on the open slopes with the wind contained and gentle at their backs and the sun suddenly vivid along each flash of steel. The English lords lounged, waiting for the cadger to bring out the birds.

The young Lord of Tewkesbury stood on his own, the falcon to his gauntlet, but watching the slow wheel of a wild bird high amongst the clouds; a buzzard hunting, bringing memories, and reborn thoughts of freedom. Intrigued, Doric stood close, watching and waiting.

Someone spoke, and he turned, jolted from dreams. "She is a little hood shy, but a fine footer," said the strongly accented voice of the cadger at his shoulder. "Will you try her, sir?" Doric smiled. The bird on his wrist was all brown beauty with her cream speckled breast and huge hungry eyes. She gazed, unblinking with the striking gaze of the raptor.

Doric stretched out his arm, taking her to his gauntlet, her jesses firm beneath his thumb, and nodding, walked with her up the slope, then stood alone where the birch trees soared. He fed her the two scraps of food he had in his other hand, speaking softly to her. Golden eyed, she listened, watching for the next shred of raw chicken to appear between his fingers.

Finally releasing her, Doric then stood in admiration, watching her sails slow spread until she seemed no more than the soft tinkle of a bell in the breeze and a speck against the high blue.

The cadger moved back but did not immediately retire. He spoke softly, as if considering. "She's a fine bird, my lord." He paused, then said abruptly, "you is here guest of Sir Thomas, my lord?"

But Doric was watching the hawk. He did not bother to correct the title of lord.

There were rabbits on the far slopes, the flick of ears above the waving grass seed, but the peregrine hovered, and without warning, swooped. She had seen a more interesting quarry. From the heights she fell, plummeting from fleck to visible majesty in the speed of her plunge. The prey was dead as her talons hit, its head crushed by the impact, the woodcock a crush of blood-stained chestnut.

The cadger, watching, stepped forward again. He seemed about to speak, then saw who else approached, and immediately nodded and walked quickly away, striding back towards the long shadows of the mews. The falcon returned to Doric's gauntlet and he fed her from his right as she perched his left, her jesses once more beneath his thumb, tearing neatly at the meat scraps with a quick thrust and an impatient flick to bewit and bell.

From behind him, Henry Tudor said, "Sir Thomas tells me this will make you happy. So are you happy, boy, to be here for the hunt? You seem confident for a wandering minstrel and trickster, I think?"

"The hunt, my lord?" Doric grinned. "Since already I seem more the sparrow than the hawk, it remains to be seen who ends as quarry."

"You are teasing, I suppose?" Henry Tudor frowned. "It is a form of humour I have never understood, and seems to me a great waste of breath. We must show strength rather than ridicule, I believe. I leave the chateau rarely, and so now I shall enjoy the day."

Doric bowed. "Yes, I was teasing," he said, "and shall remember not to do so again." He controlled the muscle at the corner of his mouth.

The bird still to his glove, he once more wandered alone, first to the crest of uneven undulations which divided forest from plain. He was seen by those who hunted and by those who watched him with more care and purpose than they watched the birds, but he did not speak. His wandering appeared unfocused and when his path took him deeper amongst the trees, there was no one who noticed the momentary disappearance of his shadow.

"A fine bird, my young friend," said the large man from beneath the larches. "Although not as I had expected to find you."

In delight, Doric grinned. "A great surprise to me too, my lord. Nor had I expected you so soon."

"I've discovered enough," Andrew told him softly, his finger scratching the back of the peregrine's neck. "I'm hoping you have plenty to add to my own discoveries. We'll leave tonight."

The falcon was restless, straining against her jesses. Doric watched her, stroking the beauty of her curved beak. "I'm expected at the chateau, but do I still play there, or let them down? Tell me when and I'll be ready," he said. "At the tavern?"

"At the tavern," Andrew nodded. "Midnight will suit, and so fulfil your obligations first and see what else you can overhear."

"Midnight then." Doric paused. "But the tavern closes by eleven. I'll meet you on the other side of the stables." As Andrew turned, nodding, and disappeared between the elongated shadows of the trees, Doric smiled, and within moments was also gone. He reappeared sauntering from forest to chateau, the bird still to his gloved fist.

The peregrine on his gauntlet locked her eyes to his. Doric saw her as an arrowed blaze of scarlet, a colour that swept through the gloom of his isolation. He talked softly to her, telling her those secrets that he had told no one else in his life. He told her about his childhood, and what he hoped, perhaps, for the future.

Doric flew her again, with the sky bright and unhazed, as he stood on the green slopes, and watched the peregrine, aware only of the Master of the Mews who kept a respectful distance out of earshot. In England, he knew, he would never have been permitted such a high ranked bird, no beggar could fly a peregrine. But here, without any idea of most men's titles, the birds that needed exercise were flown by the men willing to fly them.

"You would want her as I do, if you knew her," Doric said to the bird, or perhaps only to himself. "She is the daughter of some nobleman, though I don't know which. Our introduction was improper, to say the least. Your eyes are magnificent. Fearless. But Louisa has eyes a richer blue than the sky."

The peregrine sat motionless, regarding him, so he smiled. "You take me for a fool. No doubt you are right. But I had already learned a little about falconry as a child and loved it before I left. If you don't object, I might say that I am learning to love you, Rosalind. But if I close my eyes, it is Louisa that I see. Your eyes are amazing, but hers more beautiful still."

Doric walked with her a little higher on the slope, looking to where the long line of trees etched against the rise of the horizon, blocking the dip of the forest beyond. From there he flew the peregrine one last time, sending her up in the ring to wait on, searching for the quarry she preferred, her slow wings combating the feint of the wind, a small shadow against his own face as he watched her solitary hover. "Am I truly a fool, then? To suppose I love a girl I've not seen more than twice. Even if she came to me, she owes it to her station to marry property and title. Her family would disown her if she spoke of marrying a penniless wanderer."

He sat then, risking grass stains to his borrowed doublet, stretching his legs, easing the toes in the worn-out boots. "You are the most beautiful thing I've yet to see in Brittany," he told the raptor's lazy wing beat and tiny shadow, straining his gaze up into the glitter of light above. "But the most beautiful in England is the Lady Louisa, who I shall probably never see again." Leaning back and clasping his hands behind his head, he watched the sky, eyes hooded against the glare, adoring the bird that hung there like a candle flame. "Henry Tudor listens to his mother's ambitions, and thinks himself the Lancastrian heir, even though he stands at least twentieth in line. But who knows, Rosalind, what the wheel of fortune holds for any of us. I believe Tudor has no understanding of humour and I think no love, but he is not a fool. And he must have the courage of a peregrine falcon, if he thinks to invade England to claim either the throne, or his own death on the battlefield or the block."

The peregrine had seen her quarry. A jay flew, a little wild, cutting across. Again the peregrine swooped, a drop of two hundred feet at least, and smashed the jay's breast in her claws.

"But watching you, I learn my own moves," Jack murmured. "For your great strength is not your beauty, but your skill, and how, when you swoop, you strike not where the quarry was when you saw and desired it. You aim for where the quarry will be when you reach it. In an instant, you judge distance, the current of the air, wind and cloud, and most of all the speed of the thing you plan to kill. All this in a blink. And since you have never missed, it is this, then, that you must teach me."

She returned swiftly to his hand, and Doric took her prey and fed her, smiling. "You are remarkably beautiful," he told her, voice soft as the whispered folding of her primary feathers. "But it is time I went home,"

Returning the peregrine to her perch, he smiled at the cadger. "Rosaline is home," he said, "and well fed. She is more glorious than any bird I've flown. I thank you all for an unforgettable experience."

The Breton shook his head, puzzled. "The peregrine ain't called Rosalind, my lord. She's Agnes, just four years old, and moulted a month back."

"She told me her name was Rosalind," Doric smiled, "I see no reason to disbelieve her." With no sight of Thomas Tewkesbury, he strode through the waning sunshine and back to the tavern.

It seemed the chateau welcomed him as he entered and was taken to the great hall and the tables set for dining with at least forty men on the benches and as many platters set with food, a dozen candles scenting the air with sweet wax and not tallow, and jugs of deep crimson wine overflowing to the linen beneath.

Doric knew he was watched, and saw Tudor staring from the high table. Doric bowed, then found Thomas of Tewkesbury and bowed again. Then he eased his lute from its nest, and began to play.

Knowing the night would soon carry him home, Doric played fast, and sang fast, and heard more than he had expected of the Tudor plans and ambitions. But as Henry Tudor rose from the table, pushing back the sweeping velvet of his coat, and the other men rose too, bowing and repeating the prayers for sleep, for waking strong and healthy in the morning, and for a blessing which might bring all their hopes and plans to success, Doric also bowed, packed his lute and turned to leave.

He found a double row of armed guards blocking the outer doorway. Puzzled more than alarmed, Doric stared, then turned. Thomas Tewkesbury stood behind him.

"Well, young Doric, lord of nowhere," Thomas said, "since you were never going to answer our questions with honesty and truth, we tested you and have found you as guilty as a hanged man on the scaffold. It has all been lies, sir. A master of the lute and a predictor of failure in battle could, perhaps, be truly a common lad and a wandering minstrel looking to make his own fortune. We could not be sure. So we thought of another way to test your means and motives."

"You accuse me of dishonesty," Doric demanded, "when everything you said to me was a calculated trap?"

"No penniless fool speaks and acts as you do, sir." Thomas stabbed out with one finger, pushing Doric back towards the watching guards. They raised their pikes, one foot forward and ready to rush. "And the final proof," Thomas continued. "No village blunderer, not even a poacher, knows how to handle a hawk as you do, fool. Or have you spent all your life taming falcons, and another life learning the lute, another speaking with confidence to lords in the tongue of the royal courts, and another practising how to tell lies with a face of innocence?"

Without time or desire to answer, Doric ran back and leapt to the nearest of the benches, then sprang to the table. He grabbed up two of the meat knives lying there and faced the guards. Not bothering with speed, they stepped slowly forwards, their pikes aiming directly at Doric. But he ran backwards again, jumping to the high table where Henry Tudor had sat. Pushing around the lower table, the guards followed.

Then a flat and sour voice behind him interrupted his concentration. "You think us all fools, sir, to accept an English spy in our midst without suspicion? I have trusted no man except my uncle, nor any woman except my mother. Nor do I believe in coincidence, for life is not the joke you imagine it. You will forget the constant laughter as you learn, and we shall teach you." Henry Tudor turned and nodded to Thomas and then the guards. "Take him down to the dungeons, and lock him in." He looked back to Thomas Tewkesbury. "Then find out precisely who he is. I want to know as soon as possible what title his family holds, and whether this was a plan from Richard the usurper to take me prisoner."

With Doric still standing high on the table amongst the uneaten food, with a blade inn each hand, abruptly other voices echoed, not from the outer door, but from the doorway leading within the chateau to the stairs, bedchambers, and on to the kitchens.

These voices were cheerfully interrupting both each other and their leader, and somebody laughed. The guards whirled but stopped mid-stride. There were many accented curses and insults in French, Breton and English.

"Life is never quite so straightforward," said Andrew, raising his own sword into the candlelight. "And since he has done you no harm, you will release my young friend, and tell your men to drop their weapons."

Staring as wide eyed as the falcon, Doric hopped down from the table, kicked off a chicken carcass, and grinned at his saviours. "Henry Tudor," Doric said, "does not believe in miraculous saviours. But I most certainly do." Behind Andrew stood a crowd of armed men, pushing to pass their leader and surge forwards. They were calling out, cheering and cackling, describing the terrible bloodshed they were surely about to cause.

"Take him," roared Henry Tudor.

Andrew's men rushed forwards and the guards sprang up, their pikes directly into their attackers' eyes.

CHAPTER TWENTY-ONE

"I have no idea," Charles told his sister, his voice softly menacing. "That is the name I do not wish to hear ever again. As far as I am concerned that whore does not exist."

"No whore." Louisa glared up at her brother. "The poor girl works hard for a living, long hours. Yes, perhaps her mother was a street girl. I believe that was how Joletta was born, and why she has no father. That is all the more reason to pity the girl. I truly believe she is not the right wife for Francis, I doubt such a marriage would bring happiness to either of them. However, she should be told and given some small form of compensation. Above all else she must be found. Her mother is desperate. Joletta has entirely disappeared, and there seems no reason for it."

"Speak to me on this subject again," Charles told her, "and I shall punish you. A lady does not speak of trash and I shall treat you as trash yourself if you dare do so again."

He walked off his back stiff and did not turn around. Louisa sighed. She was not surprised. She remembered no moment when Charles had ever seemed remotely kind, nor had he consented to answer questions. Besides, she assumed, and hoped beyond hope, that her brother had taken no action in this situation and that Joletta's strange disappearance had nothing to do with Charles.

Louisa returned to give her younger brother the news. "He says he had nothing to do with it," she said. "Actually, that's not quite true. He just won't listen to her name and refuses to answer my questions."

"That means he may have done something," Francis said, hands trembling.

At least now they could look at each other. They sat together on the edge of Louisa's bed, the door shut tight behind them. Louisa flung her arms around her little brother. At once he buried his head into her shoulder and burst into loud breathless sobs. She kissed his brow and wiped the tears from his cheek with her thumb. He was, after all, still only 14, she wondered if Charles, with all his brutal control and frequent punishments, had actually made Francis into a frightened little boy instead of a mature and growing man.

"Hush my dear," she told him, "we will find Joletta somehow. Now you have decided she is not the right wife for you, everything will be easier."

"But it's all my fault," Francis continued to cry. "I didn't mean to be an idiot. And I didn't ever mean to hurt Joletta. But I did, didn't I? I'm to blame for all of this. When we find out where Joletta is I will apologise on my knees."

Each day, after Charles left the house, usually refusing to say where he intended going, Louisa and Francis went together and searched for Joletta. They walked endlessly, to the tanneries and beyond, and took money whenever they could get their hands on some, for Annie at the ale shop. She was in a continuous state of bleak misery since she could not believe that her beloved daughter, would run away and leave her like this.

"I accept," Louisa sighed, staring at Annie, "I can't be suffering the way you are. She's your beautiful daughter, and I understand. But we care, I promise we do. And we'll find her." She did not add that each day they spent searching, meant a return to misery as Charles punched out or refused them food.

Annie had not combed her hair for days, nor bathed, and her face showed the streaks of endless desperate tears, and admitted that alone, she could not work nor carry buckets, nor continue the long hours without breaking her back.

So Francis and Louisa scoured the dismal surroundings, from the old house owned by Lord Leys, where Louisa had stayed, to every part of the stinking tanneries including the foul pits, and Louisa was frequently sick into the river.

Andrew's house was the dark but welcoming home as Louisa remembered it, and Francis was intrigued. But Joletta was not living there, and Eva was not at home. The old man on the ground floor, however, called out when Louisa walked in. "I hears them footsteps, mistress, and knows tis a lady and not my friend Evie, for them shoes is not the same."

Louisa, Francis behind her, peeped into his room. and smiled at the scarecrow on the bed. He looked up with an expression of strong disappointment.

"Perhaps you don't remember me," Louisa said, taking a step back. She was trying to remember his name.

"Yes, I knows you, mistress," the man said with sorrowful disinterest. "But I thought you was the Lady Tyballis. She bin here this morning and I were hoping she'd come and see me afore she leaves." He turned away, head into the pillow and his few scraps of hair falling back into his eyes.

For Louisa, this was good news. With a nod to Francis, she ran up the stairs, but found nobody in residence. Then it meant a run down the stairs, more tricky, since many of the old cracked steps were broken or missing. Indeed Tyballis was in the kitchen and Francis watched in impressed delight. Since leaving the nursery, where sometimes he felt he still belonged, he had been permitted few visits to court and no important visitors came to the house, and none at all in a social manner. Tyballis was staring a rich perfume hot on the trivet, the small flames dancing beneath. Smiling, clearly she remembered Louisa and was pleased to see her.

"I do feel rather alone at present," she admitted. "since Andrew and his new assistant have both gone to Brittany. It's a secret expedition so I shouldn't be talking about it."

"His new assistant?" Louisa was immediately riveted. "Can I know his name?"

Removing the wooden spoon from the pot, Tyballis tasted the pottage she had been stiring. Seemingly satisfied, she removed the pot from the trivet placing it on the tiled floor. She looked up at Louisa with faint doubt, but then decided that doubt was not needed. "Well," she said quietly, "it's the young man you have met already. His name is Doric. My husband thinks him extremely efficient, so has taken him on this most important mission abroad."

Louisa, attempting casual interest, murmured, "Ah yes, Doric, the one who laughs a lot. And nice brown eyes."

She, Francis and Tyballis sat and shared the pottage, grouped around the small kitchen table, squashed on benches. "Lord Leys seems to be a remarkable man," Louisa continued, mouth full. "You are so lucky to have such a husband. And clearly you adore each other, which seems so rare these days. Arranged marriages don't bring adoration and sometimes not even vague affection."

With a small smile, Tyballis shook her head. "Yes indeed, I think he's wonderful, and so do a lot of other people. He truly is a master of subterfuge and I think he's a political genius. His Majesty the King seems to think so too. However, this means that he is often away from home for months, and I miss him so much. When we met and got to know each other, which wasn't all that long ago, it was a time of great danger and rebellion, and not only was Andrew nearly killed but so was I. Of course, from the old king's death, there was nothing but conspiracy and fighting."

This seemed so intriguing to both Louisa and Francis who had been blissfully unaware of anything at that time except their older brother's temper, that they asked a hundred questions and buried their heads in conversations and explanations. It was quite some time, an hour or more, before Louisa remembered the most important responsibility and why they were there. She looked up suddenly at Tyballis and asked, "Where would someone hide if they were frightened? There's a young woman who was living near the tanneries at a brewery, and she disappeared. We don't know if she was dragged away, or if she ran away. But we know she has no money. Do have you any knowledge of where we should be searching?"

But Tyballis had very little idea. "That could be anywhere. The folk of the tanneries can be very obstinate, knowing they're despised by virtually everyone else. Just as easy to run out into the surrounding farmlands, perhaps the forest beyond. Then there's the tenements. More than a hundred folk of all kinds live in those squashed little rooms. If I had to find a place to hide, that's where I'd go."

They had left the old house when Francis began to sniff loudly. Louisa held out her hand. Doubtless poor Francis was never going to stop crying. She sighed, but said nothing as she felt her brother's damp grip around her fingers, while dragging his feet through the oozing muck.

After a further pitiful day with no success, Louisa took Francis to the tenements where Isabella's brother-in-law lived. She remembered the right lodgings since there was no door and the opening to the room was simply a dirty curtain.

It was evening and the tenants were without light except for a few tiny cooking fires, but having decided that a daytime visit would be pointless since Robert Rudge would surely be at work. But having arrived at the recognisable curtain, and while looking for someplace to knock the, Louisa and Francis heard a recognisable voice from within and paused, not wishing to enter further.

It was Isabella they heard speaking. "Idiot," she was yelling. "I've told you never to repeat such things and the danger is just as bad now as it ever was. In fact, after deciding to leave, I was quite ready to go all the way, denounce Charles, and set off finally to find my darling Gisella."

Louisa distinctly heard as Isabella collapsed into tears it seemed that everybody was crying except herself. Her brother's eyes were still red and swollen, Tyballis had almost broken down, the old man trapped in his bed was on the point of the same, and now here was dear Isabella. But more interesting than that, was her conversation.

Louisa had no idea who Gisella might be and she looked up at Francis, one eyebrow raised. But Francis shook his head with another sniff.

It was the man's voice which answered. "None of my business now, lass. And me, I's don't need to know none of your secrets."

"Yes, they are my secrets," Isabella said softly, "but they aren't secret from you Robert, you know it all. If I ever tell, then that's up to me. This bit of misery, like a great grinding stone in my belly from morning to night, is my own private business. One day it may kill me, and no doubt Gisella will be better off without me."

"Reckon I might go off and kill the bugger once I knows you done gone."

"Once I'm gone," Isabella told him, "I won't know and I won't care."

"You ought never gone back to the house and those bleeding memories and that bastard man," her brother-in-law complained.

Another bout of tears "I had nowhere else to go. How could I stay here with you? And where I stayed was not my house and I had no right there. My only other choice was to live as a homeless beggar or take my own life."

Louisa gasped, clutched her hand over her mouth, and stepped back to the stairs, beckoning Francis to come with her. He hurried down the steps and didn't breathe again until they were out in the cool evening air. Francis stared at Louisa and she stared back. "What was all that about then?"

"I have no idea. It sounds so sad and terrible." Louisa stared up into the dark opening sky. She felt that any minute she was going to cry too, the last one to collapse in misery. "I know Isabella has secrets about our family. But she promised Charles she wouldn't tell me unless she left the house and stopped working for him. Not that she was doing any work any longer, just living nice and warm and getting paid. And that was what Charles did to keep her quiet. So I imagine there was some big secret about our mother and father. I have a recollection of Grandpapa being as disgusting and cruel as Charles is."

"And Gisella?"

The thin Halo of moonshine was now reflected in Louisa's eyes, and the moisture collecting from unshed tears. "Did she have a baby?

Or is Gisella her own mother? She's keeping that secret too, perhaps we'll never know. For now, I just don't want to think about it."

Francis gazed upwards, as if dreaming or despairing. "We can't find Joletta." He was standing still, staring into the smoke winding up from a hundred thatched roofs. "Now there's a whole new parcel. I just want to go home and go to bed."

"I think we should do just that," murmured Louisa. She had no energy left. She wished she could be alone and cry in peace.

CHAPTER TWENTY-TWO

Three of the candles blew out. Henry Tudor was bustled from the hall and taken into safety. But one of his followers shouted, "it is the last thing wc want here," and pointed at Andrew and Doric with the crowd of men pushing behind them. "No doubt of it, there will be death amongst us if we don't step back now."

One mand strode forward addressing the armed guards. "The younger one can't leave. Clearly, he knows more than he should. You three grab him and the rest of you chase the others out of here and back into the streets."

Immediately the guards, pointing their pikes towards Andrew and the men behind him, left Doric free as the other soldiers rushed to grab him. But Doric lashed out. Perched high on the principal table, he slashed down, aiming wide. His two small knives were neither so sharp nor long enough for serious battle, but dancing and dodging beneath the threat of the pike shafts, he lurched upwards and stabbed out at both men. While momentarily clutching at the pain of their sudden wounds, one with a gash from ear to mouth and the other with a small bleeding hole in his neck., Doric was free once again.

So dodging and dancing backwards, kicking out, Doric managed to trip one of the guards and grabbed his pike. They both wrestled to claim the weapon, but as other guards tried to interfere, Doric won the wrestling match, grabbed the pike shaft, and swung the heavy wooden handle, knocking out both men trying to grab him. The guards, noses bloody, tumbled backwards into the oncoming swordsmen. Doric grabbed the opportunity, leapt from table to bench and from bench to floor, then racing from the hall, he stood back against the shadows and waited for Andrew.

Meanwhile Andrew and the furious men with him, were fighting with both the guards and anyone amongst the Tudor supporters willing to face them. Blood splashed puddles on the floorboards and stains on the walls. But before anyone was killed, Andrew's men pulled back and he was able to slam the door in his attackers faces. With his sword still upraised and ready, and Doric with the Pike safely under his arm, they left the château at a run. The angry crowd who had accompanied Andrew, now disappeared into the wind strewn darkness and returned to their homes, satisfied with the resentment they had clearly shown towards those over cossetted foreigners. With Doric close behind, Andrew led the way to a small stable where, tethered outside, two horses stood waiting. Within seconds they were mounted and galloping South.

Laughing again, "Now that was a rescue I appreciated, and I thank you." Doric dropped the bloodstained pike, not being a weapon to carry any distance nor easily on horseback. Andrew had sheathed his sword, both raced towards San Marlow and their expected escape home. It seemed no time had passed, with neither of them wounded in any manner except for bruises, scratches and grazed hands

The weather was mild, and the small sailing ship waited, docked in the rolling flurry of tiny waves. They returned their tired horses and strode the short pier to where the sailing ship was roped. A a larger vessel than the little fishing boat which had brought them, but even with the sail wind strained, and the dozen men at oars, it was more than one day before they arrived back on English soil.

"We wast no time," Andrew said as he marched the gangplank and led Doric from the Portsmouth docks. "There is a great deal I have to impart to his Majesty, it seems the Buckingham rebellion is not far off. The King has already been warned of Buckingham's treachery, but we had no date. Now we do. And what you have overheard at Tudor's home, we know a great deal more. I have to get to court and speak to his Highness in private."

Doric was marching close, as exhausted as a sparrow in a gale, but willing to walk to Scotland if he might then fall into bed. He turned, looking towards the inn at the port. "We stay here and rest? Or we buy horses and ride to London?"

"Neither," Andrew told him without pause. "My horses are waiting, we ride directly for Westminster."

The English weather had retraced its steps into a second summer. Though late September, the sun remained brilliant and the rich colours of the autumn leaves blew with pride. As they galloped north, the fresh sparkle of air brought energy and enthusiasm.

Riding each day, the horses were quickly tired and by the time the two men reached Suffolk and felt the hope of home coming closer, Andrew had begun to look out for a small inn where they might sleep a few hours until dawn. It was late afternoon when a long narrow shadow told its story across the road before them. The two gibbets, only one now occupied, crested the rocky hillock on the roadside, but this time there were observers standing below.

The figure still hung by the rope, unrecognisable even as female, but not yet fully bone alone.

Three people stood, a groom holding the tethers of the horses, his master who stood seemingly gripped by shock and horror, and a young girl, her face hidden by her hands.

Turning away, Andrew continued to ride, but his pace slowed. A little ahead, Doric stopped abruptly. His breath caught in his throat, and he sat motionless. Andrew also stopped as Doric dismounted, holding loosely to the reins, and walked silently up the slope.

The gibbet was not so tall, and as he stepped through the long grass, Doric faced the dead woman's feet, now just tiny ankle bones wedged into cheap shoes. The bones of her fingers drooped from a long-torn sleeve. The left thumb had fallen and lay below like a tiny twist of ivory at Doric's feet. He stepped quickly backwards but did not look up at the clothed remains. He looked straight at Louisa's tear stained face. His own shadow fell across her shoulders, and she shivered, unmoving.

Doric whispered and immediately Louisa turned, shaking as though frightened. Then she saw his face and burst into tears.

Francis, already crying bitterly, also whirled around, but seemed puzzled, and quickly gazed back to the gibbet. Louisa reached out and grabbed Doric's hand. He clasped both arms around her and pressed her cheek against his.

Her whispers tickled the side of his face like tiny kisses, and he hugged her closer. "You knew her?" he murmured.

"It's – Joletta," she told him. "The girl my brother loved. But she was, well, my older brother didn't approve. Then Francis stopped loving her. Not because of Charles. But because of himself. So we set out to find her. She disappeared. That was weeks ago. And now we've found her."

Not entirely understanding, Doric asked no questions. He simply held her, watching over her head the slow swing of the corpse above. Francis slumped on the grass and pebbles and cradled his head on his knees, his hands clenched and his sobs loud. Looking over, Louisa called, "Oh, Francis, my dearest. It isn't your fault. None of this is anything for you to feel guilty about. Perhaps – just perhaps – she was caught stealing. We can't know."

Glaring up from his cobwebbed knees, Francis muttered, "Stealing? Maybe she did, maybe she didn't, but there's no sheriff would grab a thief in the tanneries. This is Charles. It is, isn't it. Bloody filthy vile murdering Charles. I know it is. I'm going to kill my brother."

Pulling away from Doric, Louisa ran to Francis and bending over him, both hugged him and shouted. "Don't be stupid, dear. He couldn't have. He'd be executed himself. This has to be something else. A mistake."

Down on the road, Andrew still sat astride his horse, but waved, calling. "Doric, my young friend, we need a bed for the night. There's nothing to be done here, so bring everyone and we'll find an inn.

Tomorrow I shall leave early for Westminster, and you can decide whether to come or to stay. Over supper we can discuss what has happened."

It was a small tavern, thatched, with the loose reeds almost hiding the row of tiny windows beneath. Inside it was busy and the clank of pewter tankards barely interrupted the laughing, chattering and calling.

They left their horses at the over-crowded stables, Louisa's groom leading them as Andrew marched inside to speak with the landlord. They sat at the long table outside where the last light sank into the gloaming, quieting the now sleepy flies, bees and wasps, and sending the crows and starlings to their roosts.

Andrew pondered the story Louisa and Francis told him, but his interests lay with the palace and the king and the imminent rebellion. He missed his wife and wanted his own home. Yet the story reverberated, and he heard more than he wished to hear, absorbed the details, and knew he would follow whatever had happened when he found the time.

CHAPTER TWENTY-THREE

As Andrew left , riding off as the first blink of dawn peeped golden, and Francis continued to sleep through his miserable dreams, Doric tapped on the door of the other bedchamber where Louisa had slept alone, the only female amongst the tipsy revellers.

She jerked awake, huddled back under the covers, and then changed her mind. Tip toeing to the door, she whispered through the keyhole. "It's you, isn't it?"

He smiled and in case coming to her bedchamber seemed shockingly intimate, he lied, "I've no improper thoughts, I promise. But yes, it's me. I simply need to talk."

The door squeaked gently open and before even seeing her, Doric found himself embraced in warmth. Her arms were around him and her breath was soft on his neck.

The improper thoughts he had disclaimed were indeed springing all through his body. All night Doric had felt the insidious creeping excitement and the tingling in his stomach. With the touch of her against him, those feelings exploded. After meeting his royal highness, and playing the lute for the great man and his court, the exhilaration had been enormous. Yet this was greater. After the discomfort and risk of sailing the Narrow Sea in the smallest boat he could imagine, and then risking his life in subterfuge and combat, the danger and high adventure had seemed to fulfil the emotions he needed. But this exceeded those, and his entire body sang. He rested his fingertips against her cheeks, and they seemed to spring alive.

She whispered, "Oh, Doric, finding Joletta was such a nightmare. But finding you is a miracle."

He had to leave and didn't know how to tell her. For some moments, he didn't know how to tell himself. "I work for Lord Leys. We've been in Brittany and were riding back to Westminster. It was luck – coincidence – seeing you there. A glorious coincidence. You know – don't you – how I feel?"

"I think I do. Tell me."

He kissed her eyes, taking the moisture of her tears onto his tongue. It tasted like wine. Feeling the press of her breasts against his chest was a flash of pure desire. Now he wondered if lust was stronger or love the strongest. He breathed hard with his pumping heart sounding louder than his words. "I can tell you I love you, Louisa." He couldn't pull her any tighter. "I hardly know you. You don't know me. But what I know, I love."

"Then come here and know me better."

"It's the last thing I want to say." he stared into her eyes and felt almost sick, "but I have to leave." She stared back. "I don't want to go," he said at once. "I want to stay and hold you. I just want to hold you forever, but, my love, there's danger. An invasion. A rebellion. I have to go. But I'll see you safe first."

Swallowing the news while holding back the tears, Louisa stumbled towards the bed. Doric refused to let her go, and together they both sat entwined on the edge of the mattress. "If you get killed," she said, "I'll never forgive you."

"I'd never forgive myself."

"You know I've never stopped thinking about you."

He hadn't known and it seemed almost impossible. Clutching her, unable to resist the explosive temptation, he lay back on to the mattress, every curve of her body fitting to his. He stared up at the underside of the blue broadcloth tester above them, clearly heavy with the years of dirt and dust, smoke and falling insects, mouse excrement and anything else which had dropped from the beams over the years. The faint smell of collected filth was common enough in small roadside inns, but it was the smell of Louisa's skin he was drinking, the faint sweat of the night and the delicious silken softness of her hair.

"I'll do anything I can to help," he insisted. "I'll help you and Francis move away from your brother if that's what you want. I'll face him and accuse him if that would help. Or I'll see the sheriff and tell the tale of the hanged girl and say who may have murdered her. I'll be away, but I have lodgings beyond the Fleet where someone could stay. But it's small. One bedchamber only and no place for staff. But Lord Leys has a great house out beyond the Wall."

"I know. I've stayed there. It's where I first saw you and I remember calling myself an idiot because you were a stranger, and I should have forgotten you, but I couldn't." Her voice, murmuring to his shoulder, seemed as comforting as a scented pillow.

"I couldn't forget you either," he whispered. "You slipped into all my dreams. You danced through my skies. Your eyes are bluer than any sky."

She gulped, pink faced. "But I'll go home, and I'll face Charles. I want to kill him. I might do it."

He leaned down and kissed her forehead. "No, call me. I'll do it. I'll not see you blamed."

It was Francis who interrupted them, striding in without knocking. It did not trouble him to see his sister and a man he did not actually know entwined on her bed. Sitting beside them, he muttered no apology but said, "It really was Charles, wasn't it?"

"We have to go and see poor Joletta's mother. And help her if we can. She can't carry on the business without her daughter and she hasn't a penny."

"I'll do something. I'll get her money." Francis stared at Louisa, who had sat up in a hurry. "Charles did it, I know he did, but it was my fault. If I hadn't fallen for someone so unsuitable, Charles would never have met her. And because the bastard doesn't ever speak to me sensibly, he didn't know I was going to break off with her anyway."

Lying back in slightly amused confusion, Doric clasped his hands beneath his head and said, "Tell your brother to join the king's forces against the imminent rebellion. That way he can die without anyone being accused of murder." But something else was leaking into his thoughts. It seemed the dead girl had been below station for Francis. Similarly, Doric well knew himself to be well below station for Louisa. She deserved better. Unless – but he could not consider that.

"What rebellion?" Francis was demanding.

"This is not news to be spread until the king speaks," Doric said quickly. "But the Tudor exile intends an invasion to back up a local rebellion with the Duke of Buckingham leading."

Francis frowned down. "Buckingham's a simpleton. I've met him. He follows whoever tells him he's a good boy."

"So I've heard." Doric nodded, head still on the pillows. "Married at ten to an older woman and used to following like a lamb. Now the influence has shifted to Bishop Morton, who loathes our king."

Staring first down at Doric and then across to her brother, Louisa sighed. "I don't know his majesty, I don't know Buckingham nor his wife nor somebody Morton. But if we're all in danger, then we should all go home. But I imagine Charles would side with the traitors."

Doric lifted one eyebrow and sat, inching himself from the bed and finally standing, looking down at Francis and Louisa. "Interesting. Since I work for Andrew and follow both him and the king, I may have the pleasure of killing your brother after all. But in the meantime, I've no choice but to ride to court."

"I'll join you," Francis jumped up, tears turning to sparkle and the red rims bright as fire.

"I'll escort you both to your home," Doric said. "But I must leave soon I need to be at my own lodgings by tomorrow."

"But first we have to speak with Mistress Smithson," Louisa sighed. Francis slumped back.

"Yes, I have to do that. I've been horrid and stupid and selfish." He dropped his head into his hands once more, sniffing tears. "How could

I have been so ridiculous? I mean, I did love her. Joletta was wonderful. I should have married her and then Charles wouldn't have been able to touch her."

"I imagine he would, and just as quick." Louisa told her brother, and turned to look up at Doric. "Whenever I see you, I'm always so pleased, but you're always leaving. Please come back soon."

He leaned over her, grasped her fingers and kissed each tiny smooth tip. "I will. Tell me where you'll be."

"In Newgate," muttered Francis into his palms, "for murdering Charles."

Doric swallowed hard, turned and left the room. Within minutes he was mounted and riding north east into the glow of the rising sun, stomach empty and his head pounding. He took off his hat and let the wind swirl through his hair. It cleared his sight and wiped his headache clean, but it could not clear his thoughts of Louisa.

Francis closed the door of the inn's bedchamber and surveyed his sister. "I get myself embroiled with a girl who's gorgeous but utterly unsuitable. It all ends in a nightmare and I feel sick and guilty as hell. And before we have time to clear up the mess, you've gone and done the same thing. You're in love? And with someone who looks as unsuitable as my poor Joletta. What is he? A spy? A tinker? Lord Ley's servant?"

"All of those," whispered Louisa. "And a minstrel too."

CHAPTER TWENTY-FOUR

The small fleet of Henry Tudor's intended invasion sailed from the Breton coast on the 19th day of October, which the church had allotted to Fritheswida the virgin. Seven small ships headed across the Narrow Sea, led by Tudor, his uncle, and others who had once crossed the Narrow Sea in the opposite direction, either to join the Lancastrian cause and deny the Yorkist King Edward IV, or later when Richard III was crowned and the Woodville's in spite of the previous queen having been of their family, returned to their original Lancastrian loyalties.

One day previously, from his great castle Brecon, on the Welsh Marches, the Duke of Buckingham rode out with those who had already sworn to follow him. First under cover of self-righteous indignation, the duke abruptly repented his support for Richard of Gloucester and claimed a sudden love for Woodville honour.

Woodville and Stafford, first pronouncing pretensions to restore the child king Edward to his rightful crown, then swung quickly aside to delve in rumour and innuendo. No Edward V could be set upon the throne, it was said, for he was murdered and his younger brother with him. Rumour had begun to leak, and the leakage took force like the shit in the city gutters when a north wind blew low. The late king's heir must be produced, rumour announced. Three weeks, perhaps four, had passed without sight of the boy born to the crown of England. If still alive indeed, why not be brought to sight of the people? If not, then no further proof was needed. The usurping king had perhaps murdered his own nephews.

The king of France, the eternal festering enemy, picked at rumour and nurtured the startling news that Richard had caused the disappearance of his nephews. But there was no outcry over the forgotten bastards of dead royalty. England was learning to love peace and the king who fashioned it, and besides, both boys had been seen shooting at targets and playing on the greens of London's Tower until early autumn, and with Richard already on the throne, why would those boys have been in danger.

Already forewarned by those he trusted, King Richard left Westminster two days earlier and led his troops to where he surmised the uprising would congregate. Behind him rode Andrew, Lord Leys, and behind him, rode his young companion Doric Fleet, surrounded by a thousand others armed and ready to protect their king, their land, their families and their futures.

Yet while King Richard travelled north, pockets of the disaffected south had risen. On receiving news of the Buckingham rebellion, a convergence of troubled treachery wound through its varied paths to unite beneath the crowned swan's crest of Stafford, to join the revolt. The king's reactions, were immediate. Sending trusted messengers to inform the Duke of Norfolk, who was already residing in London, his highness requested sudden and forceful retaliation.

Gathering large bodies of men from among his own followers and those loyal citizens of the capital, the Duke of Norfolk ordered a series of excellently timed sorties through Kent to undermine the actions of the traitors, cutting them off from each other, from their leaders and supplies. Within a few short days, the situation around London was safely under control.

Although Buckingham had unfurled his banners and marched east from Brecon, the crown's spies brought information that few had been inspired to join him and of the common soldiers in his train, most had been rallied by force.

At the Angel Inn at Grantham, the king received the Great Royal Seal in its white leather pouch, which he had sent for as symbol of authority to summon the country against the traitors. It was in dictation to Chancellor Russell that the royal demand was carried, but it was in the king's own hand that Richard had taken pen and added a postscript with an expression of bitter emotion. *"Here, loved be God,"* he wrote, *"is all well and truly determined, to resist the Malice of him that had best cause to be true, the Duke of Buckingham, the most untrue Creature living."* It was rare that his majesty communicated his feelings so openly, but again in writing his proclamation to the southern counties, he made his feelings remarkably clear. In accordance with his coronation promise and his full intention of continuous weal to confer full and absolute impartial justice to all men of England, he would now pardon any citizen in service of the rebel traitors who withdrew at once from their cause. He denounced *"the Duke of Buckingham, and the Bishops of Ely and Salisbury and their damnable maintenance of vices"*, announcing rewards for their capture of up to one thousand pounds for Buckingham and lesser amounts for the others.

So with the combined forces of those who had come to his summons, among them the massed men of Leicester, York and Northumberland, King Richard III rode forward on 24th October to face the first assault against his reign.

Henry Tudor, with Breton soldiers supplied by the embittered Duke Francis of Brittany, had already left that wild coast, aiming for the mouth of the Severn.

Elsewhere, it was one Humphrey Stafford, being unrelated to the duke of similar name, who immediately undermined Buckingham's progress, destroying bridges, blocking free passage by ambush and leading parties to disrupt and harass. The Vaughans, chieftains of the surrounding countryside and loyal to the king, continued to threaten and hamper, even raiding the treacherous duke's own lands behind him, while his few remaining men began to desert. Now late October, the weather was foul. The rains flooded river and road, frequently all ways forward were impassable, and even the deserters lost morale and fled to hide from all comers on both sides. Buckingham's leadership, sadly unskilled, fell flat. He was, indeed, a natural follower. As a leader, he lacked conviction and could not inspire others with the new cause.

It was during the days following when the storm swept the coast and a gale of freezing force smashed against the Breton ships, Their sails were ripped, the masts smashed, and many men were tossed from the gunwales as they tried to change course. One cob sank, the keel battered against the waves, and the men were tossed, screaming, frantic, beneath the darkening and greedy waters.

Already Buckingham had marched his small group of supporters through the fields and country roads, attempting to rally more followers, calling his neighbours to muster. Yet none were now prepared to risk their lives for a man they neither knew nor admired.

The storm out at sea continued, cracking the hulls of the smaller ships. Drowned corpses were thrown up along the beaches or dashed against the rocks. Those few survivors managed to wrap their oiled capes around their sodden clothes, and hide themselves until they dried, and could then walk to the nearest town without being recognised as invaders and enemies.

Broken planks floated the water's surface before being swept further out to sea. The remaining ship's captains screamed for a change of course, ordered the men to the oars as the sails ripped in threads, and arranged a direct return to Brittany.

One ship, the larger, although also lacking both sail and some of its oars, tumbled through the buffeting waves, was tossed and spun, its bilges overflowing, until it was able to anchor finally within sight of the coast off Plymouth. This was Henry Tudor's vessel and he anchored well beyond the English beaches and sent men to spy out the land while arranging for the ship's quick repairs and restocking.

Within the week's anchorage, hope died for Tudor as he was told of the destruction of his fleet, Buckingham's military failure, and the impossibility of any fruitful invasion. The storm having subsided, the return to Brittany was both successful and depressing. Tudor, who called himself the Earl of Richmond, had never been an optimistic man, but the preparation of the fleet had been arduous and expensive. Without options, he returned to semi-imprisonment and an empty future. So both arms of the rebellion were dead, quickly suffocated beneath Buckingham's futile conceit and Henry Tudor's ambition.

Once Buckingham's forces had been beaten back by the king and his men, he escaped into the countryside with little more than his sword and his helmet. Unable to return home, he hid where he could, farming sheds and the attics of his few supporters.

Andrew sat on the damp grass and regarded his companions. Doric was lying back on his cape, gazing up at the silver pricked clouds and the vague mist of sunshine. The third man sat cross legged, chewing on a long flat piece of weed which he had plucked from the banks of the stream an hour since.

There was no one to watch them except the birds. A kite was wheeling high, a dark gliding fleck of intensity just under the sallow clouds. She had seen a mouse peep from the moss smeared rocks. The kite broke the little creature's neck and rose again immediately, the dead fur, rain speckled, gripped in her claws. She would take it back to her mate and the nest they would now be repairing for the next spring's chick.

In the red rusty treetops, the ravens squabbled, jabbing at each other's eyes, irritated by the kite's violent intrusion and departure too quick to steal the prize. It had started to rain again.

On the far balustrade of the highest points of the Brecon turrets the pair of kites had nested, feathers ruffled against the whine of the wind, the female, broody eyed, almost ready to lay her precious single egg.

But Lord Leys and his companions were concentrating on matters of little interest to kites or ravens.

"It looks as though tis raining again," decided Casper, discarding the chewed green string and raising his hood.

"If," Doric said, opening one eye, "You didn't notice, it started ten minutes gone, then you should probably try chewing less and noticing more."

"Such intelligent conversation," Andrew sighed, "is exhausting. And I have considerably more interest in tracing that fool Buckingham before he ignites some other nonsensical skirmish."

"After the old king's death, he was well treated as far as I hear," Doric said, seemingly addressing the treetops. "Why the devil did the fool turn against his king, who had befriended him, given him more power and position than he'd ever held before, and treated him with rare respect?"

Stretching, Andrew stood but smiled down at Doric's cheerful gaze. "Because Buckingham was never capable of straight thinking nor logical understanding. First, he followed his Woodville wife as though she was his mother, and he a child of eight or nine. Then, offered friendship by a great new king, he grew a little and felt both empowered and matured. Seeing one's mistakes is always easier in retrospect, and I fear his majesty made one mistake with Buckingham, by giving him the responsibility of holding an important prisoner. Richard thought this would grow the fool's sense of loyalty and responsibility, but the prisoner was Bishop Morton, and Morton is as good at influencing fools as the king."

"Seduced by a bishop."

Casper stood, rubbing his backside. "Me arse is wet," he complained. "If we gonna find this bastard, then I reckon we gets going."

"I did not suggest a pause simply to rest your backside," Andrew told him. "We are here for a purpose. I wish to gather our knowledge, and decide the best direction. Do we separate, or stay together?"

"Separate," said Casper.

"Remain together," Doric said. "We risk being outnumbered if we search alone. Buckingham won't be without friends at his back."

"And wiv only one search party on one bloody parf," objected Casper, "reckon we risks never finding the bugger anyways."

"Not," said Andrew, "if we can trace his movements first. So where are this man's friends?"

"Do he have any?"

But Andrew smiled. "When there are few, those few can be easier to find."

"Sadly," Doric pointed out, "I never mixed in ducal company. I have no knowledge. I couldn't even guess."

Casper looked smug. "Ah," he said, plucking another long streak of pliant piece of grass, "but that be where I's different, ain't I, for I knows a bit. While you two was in that Breton slum, I were here and sneaking into them Brecon kitchens. I knows where to go. Follow me, my friends, I just bloody hope t'will stop bloody raining."

Andrew smiled, Doric rolled over, and, hoods up against the sleet, they untethered their horses, mounted, saddles wet, and the horses, shaking the rain from their manes, accepted destiny and began the trudge north.

So they rode on through Shropshire and stopped only once on the way for a few hours' sleep at a wayside tavern. The countryside was blurred under a mist of rain clouds. Spread across the hill and nestled between the dark flooded arms of Teme and Corve, their road was puddled into wet filth, and fording the streams seemed more like a swim than a plod. But the horses stamped off the mud from their hooves and accepted the long days, especially when heading directly for the first hostelry on the main thoroughfare.

It was later than usual when they finally came to a dark windowed inn. The innkeeper, startled from his sleep, forgot to complain and in the guttering light of his high-held tallow lamp he saw the manner of Lord Ley's clothes, and paused. "My lord, excuse me, I'm at your service I'm sure." He could charge thruppence farthing for a private room to such a grand lord and perhaps even a little more for the supper and the hay and grooming for the horses. "I've only one vacant room at the back, since I doubt your lordship will be wanting to share a chamber with my other two guests," he bowed. "I'll get the wife to make up the bed linen my lord, and fix a bite to eat while my boy tends the horses. Forgive my being unprepared, but we've had no custom here for many weeks till today when two fellows come in from the north. What with the weather and the troubles from the rebellion we done closed our doors and locked them too."

"Why should the troubles have affected you out here?' demanded Andrew, narrow eyed. "The king rests at Salisbury these several days, and the fighting on the Marches is well passed."

The landlord chewed the insides of his cheeks. "Best not talk of it, my lord," he said. "I'll call my Ellen to get the chamber ready."

"Hold on," said Andrew, striding forwards. "Have you seen fighting here lately? What are you nervous of?"

"The troubles are over, thank the Lord," the man hung his head. "And what I say or don't say, is always a matter of nerves for a poor man, sir. It can get you stabbed in the night by one side or lose your head from the other."

While Doric followed Andrew up the rickety back stairs, Casper followed the horses over the courtyard cobbles to the stables, where he also arranged his own bed in the straw above.

It had stopped raining, but the sky swung low with the steel weight of stars and cloud across the moon. "A good fire, a jug of wine and one of ale, and the bed proper aired," instructed Doric. "Then a good supper for three served in the chamber. We're on the king's business so mustn't be disturbed."

"You're getting good at that," smiled Andrew, throwing his sodden cloak to the chair and placing his back full square to the fire once lit. It was smoky and spat and fizzled where the logs were damp, but the heat flared well in its central scarlet.

"True indeed," Doric acknowledged, "particularly for someone who rarely stayed in an inn until a couple of months back, and didn't know the meaning of giving orders." Laughing again, he poured a tankard of ale, and one of wine, looked up at Andrew's face, nodded, kept pouring and filled the cup. He then stomped over to the bed, pulled back the upper blanket and peered at the new laid sheets. "If you want the bed to yourself tonight," he suggested, "I'll take the trestle."

"Why?" said Andrew with immediate suspicion. "What's wrong with the bed?"

"Damp," said Doric. "You drink your wine, and I'll go and order a hot brick and hurry up those suppers. And I suggest you get those soggy boots off too. I'll have them dried off for the morning. Leave them by the fire and the leather will surely crack."

Andrew grinned. "I know how to look after my own boots, Doric, and had no page or squire nor servant of any kind for long enough." He wrenched off his boots and slung them towards the door. "But you're no servant either, my friend, So make yourself comfortable."

Stretching out on the despised bed, hands clasped behind his head, he closed his eyes, picturing Tyballis curled beside him. But it was only moments before Doric returned, carrying two platters of stuffed cabbage, crab meat in hard baked pastry, bread rolls, matured cheese and apple dumplings. Under his arm he held a brick, which he now threw into the fire's ashes.

That night, the hot brick well wrapped in wool beneath their feet, the vibrations of snoring from the next door chamber now an accustomed rhythm like the wind in the timbers and the smoke down the chimney, they both dreamed. Andrew of Tyballis, and Doric of Louisa. What neither man realised, was that both those women also dreamed of them.

CHAPTER TWENTY-FIVE

With her palm to her cheek, fingers trembling, Louisa glared up at her brother.

"Get up to your chamber," Charles shouted at her, "I'll have you locked in for a week at least. This is disgusting behaviour. I shall no longer allow your defiance and appalling displays of self-will."

She demanded, "What have you done with Francis? And what have you done with the woman we brought back with us?"

"What I choose to do as master of this family," he yelled back, "is entirely my own business. Now go immediately to your room."

Turning on her heel, Louisa marched from the hall. But she did not go to her room nor approach the staircase. Instead, she walked the long corridor to the back of the building and through the kitchens, where the cook, five scullery boys, the spit-turner, the assistant cook, the three maids and the steward all blinked in astonishment, stopped working and turned in startled silence to stare at her. Louisa waved one apologetic hand.

"Don't let me interrupt," she said hurriedly, "I'm just looking for Isabella. Have you seen her?"

"Yes, my lady," said one of the maids, rushing forwards. "Mistress Isabella is in the large pantry, crushing garlic cloves for this afternoon's supper. May I take you to her, my lady?"

"Oh, I know where the pantries are," smiled Louisa, brushing the girl aside. "I used to help her with the spices when I was a child." And she hurried through the back door and out into the fading glimmers of sunlight and across the rimed cobbles of the rear courtyard. On one side stood the stables, echoing with the neighs, coughs, stamping of hooves from horses, and calling of the grooms as they filled their buckets from the well, grabbed up their brushes, and polished the three principal saddles. On the opposite length of the courtyards were the pantries, the laundry, the buttery and the doors down to the wine cellar.

"Darling Bella," Louisa burst through the pantry door, "I need your help. Where's Francis? And what did Charles do with poor Annie, the elderly woman we brought back with us yesterday? You know her, and what she's been through. We promised she could work here."

The scent of fresh garlic was sweet on Isabella's fingers, but she lowered her head. "I have no influence over your brother, I'm afraid," she said. "I knew who Annie was, of course, and tried to hide her away. But his lordship was up and shouting even before I was dressed. Evidently, he recognised her too. He called her an old witch and a whore and a slut. I could not intervene."

"I got up too late." Louisa sniffed. "I should have known, but I was so tired, I slept in."

"She was thrown from the house, poor woman, and in floods of tears she was too."

"Bother," said Louisa under her breath. "I have to find her. I'm always searching for someone or something. It's crazy. How long ago was poor Annie thrown out?"

"Well-nigh an hour, my dear. And young Francis already locked in the cellar." Louisa stared, mouth open.

"Not even locked in his bedroom? The cellar? Like a dungeon?"

"I saw it happen. I was so upset."

Knowing how Isabella had sworn to keep silent regarding the

family secrets, she wished her old nurse had at least shown the courage to intervene now. But she said simply, "Francis is still down there?" And Isabella nodded. "And he told Charles about Joletta? Did you hear that too?"

Again, Isabella nodded, wiping her moist fingers on her apron. "Yes indeed, and I fear it may have been Charles indeed –"

"I don't fear it," muttered Louisa. "I know it. Who else? Charles strung that poor girl up. Yet nothing was ever her fault, it was all Francis." She paused, then said, looking up, "Well, he's only fourteen and she was twenty-three so I suppose she may have led him on. But that doesn't deserve the gallows, for pity's sake. Charles deserves execution for murder."

"We have no proof, my dear," Isabella pointed out.

"First I'm going to get Francis out," Louisa said. "Then we can look for Annie. Honestly, I've spent months trudging London for that woman. But it has to be done. She's entirely innocent and the poor wretch will die of starvation if we don't help. So where do they keep the key for the wine cellar?"

"Only the master and the Steward, my dear. There are only two keys. We can never get him out."

"I will," Louisa announced, and strode back out into the chilly courtyard. The frost between the cobbles was melting as dawn rose, but a shrill wind was blowing up the Thames from its estuary. She rattled the door to the cellar steps and scrambled down into utter darkness. At the base, it was freezing, the stone floor felt like ice. Louisa banged on the door in front of her and called. "Francis, darling. Are you there?"

A small grunt of misery answered her. Then a mumbled, "Yes. Here. Probably for life."

The voice was muffled. "You've been drinking," Louisa suggested.

"What else is there to do in a wine cellar?" demanded Francis.

"Put the mug down, turn off the tap, and help me work out a way to open this door," Louisa told him. "How about battering it with the kegs you've got in there?"

"We'd just have puddles of spilled wine," Francis pointed out. "Go get an axe or a chopper or a cannon or something."

"I'll get an axe from somewhere since we're a bit short on cannon." She sniffed, kicking at the door. "Do you know what happened to Annie?"

He did. "I was screaming my head off, but he kicked her out of the house. I mean really – kicked. Big leather riding boots on her head and her back. She cried, crumpled over and then she just ran."

"'I'm getting you out. Then we'll look for her." Louisa thought a moment. "We have to put her up somewhere, but we don't have any money."

"Nor does she."

"That's the point," Louisa sighed. "So we have to help."

"Charles must have a money chest somewhere," said Francis. Louisa heard the faint sound of a wooden tap turning, and the fall of liquid into something solid. "So we wait till Charles goes off somewhere, then we steal all his money and we give some to Annie and we keep all the rest and run away."

The black chill was almost frightening. Louisa leaned back against the locked door and heard Francis slurp at whatever he had poured himself. "I need you sober. Not tipsy. Now wait while I find an axe."

"Getting pissed is the best way," muttered Francis. "You won't be strong enough, even if you find an axe."

"I'll get a groom or two to help."

"Don't be daft."

The servants would be far too fearful to act against their master's wishes. They risked being whipped and cast off. Charles never permitted his household to forget his powers of discipline. But the cellars were old, and the door might not need any crashing blows. Louisa ran back up the stairs. The sudden light made her squint, but she raced across to the stables and glared at the bustle, horse's tails swishing in her face, and the clink of so many bridles sounding more like a battle charge. The grooms stopped and waited for orders.

"You want your horse saddled, m'lady?"

"No." Louisa shook her head, still shivering. "I want an axe. "

"Not sommint we keeps here, mistress. No need o' axes in the stables."

"Then find one," Louisa raised her voice. "Ask the gardeners. Doesn't anyone chop trees around here? I have no idea, but hopefully you do. Just get me an axe."

The groom who had already spoken looked reluctant and frowned. But with a loud sigh, he put down the saddle he was carrying, accepted his fate and marched out towards the green hedges and the slope to the river.

Louisa glared at the other boys standing and watching her, puzzled. "Would any of you like to help me open a locked door?"

The shuffling of feet and embarrassed grunts broke the silence. "Sorry, m'lady," said the head groom. "But we ain't allowed to do fings like that. I doesn't like to disappoint, but no one here gonna help. T'ain't our fault, m'lady."

Accepting what she had already expected, Louisa waited by the open doorway, hoping that Charles would not decide to ride out while she was there.

The chief gardener appeared in a tunic and wide brimmed hat which made Louisa shiver even more. She supposed he kept warm by chopping stuff. The man was carrying two large axes, one in each hand, which he then placed carefully on the ground at his feet and bowed.

"These be heavy, my lady," he said softly. "Can I help by doing whatever you be wanting cut down, my lady."

Louisa smiled immediately. She picked up the smaller of the two axes and pointed to the other. "Oh yes please," she refrained from hugging him although she considered it, "that would be extremely kind." And she led him down the stairs to the cellar. Stomping into the lightless space before the locked door, the gardener was distinctly nervous.

"Wine then, my lady?"

"No, certainly not," answered Louisa. "My young brother has very carelessly got himself stuck in there and I have to let him out."

The gardener wheezed slightly. "But my lady, don't his lordship have a key? Or if his lordship be out, then there bound to be some other gennleman what can unlock the door."

Louisa shook her head. "I'm afraid not," she said, widening the smile. "The lock is stuck. It's bent. I mean, the key's bent. Something like that. We have to break down the door. Don't worry. You won't get into trouble. I shall inform his lordship, when he returns, that this was done on my orders."

It took very little time. With the larger axe, the gardener swung twice against the wooden planks while Louisa used the smaller axe with little effect. The door splintered and cracked down through the centre, then split and with a final crash, fell apart.

"Have some wine," said Francis, holding out the cup.

With considerable suspicion as to the rights of what he had just done, the gardener willingly drained the cup, grabbed up both axes and quickly disappeared back into the grounds. With even greater speed, Louisa and Francis raced back into the house and used the servants' backstairs up to the corridor to the family bedchambers. With no noise to hint that Charles might be close, they peeped into the grand master chamber. This door was unlocked, but the garderobe was padlocked.

"Bugger," said Francis, tripping over his own feet. "I bet that's where the money chests are."

There was definitely no sign of any such thing in the bedchamber itself, but Louisa beckoned her brother and they left the room, dodging quickly down the passage to her own chamber. Stopping suddenly, they found her door with the key on the outside, evidently her chamber had been locked, presumably on the assumption that she had obeyed her brother, and was now sitting meekly inside and unable to leave.

They let themselves in, snatching up the key. "Listen," she whispered. "if we can't steal his rotten coin, then I have another idea. We can threaten to tell his horrid secrets. Isabella seems to know dreadful things about him, but she won't tell me. If I pretend I know anyway, perhaps he'll think he has to pay us off."

Interested, Francis sat on her bed and grinned. "Dirty secrets?"

"Well, I suppose so, or he wouldn't care about people knowing. But he swore Isabella to secrecy."

"Great," said Francis. "Now, as it happens, I know something else he wouldn't like known. I know he supported Buckingham's rotten rebellion, and the Woodvilles and that French person from Wales too. Trouble is, he never went to fight for any of them. Just stayed at home and plotted. But I know what he plotted and sent messages and nasty stuff. I know he's a traitor."

"We threaten him then," said Louisa with eager enthusiasm. "Vile slime-ball worm-face traitor."

He admired her turn of phrase. "But," he decided, "he won't be frightened, will he! Not that he's the sort to easily frighten. And he never went to fight and if we told someone he supported Buckingham, he'd just deny it and say we were being nasty because he'd punished us for our shocking behaviour."

Sitting together on the side of the as yet unmade bed, they abruptly heard the door downstairs open, and the steward welcome his master home. It seemed several people had entered, and Charles' voice called for refreshments, and seemed to be ushering his guests into the principal hall.

Francis and Louisa stared at each other. "Just as well we didn't run out a minute ago," Louisa whispered. "We'd have run straight into him. "

"And he'd have grabbed me and whipped me again," Francis whispered back. "But when he sees the smashed cellar door – shit. What are we going to do? Climb out the window?"

She had thought of that several times over past years. Once, locked in her room as a child, she had tried it and had nearly broken her neck. Now she shook her head. "Impossible. So I'm going downstairs to talk to him. You stay here and lock the door from the inside until you hear it's me."

But halfway down the main staircase, Louisa realised that Charles was already on the lower steps and clearly intended coming up as she went down. They came face to face. Charles wore his usual scowl. Louisa smiled.

"No, not locked in yet, big brother. In fact, I was just coming to speak with you."

"Since I locked you in myself," Charles said with smothered fury, "I should like to know how you managed to get out."

For a moment, Louisa wondered if she dared. Then she decided that she could, and said, "Just as you said earlier today, Charles, What I do is my business."

He was keeping his voice low. "I came to release you. You have simply spared me the trouble. Now – ," he grabbed her arm, "come downstairs and meet your intended."

For some moments she had no idea what he meant, but allowed him to escort her into the great hall. Two small shards of broken wood were attached to the outer skirt of her gown, but Charles did not appear to notice. He stood beside her. "My dear little sister," he said with obvious sarcasm, "may I introduce the young man to whom you are now engaged to be wed. This is young Bryan Sudbury, and this is his father, Lord John Sudbury whom you already know to be my greatest friend in these fretful days. And the young lady Is Beatrice, Bryan's twin sister. She is engaged to be wed too our young Francis. These arrangements are already settled, although I may tell you now, you and your brother are getting the better deal."

CHAPTER TWENTY-SIX

It was long before dawn, when the night was darkest and the rain just a pale patter against the shutters, when Andrew woke to a rattle at the door. Doric was still deeply sleeping. The remains of their supper and two empty jugs were strewn across the table and the fire was a scatter of low embers, a hearth of flickering pink lights in a black shadowed room. The weird shapes of clothes spread to dry across settle and chair backs seemed like silent steaming monsters, their wings open in prayer.

Andrew sat suddenly upright and watched the door handle turn. Then he leaned over and silently retrieved his dagger from beneath his pillow where he had left it the night before. The door edged open and a nose appeared with the accompanying draught. "If you take one more step," Andrew said in a conversational tone, "I shall kill you."

There was a gasp and the nose retreated to the other side of the quickly closed door crack, but Doric had woken and leapt to the door and thrust it open, dragging in the small elderly man from its step.

"Don't kill him yet," ordered Andrew cheerfully. "I might as well find out who you're killing first."

The small man shivered. "My lord, forgive me, I meant no harm."

"So you say," Doric peered down at him while keeping a tight grip on his collar. "But so you'd say, true or otherwise. There's few who'd say, yes I'm meaning harm my lord, finish me off now."

The captured man, increasingly confused, tried to wriggle free. With Doric's firm grip at the back of his neck, there was no release. "My lord, forgive me," he squeaked again, "but Jebbe said you was the king's man, so I had to come. Is it true, my lord? About the amount advertised as offered?"

Now sitting comfortably back against the headboard of the bed, his dagger on the quilt across his knees, Andrew said, "I have absolutely no idea what you're talking about, nor have I ever heard of Jebbe. I presume you are completely insane. It's most unwise, you know, for deranged souls to go breaking into people's bedchambers in the middle of the night. It gives the wrong impression. And incidentally, you keep begging my forgiveness, but you're not at all precise about what for."

The prisoner was taken aback. "Why, forgiveness for disturbing you, my lord and I'm as sane as any poor man can be, I swear. Jebbe said as how you mustn't be disturbed, but I had to come at night and couldn't get away in daylight, as I'm sure your lordship will appreciate. It's the truth then, sir? The full reward? One thousand marks must be an exaggeration, but I'm an honest man, my lord, and would like to know."

"Buckingham?" Doric asked without releasing either the collar or the man's wrist.

"That's right, my lord," nodded the man urgently. "He's taken refuge at my little house not a mile from here, for I was his grace's personal servant many years back, by name of Alred Cooper, though now retired in honour. So, about the reward, my lord?"

Doric grinned. The smile began in his eyes and drifted slowly to the corners of his mouth, where it widened into full delight. "Well, well," he said. "How interesting. No such thing as coincidence, perhaps. Reward? Yes, indeed. A thousand marks from his majesty, but the duke must first be taken into safe custody."

"I can't take him on my own, sir," explained the man. "Jebbe has offered to help, but I doubt we could take them, just us two."

"So, he's not alone?" said Andrew, nodding to Doric to release his grip on the tufts of threadbare sheepskin collar. "How many with him?"

The man dusted himself down and reset his neck within his jerkin. "There's four others with his grace," he said, a little breathless. "And well-armed, too."

"I believe we're most eager to meet all five of them," Doric grinned, leaning against the door frame.

Thomas Jebbe, the tavern landlord, was heaved from his bed and sent out into the night's chill to bring back the Sheriff of Shropshire, a ride that was likely to take some hours. Cooper led Andrew, Doric, and the gleefully wakened Casper onto the mud paved road to his own home, a slow mile tramped on foot. No horse could travel faster with the way rutted and bogged, and without them, the approach assured a greater silence and a better chance at ambush. At first the men's ruined buskins squelched through the sucking wet but then the ground rose a little and the drizzle dried into a sibilant breeze. The stars kept behind the clouds; there was no moon and no light. Casper, even shorter than the man who led them, was striding out joyfully.

"I told yous," he pointed out with glee, although both Andrew and Doric ordered him to keep quiet in case they were overheard. "I knowed it. I heard as to how the lord has friends in Shropshire. Tis thanks to me, my lord, we's about to get our hands on that treacherous bastard."

Then in the blackness of a waning night under storm clouds, they came to the cottage, set back from the road behind apple trees and a cluster of barns.

A brief plan had already been discussed at the inn. Now Cooper crept forward to his own side entrance, and under cover of the porched doorway and its scrabble of bushes, led the others inside. There was a faint smell of enclosed dampness and dust within, and the narrow stairway to the upper story was deep in shadow. Aldred Cooper peered up, then took the stairs, each step wary, while the others scuffled into the small front solar, pulling the door almost closed behind them, Doric tight against the wall behind the door jam.

His knife was unsheathed, his other hand ready at the hilt of his sword. The stairs creaked their rotten boards.

They waited, with the uneasy breathing and shuffle of men trying to keep very quiet. Then voices cut the echoes of suspense.

"What are you doing, man?" someone asked softly from the stairway landing. Doric peered through the crack of open door.

"My lord," Aldred whispered, "I couldn't sleep. I came downstairs for ale and a hot brick."

"You're fully dressed," the other voice pointed out, heavy with suppressed suspicion.

Aldred retreated backwards, followed downstairs by the man who had interrupted him. Both entered the solar where Andrew stepped immediately from behind the swinging door and clamped one hand over the taller man's mouth, a knife blade sharp against his neck. "Make any noise at all, and I kill you at once," Andrew whispered.

The captured man was elderly, tall and thin and wearing a bedrobe considerably too small for his figure. His hair, matted from sleep, was grey streaked and his short beard was already silvered. He slumped and sighed. Andrew pulled him to the back of the darkened room and handed him over to Casper with a nod. Immediately Doric stepped in to take Andrew's place.

Another voice called from the top of the stairs. "Where the devil are you? Why all this creeping about in the middle of the night?" Silence, and then the patter of footsteps, the squeak of wood. Doric took hold of the second man as soon as he poked his toes into the solar.

Bare foot and swathed in the faded velvet of his dismantled bed cover, the Duke of Buckingham glowered at the sword point hovering inches from his face. Doric's order for silence on pain of immediate death had not the slightest affect for the duke howled.

"I have to inform your grace," said Doric, abandoning the whisper with a shrug, "that in accord with the official warrant for high treason signed personally by his highness, I hereby arrest you in the name of the king. You are now my prisoner."

"Rabble," spat the duke through the gap in his front teeth. "How dare you wave your steel in my eyes and put your grubby fingers on my person?"

Smiling, Andrew nodded to Doric and Casper. "Take over," he said. "I need to see who else is hiding upstairs." He took the steps two at a time, leaving thick wedged mud stains on the tired boards, then slammed open the door of the first bedchamber to his right, and smiled again. "So, three in the trap," he said, "and two to go."

A young man was sitting on the edge of the bed, trying desperately to pull on his boots. He had managed his doublet and hose, but the points were unhooked and the shirt collar wrong laced. He was very young with a flop of uncombed blonde hair over a confused expression. "There isn't anyone else," said the boy, pink faced and chin up. "And I hereby surrender. But I warn you, you'll get no reward from my capture, for there's been none posted."

"Not worth it, eh?" grinned Andrew. "But it's Buckingham we were after, and now we have him."

The boy kept his chin high. "I know nothing of the insurrection, sir, and you can use red hot pokers if you wish, I'll tell you nothing. I'm not one to betray my friends."

"Indeed," Andrew laughed. "But my red-hot pokers are kept for lighting my winter fires at home, and I've no interest in what you could tell me, boy. I might even admire your courage, had you simply had the sense to give your loyalty to your king and country."

He then made a quick search of the other tiny chambers, but they were empty, it would have been impossible for anyone to remain unseen. Andrew returned to the boy who was now attempting to hook the points of his hose but with trembling fingers, was finding the task somewhat beyond him. He stood in a hurry, and his hose wrinkled to his knees. "Downstairs," Andrew ordered with a wave of his sword. "And if you want to keep everything you're now showing off in one piece, I suggest you sit quietly down there and consider yourself under arrest."

The boy gulped and hoisted his hose. "I'm not afraid of torture."

Andrew sighed, "No doubt," he said, "you seem almost eager. But torture is not something we have the time for indulging. You'll have to manage without it."

He followed the boy downstairs into the solar. The duke was seated on the long wooden settle while the other man remained standing, his hands tucked into the sleeves of the undersized bedrobe. The duke glared as Andrew entered, Doric's knife hovering at a disrespectful distance from the vulnerability of his bare neck, rising white and plump from the faded velvet.

"No sign of anyone else," said Andrew, as the boy hurried to the far shadowed corner. "Casper, take Aldred with you and search the place, inside and out. Check on the number of horses in the stables. Check everywhere." He turned to Alred who was busy pouring ale, alternating between suppressed glee and timorous disquiet. "You," said Andrew, "you've told me the truth? There were two others here?"

"I know exactly who you are, sir," said the duke, rising suddenly. He had been ignored long enough. The flounces of worn pink velvet around his shoulders slipped a little. He was not a tall man. "And I therefore know it's pointless attempting to bribe Richard's precious spy. I wish you joy of the reward, but I could pay you double that, to let me go. Otherwise, be warned. For this night's work, you earn the hatred of every Lancastrian in the land."

Andrew sheathed his sword. "I've no interest in Lancastrians, and absolutely none in rewards," he said. "In fact, your grace, in truth you are the prisoner of Aldred Cooper here, your own man to whom the reward will go, and as the greatest traitor in the country, you'll appreciate his treachery I'm sure. As for bribery your grace, you've been attainted and every inch of land and particle of your property has been claimed by the crown, and much of it already promised to Thomas Stanley. I use your title only from courtesy, since you are no longer entitled to it. You have nothing with which to bribe, sir, and should accept your fate as the justice you must know it to be."

Aldred and Casper returned, shaking their heads. "Only three horses in them stables, wiv Cooper's old nag," said Casper. "Them others bin gone if they was ever there."

"Very well," Andrew said. "If you'll finish getting dressed, gentleman, we have a long day ahead of us. The Sheriff of Shropshire should arrive within an hour or two, and then we'll be heading for Salisbury and the royal camp. Since I'm damned sure it's raining as usual or if not, it soon will be, I suggest we have a hot break-fast to start us off. Master Cooper? As a soon to be a wealthy man, can you supply us with anything edible?"

"They've eaten every chicken I had in the coop already," muttered Aldred, avoiding the duke's direct gaze. "But I've some cheat rolls and a side of salt bacon and I can boil some cider with a little honey, my lord."

"Bread rolls?" snorted Casper. "Bloody stale and no bloody good fer nufthing 'cept trenchers. I reckon tis just as well we be leaving."

"No one is asking you," snapped the duke.

Doric, having accompanied each prisoner separately while they dressed and gathered what few belongings they had brought with them, now leaned back in his chair beside the cold hearth, put his feet up, his heavy sword unsheathed and prominent across his knees, and waited for Aldred to finish preparing break-fast. Doric had never cared much for the quality of the food he ate just as long as there was something on offer, more than once coming near to starvation. The three captured men sat at the cramped wooden table, eyes downcast to the etching of old scratches and stains. There was now little to say.

Aldred was spreading the table with platters and a jug of steaming cider. "I imagine the other two we know were here," Doric nodded, "are now galloping for that and the Norfolk coast, hoping to get a boat to Flanders. After we've delivered the duke to his fate, do we follow? I imagine they'd have sailed before we'd arrive."

Andrew nodded. "Flanders to Brittany, and off to Henry Tudor's cosy rookery. But these three we deliver, and the traitor can say goodbye to his arrogance."

While his camp spread wide beyond the city walls, his majesty had taken residence at the great manor owned by the Bishop of Salisbury, and immediately arranged for Lord Leys and his retainers to be accorded the same comfort. Henry Stafford, once Duke of Buckingham, was taken, heavily guarded, to the upper room of a hostelry overlooking the market square. The other two prisoners were housed together in a chamber above the sheriff's offices. It continued to rain.

The king drained his cup. "Not that peace is what I expect," he said softly, "with this as an example, even from one's closest supporters. I have the Stanleys at my elbow, which is the only place I trust them to be. Edward's damned widow still hatches plots, brooding in her web of sanctuary, and now Francis of Brittany dares to back the Tudor bastard." He sighed. "My dear Andrew, your service is as exceptional as any man might wish. I have plans for you, my lord. Interesting plans. I trust you will be pleased."

Raising one eyebrow, Andrew bowed. "As always, sire. But I have no special needs. It is just a short time ago that I lived in a ruined slum and employed criminals to help my business. But it was then I met the woman I love, and I have no complaints."

"Your conversation cheers me," murmured the king. "Treachery is the most heinous response to friendship. It leaves me more than usually weary. Disillusioned, perhaps. But I am becoming a dull companion. We should celebrate. Call the page to pour the wine, my friend, and I'll relax for an hour before the trial."

"Honest loyalty," Andrew continued, pouring the wine himself, "is admirable under all circumstances," he said. "And carries a certain fascination at times. Naturally I did not capture Henry Stafford alone, sire, and was helped principally by the young man who accompanied me to Brittany, and to Shropshire after fighting beside me. He interests me since he does not act in the least like the suspected criminal and wandering minstrel he originally claimed to be. His talent is remarkable, but there's a good deal more than that. You have met him at court, sire, and heard his skill on the lute."

"Doric, you call him?" The king looked up. "I shall also take an interest in that case, my friend, and shall find out more. But first there is the trial and the execution, and that will be all I can think of until it is over."

"And you speak of loyalty," Andrew added, draining his cup. "I and my friends were instrumental in catching Stafford, but the personal success here is due to the loyalty of your people, sire. You are now loved by your country."

The King smiled. "Kind words, Andrew," he said, "and I take your point, and shall remember it. But loyalty is so often bought and paid for, and that's a sad side to this world of ours. Stanley sits and mutters in my ear about loyalty, claiming to refute his wife's strategies and his son-in-law's scheming, but I know what is expected of me in return, and a good part of Buckingham's confiscated properties must go to Stanley's honour, a barter of power for peace. Yet, as Stanley's power grows directly from the rewards I give him myself, so his threat becomes the greater. It is a strange irony."

The low afternoon's sunshine slanted down through the high casement, leaving the intricacy of the vaulting above in its secret shadows. The soft lemon striped across King Richard's face, along the determined square chin and thrust of jaw.

"Yet you've backed the Lancashire Harringtons, common gentry, over Stanley's demands for Hornby Castle," said Andrew. "If you're prepared to set Stanley's rights aside in that matter and support his enemy, then why pander to the man over his other ambitions?"

"Because," said Richard simply, "it is a matter of justice. Only the greedy despise justice."

CHAPTER TWENTY-SEVEN

Although neither as ludicrous nor as vile as the ancient lecher who Charles had previously introduced as her future husband, this boy, almost the same age as herself, immediately seemed unlikeable. He regarded her with answering contempt. But Louisa curtsied as was proper, sat down at some distance from the visitors, clasped her hands in her lap and stared down at the splinters in her skirts.

Doric sped through her mind, grinning at her. She smiled to herself and refused to look at the silent Bryan Sudbury. She doubted whether Francis would accept the haughty Beatrice, but could not be sure. Yet she was quite positive concerning her own imminent denial. Although Doric Fleet was little more respectable than poor Joletta Smithson had been, she had every intention of marrying him, whatever that entailed. And so Louisa continued smiling into her lap. Bryan, misjudging her evident pleasure, was now also smiling.

His father patted his knee. "My talented young son," said Sir John Sudbury, "is a good boy and will certainly prove a good husband. Normally, of course, we would expect a bride price, but since my dear little Beatrice will be wedded to the brother, each bride price will cancel out the other. A good arrangement, I believe."

Charles nodded vigorously. His smile disappeared and turned to scowl as he gazed down at Louisa. She refused to look up. "And so, my girl," Charles said with looming insistence, "I shall arrange a double wedding to take place in early November. I shall inform Francis later this day. Now I suggest you and your intended take a walk in the gardens and get to know each other."

"It's pouring with rain," Louisa pointed out.

"Not at all," Sir John stood, nodded towards the window and smiled. "Just a faint drizzle. A little chilly, perhaps. I suggest you both wear your capes. In the meantime, Charles and I have a great deal to discuss."

Louisa looked up, staring at her brother. "You mean concerning the recent rebellion led by the Duke of Buckingham, which you secretly supported?"

With glowering dislike, Charles stared down, bendin, he slapped her face first to one side and then to the other. her cheeks were inflamed and scarlet as Louisa bit her lip, made certain not to cry, and stood. "I refuse to walk in the rain with that boy," she said, "and will now return to my room. Nor have I any intention of marrying anyone you choose for me, including him. You may be master of this household, but you cannot force me to stand unwillingly at any church porch. And since you're a flagrant traitor, you should be careful what you do."

As she turned to run back up the stairs, the Sudbury girl stood abruptly and came to her side. "My dear Louisa, this is the right and proper decision," she said, smiling at Louisa and then glaring back at her father. "May I walk with you instead of my brother? I promise to be a far more understanding companion."

Now Bryan was also standing but was held back by the flat of his father's hand against his chest. "Leave them be," he ordered, and frowned at Charles. "No point forcing the situation yet. Especially since our original plan appears to have failed."

"That brat has no right to know of it," seethed Charles.

"But evidently she does," Sir John nodded. "Now we have time to rethink a little, and put matters back on the proper path." He moved back, taking the boy with him. Charles scowled at everyone, but Beatrice took Louisa's elbow, and together they walked to the front door, retrieved their cloaks, and slipped out into the rain.

Accepting, interested, Louisa looked aside, her eyes half obscured by the hood of her cloak. "You dislike your father's arrangement of your marriage to a total stranger younger than yourself?"

"Yes, I do." Beatrice was watching her feet as they slipped into the muddy grass. "I always intended to refuse it. But I wasn't sure how. My father is as strict as your brother appears to be."

"He hits you?" Louisa's face was still discoloured.

The other girl swore beneath her breath and Louisa blinked. She'd never heard the words from a woman before. "Shit scum of a man," Beatrice muttered. I even doubt he's my father. My mother almost admitted as much once, but stopped at the last minute. Anyway, I've no intention of marrying some little boy." She turned back to Louisa. "What's your little brother like?"

"Lovely and kind and sweet," Louisa insisted. "But – well, rather childish at times. Not mature yet. When I think of fourteen-year-old boys being sent into battle to hack at someone hand to hand, it's ludicrous. Francis had plenty of training and he's not an idiot. But in some ways, I can only admit, he is an idiot after all."

"So not the ideal husband?"

"Perhaps he is. He'd do the right things and want to have lots of fun."

"A virgin?"

Louisa blushed. "I'm sure he is." She paused abruptly thinking of Joletta. "Actually, probably not. Is that better or worse for a boy?"

"I've no idea," said Beatrice. The girl was tall, slim, and dark haired with slightly narrow brown eyes and plucked eyebrows. Neither beautiful nor unattractive, she appeared more intelligent than luscious. Louisa was slightly envious.

"I'm surprised we've never met before," she said, "since my brother seems to be a great friend of your father. But then, I'm afraid Charles has always tried to keep me at home like some chained dog." She looked back towards the house, but no one appeared to be following them. "This may sound a little childish, but I ran away a few months back. I had a special reason, but then I had to come home. Charles is not a tolerant man. I was severely punished."

The disdain returned. "No woman should ever permit a man to beat her."

"I do." Louisa bit her lip again. "I mean I don't. The trouble is, I fight back but he locks me in my room and he punches me. I can't stop him. And anyway, there's plenty of men out there who beat their wives, their daughters, and even their staff. It's legal."

"It's disgusting." Beatrice leaned back against the stable wall. "I'm not keen on men. Actually, I find them pathetic. They can't achieve a thing without lashing out – sword – fists – spoiled babies. I've not the slightest intention of marrying one."

The two young women stared at each other, warmth increasing as though the rain had begun to simmer like hypocrass in the pot.

Louisa almost bit her tongue a third time. "I can't say the same. Oh, I respect you for thinking it and saying it and so on. I'm in love. Does that sound soppy and stupid? But I am. He's no lord, though I love him anyway."

"So go off and marry the man."

"He's off west with the king." She laughed softly. "Besides, I hardly know him, and he hasn't asked for marriage yet. I expect all he's thinking of is the Buckingham rebellion."

"He doesn't side with my father and your elder brother?"

"Oh, gracious no." Blushing, Louisa shook her head and the raindrops flew. She brushed them away. Beatrice, a little taller, faced her, smiling, and reached out slender fingers to help wipe the last trickles from her face. Louisa stepped back for this felt too intimate and she stared, nervous.

Beatrice turned, beginning to walk down the long-hedged path towards the river. With her back to Louisa, she called, "The rain's getting heavier. Come and get drenched with me. Then we can tumble back inside and drip onto your brother's rugs."

Catching her up, Louisa laughed. "I could take you to meet Francis. I'm sure you'd like him. But the girl he thought he loved is dead. I'm sure Charles killed her." She paused, staring around in case overheard by gardeners, grooms or some wandering scullery boy emptying rubbish into the river. "Listen," she said as they once again walked side by side, "I think Charles murdered the girl to stop Francis from marrying her. And we went to find the girl's mother, who was desperate, and brought her back here to work. But Charles sent her off with threats and now I've got to go and find her all over again."

Interested, Beatrice stood gazing across at the river, a grey slop of dizzying droplets dancing grey on grey, reflecting a grey sky. "So You won't marry my vile brother, and I won't marry your baby brother. That sounds perfect to me. You wait until your hero comes back from the battles. I shall never marry any man." She turned suddenly. "But since they don't allow women to marry women, I shall live a solitary life. At least, solitary as far as the public imagines. What I do in private is my own business. And I like you, little Louisa, but you are in love with a man, so we shall remain just friends."

"You're laughing at me." The rain now streamed from the rim of her hood and slid down her nose as though skating, then dripped from the end. Beatrice resisted the urge to reach out as Louisa smiled. "I don't entirely understand you, but I'm delighted if we can be friends. I don't have many friends except my brother and my nurse. And Doric, I hope, if he comes back to me."

"I'm sure he will. You're too pretty to leave."

Both blushing and biting her lip, Louisa said at once, "Beatrice, you're the lovely one. You have such elegance, and your face shouts clever. You have gorgeous cheekbones. Me – I'm all round and childish and none of my bones even show through, I have a round chin and a round forehead and big round cheeks and even a round nose. Round eyes too. And Charles never let me pluck my eyebrows."

Beatrice sighed without explanation. "My dear, you're as pretty as any man could dream of, and those big blue eyes are utterly bewitching. Besides you have an adorable little nose and chin, so there's something wrong with your mirror. You say your face is round. I say that mine is thin and sharp."

Louisa was laughing, although not quite sure why. "I'll remember those nice kind words while I wander the wretched tanneries."

Interested once more, Beatrice raised an eyebrow. "Who goes to the tanneries unless they are a tanner by trade?"

"It's a horrid place indeed." Louisa turned from the river, which had begun to swell towards the lower edges of the banks. With Beatrice beside her, they began to walk back towards the house. "It's the destitute mother I was telling you about," she said. "She worked there as a brewer. It's the only place she can go. And I have to go and get her. Save her, if you like, since it was one of my brothers who started all the trouble by falling for her daughter, and my other brother who I'm almost positive must have murdered that daughter."

"I've never been to the tanneries. An adventure, then? I shall come with you."

They had started to run as the rain began to thunder. Racing, grabbing at each other and laughing, they arrived hand in hand and both entirely soaked at the back doors. Francis was waiting for them, his face equally wet.

It was only as Louisa introduced her little brother to Beatrice, that she realised that it was not rain that shone across her brother's face. As was becoming usual, Francis had been crying.

Putting her arms around him, Louisa asked, "It's, him again isn't it." He nodded into her shoulder. "Charles found where we'd smashed in the door, and you weren't his prisoner in the cellar any longer?"

"He found me under your bed," Francis hiccupped. "He dragged me out and started hitting me. I mean really really hitting. He bashed my nose and grabbed my hair and threw me against the bedpost and thumped me again. And all the time that disgusting boy stood in the doorway sniggering."

"My brother," said Beatrice calmly. Louisa sniffed and started to apologise for the description but Beatrice stopped her. "Of course he's disgusting. I tell him that too. We're twins, but it's like one person cut down the middle, and I'm weird but nice, and he's just vile."

"You're not weird," Louisa looked at her over her brother's

quivering shoulder. He was still crying. "But your Bryan, he's a vile brat."

"You don't know me yet," Beatrice said. "And you don't know the rest of us either. I suppose Papa is normal enough but he's too strict and he doesn't understand love. But my brother is exactly how you saw. He's disgusting. Hang him from the nearest tree if You like. I'll help."

CHAPTER TWENTY-EIGHT

H enry Stafford, previously Duke of Buckingham, was placed
under close arrest in a small upstairs chamber of the Cock Inn,
which he shared with his two watchful gaolers. He paced the sad little
room, five steps covered with worn rushes and the smell of rat's urine.
He slumped on the narrow bed, stared at the low beams above his
head, rose, and paced again. His final bravado disintegrated. Misery
and fear engulfed him like the great black wings of a raven at his neck,
its beak in his throat. He begged to see the king. Word was eventually
brought back to him. The king had refused.

In the absence of the Constable, the trial was conducted in the city
Guildhall by the Vice-Constable of England, Sir Ralph Assheton. The
original Constable at that time had indeed been the Duke of
Buckingham.

He was brought to trial in silence, but his eyes were rimmed in
blood moist carmine. The king was not present. Buckingham
willingly confessed to everything of which he was accused, to high
treason against the crown, to taking up arms in rebellion, and
attempting to escape justice. He named his fellow conspirators.
Panicked tremors shook his hands and his voice as he said and did
exactly what was asked of him and as he requested, repeatedly, just

one thing in return. To see and speak with his king. Permission was again denied.

Henry Stafford was found guilty of high treason and sentenced to death. Building of the scaffold to hold the execution block was begun immediately in the main square. The sound of the busy carpenters was audible from the Cock Inn, and the steady growth of the erection was visible from the upstairs chambers. For an hour, the prisoner crouched at his window and watched the inevitability of his own death materialise before him. Then he abandoned all remaining dignity and collapsed.

He became ill, suffering from a high fever and violent stomach cramp, then vomited into the chamber pot, and was brought wet cloths by the hostelry's nervous landlady. The two gaolers watched, shrugged, and continued with their game of dice. A terrible state of terror to the point of delirium began to overtake the duke and he trembled uncontrollably. It was the first day of November, the room was unheated, and the day was stark and frosty, but it wasn't the cold that affected him. He pleaded again and again to speak with the king. This time, his majesty did not deign to reply.

It had been a long, dark night and his highness had not slept. But he was accustomed to not sleeping.

It was once again Lord Leys who spoke briefly to his king , since neither had slept. "If you feel so wretched about this whole business, why not see the man? They say he's been begging and pleading like a lunatic to speak to you, gone into a virtual seizure and does nothing but shiver and sob. I knew the man was craven. On the ride here, he switched from arrogance to abject self-pity backwards and forwards a hundred times."

The king shook his head. "I won't have some pathetic creature sobbing at my feet, begging for his life, which I cannot allow him. This extent of outright treason could never be forgiven, although I accorded him a trial. Whatever he said, I would believe it lies." Richard reached across the table and grasped his cup but did not drink from it. He ran his finger around the golden stem, tracing the embossed relief of eagles and lions, staring unblinking at the polished surface as if he saw visions. "I never expected this," he said. "I've always considered myself a good judge of character, since that seems a prerequisite of princes. When we are wrong, it can be disastrous, as you can see. I trusted Henry. Oh, I knew him pompous, puerile and inept, but I believed I understood him. I even grew fond of him."

Standing, Andrew nodded. "But if you think about it, sire, you never really trusted him. Otherwise, why heap him with all those honours and rewards? As with Stanley, your highness simply paid for his loyalty. Sire, you don't do that with a man you trust."

His royal highness remained focused on the high polish of his cup. "You're right, of course, Andrew," he said. "But I considered him honest. He craved riches as many do, and I gave him what he wanted, to give him confidence as well as to keep him at my side. It seems that the confidence he gained was far in excess of my intentions."

"Sire, you're an idealist," Andrew sighed. "And that's a dangerous thing to be in a world dedicated to hatred, greed and intolerance. But you never felt this strongly about Hastings' defection."

Richard looked up at last. "Hastings? He owed me no loyalty," he answered. "He'd always hated the Woodvilles because he was jealous of them and their influence with my brother. When he became more jealous of me, he naturally befriended the Woodvilles. It was the logical reaction. He was capable of great trust with Edward and disliked my setting aside Edward's bastard sons, but he was always corrupt. He was lascivious and spiteful, and made a fortune denying any man association with the king until paid an entrance fee. It made him rich but it consistently blocked justice from those who needed it. I admired him purely for his extreme loyalty to Edward." The king paused, then added, "Yet even accepting that, both Hastings and my brother quarrelled before the end, principally concerning gifts, honours and titles given – or not."

Andrew regarded his king. "You know, don't you Sire," he continued at last, "that if this had not happened, in time Buckingham would have become your Hastings." Then he grinned suddenly. "Do you want me to tell you in just what esteem I hold you, my king?" He shrugged and stretched, reaching at last for the wine jug and cup.

"Sire, you're the first king in history who insisted on having your coronation speech translated into common English, so that every man, literate or not, can know what oaths of fealty and weal you've sworn and the promises you've made to uphold justice and give equal rights to every citizen. Do you want me to list the other stream of accomplishments I respect you for? Having known you before the coronation, I may say, if you will allow it, that I have always considered you a man of great honour."

Saturday afternoon, as the clouds gathered once more in a black tempest of threat, Buckingham lost all hope and slumped to his knees. He had been served a warming pottage with manchet and cheeses for midday dinner, but he had eaten nothing. The priest, who had accompanied the return to his confinement after the trial, had come once more to his room. "In the name of God," pleaded the duke, "have pity. I have confessed everything. Tell his majesty, I'll say more. Anything he wants of me."

Within the hour, the priest returned, trudging puddles, his hood up and dripping. "I was refused admittance, your grace," he said quietly, "but I passed your message, word for word. The answer came immediately. It will not be permitted, your grace. His highness has made it clear, saying that under no circumstances will he see you, either in private or in public. I am to inform your grace that the king will never forgive nor condone and cannot accept any matter whatsoever that you might wish to plead."

Henry Stafford's head sank, and he began to sob violently. The priest helped him return to his bed and then left. At five o' clock of the evening, a light supper was served. Once again, the duke could not eat but he drank some hypocras and asked that the priest return and his gaolers leave, so that he might make confession. After this he slept a little, but his dreams were tortured and he tossed, crying out, waking wild and terrified, before managing to close his swollen eyes again.

A few minutes before dawn he was woken. It had begun to rain, a light silvery sleet that shimmered like moonshine in the dark. The duke took ale and a manchet roll for break-fast but could finish neither. His throat seemed closed against him and he could barely speak. "It was never my idea," he whispered. "It was Bishop Morton who convinced me. He lied to me, telling me stories against my king and convincing me what I should do. I beg you, in the name of the Almighty Lord our God, inform my king that I'm sorry and it was never my idea. It was Morton who told me what I should do."

The senior gaoler, having slept very little himself due to the constant disturbances, was neither sympathetic nor prepared to risk his own position by carrying such a worthless story. "No time for that now, your grace," he said, "As for the name of the Lord our God, well it's Him as you'll be accountable to within the hour, and so best make an honourable end of it."

The duke had pissed his hose during the night, crying out against those nightmares of hellfire and brimstone. The stale sour smell of it was in his nose as he dragged himself from the bed.

It was still raining as he left the tavern, flanked by the two guards and the fluttering priest with the last muttered sacrament of penance. He had been stripped down to shirt and hose, leaving his neck exposed for the axe. His boots were now the property of the executioner and his stockinged feet slipped on the wet cobbles, his hair slicked to his ears and forehead. But it was also the cold that made him tremble. He had no control over legs or bladder as his guards supported him, half dragged, half carried, towards the scaffold.

Across the square he could see the small huddle of townsfolk who had come to watch the death of the traitor. Because of the weather, there were few of them, but one young man was wiping his hands on his leather apron and selling hot pies from the wooden tray hanging around his neck. Stafford could smell the meat and gravy and thought he would vomit. A thin woman was selling ale, filling the same bent tin cup from the jug she carried, and passing it through the crowd.

Henry Stafford climbed the steps to the block and looked briefly up at the sky above. Dawn was a new pastel stripe behind the fluted roof tops and their crooked striped eaves, a little pink flurry between the lowering clouds. He looked back down at the block and its carpet of straw. The rain obscured the tears streaming down his face. He had to cough a little to find his voice. "May God have mercy on my soul," he whispered, and knelt in the straw which had been laid to soak up his own warm life's blood. He stretched his arms horizontally behind him and lowered his head, carefully placing his chin beyond the base so that his neck rested in the hollow. It was so cold and very wet. He shut his eyes. It took three strokes of the axe to sever his head from his body, but he was quite dead after the second.

Both Andrew and Doric, having been required as witnesses, now turned away, Doric felt sick. "He was a terrible fool, and deserved to die for what he did. Accepting the king's gifts and friendship, to then turn against him in such an arrogant manner was a vile act. No king can ignore such blatant treason. But I believe Henry Stafford was a born simpleton. A ten-year-old child in an adult body. First too long ignored by King Edward, and then ignored too little by King Richard."

"Nine years old," Andrew said. "Or perhaps eight."

"Having watched the piteous death of the eight-year-old," Doric said, "I now have a mission of my own to complete. But I seriously hope, my friend, that we continue to work together."

"Without doubt," Andrew smiled, his hands moving to Doric's shoulders. "I miss my wife and intend returning to her this morning. But you, my friend, have also become important to my life. I shall see you soon at court. Bring your lute."

"She never leaves me," Doric inhaled deeply, and needing to forget the brutal death he had just witnessed, managed to laugh. "But I have another woman I love, and I dream she won't leave me either."

CHAPTER TWENTY-NINE

North of the River Thames, east of London's Tower and the city wall, the tanneries lay spread over several miles of flat land. cradled between the arms of two vast blocks of tenements, five great pits sank into the ground, three of which were stone walled below the surface, stopping the absorption of liquid into the earth. These tanning pits stank with the urine and excrement used on hides cut from dead animals, left to soak, cleansing away the stench and the debris hauled from one pit to the next. Other substances were stored, lime and tannin, oak bark and the leaves of hemlock. Huge wooden tubs were piled within the shadows. The animal skins were also piled at each stage of their soaking, curing and cleaning. Where they had been scrubbed on arrival, stone-soaked splatters of dead flesh and the filth of the abattoir remained.

Beatrice gazed in disgust at what lay before her and claimed that breathing was entirely impossible when breathing meant drawing in the smell of every vile thing she could imagine.

"Lou said as how you were a practical woman," Francis objected. "I mean, I'm not saying it's a wonderful perfume. But these people have to work here every day. They get used to it. I stayed a few days and I got used to it as well. Not entirely, perhaps. But more or less."

"Less or more?"

They were waiting outside the larger of the two tenement blocks, since Louisa was visiting a tiny home on the first floor. Although Beatrice found this both strange and unpleasant, she had decided that moaning and complaining was sufficient diversion, and that leaving entirely would be an exaggeration, and spoil all the pleasure of what might follow.

When she asked what they were waiting for, Francis replied, "I don't have the faintest idea. Louisa gets her own odd ideas, and I never really get the point. This time she says she needs to speak to someone related to her old nurse. Sounds daft, doesn't it. But I doubt she'll be long."

Climbing one flight of steep and rickety steps, Louisa had approached the curtain which served as a door to Isabella's brother-in-law, and had called. At first there was no answer, but as she turned to leave, the dirty rag of a curtain was pulled back, and Robert Rudge appeared abruptly, a long-bladed knife held up in the candle light.

"No, no, I'm not a thief," said Louisa. "I'm a sort of friend of Isabella's. Don't you remember me?"

"I does, I does," Robert quickly sheathed his knife, apologised and drew Louisa into the tiny room. "But there's bin trouble around, see! Wot with uprisings and troops and bothersome squabbles as folks takes differing sides."

Nodding her sympathy, Louisa sat as indicated by the little central fire slab where a tiny collection of faggots were burning, the warmth delightful but the smoke in billows disguised all else. "I came," she said with faint guilt, "to ask you about two different things. You see, it's my brother."

"Young Francis?"

"Charles. As I think Isabella told you, Francis was infatuated with a brewster's daughter who came to work near here in the ale shop on the southern edge of the tanneries. Joletta. She has been killed and I think Charles killed her."

Vehemently shaking his head, Robert declined all such knowledge.

"I knows about your family," he admitted. "But I ain't seen naught o' Charles Hylton fa nigh on a seven year."

Louisa was surprised that he had ever met Charles at all, but instead explained the situation. "I'm sure it was him. But of course, I could never prove it. He's – well, Charles is not a good man."

"I surely knows that," Robert told her. She was even further surprised.

"I need something to hold against him," Louisa said. Choosing to blackmail her own brother hardly seemed an act of sweet moral Christianity, but she didn't care. "I need him to confess, but he never will do a thing for me unless I threaten to tell about his awful sins. I know he backed Buckingham in the recent rebellion, but I have no proof of that either, since he plotted and planned but never had the courage to go and fight. Dearest Isabella knows more provable secrets against him, but she won't tell me. She swore not to, and so I thought you might tell me instead."

"Ah." Master Rudge whistled into the dark swirling smoke in his tiny room. "Tisn't as easy as might be supposed, lass. Or, m'lady as I ortta say. See, Isabella is a mighty good lass and I don't want to be upsetting her." He sighed. "But I has to tell you, t'would be a mighty fine feeling to do summint agin that bastard Charles, forgive me language. He done a load o' wickedness."

"Tell me," Louisa smiled, "and I shall absolutely promise not to let anyone think Isabella told me. I won't mention you either. But it should mean that Francis and I could live happily and peacefully in our own home, I wouldn't have to marry some horrid brat, and Isabella could be happy too. I should arrange to have Annie, that's Joletta's mother, come and work in the house". She paused, thinking, and said suddenly, "Perhaps you could too, since you're close to dear Bella. I mean, this is a nice safe little room, But just a little small. You might appreciate a move."

"Hum," said Robert, shoving a few more twigs amongst the others on the stone slab. "Well, tis a long story. You got an hour or more?"

She remembered Francis and Beatrice still waiting downstairs. "Would you consider coming with us to a large house nearby? It's not far, and it's absolutely safe. Charles knows nothing about the place, but I have permission to go there, and so we could talk for however long you wish. But my little brother and a friend are both waiting for me out in the cold, so I have to think of them too. I can't leave them outside for a whole hour."

He cackled. "You thinking I gonna be shamed o' this where I lives? And so wouldna want yer friends and such to come in here? No, lass. You invites them in here, and I got wine in me locked chest, and cups too, and enough stools fer another party or such. You go tell them to come in if they wants."

She had assumed that Beatrice would be appalled at the dirt and size of this tenement building, but it was Francis who walked in and stared in shock, saying, "Just a touch crowded, don't you think?" When invited to sit, he first rubbed his hand across the top of the stool, expecting a surface of dirt.

But Beatrice said, "Well, Master Rudge," I appreciate the kind invitation. And if you allow us a cup of wine, I shall be even more appreciative. But I will also arrange to replace the keg."

They drank as the story stretched, uninterrupted, except by the gasps of Francis and Beatrice, and finally the soft sounds of Louisa crying.

"We starts wiv yer Mum and Dad," Robert sighed. waving the poker. "Tis not easy to remember all them names, but I recons yer Dad were Lord Hylton like yer brovver, and he were a terrible man. O'course, life were a touch different back then and the rich was one way and the poor were anovver."

The fire spat and the smoke snuffed out the only candle, yet the flames lit the room and as Robert bent over, poker in hand, his face was shining with sweat and the sheen reflected scarlet, as if an ogre was telling the tale of another ogre even more terrifying.

"It was only thirty years gone," Francis objected. "Though I'm not sure how old my father was when he died." He paused, scratching his head, then added, "I suppose I'm not really sure of anything."

"This is bound to be an interesting story," Beatrice murmured into the crackle of the fire, "but hardly my business. I can leave, if you wish."

Both Louisa and Francis shook their heads. Louisa said, "I don't care who knows how horrid my father was, and as for Charles, the more folk who know he's a vile traitor, the better."

"I know naught 'bout traitors," Robert said. "But I can tell yer all 'bout the past, for that tis all I knows." He sat forwards on the small three-legged stool, knees wide, and squinted through the spit of the flames. "T'was Percival, yer dad, and the lasses thought him a fancy man wiv bright silks and a 'tash, well combed and black as his heart. Percival Swells, Earl o' Hylton, what looked down 'is long nose at all the rest o' the world. He were just an earl, not a bloody duke, but the man acted like he were a king. But," and Robert leaned back from the fire and sighed, "there were one big problem. The fellow didn't have no money. Had a big house, being wot you lives in now, and anovver too. Fine robes, but he never paid fer nuffin if he could help it, and when his own pa died, he left debts and all. The first earl, he were a gambler and not much good at it, truth be knowed."

"He had a wife? My grandmother?"

"Dunno," Robert shook his head. "Reckon some lass bin there, fer getting the son Percival. But Percival growed up wiv naught but a title, and no wife wanted a gent wivvout a single coin. So young Percival, he done it a different way. His pa died by his own hand, he did, deep in debt and bloody down on his luck. Did it wiv his own knife, in the stables. But t'wer such a sin, the lad Percival had to pretend it weren't self-done and made out the earl done felled from his horse. Ovverwise, the dad wouldna get no buriel fer suicide ain't permitted as I reckon you knows. So Percival, he inherited house and title and a couple o' bits o' furniture and horses but naught else."

Frowning, Louisa muttered, "But Charles is rich. We are a wealthy family, even if Charles never gives us a halfpenny of it."

"Ah, that be the point," Robert continued. "There were two young lasses, mighty pretty sisters, they was, wot lived wiv the family up north. Real special wealthy, they was, but had no title being as the pa were a trader in spices and such like, and done made a fortune in takin' prisoners after the war in Agincourt, four o' them Frenchies, and got huge ransoms from every one o' them. Made a fortune. Well, he done wed a lass and bought a castle. Had two daughters, they did. Happy families, no doubt. And were well heard of, being so rich, but weren't no friends wiv Percival Swells. But when the pa got old and died, them daughters got all the coin. There were Margaret, who was eldest, and there were Alice, wot was only thirteen and pretty as a lark, she were. "

Francis sat up straight. "My mother? She was young when I was born, and she died in childbed, poor lady."

"That be it," Robert said. "But no so easy. Fer she didn't want him, knowing he were cruel and broke, and wanted her money fer hisself. But Percival, he got his men and a load more, promising coin, and they besieged the castle. He wanted the eldest, being Margaret, I reckon. But she hid in the privy. I weren't there course, but I knowed that be true, though Percival said as how she killed herself o'cos he chose the little sister instead. But I knows he killed her. But after he done it, he grabbed little Alice and rode off wiv her. Took the lass home and chucked her into his bed."

"Abduction?" Louisa shivered. "And then rape?"

Robert nodded. "So the lass had to agree to marry the bastard. Didn't have no choice, did she, poor lass. Wiv the elder sister dead, and the mother gabbling demented wiv Percival saying as how it were all lies, he got all the money and a pretty wife wot he bullied and beat. But she had his son. She were still just thirteen, but had a fine boy and struggled through, she did."

"The son was Charles?"

"Oh yes, indeed," Robert answered Francis. "Born o' rape, he was, yer big brovver. And I reckon that were the only bad fing wot werren't his fault."

"He was beaten too, wasn't he?" Louisa murmured. "Father gave him a horrible childhood. But I had little trouble from Papa, since he died when I was young. And Francis was only three or four."

Robert nodded vigorously. "Yer," he agreed. "But yer brovver

Charles were about fifteen, I reckon, and that were when he killed his pa."

The shocked silence continued until it was Beatrice who stuttered, "Charles murdered his own father?"

"Wiv a hot brick from his bed, on top o' the stairs. Skull walloped, and down them stairs the bugger fell. Proper dead, he were."

"Oh, gracious me," Louisa gasped. "I didn't expect such a terrible story. No wonder Charles insisted on keeping it all secret."

"That's a truly dreadful tale," Francis said, half choking. "And that's my father Percy. How vile. I almost feel sorry for Charles. And I certainly feel sorry for my poor wretched Mamma. What a truly desperate life she had. And I'm sorry, but I can't feel Charles was wrong to kill his disgusting father. I would have wanted to do the same."

"But now Charles has turned into our own horrible father," objected Louisa. "He's just as bad."

"I'm so sorry," Beatrice whispered. That's an even worse story than my own family's."

"But there be much more n' that," grinned Robert. "That be only the beginning."

CHAPTER THIRTY

Even deeper into the tannery, the small group trudged onwards, their capes held up to their noses to escape the encroaching stench. This, her first visit ever to this outlying area of virtual exile, fascinated Beatrice and she refused all offers of returning to the city's comparative safety. Francis spoke to no one and stared down at his boots as they walked the muddy lanes.

Louisa had been crying. Now her tears were hidden within the new sluice of rain, cold and continuous. She gazed as Beatrice beamed. "You know a lot about us now," she murmured. "You won't tell your brother, will you. Or – anyone."

"I am a creature of trust," Beatrice assured them both. "And I'll help all I can. I'd be delighted to meet this wandering minstrel of yours sometime."

Slightly embarrassed, Louisa tried to smile. "But then you might fall for him too and he might choose you instead of me."

"That," Beatrice laughed, "is entirely impossible."

The streets were crowded as usual, carts delivering newly skinned hides from the abattoir, the stink of recent death. Skins were carried on the men's backs, bending over to take the weight, arms over their heads to steady both the man himself and his load.

Squabbles were frequent with shouting, bunching out and the barrage of insults repeated, but the work needed what the men called relief.

"Tis hard, this buggering work, and breaks our backs. Soon we stinks o' the same stench as we got here and our tunics is bathed in the muck so we can't visit nowhere 'cept where we is. If we didn't break off sometimes fer a bit o' cursin' and quarrels we'd all go bloody crazy."

Francis saw Annie immediately as she crossed from one pit to another, hauling overflowing buckets in each hand. Louisa and Francis ran over at once. Francis took the buckets from her, but blinked, and set them down at once.

"Piss?" he smelled.

Annie nodded. Her eyes were swollen and blood rimmed, her nose leaking like a baby's, and she clutched at Louisa. "You mustn't come here, my lady. Tis filth, all of it. You done what you could, and I thank you for it. I don't ask for no more."

Shaking her head with miserable vehemence, Louisa looked down at the small woman. "And now you're working for the tanners, not the ale shop?"

"Without my Joletta," Annie said, half crying, "I'm too slow. The shop's got a new lad and his pa. I got took up by the fellows here, being as they know me from the shop."

"And you carry buckets of urine for a living? How interesting." decided Beatrice.

Annie took no notice. "I understands," she told Louisa. "Tis yer brother don't want me, just like he shut out my lass. There ain't a lord o' the whole land what wants a brewster's daughter in his family."

"Perhaps," Louisa admitted. "But you'll come home with us, and have a decent life doing a bit of gardening, or even making ale if you like. And this time my horrible brother won't be able to stop you."

Annie looked disbelieving and dropped her gaze. "I can't think yer brother wouldn't notice, my lady. Honest, tis not needed. I got a job."

"Where do you live?" Beatrice asked.

"I ain't got no home yet," Annie said, half whispering. "But I sleeps in the tannery hut over there and tis right warm and cosy. Plenty o' straw, and I collects me own water from the well."

"You're coming home with us," Francis insisted, taking her elbow after Louisa had released her. "No argument. Losing Joletta was my fault, and all that dreadful bad luck, just after you'd had to leave the Fleet shop when that bastard wherryman accused you of cheating. It's time you had some good luck, mistress, and we owe it to you."

Annie, now clinging to Francis, immediately burst into loud sobs.

Beatrice looked at her companions with a faint smile. "First Francis," she murmured. "Then Louisa. Now Annie. I don't remember crying my eyes out since I was about six."

"You didn't see Joletta," Louisa muttered. "But you heard Robert's stories. "

"It wasn't my family," Beatrice answered. "But what I suggest is that I stay witness while you take this poor woman home. Charles will be limited in what he can say and do if I'm watching. I'll join in and say how clearly she needs help." She smiled. "I might even cry."

Four of the men working close by had gathered, listening, nodding and adding their own encouraging grunts. "The lass deserves better," one man said. He patted Annie's shoulder. "You goes to a grand house, Annie lass. Why not. You takes wot you can."

Annie had begun to argue when another of the men loomed over her. "Mistress Annie, you done good by us, now get summint back." He turned to Francis. "Good words, lad," he continued, "I reckon you weren't the one wot killed the little lass after all."

White faced, Francis stared back. "You thought it was me? Me? I was the one who murdered dear Joletta? How could you think such a thing?"

The man shrugged. "Usually is, ain't it? The gent gets the little lass wiv child, and then has to kill the lass off so no suspicions. Tis the usual tale. Tis always the fellow what kills the girl. But wiv you – well – I reckons you didn't do it."

"He's a lovely boy," Annie interrupted. "Son o' a lord and all. He would never have hurt my beautiful lass. But per'aps –coulda bin the other brovver."

"Then bring that bastard brother here," said the man, "and I'll drown the bastard in one o' me vats."

Crowding close, now there were five of the tanners nodding and murmuring. One said, "I's Ned Taylor, mistress, and you calls if you needs me."

"And me, I's John Smiff," said the tallest. "I reckon I could beat any little lord into a pulp."

"Me too," the first man said. "I be John Wesst. "And mighty good wiv me mitts, I is."

"I's a John too," another said, pushing closer. "Remember me, mistress. John Beatty. I's here when you wants me."

Beatrice was wondering whether crying might be a good idea. "Let's get going," she said, smiling at Louisa. "I don't wish to sound rude, but I do think Mistress Annie might enjoy a hot bath before we have to face your brother and my father. And perhaps a new gown as well. Indeed, if she will allow us to help with a few small alterations, I doubt Charles will even recognise her, and will produce no objections to her joining the staff."

"That," nodded Louisa, "is a very good idea."

Annie shivered.

The walk home was tiring, and the early twilight of mid-autumn was sinking as they pushed through the Aldgate into London, trying to hurry in case the walls would contain them for the night if the Ludgate locked before they arrived. Annie's legs were short. She was scurrying to keep up as Beatrice and Francis strode ahead. Louisa had walked a good deal that day and was exhausted. Annie had worked from dawn and was now out of breath.

"We could stay at an inn," Louisa called, stopping in sight of Lower Thames Street. "Get a decent meal, and the bath too. We can talk for hours. And be energetic for the morning."

"And have Charles furious for being out all night, ready to lock us in and smash our heads against the wall when we see him tomorrow." Francis walked back towards Annie and his sister. "But to tell the truth – I like the idea. Charles tries to get rid of Annie again, and I'll hit him over the head with a stool."

"Hot baths for all of us," Beatrice said, also walking back to join the others. "I know a good tavern at the start of the Bridge. The rooms are spacious and the food's good."

"That's it, then," said Louisa, smiling and changing direction. "A night of luxury, and then back to hellfire in the morning." He grinned, considerably happier at the prospect. "But sometimes Charles doesn't even come home. I believe he has a mistress since he's always going off without saying where he's going or when he's coming back."

"All lords have mistresses," smiled Beatrice.

"One small problem," Francis remembered. "None of us has more than a mouldy farthing."

Beatrice shook her head and showed her purse, bulging beneath her cloak. "Your brother denies you what's yours by right," she said, slightly smug. "But my father's scared stiff of me giving him a bad reputation by appearing penniless. I shall pay for all of you with the greatest pleasure." She smiled directly at Louisa. "Of course, you can pay me back with kindness one day. I don't need money."

Within the hour, Louisa sat up to her shoulders in the steam of simmering water. A fire, still burning high, sat cheerfully in the centre of the hearth, and between bed and fire stood the bathtub. The bedchamber would be shared with Beatrice and Annie, Annie taking the truckle bed, and all three to share the bath water. Beatrice had already indulged, being the first since she had paid for the lot. Now she was downstairs enjoying a hot supper with the others. Louisa breathed in steam. The water was still without scum or grime since Beatrice presumably washed often. Annie would be the last, and the water would be left unusable by anyone else.

The flames crackled as the logs slowly burned from dry bark down to scarlet ashes. She dreamed, half forgetting to keep the water hot for the next bather, thinking only of Doric and her future.

"I am," she thought, "changing, almost each moment, while the deepest part of me watches. I can refuse Charles now. I have that confidence. I can threaten him and tell him how vile he is. Perhaps I can even make him change."

She reached out and grabbed the thin towel waiting folded on the end of the bed, avoiding splashes. Having dried and redressed herself, she spread the towel to dry in front of the fire and hurried downstairs to tell Annie it was her turn. She found Beatrice, Annie and Francis with three large jugs of best wine, their table cleaned of the supper platters.

The smell of the tanneries had faded, and as Annie hopped up to take last place in the bath water, so the final stench faded. "She needs new clothes," Beatrice said. "I have plenty spare at home but I'm not going home now. I could do so in the morning. But they wouldn't fit. I'm twice as tall and half the width."

"Then we'll go shopping in the morning," Louisa said. "It won't take long. We can't have her looking like a lady in silks specially tailored. She needs a clean shift, a new bright gown and a nice headdress."

"And new shoes," commented Francis, refilling his cup.

"And then we march home," Louisa grinned, "saying - what? We got lost and this kind woman helped us, so we've promised her a job and a bed?"

It was Beatrice who shook her head sufficiently to spill her over-filled cup. "No lies," she said. "Tell the bugger the truth and make him take it."

"Swallow it?" Francis was not convinced. He seemed a little tipsy.

Louisa smiled, shook out her long wet hair and raised her cup. "I have a different idea," she said softly. "We know about Isabella now, but we can't tell Isabella herself. But we can use the story to make Charles do what we say. That was the whole reason behind getting that story in the first place, wasn't it? So we tell Charles that this is a friend of Bella's, and she will be so delighted to see her again. They can share her room and work in the gardens. If Charles objects, we can hint at what we know."

"And first warn Isabella."

But Louisa said no. "She'll go along with it, but I don't want her to know we've heard all her secrets from her brother-in-law. I'll tell her afterwards when I introduce Annie, and just say it was a spur of the moment idea."

"And I shall stand beside you all, smiling," Beatrice declared, "so it will be very hard for him to get nasty. And if he does, I shall start screaming and spit in his face. He won't dare hit me and I don't think he'd dare actually hit you in front of me."

As far as Louisa could remember, he had already done this in the moment of greatest fury, but this time faced with herself and Francis, then the fearsome Beatrice and the unknown woman who was a friend of Bella, surely he would remember to hold onto his pride and reputation. How Bella had already permitted Charles the appalling behaviour in the past, she didn't know. But faced with a lord, strong, youthful and arrogant, she supposed it would seem extremely intimidating. She found him intimidating herself.

"No longer," she told herself. "Or at least, I have to pretend as hard as I can."

CHAPTER THIRTY-ONE

The new oak panelling around the old hall was buffed to a gloss and the heavy beams supporting the high ceiling had been repainted, with the plaster above whitewashed and coruscated in scrolled triangles. The rushes were replaced with rugs from Turkey, Persia and India and the boards beneath were scrubbed and varnished with thick dark resins. The main table was replaced by one even grander that ran the length of the dais, and the minstrel's gallery was redecorated in green and gold.

"I suppose I should be up there," Doric pointed and Tyballis laughed.

New real glass windows and grand new shutters completed the renovations. Chairs, settles and cushions were drawn close to the expanse of marble pillared granite, with the raging firelight dancing crimson in everyone's eyes, making reflected monsters of them all.

Such marks of appreciation from his royal highness were accepted with enormous gratitude, as would be expected. But for Andrew and Tyballis, the king's generosity counted for considerably more. Not the donation of power, or a seat on the royal council, but a gift more private which signified respect and friendship.

Andrew enjoyed such evenings with his lady tucked improperly and intimately tight, her head on his shoulder as he held her close to him on the padded settle and looked down on the gently contented rise of her breathing.

"His royal highness is a gentleman of exceptional generosity," Doric grinned. "Getting Norfolk to arrange for refurbishment while we were off fighting Buckingham, was a remarkable idea. Now your home seems brand new."

"Not the bedchambers," Tyballis said, "and I'm pleased about that. I like my bedchamber. It's my design."

"Whereas the old hall," Andrew waved an explanatory arm, "was a dusty heap. Now even the cobwebs on the beams have been wiped away."

"Amazing," Doric was still grinning. He could not remember being so comfortable, or so warm as autumn crept towards winter. But it was a completely different pleasure he had in mind.

"As it happens," Andrew said. raising his wine cup in salute, "I enjoy indulging my own pleasures of generosity. Since our dear king has blessed me, I thought I might do something interesting for you, my friend."

He was still laughing, saying, "But I have no home to renovate, and have little interest in renovations anyway. No need to reward the one who simply obeyed your orders."

"Untrue," Andrew said, his feet stretched to the fire. "Amongst the Breton rabble you discovered more than I did, and indeed, spied out matters of absolute urgency. Then you became not only the faithful companion, but a most entertaining one. You protected my life on more than one occasion while fighting in the west, and you play the lute and sing like an angel. What more is there to praise?"

"It was Casper," Doric, although without particular enthusiasm, "who led us to Buckingham's capture."

Andrew nodded. "He has received his reward, as always, but desires very little except acknowledgement and freedom."

Doric thought a moment, then looked up. "I met him for the second time in that wretched cell," he said, "during that summer of glory for the king, but discontent for many others. I have no idea why

Casper had been arrested. But I had been accused of murdering the girl I travelled with for a couple of years. I have no idea who killed her, but it wasn't me. I didn't love the girl, but we worked well together."

"I wonder," Andrew raised an eyebrow, "if you have suspected Casper of that same murder?"

Doric looked down. "I have wondered. Casper and your lady wife were on the same road and I met them myself before Lizzie's death. But I have no real idea. When she was cross with me, Lizzie whored herself, and some late customer is probably the culprit."

"It would not have been Casper," Tyballis said, looking up. "We travelled together for a long month, and I know what he's capable of, and what he'd never do. I know exactly where he was each moment of that month in the west. He'll kill, I'm afraid, without compunction. He's led that sort of life. But only if attacked or ordered by Andrew for some matter of national safety. Neither situation is common. But I remember meeting you, Master Doric." Tyballis sat up, extricating herself from Andrew's embrace. "You gave a prediction which I then found remarkably accurate, even if a little vague."

Andrew nodded. "And she told me of it, Doric. It seems you have magical talents."

"Unfortunately not. Those words come into my head, but invariably they turn out to be nonsense." He sighed. "And I'd never accuse Casper. It was just the coincidence of meeting him in gaol. And it was him who asked you to get me out when you came to reclaim him. As if he owed me something."

"An interesting hypothesis," Andrew replied, pulling Tyballis back into his arms. "But inaccurate. He was in that cell for having cursed the sheriff, a bad-tempered man who harbours grudges. And Casper suggested I free you too, if I could, since you were a brilliant minstrel of exceptional quality, and a young man he considered both clever and possibly capable of helpful predictions." He smiled at Doric. "Meanwhile, I am planning your reward, my friend. And it is Casper who has given me some ideas."

It was the following morning that Doric left the Leys household with the young mare that Andrew had given him, rode east through the winding streets and wide squares of Westminster towards The Strand. Although it was in very different and far less inhospitable places that he had come to know the Lady Louisa, it had been spying of a far easier sort to discover where the lady lived.

No longer dressed as a minstrel, Doric now wore a white linen shirt beneath a doublet of damask and embroidery of gold thread, black silk hose, and a cape of rich blue velvet. His black hair was cut and combed back beneath a soft blue hat, feathered in one single spread, all of which remained as grand as he'd hoped as it neither rained nor blew gales.

He dismounted at the Leys Mansion, and Doric led his horse around to the stables. He then marched to the front door and was about to raise the large brass knocker, when he paused, realising that the door was already ajar and the terrible din from within would make knocking impossible to hear. Most improperly but with considerable confidence, Doric walked in.

As he stood, hesitating, in the corridor leading to the main hall and the staircase beyond, a small terracotta platter sped over his head and crashed against the half-closed door. The smell was distinctly parsnip as a creamy liquid slipped pale down the wall amongst the jagged scrunch of pottery.

Aimed from within the main hall, the platter and the noise were easy clues to follow. Doric walked in. Stood still for a moment, smiled at the chaos, recognised Louisa, raised his voice beyond the discord, and with studied calm, asked, "I wonder if there is a Lord Charles of Hylton present here? I hate to interrupt such a delightful gathering, but I bring a message from his Royal Highness, King Richard and his excellence, Lord Andrew Leys."

The company slumped into sudden silence, each caught abruptly in a variety of positions. Doric grinned at Louisa. She stood by the vast hearth, her skirts perilously close to the flames. Staring at Doric's appearance, her open-mouthed shock gradually changed to a vast smile of thrilled surprise.

Francis knelt on the wooden floorboards where it seemed he had fallen, but peered up at the newcomer, remembering Doric from the hill where he had discovered the awful death of Joletta. Beside him stood a tall man, roughly Doric's age and height, who had been brandishing a poker and was still holding this, mid-swing. Behind him stood another young woman whom he did not know, nearly as tall and seemingly as furious.

Sitting on a settle, well away from the others, two more elderly women perched. Doric vaguely recognised the nurse Isabella, who sat straight backed, her headdress so stiff starched that it had a small life of its own and swayed like a cog's sail in the breeze when anyone came past. She also kept her hands tight clasped in the neat white of her aproned lap. Next to her on the settle another woman huddled, seemingly timid and perhaps even frightened.

Charles stared at Doric, and with a surge of immediate excitement, Louisa began to run towards him. But Doric, keeping his movements from the sight of most others, warned her back. He then nodded at Charles once more, guessing him to be the elder brother.

"The message I bring is amicable, my lord. But I believe you would prefer to receive this in private." Doric leaned one elbow to the mantle as though very much at home, smiled at the company paralysed around him, and nodded. "Your choice, my lord."

With an attempt to disguise the scowl and change it to a polite and interested smile, Charles lowered the poker and turned to his now murmuring companions. "Out, out," he told them. "We'll finish this – discussion – later."

Waiting patiently as everyone scurried from the scene, Francis with a wink, and Louisa with a flashing smile, Doric continued to lean beside the hearth. Finally, Charles faced him, saying, "You are a messenger from the palace, sir? This is not what I would expect. By your clothes, sir, you are neither guard, nor personal servant but you state that your message is amicable. Therefore, sir, you will explain quickly since I am in the midst of important family affairs."

"So I noticed," Doric smiled. "But my message is more urgent and cannot be delayed. It is not written, since his highness has as yet no wish to make this matter official. Let me explain, my lord."

Charles sat abruptly and stared up, frowning. "Speak, sir."

Doric's smile held fast. "This concerns the recent rebellion led by Henry Stafford, once Duke of Buckingham," he said, now standing directly over Charles. "I am sure you are aware, my lord, that this disturbance was quickly culled by the royalist troops, while the attempted invasion from Brittany led by Henry Tudor, the exiled son of Lady Margaret Beaufort, failed miserably. Henry Stafford has been executed for his part in this treachery, and so have two others who were considered particularly culpable, but as usual, the king pardoned those other traitors who took less part in the proceedings. His highness is indeed known for his leniency in such matters and wishes to encourage peace in the land."

Charles clutched at the arms of his chair, staring red faced as he waited for accusation he knew must be coming. "I had no part in these uprisings," he said with what conviction he could muster. "I assure you, sir, I am a loyal citizen."

"Sir Andrew, Lord Leys," Doric continued, "who studies matters of this kind in company with his highness, has heard an opposing argument. It seems, my lord, that in partnership with Sir John, Lord of Sudbury, you plotted to back Henry Stafford in his treachery and offered to stand with him should his rebellion be successful in arriving at London."

Charles had no answer. He glared. Doric had once again started to speak when Charles rediscovered his voice and muttered, "Not true, sir. I cannot answer for Sudbury, but personally I would never have done such a thing. I naturally supported the king but did not engage in the fighting. I took no part."

"I wonder if you are acquainted with Lord Leys," Doric said, knowing quite well that he was not. "I suggest you visit him, my lord, at your earliest convenience. As I explained, his majesty has no intention of ordering further executions, especially regarding those who took no part in the fighting. But encouraging treachery is treachery in itself, my lord, and the king wishes to speak with you depending on the report first sent by Lord Leys."

"I do not know his lordship," Charles was flushed, both angry and nervous. "And have no idea where he lives. This is not a lord of long standing, sir."

"That is surely of no matter," Doric answered. "His lordship abides in Westminster and no doubt you'll discover his manor if you ask. I come only to advise you and inform you that the sooner you officially explain yourself, and I would suggest you include an apology, the sooner this can be forgotten. Any delay could end in arrest."

Both Francis and Louisa had been listening at the keyhole, hands clasped tight, delighted with what they could hear. Isabella had taken Annie to her own bedchamber, and Beatrice, promising to return soon, had hurried home to escape her own father's fury.

As the door hurtled against the corridor wall, opening with considerable force, Louisa and Francis fled, hiding in the shadow of the stairs. Charles strode towards the door to the stables beyond the kitchens, calling for gloves, hat, cape, and his horse to be saddled. The steward rushed to deliver, and Charles disappeared out into the courtyard. It was not yet raining but looked as though it was preparing for a downpour. Louisa smiled at Francis and ran to the hall.

Doric stood grinning in the doorway.

"Was any of that actually true?" asked Francis. "It sounded quite convincing. Well, we know the damned man is as treacherous as a bat in a flour pot, but I didn't think anyone else could know about it."

"We do know, as a matter of fact." Doric already had one arm tight around Louisa's shoulders. "Messages between your charming big brother and Buckingham were easily intercepted. But he won't be thrown to the block."

"Shame," Francis muttered.

"That would have been awful," Louisa sighed, "even though he deserves it."

Doric was looking around. "Nice house," he remarked without apparent surprise.

"Doesn't sound as if you're impressed, "Francis sniggered. "But our father made it as grand as possible just for status, being a bit of a bastard just like his eldest son."

225

"A *bit* of a bastard?" demanded Louisa. "He was worse. Much worse. And Charles will probably get worse too. He's inherited all that terrifying cruelty."

Taking her hand, Doric took Louisa to the settle where Annie and Isabella had been sitting, and again put his arm around her. She was not resisting. "If you think me improper," Doric grinned, "which of course I know I am, you're welcome to slap me away. But," and he tightened his hand on her shoulder, "I believe we already know well what we feel for each other."

Louisa looked back, then quickly down to her lap. "I know. And I've missed you so very much."

"I suppose I should leave you to your soppy cuddles," Francis said, "but first I have to thank you. After all, my brother was trying to beat me to death. I ended up having to be protected by women. I mean – that's not right. There was my lovely sister, and Beatrice. Beatrice is really tough. She's the woman I'm supposed to marry but she doesn't want me. Actually, I wouldn't mind her, but it's not going to happen. Thank goodness her rotten brother Bryan wasn't here. Nothing like his sister."

Listening patiently, Doric finally said, "May I ask what this family fight was about? Can I help?"

"You've helped already," Louisa said while feeling the warmth if his heartbeat. "It was just that we were out all day and night looking for the mother of the girl we found hanged. And we brought her home with us, pretending she was a friend of my nurse. Bella played along but unfortunately Charles recognised her, even though we'd dressed her up. Charles went wild."

"And it's true," Francis added, "about him and Beatrice's father plotting to help Buckingham. They both hate the king, but nobody could prove that. I just want to get away. He nearly broke my skull open today. I'm damned positive he's broken one of my fingers." Francis held out one hand, the index finger drooping and bloody.

Nodding, "Call the barber," Louisa said, and turned back to Doric. "I want to leave here too. I tried to get away, that's when I first met you. But it's not so easy. A woman can't just live on her own. Your friend's old house outside the Wall is a kind offer, but I couldn't stay unchaperoned, nor just with my brother."

"No, you couldn't," said Doric, "nor with me. Worse. You'd be mistaken for – well, never mind, but unless we marry," He paused, Louisa gazed in amazed delight, which then turned to confusion, and finally she slumped back.

It had, she realised, been an offer of heroic kindness and not one of passionate adoration. Louisa sniffed. "Charles wouldn't agree. And I'm only eighteen. But thank you so very, very much for saying that. It's – terribly kind."

"It's a bloody wonderful idea," Doric grinned. "But I'll have to think of some way to make it happen. Either threaten your brother or wait until you're twenty-one." He paused, smiling down at her. "If I arranged it, would you agree?"

"I'm going," said Francis "it's getting personal,", quickly leaving the hall. His footsteps echoed up the stairs.

"At once," Louisa breathed deeply, the believable truth slipping back, "and with joy. But only if you really mean it. And I ought to warn you, I haven't got any money. No special inheritance, No property."

She had never been kissed before. For a moment she tried to see, blinking as she gazed in wonder at the nearness of his deep brown eyes and their hazel flecks, heavy lidded and reflecting her own. Then she slowly closed her gaze and drank in the taste of his mouth on hers. His lips were moist and seemed to absorb her. For a moment she felt limp, even breathless, and then she leaned towards him and kissed him back.

His tongue rubbed over hers, his hands pulled her close and she sank into the warmth of him, the reassurance of his fingers more an invitation than a force. He smelled of passion.

She knew his reluctance when he finally withdrew and released her, watching as she opened her eyes and gasped. His own breathing seemed deep and ragged. "I won't leave you," he whispered. "We could hand-fast without your brother's permission."

Wanting to agree but feeling she must not, she whispered, "We could. I'm not sure. It's an exciting idea, but would it feel real? And would Charles murder us both?"

The smile changed to ice. "He could try."

"I have one idea, except that it might not be easy." She was whispering. It felt like betraying both Bella and Francis, but for herself it was the most exciting adventure she could imagine. "You work for the king now, and for the lord of that house where I stayed with Bella. You probably have very little time. So I don't expect you to say yes."

"It's yes, if you ask if I adore you. It's yes if you want to marry with or without your damned brother's permission."

Louisa shook her head, but Doric was watching the depth of her eyes, the gleam of delight and the translucence of the rich blue excitement. "Go on and tell me. Then I'll say yes."

"We have another house, of a sort, in the family. I could go there, if you'd take me. Charles hasn't been there in years, at least, I'm sure he hasn't. There'd be no reason. It was a tiny fortress, almost a castle, but half ruined, I think. My father's family owned it for years, and he lived there more than here. But when my mother died in childbirth with Francis, my father left there, and came to live here instead. He bought it with my mother's money. It was all his then of course because her father was dead too. But someone told me about the castle, and I know where it is. Evidently, we were all born there, but I certainly don't remember it. It's been abandoned for fourteen years, but it can't have fallen down, can it? Not a solid old stone building just after fourteen years. I could get away from Charles and go and live there. And," she looked up, "you too, if you wanted to. Perhaps just sometimes when you weren't called by Lord Leys or his highness. Even Francis could come and escape Charles."

"An old castle?" At first the idea seemed ludicrous. He had lived in huts and barns, grassy slopes and small forests, on the banks of streams and amongst the cows locked in their shelter for the winter. Now he lived in the tiny lodgings supplied by Lord Leys and was under obligation. Besides, living in a property to which he had no right, and bedding a girl to which he also had no right, the building's owner could immediately have him arrested. And from what he knew,

Charles would do this without compunction. "I'll speak to Andrew," Doric said. "He'll also say yes, unless something vital has appeared from the woodwork. Then I'll escort you, my love, and settle you in freedom. Then I'll play around for permission from those with a good deal more power than your wretched brother." He pulled her back into his embrace and kissed her forehead. "So when shall we make the escape, little one? I need two days to finalise my own affairs. After that, I am entirely yours."

CHAPTER THIRTY-TWO

Having confessed to Francis, Louisa collected the few belongings she believed had personal value such as three changes of clothes, a comb and a hand mirror, and the tiny golden hat pin which Isabella once told her was given by her mother. She owned virtually nothing else except her horse.

"You can't go away and leave me," Francis objected loudly.

"Hush."

Charles was downstairs shouting at the servants. Earlier that afternoon he had returned from his meeting with Lord Leys, and his usual scowl had doubled. On his arrival home, he had marched indoors, kicked the page who had opened the door for him, and yelled at the steward who had rushed to bring a cup of hypocrass.

"Ale, you fool, ale," Charles spat, almost throwing the hot liquid back in the steward's face. "Not this spicy rubbish." He then strode into the great hall where a huge fire had been built across the hearth, smelling of rich wood and the faint aroma of old acorns. "If I succeed in throwing this wretched usurper from his throne," he muttered, "I shall have the new king's favour and I'll kill damned Andrew Leys and a few others too."

"Since you never dare lift a sword or ride to battle," said Francis who was lounging half asleep by the fire, "you'll never be any king's favourite and you'll never kill anyone. Besides, this King Richard isn't a usurper as you damned well know. Those two boys were both proved bastards. It was the Lady Eleanora's own family who came to swear she'd wed the old king –"

He was interrupted as Charles stretched out both hands and lifted his young brother by the ears, throwing him from his chair against the wall. Francis screeched, rubbing ears and forehead while cursing under his breath. His nose was bleeding. Living with Charles made this a common occurrence.

Francis limped off to find Louisa. "Charles is back. But I don't know if he's going to do anything about Annie."

"He can't," Louisa told her brother. "That treacherous pig will be too busy looking for me."

Still nursing his recent injuries, Francis collapsed on his sister's bed. "I think he knows where to find your bedchamber, Lou."

"Don't be stupid, Francis," she told him. "I'm running away and this time I won't be back." She eyed her old riding boots, deciding that she would have to wear them for the escape. "And I was going to invite you along, but I'm sorry, dearest, I'm not going to now."

"I'm coming," Francis told her.

But Louisa turned to him, shaking her head. "I can't even tell you where I'm going. And it's nothing horrid, Francis dear, and nothing against you. But I'm going with Doric, so I just want to – well – you know."

"I fell in love with a Brewster's daughter. Now you're doing it with a wandering minstrel." Francis sighed. "I hope yours ends better than mine."

"He wants to marry me, and we can do a hand-fasting."

"The church says that doesn't count as true."

"I know," Louisa said, blushing slightly. "But the law says it counts as legal. That's good enough for me even if a real wedding would have been nice. But, honestly, if even the old King Edward had two secret hand-fasting marriages, why should I complain?"

With the birth of tears in his eyes, Francis flopped his head down into his hands. "Go on then. I wish you much joy. But remember me, won't you. Come and get me when you can, if I'm still alive."

"He'll be too busy searching for me," Louisa said. "Tell him you're angry with me too, and you'll help him search. No one will find me, but it'll stop him being furious with you and he'll think you're on his side."

"I'd sooner come with you." He wiped his eyes with his knuckles.

"I wish I could. I was going to ask Beatrice too. She'll be cross when I tell her I want to go alone with Doric. And anyway, you'll have to stay and look after Annie. Be nice to her, won't you, and don't let Charles chuck her out again."

Three days later, the stars were hidden by cloud. Doric was waiting for her beyond the entrance to the stables and held the reins of her own horse which he had saddled while the grooms slept. It was two of the clock in the morning, so early that no one woke and no one saw what was happening as Louisa crept from her room and tiptoed to the kitchens and then to the back doors.

The chill was frosty and even the grass they passed was rimed. But neither cared. They had begun an adventure which would bring them together and that meant everything.

Louisa huddled within her cloak, gloved hands tight on the reins. She was a long-practised rider, but she was not accustomed to riding in the darkness where not even the blink of a star showed the road ahead. No moon escaped the clouds. But she had escaped the prison of her brother's control.

Watching her, at first making sure she rode with confidence and needed no help, Doric then watched for his own pleasure. Even within the voluptuous velvet and fur of her cloak, he imagined the rise and fall of her breathing, and the invisible rise and fall of her breasts, then inside the gloves he imagined her fingers touching him where he ached and desired. He imagined holding her beneath the bed covers, not seeing her perhaps, though a glimpse of skin in the candlelight as she stretched out one arm to hold him, while his own hands felt the swell of her, the warmth of her and the movement of her legs against his.

He awoke from the drifting dream, as they rode into open land beyond the north Wall, the wind gathered speed and strength across the rolling shadows without trees or buildings to tame it. Louisa squinted back into the ice blowing in her face, and Doric reached out, his hand to the reins. "Here we slow down, my love," he told her, "or the horses will tire too quickly. Keep close. Within the hour we can stop to break-fast."

"So soon?" Seemingly worried, Louisa gazed into the black unresponsive distance. "I don't want to be caught, dearest. Shouldn't we keep going? And besides, I'm afraid I have no money."

"You need rest, my love," Doric told her, one hand now on hers. "And so do the horses. Fryeming is not too far and we'll reach the village before nightfall, even stopping for break-fast, dinner and supper since there'll be no food waiting at your old house. I'll not have my fiancé fainting from starvation just as I claim her as my wife." Grinning, he squeezed her gloved hand. "Besides, my love, I have money enough. My Lord Leys pays well."

As first light dawned with a hesitant glint of lilac over the horizon, Doric pointed to the three-story inn, The Shepherd's Staff, well-lit on the roadside. As the horses were scrubbed down and fed, left to browse and finally to drink, Doric led Louisa into the inn, watched her gulping down the hypocrass, and delighted in watching her small fingers now free of her riding gloves. Yet after some moments of uninterrupted pleasure, he wondered if he was surrendering too quickly and too childishly to such an unlikely infatuation, just as the boy Francis had done.

She was watching him now. "What are you thinking about? You look as though you have the ruin of the nation on your mind."

At first he was silent, wishing neither to admit his sudden doubts, nor wanting to lie. Then he changed his mind. "The past months have been remarkable," Doric said with a slow sense of guilt. "From the age of twelve, I spent my life in slow contemplation, as a child does, making no plans. I wandered. I achieved nothing and lived as poor as a bat in the belfry and as unthinking as a spring blossom, blown into oblivion in just a few weeks. I was a trickster when I needed money, almost as bad as a thief, taking coin for pretending magic which didn't exist."

She leaned over the little table, eyes alight with laughter. "Tell me some. Show me magical tricks."

"You wouldn't be impressed."

"Try me."

Finishing his own hypocrass before it lost the sweet heat, Doric looked into the stained base of his empty cup. "To ask the crowd, if there is a crowd, for a question that can be answered either 'yes' or with a simple 'no', I show the palms of my hands, and they're clean, without any mark. Someone asks a question. I judge whatever I should rightly reply, then hold up the palm of either my right or left hand. There is a *Yes* written large and dark where nothing was written moments before."

Louisa was impressed. "So you can do magic."

"No." Laughing. "But you won't like my explanation." She waited, eyes bright, so he said, "Before I summon the crowd, I've written both those words on my hands in my own urine. Nothing shows. Then when I decide which word is the best answer, I take a tiny pinch of wood ash from my belt, clamping it between my fingers and then scattering it over my palm. I can show whichever word I've chosen, and where it seemed nothing was written before, now the word is large and black and easily seen."

"You like writing in your own urine?" She was laughing, hiccupping her hypocrass.

"I can't say it was my favourite trick, but it always impressed the crowd."

"Your singing and your music? If you do that for the king, you must be good."

He leaned back on the stool, chewing on the last piece of cheese. "I loved playing the soft and the melancholy, but the crowds wanted the fast and cheerful songs with the words they knew and could sing along. But it meant years of wandering, years of doing so little and sleeping wherever I'd stopped. Then suddenly there was this past summer of upheaval. The coronation followed by insurrection, treachery, a friend of mine was killed, I have no idea why or by whom, and I was arrested as a suspect. My life changed. I met Lord Leys. Then Brittany. I'd never travelled across the waters before. Then I met you, little one. That seems like only moments ago, but already I'm fast in love."

Something occurred to Louisa. "Is it too fast? Like Francis?"

"The same occurred to me," he confessed, looking into the depths of her eyes. "But I've met a thousand folk on the road, two hundred pretty girls, a hundred beautiful women and I've never been in love before. And never thought I was. This is new. And it makes me feel suddenly alive."

"Me too." Now she was excited again. "And you are so remarkable, my love, and I feel reborn as well." Her smile was reflected in the dregs of the hypocrass. "But I'm about to marry a stranger. I don't even know where you came from. What were you doing before you were twelve and took to the minstrel's life?"

He looked away again, fingering his empty cup. Finally, he sighed, "I lived in a monastery. I hated it. I ran away."

"Training to be a monk?" Louisa was astonished. "That's the last thing I expected you to say, my love. Did you grow up there as an orphan? Or left on the doorstep like unwed mothers do sometimes, poor girls?"

Doric put down his cup and reached for her elbow across the table. "We've been too long, little one." He stood, leading her with him. "We'll arrive at midnight as it is, and if we are later still, then you will be falling to your knees, my sweet, and probably the horses as well."

No rain dared flood the journey or slow their speed and they crossed the fields onto the more sheltered lanes. The first week in November, most trees had lost their leaves, their bare branches creaking in the winds and waving a bleak goodbye. Some of the thicker bushes retained their russet coats, but the cold was strengthening, and early morning frost spangled those leaves which still clung.

At midday Doric stopped again, taking Louisa into the tavern that stood at a crossroads, the smell of baked apples and roasting parsnips attracting anyone who passed those open doors. But after three portions of apple tart and two of parsnips in red wine, they hurried back to the stables where their horses, eyeing them with exhausted disapproval, still had their noses in bags of hay, with an apple each as bribery.

Here the roads were flat and well earthed as they approached the southern boundary of Essex, when the fields once again tipped upwards. The twilight fell like a velvet cloak across the tiny streams, the windmills and the cattle returning to the milking sheds. A cloud of starlings swept up into wild swirling patters against the darkening clouds, then dispersed, disappearing into their own shadows.

"Ready for dinner?" Doric asked. Their horses were ambling, as though waiting for night to hide them again. It had been a long day of excited optimism fading into exhaustion.

"I'm not hungry," she told him. "We're too close."

"Are you ready to sleep on a stone hard floor without beds, and wake hungry in the night without a kitchen to raid?"

She laughed. "There must be beds, even if they're covered in dust."

"Dust keeps an old mattress soft."

Another hour, and the hill rose before them, a gentle slope and the village topping the land like a shimmer of cream topping a dumpling. A windmill thrust its arms up into the night's sky, and the tower of the local church soared even higher. Three yew trees shadowed the village, bending and stretching like broken spires across the crest.

"We're here," Louisa whispered. "Except we're not. I mean, this is the village I think. But the castle ruins are on the other side of the hill."

"Then I shall hold my breath," Doric murmured, his eyes on the first wink of the stars inching from the clouds. "It isn't midnight yet, I'm sure, since night comes early in these autumn months. We arrive a little early then, and ready for a silent night. You need to rest deep, my dearest, for I hope it will be your last night alone."

"Really alone?" she asked, her voice still little more than a whisper beneath the whistle of the wind through the trees. "Can't you cuddle me anyway?"

"If I did that," Doric told her, "I doubt I could resist you little one, unless I wore my riding gloves and patted your mane as I do my horse."

She giggled. "I don't mind. Truly I don't. And – if we marry in the morning?"

"When we marry," Doric leaned across the pummel of his saddle, and kissed her cheek, "I shall take you into my arms whether we sleep on a broken turret, a muddy bank, or a wine cellar. I shall make a mattress of your cloak and mine, and keep you warm with my own body."

The hill rounded into the night with the stars spangled above as though singing their welcome, and a slither of moon shone as pearlized as a dove's wings. The quiet was an echo of itself, and even the wind dropped, ashamed to disrupt the expectations.

The base of the hill was elongated, and they slowed almost to a shuffle, waiting for the first glimpse of a stone wall, a broken building, fallen turrets or a cracked drawbridge. Even a moat shining in the moonlight, or an iron portcullis, its crossed bars fallen.

"Tis an old place, far as I bin told," Robert Rudge had explained to Louisa. "I ain't never bin there, but my dear Bella done told me over and over for she were there some years. Grand, she says, and mighty big inside. But she done lived in the nursery tower, and never much went into the main house. "

And she had asked, "So I was born there?"

"You all was," Isabella's brother-in-law had told her. "Yer Pa were rich as rich as a king, and he done bought the mighty manor in The Strand and all. He lived there when there were business in the city, or wiv them lords at court in Westminster and such. But t'was that there castle as were considered home. Till his wife died, that is. After you was born, young Francis, then yer poor Ma died, so yer Pa upped and moved to the city fer good, brung you little 'uns wiv him, and my Bella too. And I reckon he never went back. T'were a better house anyways, Bella says. And yer Ma were buried up on the hill in the churchyard o' St. Mary the Virgin. You goes to see what ruins be left after all this time, I reckon you can go to that cemetery too, and say goodbye to yer Ma."

It was what she wanted to do. But first Louisa desperately hoped for a blissful night's sleep, tight in Doric's arms, if she could convince him away from his virtuous determination.

They saw their destination as a jagged line of cliff-like silhouettes against the skyline as the rest of the land misted into the low clouds. The stars had once again blinked out, but the slither of moon persisted, its pale milky aura gathering it safe.

There was the great tower, as she had been expecting, turreted and unbroken, tall and dark, almost threatening. Beyond that was a half lump of what had once been a cottage, its roof now a jumble of broken flint. Behind sat the memory of whatever there had once been, parts only partially destroyed and other parts utterly sunk into tips of broken stone.

No longer beautiful and no longer welcoming, the ancient crags seemed as thrilling to Louisa as a palace might have been. She drew in a deep breath and gazed up at Doric. "We're home," she said. "This is the Castle of Hylton."

CHAPTER THIRTY-THREE

O nce there had been stables and a long block of roofless sheds sat squat in the shadows, tiny drifts of filthy straw still caught in open corners. Doric tethered the horses although he could offer them neither food nor water.

"Won't hurt them for one night," he frowned, "since they're tired out anyway. But it's a form of cruelty after they've ridden all day and must be thirsty, poor things. Luckily they ate and drank well at midday."

"But now," Louisa stared up at the black tower and shivered beneath her cloak, "I suppose we're thirsty too, and we'll get no ale or wine. But there must be a well somewhere in the grounds."

Doric nodded. "Filled with dead leaves and dead birds, no doubt." He ran his fingers through his horse's mane and wished her a good night. "But I'll come out and search for whatever there is once I've settled you inside in the warm."

No tremor of warmth leaked from the tower. Unusually tall, although not wide, it reeked of ice and threat, somehow a place which wished to deter rather than welcome. Louisa imaged a height sufficient for five floors, though she doubted if that many had remained liveable, and the tower's girth suggested only one large chamber on each floor. Without realising, she had stepped back several times and now stood at a greater distance, her fingers locked into a nervous fist. She wished quite fervently that she had not come, and yet could not describe why. "It's so dark and so lonely," she whispered. "Perhaps we should stay in the village for tonight."

"The horses would be better stabled," Doric nodded again. "But it would take us some time to get back there. That hill means a long winding road upwards, possibly hard to track in the dark. We don't even know if the village is walled, with gates locked for the night. And I'm curious to see what waits for us inside this amazing ruin. Aren't you curious, my love?"

"No. It looks strangely intimidating."

Immediately he put his arm around her shoulder, kissed her ear, and walked her forwards. "You left here when you were four or five it seems, such a young child, my love," he said. "But do you remember nothing of it?"

She did not, but she walked with Doric, approaching the first crumble of dark stone and stared up to the peaks. The crenelated battlements glowered down. She could see arrow slits, five up, two across, each unglazed and each black as unlit coal. Again she shivered. "Come on then. But I can't see a way in."

They walked slowly around the tower's base, dodging the overgrown weeds, ivy and thorny shrubs, eventually they saw what was surely the entrance. The great doors at the base were up three shallow steps behind the ruined flint cottage, and they were locked. Iron bars striped the doors outside, and a padlock hung from each, now rusted, one hanging broken, the others immovable. Louisa was unsurprised. "My father would have locked everything, back then the castle was liveable. He possibly thought of coming back one day – or giving it to his children. And there might still be other things left. Beds, perhaps, tapestries, at least items for the kitchens and a dining table."

"Let's imagine he gave it to you," Doric grinned. "But it may take some time to break in." He had withdrawn a narrow bladed knife, he pressed the point into the keyhole of the first padlock, and began to explore. After a moment he blinked up at Louisa, who was watching him with interest. "Another of my dubious skills," he told her. But," he added, still grinning, "I may have been a liar and a cheat, but I never robbed houses back in my dishonest past, not even when starving."

"Were you ever starving?" Louisa asked, fascinated.

He thought a moment. "No, not really. I could always find berries and roast acorns if I was hungry enough. I don't remember ever going more than two or three days without food."

Impressed, she clasped her hands again with a nervous twitch. "Poor darling. I've never been more than a few hours, though horrid Charles has refused to let me have dinner a few times. But I've had an easy life, apart from my wretched brother. I certainly wouldn't know how to pick a lock."

The first padlock clanked and fell open, its rust thick keyhole spilling grains of old metal. Doric shook the door, but it still did not open. He began work on the second padlock. It took a little longer, then it tumbled to the ground and split wide. The third was easier as the rust had eaten into the keyhole to such depth, that a simple twist sprang it wide. There was just one left.

An owl was murmuring from a dead tree trunk over their heads. "I thought I saw movement on the battlements," Doric said, his knife now exploring the final padlock. "But evidently it was the owl. Perhaps birds nest here, it's sufficiently abandoned. Indeed, the place seems remarkably collapsed for a vacancy of only fourteen or fifteen years."

"It is, isn't it." She was suddenly concerned. "It seems more like a hundred years. I hope I've come to the right place."

"I doubt there are too many such places around," Doric said as the last padlock fell open. "Now, let's see what dismal catastrophe remains inside." And he reached out, taking Louisa's hand.

Within there was only black. No shape emerged from the darkness and no glimmer of light entered within. The blackness seemed solid.

Again, they heard the owl outside, and Louisa peeped back around the door, pulling it further open. The creek of old wood echoed as though in a cave, and the screech of the rusty hinges shrieked out like some tortured animal. Louisa shrank back.

But it was easier now, with their sight adjusting and the door further open to the glimpse of moon, they could see the first steps of a winding stair, narrow and steep. The steps, as their enclosure, were of unrelenting stone and where once there had been plaster and whitewash, now only flakes hung in trembling reluctance as the steps climbed higher into the invisibility of the darkness.

"At least," Louisa whispered, "the ground is solid. When we couldn't see a thing, I was frightened to step forwards, there could have been a pit."

"You won't fall," Doric promised her. "I have hold of you." Her hand was held tight in his. He felt around the walls but there seemed no other doorway except that to the outside, through which they had come.

One step, and the side of the stone cracked but did not fall. Two steps and Louisa came close, although hardly daring to climb. Three steps. Now both of them were on the stairs and even where the stone was chipped or broken at the outer edge, it held their climb while moving so slowly upwards. But as they climbed, the darkness fell and they were lost in a black nothing. Hands against the wall, feeling their way, Doric felt his fingers slide into the cavity of an arrow slit, but there was still no entrance into an actual room. He continued step by step up into the depth of black nothing.

For one moment he thought he heard a rustle, the brief suggestion of movement, but as he stopped, straining to hear what it had been, the whispers had gone. He accepted the probability that these murmurs came from his own nerves and the need to protect Louisa from anything and everything.

Step by step. Louisa clung to him, strangely this sensation of trust brought him confidence. But he felt it had been a thousand steps and still no destination. No reason to climb.

But abruptly his feet slipped and for a moment he felt the slide carry him. He was falling, Louisa with him. The black waves of ice slung around them, fingering, tasting.

And then it was safe again and Doric leaned back breathless against the cold stone. He held Louisa tightly to him., telling her, whispering, "Rain puddles over these stairs. This past month has been wet and must have sliced through the arrow slits. The stone is so aged, it feels polished."

"Water on slippery stone." Louisa whispered back. "There must be a door soon. No one builds a tower with just a staircase leading nowhere."

He nodded but wondered. After years of inventing tricks, he now felt he'd found the ultimate trickery. And then, as suddenly as everything else, there was a doorway. It opened without warning, and both Louisa and Doric stumbled through into equal darkness, flat floored with space.

Following the circle of the smoothly plastered wall, they began to discover other shapes, and with an ecstatic squeak, Louisa found a bed stretched heavy and solid in the centre of the room. Then Doric called, "There's a candle," and an abrupt flash of light followed as he flicked his thumb down on the steel clip of his tinder box and held it to the candle wick. "Though this candle hasn't ever been trimmed. I doubt it will keep its flame for long."

Louisa stood behind him, her arms around his waist as he held the little bowl high. The melted tallow within began to swirl into smoking liquid but the wick flickered, holding its golden flame. Doric lifted it high and they both gasped.

The room was huge, without corners, and the rounded walls were pale and clean with a large religious tapestry hung beside an arrow slit. Through the window, now with a contrast between black night and light within, they saw the stars through a curling knot of ivy. Moss had crept through the arrow slit and crawled down over the stone wall and its lost plaster, finding the narrow cracks of damp. The wind crept through the entwining leaves, bitterly cold but utterly silent.

Standing together, they examined the secrets of where they had found themselves. The bed was grand and wide, well covered with a quilt of eiderdown and heaped pillows. The linen was clean as though ready for immediate use. The posts were bare, but a tester of red velvet protected the bed from whatever might fall, since the ceiling beams were long untouched, spiders and dirt visible even in the shuddering light. Beneath the grand covers was a chamber pot and a cushioned chair flanked one side. At the end, as though waiting for its master, sat the table, and on the table was a cup, quite empty, a jug, equally empty, and a riding whip. There had also been the candle which Doric had found. Louisa stared and Doric told her, "This tower is not as deserted as you had supposed, my love. Someone comes here, for this room is kept clean, except for the high beams, impossible to reach I imagine. Then there's the encroaching damp, of course, and the ivy."

"At least," she whispered back, "we can sleep in some comfort."

"Except for whoever normally uses this bed, might arrive at any time." He picked up the riding crop and turned it over between his hands. The handle was carved with intricate swirls of wing and claw.

Louisa stared. She was still whispering. "It's Charles's. I recognise it." She blinked up at Doric beside her. "Oh, this seems too strange. Does Charles still come here? Clearly, he knows about it. And he goes off for a day or two on his own sometimes. Why doesn't he tell anyone else? Or is it a hideaway, where he can be alone?"

"Or bring a woman?"

Louisa blushed. "Well, if he comes tonight, he'll find me cuddled in the warm. Though it's not warm, of course. It's freezing. I need you, Doric beloved. I need your arms and your body and your warmth."

He grinned and pulled back the covers, examining the sheets, and nodding. "It seems clean, my love. Climb in. But keep your clothes on. Firstly, it's far too cold for you to undress. And secondly, I could never hold you to me naked without eating you entirely, from toes to head. My powers of resistance are not so strong. I shall remove my boots, that's all."

Distinctly disappointed, Louisa sat on the bed, still gazing around. "I wonder what else there is here. The rooms above, I mean, and there's at least four up to the battlements. So three more. Are they furnished too?"

Still holding the candle as it burned downwards with a hiss and splutter, Doric walked slowly around the bedchamber, searching for other signs. He closed the one door leading back out to the endless steps, and eventually came to sit beside Louisa on the bed. "We search the rest of the tower in the morning, my love. Some light at least will enter, even if the day's dull. Creeping in such darkness shows us so little, we're lucky to have found this room. And even more lucky to have found a chamber with a bed."

"But even more puzzling."

Doric watched her a moment, then bent and untied her shoes, pulling them off and tossing them to one side of the room. "You look tired. And you have every right to be exhausted. Yes, the bed is a gift, of sorts. Sleep, my dearest, and I'll hold you safely until dawn."

He held back the covers for her and Louisa slid beneath, her knees curled to her chest, skirts crumpled. Slowly, Doric climbed in beside her, accepting the challenge, one arm beneath, the other around her waist. "Do we still marry tomorrow, my little one?"

She opened her eyes at once. "Don't you want to do it anymore?"

"I want you on the church porch, but your brother would raise hell into our heaven. I might ask for the king's permission, and then there could be no family objection. But I'm no close friend of his highness and if he refused, then I couldn't even take you in hand-fasting. I won't risk that. Yes, I want you, beloved. And I'll take your hand tomorrow if you'll let me. But finding what else is here could be dangerous. Your brother's riding crop and a bed with clean linen in a place that seems long abandoned, is telling a story that I cannot understand. The questions need answering."

"I've never understood Charles," Louisa whispered back. "But it's you I want to understand now, Doric dearest. All about you. And about what people do together when they marry."

He laughed softly. "Don't you know, my love? No explanations from your nurse? Or the maids? Or anyone else?"

"There never was anyone else, even a mother," she said. The candle spat, the tallow almost disappearing into smoke and the tired smell of burning fat. "I always wanted to know and when I saw two of the hounds, it upset me. It looked horrid. I asked Bella and she said people weren't hounds."

Leaning over, Doric kissed her. She sank back beneath his weight, opening her lips to his breath. Then she felt the heat of it, and the sudden tip of his tongue to hers. "I'll show you," he murmured to her. "Very slowly and very clearly, tomorrow after I've taken your hand. I'll answer all your questions, my love, and call you my wife. And I'll teach you exactly how to know me. And I shall spend the day understanding you as we explore this place in daylight."

"It's you I want to find," she whispered to his neck. "Not dirty rooms and wet puddles and broken furniture."

"If that's all there is, it won't take long. Shall we spend all day in bed then, my dearest?"

But as she nestled tighter, straightening one leg and curling the other around Doric's back, there was a sudden sound, and both of them ceased instantly. Doric with his hand halfway to the floor, placing the candle there, while Louisa snapped open her eyes and stared up at the beamed ceiling.

There were footsteps above. Three steps, four, then another. And then, once more, absolute silence.

CHAPTER THIRTY-FOUR

A tiny reverberation accompanied the footsteps. Then nothing. Doric and Louisa continued to stare upwards. A ringlet of dust woven web drifted down from one beam, and fell to the waiting tester, but now there was silence and Louisa wondered if she had imagined the footsteps.

"Was it real?"

"Very real, my little one. Sadly true. There is someone else here. But whether they live here, some friend perhaps of your brother, or a beggar without a home, or a villager cast out, we can't tell. But your brother himself has never been so light on his feet. That was a woman. Very young, or sick perhaps, or very old."

He still held Louisa, still bringing the promise of safety even though a greater danger now whispered from above.

"Not an animal?" she mumbled. "There must be birds trapped, or a stray dog. Even squirrels. They hibernate for winter. A bird seems likely as it could have flown through the slits in the walls."

"My darling, no bird walks with such resounding footfalls, not even an eagle. Nor squirrel. A hound might be large enough, but I doubt it could have picked the locks on the door downstairs."

"Then I'm going upstairs to find out." She sat up a little, wedged on both elbows. "I can't sleep now, Doric. I have to know if it's robbers. Or Charles. Or his fancy woman. Or something trapped."

"I'm impressed." Doric held both her hands. "Very courageous of you, my sweet. But you'll go nowhere alone, and I'd prefer you go nowhere at all. You stay here and wrap warm. I shall go up and see what hides in the room upstairs."

It was quite dark again now, since the only candle had fizzled out. The wick had burned away, and the tallow had melted into hot sludge. "No, we go together." She grabbed at his arm. "It's not courage, it's being scared. I don't want to be left here alone. Someone might come in. Charles might appear. Or the ghost."

"You think it's a ghost?" Doric dislodged her fingers and swung both arms around her once more. "No ghost, my love, I promise you. But we'll both go to see, if that's what you want. I promise you, whoever it is, I can keep you as safe as you would be in your own bed, whether we have burglars, ghosts, or Charles himself. Charles can be cruel, I believe, to you and to Francis. But he's a coward who won't fight for whatever he believes, and without the courage to face the truth."

"That's right," Louisa told him. "But I'm the coward who can't go to sleep, not even in your arms, while footsteps echo from ghosts upstairs."

He brought over her shoes and began to haul on his boots.

Leaving the comfort they had so blissfully and unexpectedly discovered, was a madness both regretted. First the gift of the room, the bed and the candle. Then thrust once more into fear and the bed perhaps lost.

Back on the ice of lightless steps, Louisa shivered. Having seen with the glimmers of the candle, now the freezing black swirl of the staircase seemed even worse. It wound ever upwards, narrow, steep and relentless. Back into nothingness. She wished she had wrapped herself in the eiderdown from the bed, as even her fur lined cloak no longer seemed warm enough. She wondered if the ghostly soul above could hear her own footsteps, but the stairs she climbed were solid stone and she heard no echo. Doric had attempted to relight the candle, but this had been impossible. She had the security and comfort of his hand, but the wind through the arrow slits had begun to whistle and chilled her even more.

She wished desperately that she had stayed in bed after all, and yet knowing she would have been even more afraid, she could only follow the warmth of Doric's black shadow on black walls. Feeling as though she had climbed a hundred stairs or a thousand perhaps, her back aching and her knees unforgiving, abruptly another door was suddenly clear to their right. Too dark to see, but easy to feel. Both of them stopped.

"Here," Doric told her.

She traced the outline within the rugged surround of stone, plastered in places, but mostly worn away. The wooden door itself was solid but narrow, just wide enough for one person to squeeze in, and hinged in rust.

Still whispering, "We have to go in. Where's the handle?"

"It's locked," Doric said his voice a soft whisper, "but the key is here on the outside. You're ready to see inside and face whoever is there?"

"Whatever is there." She nodded. "Yes. But please stay close."

His fingers felt along her cheek, then he leant and kissed her there. His mouth remained warm, but she was sure that her own was blue with cold. This time, clutching his hand brought no confidence at all.

The spirit world and the pitiful ghosts, trapped in purgatory, who still walked the earth, searching for the gateway to heaven which they would never find, had never before haunted her. What happened in the living world had been her enemy almost since birth, with Charles as her appointed and only guardian, his cruelty a constant threat, and his behaviour a persistent accusation that she was so unlovable that no one existed, except perhaps little Francis and Bella, who might ever care for her.

But for a sudden moment she remembered the priest's sermons, telling her that any child which died before receiving God's blessing during the Christening at the font, would wander purgatory for evermore.

It had seemed wicked to her then, and even more unjust to her now. It was many years since she'd attended the local church as Charles disliked allowing her out while young, but now those words echoed in her mind. Louisa stood very still, her hands clenched, prepared to protect herself and Doric too. She heard the key grate in the lock, the click of the spring, and finally the creak of the opening door. A long shadow, blacker than black, slid from the slowly widening slit, swamping her and flooding over Doric as he entered. The door creaked and the hinges squealed.

Someone inside screamed.

The shrill horror of it stopped as if swallowed back and was followed by utterly empty silence.

Louisa grabbed the back of Doric's collar, and he half turned, his arm immediately around her waist while they both stared into shadows and an unmoving emptiness.

And then, unmistakeable, the faintest sound of something pushing backwards, cloth scratching against the stone, and deeply uneven breathing.

Doric whispered, "My love, stay back."

But a departed soul forever trudging purgatory seemed the greatest sadness she could imagine and with abrupt determination, Louisa walked past Doric and stared into the silent indoor night. And she softly asked, "Can I help, whoever you are? I will try to help, whatever that entails, whether you are living or dead."

She heard the breathing, but there was no answer. Now Doric stood close beside her once more, and again she felt his arm slip warm around her waist. "I stand in the company of Lady Louisa Grange, sister to the Earl of Hylton," he said, raising his voice, "one of the family who owns this tower and the ruined castle surrounding it. "You stand in no danger from us. Please tell us who you are and what help you need."

The faint gasp in return sounded human.

"Not a bird," Louisa whispered.

"You believe in ghosts, my love," Doric answered, "but I do not. This person lives."

"Then she's come for comfort and shelter."

"But could not have locked the door from the outside." Doric spoke to be heard. "She cannot be her own prisoner."

Another gasp, almost a sob, and suddenly Louisa ran forwards. "Whoever you are," she called, "you must not be sad. There's so much sadness in the world," and she pushed into the absolute darkness of the far wall. Louisa found herself pressing against human warmth, shivering humanity but no spectre nor creature from the world of the unliving. "You – you're real," she stuttered.

Doric was again instantly beside her. "Is there light?" He reached out. He felt a shudder of silk and behind the silk there was a woman. For him, this was impossible to mistake. "My lady," he asked gently, "will you trust us, and come out from behind the curtain? I swear we mean you no harm." And he tried to pull back the drape of silk, curtain or quilt, and know whatever poor woman seemed so terrified. He grasped the long swing of covering, and stood, holding it wide.

Again, pushing forwards, Louisa recognised pulse and breath, arms thin as sticks reaching out to push away whatever might hurt her more. And at the same moment, moving back with the curtain in hand, Doric felt the swing of something hard behind his head, and called, "I think there's an oil lamp. Let's have some light."

The tinder box clicked three times, and then the spark rushed into flame. An oil lamp strung from the ceiling beams now swelled in brilliance and everything in the world changed.

They stood in a great space, but against the circle of the Far wall stood a huge bed, almost a room in itself, curtained in ancient silk, torn and striped in the filth of many years, and behind the curtain, desperately hiding, was a woman, neither young nor so old, but unbelievably thin and utterly terrified.

Once more, Doric pulled back the curtain and the woman released her grip on the shelter. Her fingers were tiny bones without flesh, and her face in the lamplight seemed tight to her skull, ugly in its wretchedness. But the eyes, deepest blue, were beautiful.

251

Whispering again, Louisa begged, "Tell me, please, who you are. And why you are here."

She had either lost her voice or was too frightened to answer. Gradually, as if she had forgotten how to move her hands, she raised one fragile finger and pointed at Louisa. Quickly, Louisa nodded. "Yes. I'm Louisa Grange. I was born somewhere here. My mother and father are both dead, but perhaps you knew one of them? You seem so – so scared. But I really want to help. Did you get locked in by mistake? Are you – starving?" Louisa was sure this must be true.

The woman sat on the corner of the bed where the ripped silk of the curtain had been hanging. She sat very still, yet her hands and arms trembled violently. Her hair was long in an unwashed straggle of silver strands over her shoulders and down her back almost to her waist, uneven and in places threadbare. Her knees protruded in jagged bones beneath her skirts. She wore only a shift of old linen, covered by a loose tunic of colourless flax, shorter than the shift, with wide shapeless arms. The shift below did not reach to her wrists, which were tiny lumped bones, hardly supporting her hands. Her feet were bare, the toenails long and ragged.

"Please, oh please, tell me who you are, mistress," Louisa asked again, almost crying.

Doric knelt at the woman's feet and reached up for her shaking fingers. "Mistress, I swear we'll bring the help you need. Have you been trapped here so long?" She still did not answer, and he spoke again, very softly. "I believe you need care, madam, and food. Sadly, we have none with us, but in the morning I shall ride to the village and bring whatever you need. May I ask, mistress, when did you eat last?"

There were tears bright in her eyes, reflecting the light of the flickering oil lamp. Her fingers, where Doric reached for them, twitched and moved forwards over her knees as if she craved the touch of another human being. He understood at once, recognising both her desire and her nervous hesitation. Immediately, but slowly and gently, he put the warmth of his palm over hers, then curled his fingers around, steady though not tight. Again he asked, "Do you need water, mistress? I carry neither wine nor ale, but there must be a well here and I can bring you water if it's clean. After dawn rises, I'll ride for food. But first won't you tell us who you are?"

Waiting, Louisa and Doric stared at the woman's misery and confusion. Doric remained kneeling. Receiving no reply of word or sign, Louisa turned, looking for the first time fully around the room. Aside from the bed and its once fine but now ruined coverings, the hanging oil lamp, and a stool by the bottom post, it seemed there was no other thing there. Large as it was, the chamber was virtually unfurnished and lacked all comfort. There was neither rug nor wall hanging, chair nor settle nor place to light a fire. Louisa looked back to the virtual skeleton who had been locked into this vile tragedy. Facing the obvious signs of cruelty, she thought only of one person, and she knew that the riding whip seen downstairs had belonged to Charles. Now one awful but most likely possibility crept into her head, and she felt sick.

But Charles himself had been married for just two years and no one had seen much of the woeful bride. It was soon believed that the woman could not have children. The cause of her death was never clearly explained. Gritting her teeth, Louisa dared to wonder if the rarely seen wife had not died at all. Or, if not his wife, whether, in his madness, Charles had taken a mistress but chose to starve her and keep her prisoner.

Louisa sat beside the woman, touching but not too closely in case she might cause more nervous confusion. She repeated Doric's question. "My dear lady," she murmured, "you must realise by now that we aren't here to hurt you. We never expected anyone to be here. I was sure this whole place was empty. But that's beside the point. I'd love to know your name. And like I said, I'm Louisa, and this is my friend Doric. We are – engaged to be married, which is why we came here."

One fleshless hand still clasped by Doric, the woman reached timidly to Louisa and laid her own hand on Louisa's lap. She looked for a moment into Louisa's eyes, then lowered her gaze and for the first time managed to speak.

Her voice was the crunch of gravel, words forced from a throat so dry it could barely croak. But with her eyes lowered as if ashamed of herself, she said, "Alice. I am – Alice." And then she tried to clear her throat and looked up once more at Louisa. She waited another moment, and then she whispered, "I'm – your mother."

CHAPTER THIRTY-FIVE

T he child hesitated. "But Uncle, sire, my lord, I'm happy here. I prefer to stay. Can't I stay?"

King Richard shook his head. Behind him, Andrew of Leys and Francis Lovell stood, waiting and silent.

"My dear nephew," said the king softly, "This small Norfolk property is no longer as safe as I had hoped. As the most in peril, your elder brother already sits quietly in the court of Burgundy, as you know. In my sister's custody, he will be most royally protected. You, however, as my namesake, seemed in less peril and indeed, seemed of less danger to me, so remained comfortably in your homeland. Yet we threaten each other as rumours whisper abroad. The king of France, always an enemy, especially since I refused his bribes some years back, now plays the fool, claiming that I have ordered both of you murdered for my own satisfaction, ensuring that no other claimant to the throne may threaten the safety of my crown. This slander puts me at some risk, if rebellion is again mounted in your name. Henry Tudor threatens the same. But you are equally threatened, Richard, for if one of my enemies, especially amongst the Woodvilles who call you one of them, finds where you now stay and is able to abduct you, then your life is in doubt. Tudor whispers from abroad that my crown should be his. His Lancastrian claim is I believe, the twentieth in line, and so his claim is absurd. But those with better Lancastrian claims are either unsuitable, or do not wish for the title. He calls himself the rightful king, but if he can make others believe that I have unlawfully stolen the throne, then he can only admit that you and your brother are the rightful princes of the land, and not himself. Thus, your lives are in great danger from him, and I must move you to your brother's side."

Young Richard hung his head, fidgeting with the ring he wore on his left thumb. "Must I go so far? I like my brother Edward. But I hardly know him. We never lived together until our father died. And I like it here. You've been kind."

"And I'll not be unkind now, Richard." The king smiled. "I shall arrange for your return once I can be sure that the threatened invasions and rebellions are abandoned entirely. Meanwhile my sister will love you, I'm sure, especially since she has no children of her own. And I cannot keep you here where your life is in considerable danger." He turned to the two men standing behind him. "Francis, Andrew, you know the situation. I shall leave it in your hands, but don't take too long. Sir Edward Brampton will sail with him as his protector."

His highness left abruptly, joining his small escort that waited outside in the courtyard, the king's horse ready saddled and stamping, impatience.

Andrew looked across at Lovell, smiling both at him and at the eight-year-old boy standing between them. "I believe," said Lord Leys, "we have a task of some urgency. I'll see to the guard here and double it of today." He looked at the young Richard. "You may dislike the idea of leaving this house and your present protectors," he said, "and I both understand and sympathise. But if a mob of cut-throats paid by Tudor came rushing into your bedroom one night, I imagine you'd feel less comfortable."

The boy sniggered, wrapping his arms around himself. "Yes, alright, I admit it. And Edward can protect himself a bit, but I'm not so good. I mean, I wasn't ever brought up to be king. I'm good with a bow at the target, but nothing much else. So I suppose I don't have any choice."

"Tudor failed in his first attempt at invasion," Francis Lovell said, sitting back at the table. "But he's backed by his mother, and she's one of the richest in the land. The French back him too. Not a shy country, I'm afraid. The Buckingham business was well-nigh a joke, but if they'd won any ground, it would have been Tudor on the throne, and Buckingham relegated or killed off. Morton arranged the whole uprising of course, but he escaped as soon as he saw failure written large. Yet Tudor still has backing."

Andrew nodded to Lovell but spoke to the boy. "But Tudor can only claim the throne, even by invasion, if he states that Richard stole it from Edward, your brother. And if you and he then suddenly pop up alive and ready for your own coronation, then guess what Tudor will quickly have to do."

The boy hung his head. "But going abroad. Do they even speak our language?"

"I imagine you've been taught French? Margaret of Burgundy is your aunt, and always close to her brothers, speaks four languages, including French and English, and knew you as just a baby." Andrew folded his arms, hands tucked in his opposing sleeves. "You will enjoy her court, I'm sure. Shooting at the target perhaps, and some of the best food you've ever eaten."

They passed an hour, amicable in the presence of the boy Richard, explaining to him and ensuring his comfort with the idea of leaving his homeland.

Lovell said, "You've spent some months with your brother earlier this year, Richard. I imagine you'll enjoy his company again."

"And still keep a comparative sense of freedom," Andrew added, "as long as your identity is kept secret. There would be little point in going abroad if the whole country knows who you are and where you've gone."

Eventually Lovell stood. "I'm risking complacency. I should travel south immediately and speak with Brampton. He needs a ship, and must leave these shores under cover of night, and with his passenger unnamed."

"He'll know all this already," Andrew said, also standing, and again smiling down at the boy. "This is an adventure," he told him. "You've never sailed before, nor lived at a foreign court, watched over by a duchess. You will enjoy every moment, I'm sure."

"I'll be in danger." Richard swallowed hard and looked up. "I'm not a coward. But only a fool enjoys danger."

Andrew grinned. There had been times when he'd enjoyed it himself. Instead he turned to Lovell. "Go south and meet with Brampton. I'll settle matters here, and then follow you back to Westminster."

It was two days later when Andrew of Leys left Hawkbridge Manor where the late Edward IV's younger son Richard, now proven illegitimate, was living. He rode with only one companion, needing neither guards, trumpeters, nor guides. His companion, Casper Wallop, spoke constantly but received few answers. Andrew stayed overnight at the Saddler's Arms on Norfolk's border with Suffolk but left at dawn the following morning. Nearing Essex, they stopped for dinner, then rode onwards with the intention of spending the following night at the Cup and Grape, where he had spent many comfortable nights in the past.

It was late when they came to the burned shell of the wayside inn, and remaining mounted, stared at the ruin of blackened beams and fallen walls. the thatch lay in tumbles of scorched reeds and where the front doorstep and the heavy stone archway beyond still stood as though welcoming guests, the way led only to charred destruction.

"Damnation," said Andrew loudly. "So, do we ride all night and look suitably diligent when we arrive exhausted at Westminster? Or do we indulge ourselves, accept the urgency, but stay at some other hostel along the way?"

"Don't reckon you really wants me ter answer that," Casper grinned. "For you knows bloody well wot I'd be saying."

"Since I so greatly value your wise advice," Andrew said, "I shall naturally stop at the next suitable inn. And if we are late back tomorrow, then it will, of course, be your fault."

"Reckon I's always at fault," Casper said. "'Tis my favourite occupation, fer sure."

"Although," Andrew added, still smiling, "we still carry plenty of food in both saddle bags, if riding all night becomes the only alternative, we will survive."

Andrew turned his horse, laughing, and headed south.

It was a little after midnight and the night was coldly hostile when they came within sight of the hill, and the village of Fryering atop it. It was Casper who pointed. "I know the village," Andrew said. "A delightful place, and the tavern rents bedchambers by the dozen. But it's a long winding road up that hill."

"Better'n naught at all," Casper insisted.

"Very well, your advice then, my friend, and naturally your fault if the place is full for the night. So, we head for the hills."

But it was before arriving at the first rising slope, that something else interrupted their intentions.

Taking no interest in the ruined and tumbled stone and the huge blackened tower rising beside the rubble, which they had passed often enough before and knew it abandoned, both men rode on until, swerving back in shock, they heard the echoing scream. Casper stared, blinking, mouth open. Following the scream, there was once again complete silence except for the wind in the treetops, and the hooves of Andrew's horse. For even before the shrill echo had faded, Andrew had already loosened the reins, kicked his spurs to his horse's sides, and was galloping towards the tower. Finally, dismounting, he threw the reins to Casper, ordered him to tether both horses and follow. He then dismounted, entered the tower door, left unlocked and open, and ran the staircase.

Already he heard the snort and disturbance of other horses and knew that others were here, but it was the echo of the scream that he followed.

As the stone steps wound endlessly upwards in bleak lightless chill, he slowed, listening carefully. He heard Casper behind him. Eventually at the first doorway they both entered, seeing the solitary bed and the signs of recent occupancy, Andrew lit the tiny torch he always carried ready, and it was clear the room was empty.

They left and followed the continuing staircase. Now, faintly and almost like whispers in the breeze, they heard footsteps as they climbed higher. Andrew held his torch upwards, its flame reluctant in the ice.

In the chamber above, both now crouched at the woman's feet, Louisa and Doric held the sobbing woman's hands, her stick-like fingers entwining with theirs.

Louisa stared. "My – mother?" she whispered. "I don't understand."

"I am Alice," the woman wheezed, gazing through her tears. "No one else. Don't you want me? I would understand. Shall I say I am someone else?"

Even more perplexed, Louisa said, still whispering, "Are you Blanche, perhaps, mistress? She was married to Charles for such a little while, and then he announced her dead, but my mother – she died fourteen years ago."

"Have I been here so long?" The woman's voice was faded and pitiful, and as Louisa stared into her eyes, the lines on her face and the fragility of her hands, neck and wrists, she realised that what seemed impossible was true indeed, and with a howl of intense pity, she flung herself up into the woman's arms, and frantically kissed her pale face.

Her whispers now struggled through as she choked, disbelieving even though she knew it was true. She saw her mother in her mind, a young woman when Louisa was little more than a baby, slim and intensely pretty with huge brown eyes beneath long lashes, her warmth tender and her embraces loving. "You are, you're my mother," Louisa spluttered as Doric knelt back. "You're truly alive. You're truly real. But how? And why? My darling Mamma, you look, my dearest. Is this some sort of hospital?"

Trembling again, the tears in rivulets, Alice whispered back, "It is a prison. It is a cage. I am not permitted to leave." She leaned against her daughter's cheek as though lacking the energy to sit alone. "You may be in danger, my beloved. But to have you here is a bliss beyond words. I believed I would never – could never – see you again. How is Francis, my baby? Did he live?"

"Oh yes," Louisa said in the rush. "He's fourteen and very well and awfully nice. We used to talk about you because he was so sorry he never knew you. We were told that you – died – in childbirth. I don't understand."

It was Doric who stood and leaned forwards, his hands soothing on Louisa's shoulders. "Lady Alice," he asked, "May I ask a question you might find difficult to answer? But is it your elder son Charles who has locked you here for so very long? Do you know? Have you seen him, or anyone else during these years hidden away?"

"I'm not hiding," she mumbled, still clutching Louisa. "It was this bed, where I live now. My little baby was weak, but he suckled, and I held him with my arms and all my heart. He was so beloved to me. But the medic said I was unwell and needed to rest. My husband – how I hated my husband – locked the door and would not allow me out – until I had recovered, he said. But did I never recover? He brought me food for some days but then that stopped. I cannot remember how soon. It was so long ago. I cried for my children, but your wretched father said they would be well cared for, though not by me. I could only rest, he said. And now it feels as though I have rested for a hundred years."

"When, what do you eat?" Louisa asked in words between sobs.

"Food? Very little. But I can eat sometimes. Food is left when someone unlocks the door, and I see a hand pushing through a platter just inside." Her fingers fluttered as though she could not control them, and the trembling of her whole body continued. Each part visible seemed only bone, a terrified but living skeleton. Her voice cracked, faded, but resumed. "Water too. A jug of water and bread. Ham. Cheese. Not very often. But I am no longer interested in food. The pain of hunger went long ago. It is love that I yearn for. It is so very, very long since I tasted love."

"And Charles?" Doric asked.

"I was excited when I saw him. I believed I was free and would run back into the arms of my children. Charles told me my husband was dead. I felt a warmth through my whole body. Relief. Rebirth."

"But Charles is so like father."

"He is his father in so many ways. He says that if I was freed, I would ruin the reputation of the family. It would be a scandal. I promised I would never tell. He wouldn't listen. One day when he came, I grew angry. It had been three years or more and I was desperate. I was sure I would die. I screamed at him and told him he was no longer my son." She tried to wipe the tears from her eyes and cheeks, but her fingers were so thin, and the knuckles too protuberant, she hurt herself. Her reddened eyes spilled tears again, and she collapsed down against her daughter. "He whipped me," she mumbled, hardly able to speak. "Now, when he comes, he brings me food. Old bread, cold pottage and cabbage soup, wedges of pastry although sometimes it is green with mould. But I must eat it or I would starve. But I hate the food he brings. It is the food of dying beggars, poor souls, and I know that is what I am. I have thought what would be best for me. I have wanted to die. But when the food comes, I grab it and I eat and I live. Hunger is such a thorn, it cannot be ignored. I say I will never eat again. But I see mouldy cheese and I cannot stop until I've eaten every crumb. I hate it and I hate wanting it, but I seem to have no choice."

"When did he come last?" Doric knelt on the floor once again, his eyes as moist as hers.

"I have no sense of time," she said, "It is day sometimes, and night sometimes, but I see darkness in both. I dare not waste my candles. He only brings me two. I see him rarely. Last time? I have no idea. A week past? More, I think. Two weeks or three."

Louisa kissed her eyes, her withered cheeks, and every wizened finger on both hands. She couldn't believe it. "And he whipped you. In God's name, why?"

In a mumbled whisper, the woman said, "To make me fear him." She cowered back as if expecting it again.

"You've been here all these years. If only I'd have found you before. But I didn't even know this place existed. I realise I was born here, but we left after Francis was born. I was four. I remember nothing of this place, and so little of you. Only once, when you read me a story, I remember. You were golden."

"And now I am white and grey and a sack of withered bones."

Doric interrupted. "I carry no food, but as soon as dawn rises, I'll ride up the hill to find a shop and buy whatever I can." Shaking his head, he sat back on his heels. "I swear you'll eat well tomorrow morning, my lady. Neither mouldy cheese nor stale cheat. Thank the Lord we came here. Louisa's idea. Charles is cruel and she needed to escape. We'll be married, Lady Alice, if you'll have me as a son-in-law."

He was also crying silent tears gazing at the two women, each so different even though mother and daughter. Louisa continued, "Mamma? Charles tortures you?"

"He hates me. But I don't know why. I gave him life. I loved him. But at least sometimes he brings me food and even when he knocks me down or whips me, he doesn't kill me. Yet after what seems a hundred years, I still don't understand. I've asked why he hates me, but he simply slaps my face."

"He seems to hate me too," Louisa sighed. "He beats me and Francis all the time. Perhaps he hates himself. Perhaps he hates you for giving him life. And he always hated father."

"He hates the king," Doric murmured. "He hates his country. I would guess he hated his wife. Do you know he hated his father?"

"He killed Papa," Louisa added softly. "But that was almost kindness."

Her words and those of her mother were muffled, each pressed against the body of the other. But Louisa, almost frightened, felt her mother's ribs, the bones of her shoulders, of her arms and of her neck. The woman seemed without flesh, and Louisa could not stop crying. Now Doric was silently crying. Yet Alice had stopped.

"Will you set me free?" she asked as though expecting to be refused. "I know Charles will try to kill me, and even you perhaps. But can we pay guards? Can you dare such a thing? Do you want me, my beloved daughter? I know I am no longer strong, nor beautiful, nor rich as once I was, which is the only reason your father wanted me. I am sure I have no family left of my own. But I swear I will be so very good, if only you would let me walk free."

"Oh Mamma," Louisa sobbed, "I love you. I adore you. Francis will faint. He will. He'll be so happy. I could never leave you here. I promise your life will change in every single tiny way and we'll bring you home with us as soon as Doric buys food. Doric has lodgings, perhaps you could stay there," she gazed up at him, questioning, "If Charles threatens us we can't stay there. But I promise with all my heart and soul, I would never, ever leave you here."

Clutching, unbelieving, Alice tried to stand, but fell back. Her body had no strength and her legs could not hold her. Louisa knew she might carry her mother in her own arms if necessary. The skeleton woman was crying again.

Then so utterly unexpected, the sudden interruption seemed like the arrival of the devil or a visitation of terror.

The heavy footsteps up the last few stairs outside resounded, and suddenly the door was flung open. Louisa whirled around, screaming, "Charles," and Doric snatched his knife from his belt and stepped towards the door. Alice, crumpled like a dying butterfly, hid her face beneath her hands.

Marching into the chamber, torch held high, the flames hid his identity but showed no likeness to Charles. Andrew waited less than a moment to see the devastation before him, and walked forwards with the flickering light, saying, "I am Andrew of Leys. Is this –? Doric, in damnation's name, it's you?"

Behind him, Casper stared. "Mistress Louisa? I reckon I ain't mistook. But there be a female well-nigh dead, and we needs a medic."

"I believe we do," Doric said, his vice half lost. "And food, if you have any."

"I got no medic," Casper replied at once. "But I reckons I got enough food fer any hungry household. Tis in me saddle bag, and in Master Andrew's and all." He sighed with a partial gargle of disgust at the thought, but continued, "I just gotta do all them bloody stairs, down to them saddle bags, then all the way up again."

Andrew had wedged his torch in the broken crack of one bedpost and sat quickly next to the woman he did not know. "My lady," he said. "You are unwell. My companion is fetching food and drink. Can you face food? I believe it is what you need." He turned to Doric, "For God's sake, man. Explain yourself."

"I think it will be a very long explanation," Doric said, brushing the stripes of tears from his face. "It's a story I can barely believe myself, but we have the proof here. May I introduce you to Lady Alice, Countess of Hylton, the mother of Lady Louisa, my future bride."

Andrew absorbed this information with one raised eyebrow, regarded the clearly starved woman crouching on the bed, and bowed slightly, pretending unphased practicality. "My lady, I am honoured. I am Andrew, Lord Leys, and am delighted to be of service. I understand that you wish to leave this wreck of a building?" She nodded, half excited and half frightened. "Once you have eaten, my lady, and once the sun brings the light we need, then there are two possibilities. Please state which you prefer, as I am happy to offer either. You can take my man's horse and ride with us back to Westminster, but I must warn you it is a long ride and we cannot arrive until late in the night. Or if you are prepared to wait an hour, I will ride to the village nearby, and hire a litter. It will make our journey slower, but you will be held safe, sheltered, and, should you wish it, out of sight. If you decide this is the better method, then we will stay tomorrow night at a suitable inn, take a hearty dinner and supper, and ride to my home the day after. It is a large house and offers considerable comfort. My wife Tyballis will be only too delighted to make your acquaintance. She spends too much time alone while I am working. From there, we can decide together which is the best course of action to take regarding your identity and wishes for the future. In the meantime, my lady, do you own a cloak?"

She swallowed, and shook her head.

"I have one," Louisa said at once. "It's very warm."

"And you wish to freeze for two days?" Andrew enquired. "I think not. There are blankets here to cushion the inside of the litter, if that's the choice you make, and I shall buy a cloak of some kind in the village."

Louisa didn't know whether to laugh or cry. She felt the crazed ripple of nightmare within her combine with utter joy and immense excitement.

Alice stared as though seeing visions and discovering emotions which she had long forgotten existed.

"We will choose the litter, sir," Doric told his bemused friend. "And I believe Louisa should travel with her mother. The Lady cannot ride in this condition."

Both Louisa and her mother were again crying in each other's arms.

CHAPTER THIRTY-SIX

The two day journey slipped into three. The litter travelled slowly across the rutted roads and winding country lanes, the potholes and puddles. The fords were unpassable as they sank below the overflowing streams and rivers and even the few bridges were a danger. Doric and Andrew discovered alternative crossings, and Casper was sent onwards with a message to his royal highness, explaining that it would be impossible, due to unexpected circumstances, for Lord Leys to arrive back at the palace within the day.

"*You are excused, my lord*," wrote his majesty in return. Casper brought the royal message, and the remainder of the more secretive words by mouth.

"I done waited in the office," Casper said, sinking down beside the tavern's flaming hearth. "I didn't hardly expect the king, now did I? But out comes this official all in bright red, and he brings this note, but he speaks an' all. '*Kindly convey to your master*' he says, '*that tis a situation now under control o' Francis Lovell and Edward Brampton. Ain't no cause fer worry no more. Lord Leys be free to deal wiv his own business, wot sounds proper urgent.*'

Andrew failed to point out that the royal official was unlikely to have used those exact words, and leaned back, content. His majesty had many loyal men who would have no difficulty taking the young prince to safety in Burgundy, where both boys would be able to enjoy life with greater liberty than they had been permitted as heirs to the throne.

The situation with Lady Alice and Charles of Hylton, was quite another consideration.

At each stop, the lady was wrapped in her new cloak and carried by Doric to her chamber, for she was virtually unable to walk. She ate either in the bedchamber, or food was brought to her within the litter. Louisa always stayed with her. Doric spent many hours with Andrew discussing the nightmare that was barely believable, and barely possible to imagine.

"Fourteen years," Andrew sighed.

"I have heard of those unjustly kept in Bedlam for many years, caged as lunatics, but as sane as you and I having been condemned by relatives who want them gone. I have heard of women treated as slaves by fathers and husbands, even raped by their own relatives." Doric paused, and sighed, adding, "I have heard of boys kept in monasteries for some years, tutored to become monks, and yet constantly abused. But," he continued softly, "not as long as fourteen years. I have little knowledge of the husband, but the son Charles is crazed indeed. He should perhaps be sent to Bedlam himself and caged for life."

"He does not deserve any life at all," Andrew said.

Following the litter each day, Doric rode in a dream of combined sorrow and delight. He had not fulfilled any of the future he had expected, and which had seemed more dream than truth, yet a dream destined to become reality. To marry, to live for weeks in a castle, however ruined, with the woman he loved, and finally to return to the work he now valued, with his wife at his side.

None of the dream had eventuated. Not one bright spangle had turned to truth. But instead the incredible had become credible, the woman he loved remained his intended, and had discovered her living mother, and the utter evil of the brother she hated.

Often he rode with tears in his eyes, both for Louisa and her tortured mother, but if asked, claimed the wind had brought those tears.

After three slow meandering days they arrived at the great house of Leys, where Andrew carried Alice to one of the larger guest bedchambers, followed not only by Louisa, but by Tyballis, astonished at the quickly told and utterly terrifying tale of the tiny woman's captivity.

Once, before meeting Andrew, Tyballis had seen a stray dog wandering the streets, more skeleton than animal, starving to death on its feet. She had brought it food whenever she could grab any, and gradually saw the dog grow flesh, its eyes turning from hopeless to hopeful. But it had disappeared after some days, and she had never known if it lived. The woman now curled on the grand bed, although half covered by a thick cloak, was as thin and as weak as the dog she had tried to save,

Louisa sat on the bed beside her mother, and Tyballis pulled up a small chair, sitting close. "We will do everything, absolutely everything," she said, 'to help. To make you well. To return you to your family and rightful home, and to take Charles to court for his vile actions. He should be executed." She paused. "Would you be sorry to see your own son die, after what he has done?"

"Charles has inherited his father's sickness," Alice whispered. "Indeed, he killed his own father, and I understand why. But I would not wish to watch his own death."

With undoubted determination, Doric left Andrew's home and rode to The Strand. At Hylton house, he followed the steward to the main hall, and watched the fury grow as Charles was first informed he had a visitor, and then realised that the visitor had marched in, uninvited.

"How dare you, sir?" Charles yelled, recognising him as the king's messenger. "You have no permission to enter here. If you carry news from his highness, then deliver it quickly and leave." Instead, Doric sat. The cushioned chair by the fire faced the chair where Charles had been seated. Staring in anger, Charles returned to his seat, and glared at Doric. "Very well," he said, accepting where there appeared no choice, "so what is so important that I must be told in such a manner?"

"I assume," Doric said, crossing his legs and staring into the rising flames, "you are aware that your sister Louisa has left this house some days back, and has not yet returned."

"Of course I know, fool," Charles growled. "I've had half my household out searching for days. Do you know where she is? Bring the slut back here, and I shall reward you."

Doric smiled. "A generous offer indeed, my lord. And no doubt you plan to punish your sister for her attempt to escape you?"

"Dammed right, I will." Charles leaned forward, one hand scraping back the thick crop of black hair, so slick it reflected flames and seemed red in colour. "I'll personally flay the brat. So where is she?"

"I can tell you exactly where she is." The smile grew but his eyes were ice. "But more, my lord, and surprisingly, I imagine, I can now also tell you exactly where your mother is. Indeed, they are together."

Charles stared. His mouth snapped shut. For a moment unable to speak, finally he cleared his throat and the fury colouring his face turned to white fear. "I don't understand you," he said. "My mother died nearly fifteen years gone. Whoever you have spoken to regarding this, must be lying. A fake, a criminal, someone hoping to grab inheritance."

"Your sister, and your true mother, ill as she is due to your treatment," Doric replied, the smile gone, "have arrived at Leys House, and I have come here to escort your young brother to his mother's side after her fourteen years of imprisonment and near starvation. What you do is your choice, my lord. Stay here, if you wish, and wait for the inevitable repercussions. He leaned so close to Charles, that their hair almost touched, "you may be sure, my lord, that you will be faced with a situation you cannot control."

He did not wait for an answer, stood again, turned and strode from the hall without looking back. His final glimpse of the Lord Charles was of the man flushed and open mouthed, gazing in terror and disbelief. Doric walked quickly towards the steward, who stood mystified at the doorway. "Young Francis," Doric said. "Where is he?"

"To the best of my knowledge, he is in his bedchamber," the steward answered. "Shall I inform him that he is required downstairs, sir?"

Nodding, Doric added, "And tell him it's me," he laughed, "the wandering minstrel."

Francis skipped the stairs and ran to Doric. "Get your cape, boy," Doric said, "and your horse. We're making an extremely important visit."

"Louisa?"

"She's fine," Doric said as Francis ordered his horse saddled. "And looking forward to seeing you. No, we are not yet man and wife. But there is more unexpected news than that."

Alice sat at the head of the high table, laughing as she took the place of the lord, since he was absent, and regarded the women seated, gazing back at her, and at her youngest son who sat on her right. Dinner had been served and a variety of platters lay steaming, their condensation mingling with the smoke of ten tall wax candles.

Although it was midday, the November weather was dull and rain was imminent, with black clouds waiting to sink lower before bursting their contents into the wind.

Duck's liver, creamed asparagus, onions caramelised with precious sugar, spinach and walnuts, roast pork nestled within the parcel of crispy crackling, sharp lemon tart with custard, figs in a yeast and soft cheese pudding, turnips stuffed with an egg and bacon mixture, and several large jugs of wine.

Louisa sat to her mother's left, and then Beatrice, by special invitation. At the end of the table, smiling broadly, Tyballis sat, her embroidered napkin over her shoulder, her knife and spoon in hand. "I think we should begin," she said, and the servers started to fill each platter as the guests pointed to whatever they wished.

"Everything," said Francis. "And plenty of it."

On his other side sat Isabella, feeling highly outranked, but adoring the sight of the lady who had once been her mistress, the mother of the three children she had nursed from birth.

Having told Beatrice the story, Louisa had invited her. "I want you to know everything," she had said. "But there's more. I want you to be a witness and tell both your father and your brother."

Sitting unaided, Alice had learned to smile. She had also learned to eat. Still desperately thin, there was now a little soft new flesh covering the once bare bones, a skeleton thinly plastered. She could walk now, slowly, even up the steps to her vast new silken bedchamber. She had clothes, a little large for her but soon to be grown into. Now she wore lilac velvet and outer sleeves embroidered in silver over the inner sleeves of white damask. She raised her cup of wine, and everyone drank. Her story was slow to tell.

"My husband was a powerful man, and a cruel one," she said. "But before I married, I was happy. My father was a successful trader in wool exported to Italy, bringing silk in return. He was one of the first to deal with the Medici family in Florence and travelled there several times. I went with him once and that gave me what I supposed to be a love of adventure. But that did not last. Because he was mightily rich and we lived well, Lord Percival, Earl of Hylton, had bought from us, and knew my father. His own family, due to gambling and the disadvantages of war, had left him virtually destitute. It is an old story, I think, of the titled yet poverty stricken gentleman and the common man with riches beyond his needs. Percival offered to marry my elder sister and become the heir to the family wealth, while making my sister Lady Margaret, Countess of Hylton. My father was flattered, and my mother delighted, but poor Margaret despised Percival, having met the beast, and refused. It was several months later that troops of armed men surrounded our home, set fire to the kitchens, permitted most of the staff to escape. My father rushed out in horror, poor Papa. They killed him. I saw him lying dead, stabbed in a hundred places and bleeding over the bushes of meadow sweet. My sister hid in the privy, but several men hauled her out. Yet as she pulled away at the top if the staircase, they pushed her back and she fell, falling every step until her head was crushed. My mother, my darling Mamma, killed herself. She stood gazing at the bloodshed stretched before her, and taking my father's knife, thrust it into her neck. Thank the Lord I didn't see her death, but I have often dreamed of it. Percival grabbed me as the only member left of my family, tied me up and carried me back to his castle in Essex. I was thirteen, just a month after my anniversary when I believed that turning thirteen after a year of being twelve, was an exciting omen and signified maturity. At Percival's home, I locked myself in the bedchamber. I did not eat for five days. But when finally a maid whispered that she had brought me food, I opened my door, and Percival rushed in. He raped me. And after that he raped me every night until I fell ill. Our marriage was a simple handfasting, but it was witnessed by two priests and the entire household, so I could not deny it. I tried to deny him, but was beaten for it so many times that I accepted beatings as part of life. I gave birth to Charles while I was still thirteen, and adored my tiny baby. But he was taken from me and brought up strictly by tutors employed by Percival. You, my darling Louisa, were born six years later, after two miscarriages. I was permitted to care for you during those years, my love, since you were simply a girl. Then finally Francis was born. That was when I was locked in the tower, at first unknown to me since I was weak, but then the nightmare was revealed. And for fourteen hideous years of starvation and misery, yearning for my children, I was caged there. Percival finally died. Charles, now adult, took on his father's image, laughed and admitted he had slaughtered Percival, but none knew of it except him and myself. I did not miss my husband of course, but I was bitterly saddened when I realised that my imprisonment would continue under Charles." Finally she looked up, smiling again. "Until my beautiful daughter and her friends came to rescue me." She drained her cup after raising it once more to Louisa, and continued, "I am old now. And look it, as I well know. But I think I still have years left to love my two sweet children and my new friends."

Beatrice stood, her own cup in hand. "My lady." She curtseyed with exaggerated depth. "As the most courageous woman I have ever met, may I drink to your courage and your beauty. You are, I believe, no more than thirty nine or forty years, and therefore young. And courage is more beautiful than youth. I shall tell your story to my own family this evening, and then I shall spread it as far across the land as I am able. Charles will cringe from the scandal, and from the hideous truth of what he has done. But his cruelty must be known, and you, Lady Alice, will be loved and admired."

With eyes again full of tears, Alice smiled. "I have no care for that, either admiration or embarrassment, which I think more likely. I want only my two younger children, my friends, including you, my dear, and perhaps – sometimes – a little food and a soft bed."

Andrew and Doric were in conversation with his majesty, a rare meeting, carefully arranged by the king. Having virtually no spare time, his highness had already explained that their conversation must be brief.

"This is not behaviour I can tolerate," he said, elbows on the small table, while tenting his fingertips. "This gentleman shall to brought to justice, and his guilt shall be decided by a jury."

Andrew was standing. "I thank you, sire," he bowed. 'This man has created untold suffering. And I believe he was only fifteen years of age when he murdered his father and took over the imprisonment of his mother. A creature so wicked at such an age is a terrifying thought."

Richard waved a hand at the two chairs, empty, on the opposite side of the table. "Sit, sit, this is a private matter and not yet official. We must speak without undue civility. Now – young Doric – I understand you wish to marry this Hylton girl? For duty or for affection?"

"I do, sire." Doric spoke softly, looking directly at his king. "And I claim both reasons. I love her. And once her brother is either executed or taken to the Tower, caring for her will also be my duty. It is her brother who has denied permission and Louisa is as yet only eighteen."

"Then you have my permission to marry the girl." His highness leaned back in his chair, fingertips again tipped together. "I over-rule her brother. He shall be brought to trial. I know you, young Doric, and I know your loyalty and the priceless work you have done for me while serving Lord Leys. I shall get my secretary to write of my permission and send the message to your own lodgings. And," he smiled suddenly, "you must play for me again sometime soon. I miss both your playing and your singing."

Standing at once, Doric bowed deeply and thanked his king. He then, not having been ordered to stay, left the chamber, walking backwards until he reached the door. Once outside, he sighed in utter delight, and waited for Andrew.

He was not long, and as they rode back together, Andrew said, "Well, young Doric, it seems your needs have been answered. I shall supply you with funds, and I believe his majesty will do the same once you announce your wedding."

Astounded, Doric said, "How disaster turns to delight. I once wandered the countryside with a girl I was fond of. Not in love, nor she with me, but when I discovered her dead, I was appalled. Shortly afterwards I was arrested for her murder. I imagined this would mean the end of my life. And at that moment, my lord, you walked in. Even earlier, when I was little more than a child, a similar situation developed. Some years of bitter misery led me to – escape. But instead of failure, I then loved my life of sunshine and singing."

"Ah, yes." Andrew nodded and raised a finger. "Casper had some news concerning the death of your young friend in the countryside. Elizabeth, wasn't it?"

"She was." Doric paused, surprised, and admitted.

"You thought him the guilty one?" Andrew smiled. "You told me once before, which was why I questioned him. Immediately he gave me the answer. He was innocent, as I was already sure, but he knew who was guilty."

CHAPTER THIRTY-SEVEN

Alice held out her arm. The skin was stretching like the knitted silk of a gentleman's hose, and beneath, soft as the fur of a new-born kitten, her flesh swelled rose pink, and no bone dared show its inner fragility except where the knuckles on her fingers jutted. The bruised black hollows around her eyes had paled, the blue of her eyes brightening as the hollowed flesh became softly convex.

"Is this truly me?" she sighed. "I had forgotten what I looked like once. How strange to recognise myself all over again."

Louisa hugged her. Francis leaned on the beam over the fire's hearth where the spit and crackle of the flames danced as if hearing music. "You're – gorgeous, Mamma," he told her. "I used to cry because I never knew you. I felt guilty because I'd killed you. As a four or five-year-old, I thought myself wicked for murdering you at my birth. And I asked Louisa what you were like, but she hardly remembered."

"A little, I did," Louisa answered. "I knew you were beautiful, and kind and your kisses were like angels. I remembered you carrying me onto your bed, where the eiderdown was so soft and quilted, I felt I was crawling over mountains and falling down the hills into valleys. To crawl over that eiderdown was so bewildering, but I kept going because I could see you sitting there beyond the mountains, with your arms out to me. I remember you kissing me goodnight. But I also remember you running from Papa."

Her smile faded. "I did that often," Alice whispered.

"I think," Francis murmured, leaning back, "that was part of why I thought I wanted poor little Joletta – because I wanted a woman who loved me – a sort of make-believe mother. And then, dear saints have mercy, I knew it was my fault that Joletta died. First I killed my mother. Then I killed Joletta." With a sudden jolt, he sat forwards again, and smiled. "But I never killed you after all. And I didn't kill Joletta either. Charles did that."

⋈◇⋈

Beatrice had returned to her own home. It was the evening when sleet had turned to ice, and a black sky had denied the moonlight. Both her brother and father were in the hall, still at the table after a late supper. Food was strewn across a dozen platters, waiting to be taken back to the kitchens, ready for a cold supper for the staff.

Bryan was thumping on the table. "You always get what you want, Papa."

"He won't this time." Beatrice judged her own entrance, marching in with the bravado of an armed guard. "Bryan, you're an idiot, even if you are my twin. I got all the brains, you got all the idiocy. And you can't marry Louisa, she's about to wed someone else. As for me marrying Francis, no, I won't. Nor would it be in any of our interests, since Charles is about to be arrested."

Her father stood abruptly, his chair falling back behind him. "What nonsense are you babbling, girl? Lies. I refuse to believe such abysmal rubbish."

"Believe it or not," Beatrice smiled at her father. "You'll hear it soon enough. Meanwhile, I shall go and entertain my mother with the whole story."

Within moments, Sir John Sudbury marched into his wife's bedchamber and stood looking down at the two women sitting

277

together on the settle. "Well?" he demanded. "Madam, do you believe your daughter's lies?"

The older woman quavered. "I have never known our dear Beatrice to lie. Only cowards lie, my lord. And from the little I know of your young friend Charles, I do not and never have trusted him. His poor little wife died so soon after their wedding day, and yet I have never heard him speak of her or speak of sadness. And he wished to marry his younger brother off to Beatrice, and never spoke of himself, being of a more suitable age. I believe he is about twenty-five years. But he does not seem to want another wife."

"Nothing to do with it," objected Sir John. "He's a man of wealth and title, and shares my political views regarding – well, you know full well exactly what I believe. Those unions will cement our agreements when the invasion arrives. It will ensure our futures with the new power to come."

"The invasion failed," Beatrice glared.

"The next one," said her father, "will not."

Kissing her mother's cheek and patting her hand, Beatrice rose and gazed momentarily as she passed him, before opening the door. "I have given you accurate information," she told him. "The rest is up to you. But I am leaving and may not return. I meant to come home, I thought it was what I wanted, but now I'm quite sure I don't. I shall arrange for Edith to pack up my clothes and other belongings, I'm visiting friends. But I will keep in touch with Mamma. I may not even see you again Papa, especially if you keep up your friendship with Charles and end up being executed at his side."

❤

Tucking up her knees beneath the blanket, Annie wrapped her arms around herself and chuckled at Isabella. "Too right, my dear," she said in agreement.

Isabella looked up. "'Tis the first time I've heard you laugh," she said, her own smile wide. "I'm delighted, Annie. We must all get over our past unfortunate events. You have a new life now."

"I shouldn't feel sorry for meself, I knows that," Annie said, her laughter abruptly fading. "Thanks to yer lovely Lady Louisa, I got luck I don't reckon I deserve, coming here and all that. And from wot I heard about the poor lady mother, well, tis shocking. Now that be worse than I ever heard. But losing my sweet daughter Joletta, it ain't gonna be forgot fer the rest o' me life. She were me life and breath, she were. Once she growed, I could give up me old work, and start wiv the brewery. She done helped wiv all of it. Wivout my lovely lass, I can't earn naught, and I's too old to go back to me old job."

With a guess at what Annie's previous work when young, had clearly been, before Joletta had grown, Isabella nodded. "Very difficult, my dear," she said. She had not intended to say any more, but with sudden impulsive instinct she added, "I know something of how terrible that feels."

Annie stared. "Surely you weren't never on the streets, Bella? You ain't the type."

"No, no," Isabella said, regretting having spoken at all. "My work has always been as a wet-nurse and looking after the children of grand ladies without the wish to do their own washing nor keep the babe in his nethercloths and so forth." She paused, her voice dropping to a whisper. "It was the terrible pain of losing a child that I meant, my dear, and sympathise with you of course." She turned away, changing the subject. "But the good lord sends us joy as well as sorrow, and we must learn to cope with both."

Annie refused to be diverted. "Bella," she said with determination, "I ain't quite sure wot you's telling me. But tell me if tis true, you be saying as you had a babe yerself. And maybe lost it at birth?"

Now there were tears in Isabella's eyes. "I have no desire to speak of this," she sniffed. "I have never told another soul, not even my dear Louisa. Why I could not resist – when you have suffered such tragedy in losing your own dear daughter – I cannot say. But I would sooner not discuss this any further. So, my dear, I shall go downstairs and start to fold the washing."

Staring, Annie didn't budge. "So I's not allowed to tell nobody nor ask any more?" she asked, dismayed.

"I'll say not another word, and you must say nothing at all," Isabella told her. "The subject is closed forever. Why I said it, I cannot imagine. Foolish. Horribly foolish."

"I ain't sure I even understands," Annie admitted.

"Excellent," Isabella told her. "Now we go downstairs and collect the washing."

Snatching up the valuable glass jug from the table, Charles threw it with considerable force at the wall above, and a hundred broken slithers fell back to the floorboards. Then he sat, almost collapsing, and buried his head in his hands., his elbows on the table. Briefly lifting his chin, he called for wine. Another jug was brought, and a cup. The steward looked down at the broken glass on the floor.

"My lord," he said with some care, "these broken shards look remarkably dangerous. May I send the girl to clean them up?"

Charles nodded, waited until the steward filled the cup, drained it and nodded again, asking for a refill. After draining the second cup, he dropped his head back into his hands. He heard the steward leaving and the maid's arrival but spoke to neither. He did not know what he should do.

He understood himself. Charles had always known why he did what he did and accepted the need for it. Having grown up beaten and kicked by a tyrant, and seen the tyrant's wife equally abused, more perhaps, he knew no other behaviour, and somehow admired what he himself had hated. Beating others was a gift of relief after struggle of any kind, and he saw no reason to surrender such logical malice. But perhaps, just perhaps, he had gone too far.

Shaking his head at himself, he drank a third cup of wine, and made a decision.

Enclosed in Doric's arms, Louisa gazed into the depths of his eyes, and saw her own future.

"I don't know why you love me," she whispered. "I'm a bit plain and rather silly and awfully immature and I've never been anywhere or done anything. You are so very much the opposite."

He grinned at her. "I don't love you for any special reason, my beautiful girl," Doric told her, kissing her ear. "I love you because I love you. Sparks in the sky, rainbows, suddenly knowing, as soon as I saw you, that we were tied together – is love ever more easily explained? With weddings usually arranged for the gain of political advantage or title, inheritance, bolstering the position of both parties, marrying for love is rare. Sadly rare. You, my sweetness, are the greatest gift and it needs no explanation. Can I say I love you because you have hair like silk? Or because my stomach jumps when I see you, and my chest tingles and I just want to wrap myself around you and stay there forever?"

"Then love doesn't ever make sense?"

"Perhaps it doesn't. Do we need something sensible?"

"Loving makes me feel very alive," Louisa said. "Isn't that sensible?"

"No. It's wonderful and exciting and unexpected and settles into pure happiness." Doric grinned, his arms squeezing. "And it makes me feel alive too. Far, far more than I ever was before."

"Even while you play your glorious music?" Louisa wore green over her shift, it covered her in deep soft velvet, yet Doric felt the swell and heat of her breasts and the pressure of her arms as she held him as tightly as he held her.

"Music," Doric murmured, "is a sort of bliss. But it doesn't make me tingle, as you do. Or imagine what I might do one day – how I might touch you, and see you, and make love to you."

"Do it then," Louisa said suddenly. "We'll be married soon. Does it matter if we do things before? I want to know what happens. I used to ask people – I mean the maids and Isabella and the woman who measured me for new clothes. Martha, my tailor's assistant. She just said I'd find out one day."

He laughed, simply because he wasn't sure how to answer. He did not feel he could tell her that his groin twisted when he touched her, nor tell her what he imagined doing once they were truly together. He couldn't explain that seeing her made his heart pump or that he felt he had a fever just holding her hand. Instead he laughed softly, and then said, "My beloved, there's something very different I ought to tell you. I should have said this before, but I've told so few. Not even Andrew. Indeed, no one, not since I was twelve years old."

Astonished, Louisa loosened her grasp on his shoulders and leaned back a little on the cushion, gazing back at him, almost frightened.

In the following silence, when Doric seemed to find words difficult once more, she whispered, "You're already married? Or you can't make love, not ever? Or perhaps you don't really love me after all?"

"God, no. None of those." Doric moved one hand and lifted her chin, the other to her hair, caressing the strands from her eyes as he smiled . "My dearest, not only have I never married, I've never loved a woman before. Not genuine love – until I met you. And once we marry, I swear I shall make love to you and discover every part of you." He kissed her, his fingers roving, then his kisses following his fingers. "It's about myself. I never told anyone before because it makes me sick. And at first, I didn't have the slightest intention of telling you either. But you have to know, my beloved. And if it puts you off marrying me, then I'll have to accept it. But it's so much part of me and the reason that I've done everything I've ever done – since I was young. I feel I'd be cheating you if I don't tell you."

With sudden and energetic passion, she cradled his face between her hands, leaned down, and kissed his eyes. They were moist.

"We've both cried enough," she whispered. "Just tell me, Doric darling. There's nothing, nothing at all, that would stop me loving you. So tell me, whatever it is, and then make love to me."

For the first time in his life, the dark mystery of his past barely seemed to matter. The one thing that had guided, pushed and restrained his every move for more than ten long years, now seemed utterly irrelevant. The movement of her breasts, the soft dimples of her skin, and the shadows of her mouth over his, mattered more than anything else in all the world.

Doric was fully dressed, and relieved that what he felt was hidden. But he reached up and pulled her against him, wishing that he could feel her breasts against his bare skin. His fingers pressed with delight against her back and the small cushions of her spine. He yearned to know every part of her, kissing instead of speaking.

But he said, "You see, Doric isn't even my real name. Nor Fleet. I made them both up. I had my own reasons, which mattered so much to me at the time."

"And your real name?" She was bemused. Had he killed someone?

"Matthew. Matthew Attlewood. You, my own love, will be Mistress Attlewood if you still agree to marry me. But call me whatever you want, for I hardly remember now what my true name is."

"I don't care what terrible things you did before I met you," Louisa said, sitting up again. "You're Doric Fleet because that's who I fell in love with. And whatever is so shameful you had to hide by changing your name, I don't care. Matthew did whatever he did, and he doesn't have to tell me because it's not him I'm in love with. But my beloved, first make love to me. That means we're married. Maybe not for the church and maybe not to the law and maybe not even to you. But after you make love to me, then I'm your wife. And then you can tell me about Matthew somebody if you really want to."

He couldn't look away from her high tilted breasts. "I was meant to be celibate. How could I ever achieve such a thing?"

"Because you said you had a girl who died?"

"I was never chaste, though originally not by choice." His fingers touched across her breasts, very lightly, almost as if he dared nothing more. "Like your poor mother, I felt myself unloved and unwanted when my parents bundled me off to a monastery. It didn't appeal. I didn't love the idea or the life, but I believed I'd been thrown from home, and was sorry for myself. I was eight. And I wasn't a baby anymore. Chastity, it seems, doesn't appeal to every member of the clergy."

Staring at him, Louisa only faintly understood. "There were girls in the monastery? Women?"

"The monks themselves. Just two of them, old, wizened, and without shame. One to hold. One to act. And then cross over. From the age of eight to twelve, I was abused. Until I ran away." He paused, moving his fingers from her body. "Does that disgust you? If it does, I'll understand."

"Why should it?" Louisa demanded. "They did horrible things – not you." And she flung herself into his arms, both arms tightly around him.

CHAPTER THIRTY-EIGHT

I n his usual manner of exaggerated politeness combined with faint disinterest, the steward opened the huge wooden front doors. They neither squeaked nor creaked, being, as always, in perfect order.

Yet what the steward faced as the doors swung open, was not what he had expected.

Three angry men of various ages pushed past him, almost knocking him to the ground. He shouted out, warning the lord of the house as best he could, and stumbling back to his feet, he hurried behind the intruders towards the main hall where he knew that his lordship and his house guests were seated.

Both Andrew and Doric stood immediately and strode forwards.

Having forced their way inside, Sir John Sudbury, his son Bryan and Lord Charles Hylton stood in the hall's vast vaulted entrance, their swords sheathed but their hands to the hilts.

Louisa, Tyballis and Beatrice had also hurried to their feet, although the Lady Alice, breathing heavily, remained seated, trembling, her fingers clutching the arms of the chair. Behind her Francis stood, his own hands protectively on his mother's shoulders.

Without hesitation, Charles shouted both at Andrew and across the room at Louisa., then noticed Francis in the shadows and roared, cursing. "you pickle-brained pig-swilling brats," he yelled. "You eat and sleep and indulge your damned selfish wishes at my expense, then run to others, without permission or apologies."

But then, in sudden horrified realisation, he saw the vision of his mother, her hair pinned in silver beneath pale blue gossamer, eyes glowing, and her slim body dressed in palest turquoise silk, catching the glimmer of the fire in its sheen.

He stared, gulping. Alice stared back. Andrew stood in absolute silence, but his hands were clenched. Then both Francis and Louisa marched forwards to face their brother. Francis had pulled his knife from his belt, but it was Louisa who stepped closer and slapped Charles across the face. He lunged at her, but Andrew and Doric stepped between. Doric forced Charles' arm behind his back, levering the elbow inwards to the spine and the wrist upwards to the back of the neck, on the verge of breaking both elbow and shoulder joints. The agony flushed across every part of his upper body and Charles, unaccustomed to such pain, screamed and staggered. Doric released him and let him fall.

Andrew placed one steady foot on the fallen man, keeping him down.

"Kick the bastard," Francis yelled. But Bryan had run at him, head down, attempting to knock him over. Doric wrenched Francis aside, and Bryan hurtled onwards, unable to stop himself as he crashed into the wall between the two great windows, catching the side of his head on the open shutters. He squealed, high pitched, and lurched backwards, holding the side of his face below the eye, where a rough bruise decorated his cheek, and below the eye it had started to bleed.

John grabbed his son, holding him up, but shouted at Beatrice. "Traitor. Treacherous bitch. You're no daughter of mine."

Calmly expressionless, Beatrice watched him. "The kindest words you have ever said to me, Papa." She faced him, snatching his sword from its scabbard. Walking back, she handed the short bladed sword to Alice. "Take it, my lady," Beatrice told her. "Hold it out. You are, in any case, absolutely protected. But if any man dares insult you, please feel free to stab the bastard."

Tyballis had collected the large solid silver platter from the table, walked behind to where her husband had one foot balanced, keeping Charles flat on the ground. She nodded to Andrew. "Poor boy," she smiled. "Let him up, Drew. He's only a young fool after all." Andrew, understanding at once, removed his foot, staring down at Charles.

Charles, half choking and rubbing the side of his face, then staggered to his feet. Immediately Tyballis slammed the silver plate down on his head. The metal was thick and heavy. Charles tumbled, unconscious. The back of his head hit the floorboards with an echoing thump.

Both Bryan and his father John moved back. John now held the sword, he had taken from Bryan, but he held it slack, point to the ground. Both backed off. And then behind them the steward and page, having brought two large copper saucepans and two long carving knives from the kitchen, smashed a saucepan over each of their heads, waved the carving knives in their faces as they lay squirming on the ground, then took the arms of each man and dragged them from the hall, kicking the door shut behind him. The front doors, still wide open, were close enough for them to hoist both men through the opening where they toppled down the two steps into the grounds beyond, and the steward then slammed the doors in their faces. The page brushed his hands together for a job well done, and returned to the hall.

"My lord," he suggested from the doorway, "your two principal visitors have somewhat abruptly left the premises. Now shall I bring light refreshments and a jug of wine for your guests?"

"Indeed, three jugs would be better, I believe, Britle. And thank you indeed. That was a job well done."

Alice was smiling. Not far from her own feet, her son lay, blinking as he began partially to recover consciousness.

"I have not laughed so happily or so long, I think, since Percival invaded my poor father's home."

Doric stared down at Charles. They had not allowed him to stand and he sat like fallen debris on the floor. Doric held his wine cup but offered none to Charles. "Your mother," Doric said, "states that you murdered your father. She does not think that wicked, however, since his own wickedness was too terrible to recount. But it seems that you copied your father's character and adopted his cruelty. Did you also murder your wife? Without accusations of outright murder, it seems that your other actions are dreadful enough that you will remain here, under guard, until I fetch the sheriff and have you arrested."

"You?" Charles snorted. "A stranger, a vagabond, a common street beggar. You know nothing of me, and should no doubt be arrested yourself."

"Sadly, some of that is true," Doric answered, "Yet, you will be horrified to know that I am soon to become your brother-in-law. Louisa has accepted my greatest wish, and we shall be wed at the Abbey in eight day's time. That may seem a sin to you, sir, but your own sins are horrific."

Spluttering, Charles smashed both fists on the ground beside him, eyes crazed with fury. "You'll do no such thing, scum. A penniless beggar will no way enter my family. And that slut is under my control and cannot disobey me."

"Not quite true," Doric smiled, voice soft. "His royal majesty the king has given written permission for us to marry, which I believe somewhat negates your own futile opinions. And while the wedding ceremony takes place, you, sir, will be held in the Tower, or in Newgate. As well as killing your father, you have killed a young woman you barely knew, stringing her up on the scaffold outside the city. And most evil of all, you imprisoned your mother for fourteen long and terrible years, virtually starving her, and keeping her in fear and misery with the obvious intention of holding her until she died. You, sir, are a monster, and will pay dearly for this, in addition to your daily brutality to your young brother and sister, and finally for your outright treason to his highness, King Richard. You will be executed, sir, and no doubt your head severed on the block and then spiked on the south gate of the Bridge, for all to see."

Staring, spluttering, snatching at his collar to loosen it, Charles sat and did not attempt to rise. There was a glaze of unshed tears in his eyes. He started to speak, but could not find the words, and finally hung his head between his legs, refusing to answer.

"I shall leave now," Andrew said, his hand to Tyballis, leading her with him as he left the hall. He turned first to Doric. "Take over, my friend," he said, "and call my steward Britle if there's anything you need. More wine perhaps?" Then turned to Charles. "I shall shortly return with the royal guard and the sheriff of the Ward," he informed him. 'In the meantime, you will remain here, attempt nothing, and await your fate,"

Beatrice sat cheerfully beside the fire and held her hands to the blaze. "What fun it has been," she said, "since leaving my own boring home. You delightful folk present a good deal more entertainment than most."

Now sitting beside her mother, Louisa curled her head to the delicate shoulder and clutched Alice's hand. Doric drained his cup and refilled it as Tyballis walked back through the door.

He had been squatting, immovable, on the ground, back bent, head flopped between his knees, forehead almost to the floorboards, his sword at some distance on the table, and was watched closely. Yet Charles sprang, far quicker than expected, and pulled his knife from the cuff of his doublet. He backed off, knife blade straight out. Tyballis was at the doorway, blocking the escape and Beatrice ran beside her. Francis kicked out at Charles but missed as Charles dashed, head towards the other side of the hall.

Doric, grabbing the surrendered sword, ran directly at Charles' back, with a thrust of the blade that did not miss. The wound bled, but Charles leapt. With one booted foot and the metal hilt of his knife, he smashed through the lower part of the window glass, bending and cracking the mullions as the glass broke and danced in sunlit splinters. Doric ran, lashing out with the long sword. but Charles had disappeared.

Doric rushed outside while Tyballis screamed for the steward. Both Francis and Louisa ran after her to the main doors, while Beatrice kicked out the remaining danger of the glass, and also jumped through the window.

Alice, holding her breath, sat very still. She could hear the shouting and the slap of metal. But after a long hour of virtual silence, she heard the return, led by Tyballis, who was panting.

"The bugger got away," she gasped, unrepentant of her cursing.

Louisa collapsed at her mother's side, half crying, half apologising.

"But the fault is mine," Doric said, marching into the centre of the room. "I was left to watch one of the foulest men in this country, and I failed." He held up the sword he still carried, It dripped fresh blood. "Once in the back, and deep, I think," he said as he pointed to the depth of red smears on the blade. "And in the back of the neck, less deep," he continued, "but perhaps more serious, since the neck is not safe-fleshed. But," his eyes seemed alight, "somehow it seems I let the bastard go. I cannot imagine how I failed with such unholy stupidity."

"I saw his actions," Beatrice said, coming behind. "He was faster than I could have expected. No one saw the first move. We were all watching him, not just you. But none of us expected what happened."

Louisa was still hugging her mother. "Charles is always such a coward. He hits and beats and slaps, but only when he knows he can't be hurt in return. He's never followed any leader in battle. He stays at home. I never, ever would have expected him to leap through a window."

"Let's hope he's badly injured," Francis muttered.

"When Andrew returns," Tyballis said, marching to the wine jug where little remained, "he'll bring the guard or the sheriff's men. They'll set off immediately to look for him."

"And he's injured," Beatrice nodded, sinking back beside the fire. "Sword wounds in back and neck, and whatever cuts he had jumping through that glass."

"For an hour at least, we searched. We searched the grounds fully, back and front, then the roads beyond." Doric sat at some distance, leaning back, legs stretched out, eyes closed. "I must apologise most sincerely," he said softly, but with everyone listening. "That creature has harmed each one of you in some manner, some most horribly abused, and he must be captured and executed for his crimes. It might have been simple. We had him. And I failed to keep him."

"It wasn't your fault," Alice whispered. "You almost recaptured him. He is a beast, as I know full well. He is a coward, that's true. But he is still capable of more than you might suspect. I don't believe murdering his father was an easy business. Percy would have tried to kill him in return. And Charles was only fifteen."

The room sank back into silence as they sat quietly but in miserable regret, for Andrew to return with officers of the law.

CHAPTER THIRTY-NINE

"There's something else disgusting and wicked that Charrles did," Louisa told Doric that night. A small fire sizzled across the hearth, sending light curls of smoke in all directions. On the trivet raised over the fire, two bricks were warming, ready to be thrust beneath the coverings for a cosy warm bed once Louisa was ready to sleep. She was rarely prepared to sleep these days, and grasped Doric's hand, refusing to let him go.

"Tell me then, my love," Doric said. "His list of crimes is already so long, would another, even another murder, make any difference? He cannot be executed twice."

"Not another murder. This time it's rape. I'm not quite sure how long ago, but he raped my poor little nurse Isabella. Probably lots of times and she must have been so frightened. She had a baby. But he was obviously worried about scandal and he took the baby away. She still doesn't know where it went. At least I pray it's alive."

"But your nurse still works for you I believe?" Doric frowned.

"Yes, because she had the courage to tell Charles she'd talk about all his wickedness and he promised she could stay there, still get paid along with a free bedchamber and food, and carry on looking after Francis and myself even when we grew, as long as she kept her mouth shut." Louisa stared miserably into the flare of the flames. "I'm surprised he even cared if people knew. But she knew about killing his father too. That would have been a great deal more serious. But I know she had no idea that my mother was still alive. He managed to keep that secret."

"She told you what Charles had done to her?"

"No." Louisa sipped her wine, still holding tight to Doric's hand. "It was who she calls her brother-in-law, I think he was her sister's husband years ago, but the sister died. Robert and Isabella stayed sort of distant friends. He knew a lot about Charles, and he told me one day when I went to see him. I think Isabella's sister must have told him. But he knew nothing about my mother. No one knew that until we found her."

Doric nodded. "His list of monstrous crimes grows longer. Sadly, lords who bed their servants and then throw them to the streets when they birth a child, are common. I've heard of this often enough, but Charles has gone further. Andrew has informed the king. There are royal guards searching for him as well as the sheriff's men."

"I always thought I had a horrible childhood after my mother died. Well of course, she didn't die but you know what I mean. But my darling mother had far, far worse. And poor Bella, raped over and over by her master, and then having her baby stolen. And you, my beloved. What you told me days ago, that was so sad."

"Strange," Doric said, gazing at her. "That was my nightmare for so long. But now I've spoken about it, the vile memory is fading. It seems so long ago. Less important. What frightened me was the thought that you'd be disgusted. I feared you might not want me anymore. But not only are you still here in my arms, but you make the past fade away,"

"Darling Doric. Only you matter."

"What matters is that Charles escaped. I'll stop raging about it being my fault – although it was. But losing him is unforgivable. Clearly he's not at home?"

"There's a little wine cellar, but I broke the door down some time ago, when Francis got locked in there." Her fingers were twirling the black ribbon of his doublet, tying it and releasing it as she tried to think. "There's all the outbuildings and the gardener's sheds. Where they store the hay the milk buckets. But the guards have searched all of those. He's not there."

Louisa was fully dressed. Doric also. They had not risked lying in bed together since the night they had spent embraced. It was then that Doric had told her why he had run from the monastery.

Now he said, "That night I saw you almost naked. That's the vision I see when I close my eyes. Those infernal priest have gone into the shadows. You, my love, are the light."

She laughed at him, still cuddled tight beside him, his arms around her waist. "Looking at me was so odd, you can't forget? Am I different? Peculiar?"

He stroked his fingers down the front of her gown, tracing the invisible curve of her breasts. Already his desire was itching at him, filling his thoughts. "My dearest beloved, you are quite deliciously beautiful when fully clothed, But undressed, you'll become a swan, a peacock, a rainbow and a smiling golden moon."

"Now you're making music again."

It had been a strange night, wrapped close in each other's arms, her near nakedness the most delicious experience, yet they had not made love. Nor had they made love since. He had caressed the firm circle of her breasts, and felt the magical thrill of her belly, sliding down to where he had not dared explore.

Instead, swept quickly into misery by his confession and the recounting of the nightmare he had never forgotten, he had kissed and adored her, but had gone no further. The telling for the first time in his life of what the two priests at the monastery had done to him, he knew that love-making would come too quickly, bringing him enormous relief but little pleasure for the woman in his arms.

The monastery where he had lived for four years, in training to become a priest himself, had not changed his life with adoration for the church, nor brought the wish to practise that religion himself. Instead the priests, two men older than his father, had held him down, abused, humiliated and raped him night after night until he had

294

escaped. He had informed the abbot on several desperate occasions, but had been punished for slander, and then ignored.

Once turned twelve, overcoming the fear of living in the fields and streets, Doric had taken his old clothes and his lute with him, and left. The Monastery of Saint Eulalia sent out no search parties, and, Doric sighed, no doubt the two aged priests would quickly find some other child to destroy.

"You don't fear me touching you?"

"Why should I? It's what I want. I dream about you touching me. I want you to show me all the secrets about making love."

He had found it difficult to talk about. His heart pumped, his belly lurched and the words stuck in his throat. "You don't - thinking of a lover who has been raped by two old men. It doesn't stop you wanting me? They laughed, enjoying – everything."

But she hadn't known that sometimes men wanted men more than they wanted women. "I just didn't know. Is it wrong?"

"The church says so. But it was men of the church that did it to me, and what I find wrong is forcing a child. Forcing anyone. It took me four years to escape."

She sighed, kissing him, enjoying the rough tickle of his chin. "You didn't go back home?"

"No," he told her. "It was my parents who sent me there. And even if they accepted my story, the abbot, had he wanted me back, which is doubtful, would have come directly to my parent's home and told them I was lying. I took to the road. That abuse haunted me continuously, but I grew happy enough. I loved my music. I enjoyed inventing the tricks of my trade. I told the villagers of anything that came into my head, and sometimes the predictions were right. I adored the freedom."

"But bitterly cold in winter," she shivered.

"There are always sheds in the countryside. Sleeping with cows and horses is warm enough. A little smelly at times, but I got used to that. I probably stank myself."

And now, fully dressed but back in his arms, Louisa asked, "Doric beloved, did you never want revenge against those priests? I would have. I think I might have slipped back in the middle of the night and thrown boiling water at them. Or told the sheriff. Or even stabbed them, if I could."

Doric shrugged. "I thought of it a thousand times. But I had escaped. I never wanted to risk being taken back. And I never wanted to see them again. No sheriff would have listened to a child speaking against men of God. I simply tried to forget."

"But never did."

"I found I loved the freedom." He smiled. "Daisies on the riverbanks, turning green grass to white. Water reflecting the sky, Sunshine on the cobbles like a golden haze over the gutters, making ugly into beauty. Breezes in the reeds. The life of the leaves with fluttering green turning to brilliance, russet and scarlet, crimson and mustard, the bay trees and leaves becoming spices, Then tired and old, crinkling as they wave goodbye and fly from their branches, joining the birds. The shrill complaints of winter but then the buds, the shoots opening, the blossom awaiting new leaves. Sun on my face again. Soft showers in spring. That's freedom. I loved the freedom."

"That's – beautiful. Will you miss it, Doric?" She pulled tighter on his ribbons, as if frightened he might leap away and rush back to the countryside.

"Love changes freedom," Doric said. "Now all that freedom seems empty. A life without meaning."

Her fingers clutched so hard at the knots in the ribbons, they began to unravel. "I won't ever stop you doing things, my love. I love your music. Your singing makes me laugh and cry and opens doors into new ideas. Go back and walk in the country. Keep your freedom."

He shook his head, wishing he could play with the ribbons beneath her arm where her bodice was tight tied, as she was doing to him. Instead he frowned. "It's not freedom I'm thinking of, my love. It's rape. No – not even that. It's cruelty. The priests – your father – your brother. And a thousand others. Why does Charles enjoy cruelty? Why does anyone? A sense of power? Perhaps to hide their own cowardice?"

She thought a moment, her fingers pausing. "Because his father was cruel to him? It's like revenge on the world."

With a sudden deep exhale, Doric straightened. "So we go to find her."

"Pardon?" Louisa stared.

"The lost child. Boy or girl? I think you told me the child was a daughter. Do you know her name?"

Suddenly excited, Louisa abandoned the ribbons and flung both arms around Doric's neck. "It's a girl and her name's Gisella. What a wonderful idea. I'd so love to do that, and I can just imagine taking the little girl to Isabella. It would be wonderful." The excitement faded a little, replaced by doubt. "But Doric darling, I don't know how old the girl might be. I don't even know if she's alive. And where n earth would we start looking?"

"I know exactly where to start," Doric told her, "since Charles is a man of little or no imagination. It may not work. Though we can try." He had begun to stand, then sat back, his embrace tightening again. "But I cannot take you, my dearest. We are unmarried. To travel together is unwise. Last time we'd planned a handfasting. But this time our wedding is planned for some days off. I think, my love, I should travel with Francis."

Louisa grunted. "That's a terrible idea," she complained. "Perhaps I can go with Beatrice. She always likes doing the unexpected. Just tell us where to go."

"Just two women? You'll need guards."

"That's a shame," as she had been imagining wild adventure and the final thrill as the little girl was discovered. "After all, I've travelled with just Bella before. All the way into the tanneries. And just with Francis. I've never been used to grand cavalcades or streams of armed guards or anything. Actually, I've always had to creep out because Charles would never have let me go if he'd known, so whenever I went out except to church, I crept away without him seeing."

"And I assume you won't tell Bella since you might fail, and she'd be devastated."

"And I want the success to be a wonderful surprise."

"Then," Doric said after a pause, "You take Casper."

※◇※

"You wants Fryerning *again?*" Casper objected. "That there same village? Ain't we more or less just got back?"

"I'm looking for someone," Louisa told him with polite insistence, but not wishing to be more specific.

"And I am coming too," Beatrice told him.

Casper snorted. "Then you doesn't need me, missus," he said.

"Actually," said Tyballis from the chair by the fire, "I think I shall come too."

"In what case," said Casper immediately, "reckon I'll be coming after all."

The last day of November dismissed the dawn and instead chose a storm which hid everything else. Lightening forked through the pelting water and the thunder sounded like the rage if the old gods.

"Reckon we has to wait fcr tomorrow," Casper smiled.

Louisa shook her head. "I have a very good cloak," she said, "with a hood. And I hate having good ideas delayed."

"The rain doesn't worry me," insisted Beatrice.

"I quite like the rain," agreed Tyballis. "Everything gets refreshed and the countryside smells reborn afterwards."

This reminded Louisa of what Doric had explained about freedom. "Then let's get our cloaks, and have the horses saddled," she said with renewed enthusiasm.

Casper glowered. "Reckon all you females is pickle-brained," he muttered as he sauntered off to the stables.

Riding north, the last triumphant clap of thunder echoed in the distance, the rain shrank back into sunlit drops and gradually stopped. The clouds faded into mist and a vast smudge of rainbow shimmered across the smiling sky. The arch of colour honed, and the promise clarified.

It was a long ride into Essex, the horse's hooves kicked up slush, the mud in the puddles, and the splash of soaked cow dung. Yet

298

following the winding road leading up the hill to the village where they wished to start their search led them to the inn before midnight, and the women crowded in through the closing doorway. Casper wandered off to sleep above the stables.

Sharing the bedchamber, Tyballis, Louisa and Beatrice ordered wine and fig-cake brought up to them, then questioned the maid.

"A girl, a baby, stolen from her mother," Louisa explained. "But I don't know how long ago. As much as fifteen years perhaps, but as little as nine or ten. She could have been put into service or given to a family without children. Her name was Gisella, but that might have been changed."

The maid pursed her lips. "Them little souls wivout no farthers," she said with faint disapproval, "they gets took to the convent. That be the big house down past the old ruined tower. Them nuns is good folk and takes in babes wot no one else wants."

Not having known there was a convent nearby, the women cheered considerably, enjoyed their wine and cake, and slept well, dreaming of orphans, nuns and of turning cruelty to joy.

"I was told – once," Louisa murmured, "that not all houses of God are places of charity and worship. I mean, there can be wickedness too. How can you be wicked as a priest? Or a nun?"

"I've met few of either," Beatrice said. "But I've met good men and bad, even in my own family."

Tyballis glanced at Louisa in the candlelight, wondering what the story might be behind such a sudden remark. "I've heard of monks raping nuns," she said. "And of monks attending brothels. As for the nuns themselves, I know nothing. But I hope we might discover true happiness tomorrow."

CHAPTER FORTY

"I am hoping," Isabella told her new companion, "that young Louisa will come back to see us one day. She is such a kind and darling girl."

With the bitter chill outside sneaking in under the door with a whistle, both women sat rather huddled, their cloaks around their shoulders and their noses hidden beneath kerchiefs. With neither the lord, the young lady, nor even Master Francis at home, only the steward remained to keep order. All the usual duties were maintained as always, but a certain laxity had crept in, just like the draughts. With Lord Charles watching every detail as though he floated from chandeliers to fire hearths to stairways and doorways, there had never previously been one moment to rest. Without him, the pace had halved.

Yet permanently lacking specific jobs of any kind, Isabella and Annie were wondering whether they should have stayed in bed.

"I had thought I might grind the rosemary with the mint," Isabella said without moving.

Sitting equally firm, Annie added, "I had a right good idea last night and I reckons I could start me own brewery here. Just a little 'un o'course since I ain't got no help. But I could do a bit on me own.

T'wer a good brew wot we made, Joletta and me. I likes to keep busy."

But neither of them had moved for the last two hours as the wind rattled the windows and the broken door to the wine cellar outside, slammed open and then shut with a resounding crash.

"Someone ought to fix that," decided Isabella, and Annie nodded.

It was not long afterwards when another crash interrupted their thoughts and after a moment, they both looked up in considerable surprise as they heard a small but determined knock on their door.

No one ever knocked on their door. With a slight tremble, Isabella stared, stood, and, pulling it open to the shadowed landing half way up the servants' back stairs.

A young girl stood shivering in the candlelight. Sweet, round faced and light haired, she appeared roughly eight or nine years of age, but extremely nervous. Behind her, and holding the candle, Louisa stood, covered by a heavy cloak. The girl was also cloaked, but beneath that she wore a threadbare smock of unbleached linen.

"Oh, you poor little lass," Isabella said, taking the child's arm. "You must be frozen. Come on in. In truth, we are cold too, but we have a little fire, and some steaming hypocrass to share." She looked up, questioning, at Louisa. "My dear, have you brought the child for us to look after? Is she an orphan, poor girl?"

"Not exactly." Louisa followed the girl into the bedchamber. "Her name is Gisella, and I believe she is your daughter."

Although lighter haired and naturally a good deal younger, the child had a look of her father.

Isabella stared at Louisa, then at the shivering child, and finally at Louisa once more. She promptly burst into tears. "It can't be," she sobbed. "How could you know? How could anyone know?" At first, she appeared to be falling but instead Isabella leaned over and wrapped her arms around the child, suffocating her and weeping into her wet stringy hair. Although still crying loudly, she managed to splutter into the little girl's face, kissed it roundly several times and asked, "Is it true my own sweet beloved? Are you really my daughter?"

Gisella had neither voice nor any idea of the truth. It was Louisa who said, "Your brother-in-law Robert told me what Charles had done. And strangely enough it was Doric who said we must find your little girl. I had no idea where we might start to look, but he suggested back near the tower where I was born, as a place Charles knew well. I expect you know about the convent. We went there and asked. Knowing Gisella's name was a great help, and we said the child would have been brought on the authority of Lord Charles Hylton. They knew at once. Poor Gisella was working in the kitchens. But she's utterly puzzled to discover her mother after more than eight years."

"I thought the nuns were my mothers," Gisella mumbled, extricating her mouth from the embrace. Her feet now rose from the ground as Isabella hauled her up tighter.

"It is me, my own precious," Isabella said through her tears as Annie watched in delight, although also crying, reminded now, and remembering the loss of her own daughter.

Louisa left quietly, slipping away down the back stairs to where Tyballis, Beatrice and Casper were waiting, still mounted, and well cloaked against the cold.'

"It's funny," Louisa said as she mounted her own horse and turned back out along the hedged pathway to the Strand, riding west and then north., "but I was just about to say, 'Good. All done. Let's go home.' But it's my home I'm leaving, which is crazy. Dear Lady Leys, it seems I feel more at home in your home than I do in my own."

"Only if you call me Tyballis," she answered, "and forget the lady business. I haven't even got used to being a lady myself. "

"She don't even like me calling her a lady," Casper shouted back over his shoulder, "wot is bloody daft if you asks me."

"Now Isabella has her daughter back, and a friend in Annie," Louisa smiled to herself, threading her gloved fingers through her horse's mane. "And I have left him, so has Francis, and our beloved mother is free and happy, I hope, and looking more beautiful every day. I feel I've become quite a traveller. I'm going to marry Doric and not that horrid Bryan, and Charles himself has had to run away and hide or he'll be arrested. His life of cruelty has almost been wiped away. The list can't grow longer anymore."

Looking over as they neared her own great manor house, Tyballis turned her horse towards the opening to the grounds, past the swinging gate, and smiled at Louisa. "He will be executed, my dear. You know that, don't you. But not only is it well deserved, you'll not suffer from your brother's reputation, for you'll be Mistress Fleet and no longer Lady Hylton."

"Actually," laughing although without the slightest intention of relating the whole story, Louisa said, "Its not his real name, you know. I mean Doric. He changed it when he went on the road. He's actually a Matthew. Matthew Attlewood. I like the name, but I'll always think of him as Doric. I'll never be able to call him Matthew, just like you won't let me call you Lady Leys."

Riding into the courtyard which flanked the stables, Tyballis, Louisa and Beatrice dismounted as the grooms rushed to take the reins and lead the horses off for food, water and combing. But Tyballis turned again to Louisa. "Attlewood. I've heard that name somewhere." She looked over to Beatrice. "You're a more practised lady, my dear. Do you know the name?"

"I do," Beatrice said, "but I daresay there are plenty of them around. Is it common? Like Stafford and Stanley? I've no idea. But this trip has been gloriously successful, and today it can rain and squall all it likes, I'm as happy as a squire when his master is knighted."

Before reaching the front doors, Louisa felt herself encircled, both Doric's arms slipping up beneath her cloak to wrap around her waist, feeling her heartbeat quicken and pound. He kissed the back of her ear, "I know, my love. A glorious success."

"Not my success. Yours. You told us where to look."

"It was simply a first probability. Charles surely knows no other place where he might be so readily accepted and have no need to explain his reasons."

"There's a convent there. At the bottom of the hill on the other side from the old tower, and that's where he'd left the baby. She was still there, poor little thing, not abused but not loved either. Now she'll be so loved, she'll be squashed breathless into milled flour."

"And hopefully," Doric led Louisa into the warmth of the main hall, "she'll never meet her father."

As the others followed, Louisa said very softly "It's funny having such a mixed up family. My own brother so cruel. My father perhaps worse. My little brother is a darling and my mother is wonderful and kind and clever and beautiful. But I keep thinking of when we first saw her. I don't know how she was still alive. Just bony sticks and too weak to stand."

"And would have died within the month."

Andrew was kissing his wife, and Tyballis was glowing like the ashes in the fire. No draughts, the hall was warm and sizzled with flames across the hearth, candle splutter, steaming jugs and the sweet perfume of wax, burning logs and the spiralling smoke finding paths up into the vaulted ceiling.

Beatrice, with no husband or lover, sat meekly and alone on her favourite chair. "I have been wondering," she said, although the four others were barely listening, "whether my own father and brother should be denounced for treason. They backed Buckingham's absurd behaviour without much fervour, you know. I don't love either of them. I don't even like them. But as long as I don't live there, perhaps I can forgive."

"I shall never speak of them," Tyballis promised, sitting on the opposite chair. "It's not my business, Beatrice. Yet Andrew and I, we both work for his majesty, you know, and that includes denouncing traitors."

Hands clasped behind his back, Francis stood at the long window, staring out at the bleak and darkening weather. "We ought to concentrate on our own lives," he said, "not everyone else's. I don't mean not to help. Finding Mamma was magical. Miraculous, thank the Lord God and all the saints. And thanking you and Doric, Louisa. Not that you actually went off with that in mind. And finding Bella's little girl in the convent, that was so good too. But I never had a chance to be anything or anyone with Charles around."

"You're only fourteen."

"You told me once, Lou, about boys going off to war at fourteen. I want to go on a crusade or fight for my king or something. Maybe I ought to go to university. Like a special school, I think. There's one in Oxford, you know. They teach you things.- I've never even been taught swordsmanship."

"You'll be lord of the house, when you decide to go back there." Beatrice looked up at him. "Charles will be under arrest. You'll be the heir, Lord of Hylton and a very rich lord at that. How does it sound? Francis Grange, Earl of Hylton. That beautiful house will be all yours. Isn't that enough?"

After a short pause while he digested this sudden realisation, Francis began to sparkle. "Maybe", he said. "And I'll get married one day and his majesty will come to visit, and I'll have hundreds of children."

"You'd better find a very patient and domesticated wife."

"If I'm so rich," he decided, "getting a wife will be easy." He looked searchingly at Louisa. "How rich is Charles, anyway?"

She didn't have any idea. "Ask Mamma, but not at the moment. She's in her bedchamber, fast asleep. Poor darling is still very weak."

"I'll go up," Tyballis said, "and see if she's awake, and if she needs help with anything."

Louisa whispered to Doric, "It's too cold to walk in the garden," she mumbled, "but I want to talk. To tell you something, just a little bit important."

Doric was still standing, and took Louisa's hand. "We can't go far. Supper's about to be served. Come onto the stairs and speak to me."

She supposed that would be time enough and followed him from the hall to the grand carpeted stairs. Here she promptly sat on the fifth step, Doric sat beside her legs on the fourth, his arms crossed on her knees as he smiled up at her. "Tell me."

"I don't know if you even really wanted to know, and I don't know a thing about your girlfriend before you met me. And I wouldn't even want to think about you with her and what you did with her, except I know she was killed and that must have been shocking and horrible. And Tyballis whispered to me while we were searching for Giseella, that you once thought Casper might have done it. So I started talking to Casper as we rode home. And he told me."

"I hope," Doric smiled faintly, "you did not tell him I suspected him?"

"I'm stupid, but not that stupid," Louisa said. "I just asked him what happened to her. He said she was a trollop. Was she?"

"I suppose so." His smile was studied.

"He said he saw her go off with the local mayor, and the mayor took her into the graveyard. Then he heard the priest run out of the church, shouting and complaining. Casper thought it was funny so he peeped around the corner and saw the priest and the mayor both fighting, and the girl in the middle, and the mayor bringing out a knife, and the priest hitting them both over the head with a big wooden cross. And he didn't know any of them, nor you either back then, so he left them to struggle and walked off. Casper didn't see the end but – well – he thought they were all ridiculous. I'm sorry, that's not a good word to say about murder – but you know Casper."

Doric nodded. "And you believed him?"

"It seemed convincing." Louisa bent and kissed his cheek. "It must have been horrid for you when you found her, and I know you got blamed. But Casper didn't know any of those people so there wasn't any point making it up, but evidently, he told Andrew ages ago. And Andrew believes him."

"But Andrew employs him. They have a partnership."

"Andrew isn't stupid either," Louisa said, wriggling her legs closer to him. "And he's always accepted it wasn't you. He wouldn't have employed you, would he, if he thought you were a killer?"

"He purposefully employs killers," said Doric softly. "But I trust him. I might even say I've grown to love him. And his wife. Casper? Perhaps even him. And living here, with you so often in my arms, is the greatest love I've ever known."

"You didn't love Lizzie?" She blushed.

"No, never. We used each other. When we argued, she went back to the streets. She was a whore and I was a cheat and a liar and a wandering vagabond."

Having ignored both his laughter and his words, Louisa added, "And Casper says you sometimes give good predictions. So predict something for me."

He was clasping her legs now, his hands around her thighs over the silken skirts and the thick linen of her shift below. "I can predict that you'll be wondrously happy with your loving husband for many glorious years."

"Oh pooh, that's just you being romantic," Louisa said. "So predict for Andrew and Tyballis."

"First a girl. Then a boy. A year away." He was still grinning.

"And the king?"

Doric frowned. "There is something wrong. A great black wall surrounds him. I see him galloping across the fields. He holds a battle axe. But I feel pain. Misery of some kind. I can't see the climax." He looked up. "Besides, it is doubtless all the greatest nonsense. I've no desire to see the king injured, and I believe little of my own visions. Anyway," he smiled again, "I can hear supper being served."

"They have a good cook here, better than we had at home." Louisa brightened, dismissing Doric's words. "We'll have to get a good cook, dearest, when we're married. Perhaps we can steal this one."

Standing, Doric led Louisa down the few steps and towards the hall. But he stopped abruptly. "You do know, my beloved, that I have virtually no money, and only the lodgings outside the Abbey sanctuary."

"I don't care," answered Louisa. "Francis will let us live there. He'll be rich. And it doesn't matter anyway because you've just predicted how happy we'll be."

CHAPTER FORTY-ONE

Without crown, sceptre or throne, King Richard sat behind the small table, his scrolls and paper, quills, ink pots and bowls of sand spread across the trestle before him. But he leaned back, his hands clasped behind his head. He was smiling. "You've been busy, sir."

"As I invariably choose to be," Andrew said, "and always in your service, sire."

"And your faithful minstrel, is he waiting outside? Very well, bring him in. I imagine this will be a tale of some length. Undoubtedly he has been involved at every stage since you travelled to Brittany."

"Indeed he has, sire, and with considerable skill."

"I like the man, and admire his many talents," Richard said. "After this marriage takes place, I may arrange a gift of property. Or title? Would the boy appreciate either?"

Andrew nodded, his smile wide. "He has no home except the small lodging I rented for him when he began working for me."

"Then," his highness said, "Once the ceremony is passed, I shall decide on my gift. If he is to continue working for you, sir, then he should live nearby."

It was a small chamber, candle lit even by day during the bleak colourless chill of winter, but used frequently when his majesty conducted private and necessary business. Andrew had been here on many occasions, though assumed that Doric had not. The chair beyond the little table, used by his majesty alone, was deeply set, high backed, and wide armed, with a tapestry cushion depicting the arrival of the three kings on Twelfth Night.

Facing the table were more chairs, eight at least, but lacking cushion or height, yet of wood both smoothed and polished and designed for comfort. Several rugs decorated both the walls and the floor, and the candle sconces were carved. There was, however, no rug immediately in front of the table, for this was where someone would be required to kneel, should he be brought to answer to his king for some crime or misdemeanour.

But at present, no man knelt there, and Andrew sat straight backed but comfortable.

"Then I shall call for wine," his highness informed Andrew, "and all you have described to me, sir, I will now discover from others. That shall be the crimes of a nobleman I barely know, who holds no position of power, yet has been seeking to undermine my own, and presumably bring to the throne some more easily influenced monarch who will befriend him. The royal guard are on the watch and have been searching for this creature for some days. Once captured, I shall order the trial of Charles Grange, Earl of Hylton, and will await the result before signing the death warrant, and then remove all rights to his title, goods and land. But first – who is this man, capable of such dishonour, cruelty and treason? Sir Harold Harcourt and Sir John Sudbury will be brought here shortly as witnesses, although I shall not permit John Sudbury to leave freely. He will be held until this wretched Earl of Hylton is found. In the meantime, my friend, I hope to find this a conversation of some interest."

The wine had been brought, but although Andrew drained his cup, both Doric and the king himself sipped as they talked.

Shortly after, the arrival of all concerned was announced. Now behind the royal chair stood three guards, unmovable, waiting for their king's demands. Andrew sat opposite, Doric standing behind, both hands to the high back of his chair. To his majesty's right, sat the Duke of Norfolk, quietly examining his wine cup as he listened to a story entirely new to him. Behind him stood two guards of his household. Between Andrew and the small table, Sir John Sudbury knelt, not daring to speak until ordered.

Harold Harcourt was brought in by another of the royal guards and remained standing, ordered to recount his part of the story.

"Your gracious highness, ever since your glorious coronation and your acceptance of the crown, I have been further threatened by the Earl of Hylton. He claimed my property while I was under suspicion of dishonourable dealings with one Bob Brickster, who was later convicted of treason and corruption. But although Brickster was sentenced to death, your majesty, I was found entirely innocent of all crimes. Yet Hylton refused to return the deeds to my property and claimed the right to do so under the old laws still standing. But then, sire, your own intention to change that specific law was announced. The country listened with gratitude and approval, sire, when the news was spread, stating that in future a criminal's property could only be taken from him and claimed by another once he was found guilty and sentenced to hang. We all cheered, your highness, when we heard that in future an innocent man could not be improperly deprived of his goods. And I bless you for it, sire, it has changed so many lives. Your highness's new laws have brought joy to all your citizens. The Earl of Hylton continued to threaten me, and even after your royal intentions were widely circulated, he harassed me. But I held to my rights according to your new laws, sire, and have not heard from Hylton for several months."

Harcourt was thanked and led out. Sudbury remained kneeling.

His royal majesty now ignored Sudbury and spoke quietly to Norfolk, Leys, and occasionally to Doric. They were four, yet the king watched Sudbury's lowered face as Charles Grange, Earl of Hylton, was discussed at length.

In conversation, each party calculating each remark and watching, wary, for its reception, Richard used strategies of battle, siege and defensive palisade, with a general's sharp judgement of character and motive. Beginning with diplomacy as all wars must, Richard imposed an atmosphere as relaxed as each man's distrust allowed him. And therefore, although it was the list of Hylton's crimes that was the subject of all conversation, Sudbury knew that he was equally the subject, and when abruptly asked the final question, he broke down and confessed.

"What has been said concerning my friend, Earl of Hylton," he sobbed, "has all been the truth, your royal majesty. But I swear I have not been involved in any of this abuse towards his family and in particular his parents, whom I have never met. Nor did I know a thing about Master Harcourt, sire. But as a poor man, since my knighthood was earned at Townton, fighting for your brother, sire, but which brought neither property nor position, I was deeply troubled that I had nothing for my son to inherit, nor anything of value to enjoy, even for myself. My marriage brought me a little, including my home, but it was when I became acquainted with Charles Grange that my sins began. I apologise with all my heart, your majesty, but when Charles offered me both his sister and younger brother as husband and wife to my children if I agreed to back the Buckingham rebellion and claim Henry Tudor as rightful king, I was wickedly tempted. May the good lord forgive me, I held no such view, and never had the slightest intention of fighting against your majesty. Nor did I. But I sinfully proclaimed myself a traitor in order to gain mighty profitable unions for my son and daughter." Still kneeling, his hands were together in supplication, but the king did not smile. "Forgive me, I beg of your royal majesty," Sudbury pleaded. "I was overcome by greed, but I never intended to honour that treasonous statement. It was a lie, my king. A stupid and sinful lie."

"For which you may be executed, sir," the king said softly and without expression. "But I shall not sign the warrant until after your trial. You will naturally be called as witness when the Earl of Hylton is brought to trial, and how you behave at that time may ensure your own fate, sir."

"I swear, sire, I shall speak the truth and denounce that traitor before the court."

"Take him away," said the king.

Andrew stood, and bowed. "I can only hope we find the man soon, sire. But I have no idea where he might be. His original home in Essex has been thoroughly searched. An interesting building, I gather. Naturally also his home in The Strand. The city too – far and wide. There is as yet no sign of him."

"My men are searching further afield," sighed the king. "I presume it will take some time to find such a man."

His majesty's official chamber was slowly left vacant as each man, accompanied by his guards, left the room, and Sudbury was led off, his arms forcefully held behind him.

Andrew and Doric strode the wide palace corridor. "My own concentration is more selfish, my lord," Doric smiled. "I believe today is the fourth day of December."

Andrew grinned. "It is indeed. And soon it shall be St. Stephen's day, my friend, the first day of the Christmas season each year and this year it will be the day of your wedding. I and my wife shall certainly be watching as you stand on the porch steps of Westminster Abbey, gazing at young Louisa Grange, and take her as your wife."

"I have one small problem," Doric admitted. "And I'm somewhat concerned. It would be utterly ludicrous to marry first, and then find that the marriage is illegal."

Andrew raised one eyebrow. "You are expecting to be taken to trial yourself, my dear boy? I ordered Casper to speak with Louisa, you know, concerning the truth he'd seen shortly before the girl Elizabeth was murdered last summer. You are no longer under suspicion, you know."

Shaking his head, Doric marched from the palace beside Andrew, heading for the royal stables where their horses waited. "No, not that. Poor Lizzie, but one of the few, vile is fortunes where I wasn't guilty in any sense, but instead profited by meeting you, and then Louisa. An indirect cause for guilt, perhaps, but not the reason I believe my marriage may be declared illegal."

"Already married, although not to Elizabeth, I gather?" Andrew waited, then added, "Time to confess, and quickly, my friend."

"Simply my name," said Doric, staring back without embarrassment. "When I left to play the minstrel and wander the countryside, I hid my name. I naturally avoided being discovered. Doric Fleet is a name I invented."

"A man who does not exist," Andrew frowned, "cannot be legally wed to a woman who does. What the devil is your real name?"

He wanted to deny it, to say only that it didn't matter, but he was sure that Andrew would insist. So he replied meekly, "Matthew. But I prefer Doric."

"And –?"

Shrugging, Doric admitted, "Matthew Attlewood. An absurd name, But I imagine it's a name I need to adopt again, if the marriage is to be legal. Louisa already knows since I confessed to her sometime ago. So, I suppose poor Doric disappears, except in private."

"Attlewood?" repeated Andrew. "How interesting."

CHAPTER FORTY-TWO

"How can I tell you, my dear Louisa, just how grateful I am?"
Louisa held her nurse's hand and smiled. "You should never have lost your daughter, Bella dear. That was wicked. The whole thing was wicked. I just tried to make the past turn out a little better for a change. Charles is a brute and a monster and an unbelievable beast. How have I lived with him for eighteen years? I knew he was vile, but the worst things I never knew. What he did to you. Killing his own father. And what he did to poor Mamma."

"My own beloved little Louisa," Isabella continued, "Thanks to you, my sweet, my whole life has changed. I have a good friend in Annie, and I have my own wonderous baby girl back to hold and love." She paused one moment, wringing her hands. "I was just wondering, my dearest, if you were hoping, in return for such great kindness, if I might leave this house now I have my own little family. I have a place to go, you know, if you would prefer that."

"Good gracious," gaped Louisa in shock. "Definitely and absolutely not. You're my lovely nurse and I've loved you since I was born. And your little girl looks like a darling, and she deserves some comfort too. What ever made you think such a thing?"

"As it happens," Isabella was blushing a little, a pink tinge across her cheeks, "it was dear Robert who suggested it might possibly be true. He's quite right of course, I live here and sleep and eat in considerable luxury, but with the agreement of Lord Charles since I promised – well, dear, you know what I promised. And now that promise doesn't count anymore. So Robert suggested that if I had to leave, he would be very happy if Gisella and I went to live with him. I said I would consider the matter."

"But," Louisa objected, "that tiny little tenement room is too small for him alone, let alone the three of you."

"There would be certain compensations," said Isabella with vague embarrassment. "You see, although he is my brother-in-law and was once married to my elder sister, poor dear, and to marry the husband of your sister is considered a terrible sin, I have heard of it happening. And since only few folk would have the slightest idea of our relationship, we thought a simple hand-fasting would bring great happiness. We are very fond of each other you know."

"I gathered that." She frowned. "I don't think it's incest, since you don't share the same bloodline. Is it really a sin? He's not your real brother."

"No, certainly not. Yet I believe it would be most improper. But," and she giggled with undisguised anticipation, "I would be so delighted. I feel – well, you know, my dear. And he never had children since his wife died in childbirth before the little girl even took a breath. So he says he will call himself Gisella's long lost Papa, and we can all live together."

"Perhaps," Louisa was starting to wonder whether sin was a natural part of the Grange and Hylton family, "You could pretend that your poor sister and Robert weren't ever truly married?"

Hands fidgeting in the large pocket of her apron, Isabella nodded eagerly. "A good thought, my dear, and will put Gisella's mind at rest when she grows."

"Then you can all live here," Louisa said with determination. "How could I lose my gorgeous nurse just when she recovers her daughter? And Robert is a very nice man too. Besides, that tenement room is hideous, please get rid of it. You are all welcome here and I won't tell anyone that Robert is your brother-in-law. I don't care and after every wicked thing Charles has done in his life, why would I care about sisters and brothers? This way you can stay friends with Annie, or she'd be left alone."

"She's out with Gisella now," Isabella said. "They have gone to the market. Gisella loves going out. I have bought her a new gown, bright red to go with her big smiles."

Remembering the stench of the tenement bordering the tannery, remembering the tiny space, the curtain of old torn and stained material, the straw bed and the tiny central fire stifling the room with its smoke, Louisa asked, "Was Robert so poor he could only rent that slum?"

Hanging her head a little, Isabella sighed. "When dear Mary was alive, they lived in a little house in one of the back lanes near Cripplegate. Robert was a builder. He earned well enough and the house was cosy. But when Mary died and the baby with her, Robert seemed to change. As if he wanted to be destitute and couldn't live in a house where his wife and child died before his eyes. But now – of mistress Louisa, you should see him now. He's like a man reborn. I am so proud to be the cause of that."

"Go and get him. I want to see that sparkle," Louisa said. She wondered if some larger space amongst the servants' quarters could be adjusted. Three bedchambers if Annie was to be included. Even a little space for a community room where the family could gather. "I am," she said to herself, "becoming quite a competent little organiser. As if I was already in charge here."

Francis and Louisa had returned home the night before. As the deep wet morning bloomed, and dawn peeped through the clouds, it was the fifth day of December, and her last day as an unmarried woman. She ran back upstairs, calling to Francis.

The wind was blowing the smoke back down the chimneys and all across London and Westminster the pages were rushing to clean up the small messes left by the hounds now they were kept indoors, and the maids ran to sweep up the flying ashes and soot. Each morning, unless the rain poured unceasingly, the hounds were let out to run and hopefully empty their bowels outside. They ran excitedly, frantically wagging tails, yapping and pushing, delighted with the prospect of freedom as the doors were opened for them. Then as they poked their quivering noses out into the squall of wind, the slash of the furious rain angled into their faces, and the sudden roll of thunder, their tails would abruptly hang limp and all of them would turn and push back into the warm, hurrying back to the great fires where they would curl comfortably or run cheerfully to piddle and shit in the corners.

One of the younger dogs, ears briskly alert, was cradled on Alice's lap. Her fingers slid through its pale coat and scratched beneath its chin. It was trying to lick her fingers, but however it turned its head, her fingers kept dodging out of reach.

"Percival didn't like animals," Alice said. "I adopted a kitten out by the barn. The mother had given birth to several, but a fox had taken two. So I took the third inside with me and the mother followed. Percy never knew because he never came to my room. He expected me to go to him and when I did not, he sent a page to fetch me."

"There was," suggested Tyballis, "a considerable number of years between your first and second born, my dear. "Did you manage to escape your husband so often?"

Alice smiled at the puppy curled on her lap. "I was thirteen when Charles was born, and remained ill for some time. I conceived children, but then lost them. The midwife told Percival to leave me alone, and for some time he did. He had mistresses enough in the village, I'm sure. I believe he forgot about me after a few years. When he forced me back to his bed, I did not conceive. When I became heavy with dearest Louisa, I was most surprised. I was absurdly pleased, for Charles had been taken from me long since. I had even been frightened that if I proved of no use to Percival, he would have me thrown from the top of the tower. But no, I gave birth to my beautiful daughter. And because she was a little girl and of no interest to Percival, I was able to keep her beside me for some years. One soft loving tabby cat, one delicious black kitten that used to climb my bed curtains when tiny, and a gorgeous baby girl of my own."

Beatrice was laughing. Tyballis said, "Six years between, I think?"

"Indeed. It seemed longer at the time." Alice had few happy memories. The birth of her daughter was one of the few. "Oh dear yes, the pain and the fear and afterwards Percy's disdain when he visited me to see my daughter. But then there was bliss. My daughter suckling, my baby in my arms. Years of uncomplicated comfort. It was a beautiful old castle before Percy died."

She had no wish to speak longer, for when the birth of her last child gave her husband a second boy, he took his family to the new grandeur in The Strand and locked his wife away.

"And four, nearly five years after that, you discovered that your husband was dead. But instead of returning to your family, your imprisonment continued." Beatrice leaned over Alice, kissing where the skin was fresh, new and plump. "But that was nearly ten years gone. How I would love to kill Charles. Wouldn't you? I'd slice him to bits, but from the bottom up so he wouldn't die too quickly."

"I don't want to think about it." Alice murmured, again staring yet not even seeing the now sleeping hound on her lap.

Tyballis stood, breaking the newly bleak atmosphere. "I have to go to Drew's old house beyond the Tower," she said, brushing down her skirts. "Casper is taking me, as Andrew is in conference with the king, and Doric is speaking to Brampton concerning the present condition of old King Edward's two bastard boys. Alice, my dear, I'm quite sure you will be comfortable here, since I believe travel at this stage is not a good idea."

Looking up, Beatrice said, "I could keep Lady Hylton company. But, in fact I should like to accompany you, Lady Leys."

"Too many ladies," Alice sighed. "I am simply Alice. And please travel with dear Tyballis. I shall doze by the fire and shut down every memory from the past. My life began when Louisa and her young man burst into my prison and changed everything. Before that, I refuse to remember. I was not – alive."

Tyballis was grinning. "My newborn friend, I am simply delighted to know you. For a child of your age, you are indeed quite remarkable."

"And more beautiful every day," Beatrice said.

"Which is true," Tyballis whispered as they left the Leys Manor, hurrying out into the cold, their cloaks wrapped in voluminous billows around them and their huge fur collars up to their chins while the fur lined hoods slipped down over their eyes. "Each day she seems a little sleeker, her big beautiful blue eyes brighten, her chin disappears into flesh instead of being a tiny pointed bone, and her fingers dance instead of trailing like spills for lighting the fire."

"I am amazed," Beatrice nodded, "that such starvation and mistreatment did not kill her years earlier. At least that vile man must have brought her food sometimes, but it was still a form of torture. But now," mounting her own horse, "I shall have the pleasure of seeing your own home."

Behind them, Casper rode, puffing clouds of condensation from his mouth into the freezing air. The horses shook their manes, snorting as they were brought from their warm stables and soon were riding east.

"Once a grand home," Tyballis told her. "But that must have been many years ago. I never saw anything but a ruined slum, but it still stays open for those who need a free home, Drew has often spoken of having it knocked down, and building something new. But it's too close to the tanneries to ever be a beautiful mansion."

The gulls were screeching, flying up from the estuary and squabbling along the river banks, but Tyballis still avoided the Thames and its Bridge, keeping to the lanes beyond the cheaps, and heading towards the Tower, its white Keep rising like a washed cloud within the rain.

"I'm interested," Beatrice told her. "I still remember how the tannery stinks."

They approached the Aldgate, but the horses were plodding, their hooves kicking up showers. "I promised Louisa I'd go to visit the girl Eva, who sleeps at the house most nights. I am hoping at this time of day, she'll be there. Louisa wishes to invite her to the grand feast Andrew and I have arranged for tomorrow after the wedding." She laughed. "I should warn you that Eva is an unrepentant trollop. There are so many girls who have no choice. Starve, or sell themselves on the back streets. But she and Louisa grew a small friendship."

"Now that," Beatrice grinned, "is a delightful idea. I've never met a whore before. Or at least, not knowingly."

"Whereas I," Tyballis laughed, "have known several, and mostly at Andrew's home. Whole collections of prostitutes. Not a wonderful attribute for the man I fell in love with."

With polite silence, Beatrice ignored this admission. "Your husband is a remarkable man, Lady Leys."

Tyballis laughed again. "They needed a free place to sleep and he needed anyone he could trust to bring him information. He has always worked for the king, you know, long before the king was a king. He is still a gatherer of knowledge, commonly known as a spy. Prostitutes make good spies and meet with a variety of people who freely gossip to woman they assume will never mix with royalty or pass on information they should not understand themselves."

"And that's what this girl does?"

"Oh yes," Tyballis said, riding through the broken gateway and into the tumbledown and overgrown garden. Weeds knotted the flinted path, and spices mixed their perfumes with those of rotten apples and the first faint corruption of the tanneries brought in on the wind.

At the old front doors, Casper dismounted and grabbed the reins from both Tyballis and Beatrice, leading the horses around to the back where a semblance of old stable shelters remained. "When I comes back," Casper shouted over his shoulder, "I shall see if there be any stuff worth drinkin' left in them kitchens."

"I doubt it," Tyballis called, "and besides, it is far too early," and led Beatrice to the front steps, also overgrown with weed and the first climbing twigs, loops and leaves of ivy.

Less than half an hour ahead, walking steadily, quickly, and with excited determination, Isabella approached the great tenement building where Robert Rudge lived behind his doorless curtain, and was waiting, almost breathless, for the news that would change his life.

Half a mile south and approaching the riverbanks, someone else walked, unseen by most. He watched the waters rise as the rain swept hard and fast, gulls and crows abruptly cutting through the heaving surface, fishing for a hard-won dinner during the winter season. The wandering man, hidden beneath the hood of his oiled cape, had stood for long moments, gazing down at the river's heightening tide, and considering how drowning might feel on such a bitter day, or whether striding out into the countryside might be a less self-pitying escape. He could neither play a musical instrument, sing, or invent false trickeries, but he knew of minstrels making their lives cheerful enough in the freedom of the wild.

CHAPTER FORTY-THREE

With thoughtful generosity, it had stopped raining. The icy wind still sliced between the rooftops and even sent some of the church bells clanking, as though the whole city celebrated the wedding of Louisa Grange to Matthew Attlewood, once known as Doric Fleet, who stood together beneath the porch of Westminster Abbey, facing the smiling bishop in his robes.

Although not expected to attend, his majesty had sent a message of greeting, and the guests in attendance were numerous, although all were squeezing together to avoid the freeze.

Sir John Sudbury remained in custody and his son was lying drunk on the floor of his bedchamber, but his daughter Beatrice stood on the steps of the great Minster, smiling with delight, and stepping constantly closer to the young woman Eva, who appeared to be edging closer to Beatrice at exactly the same time.

Lord and Lady Leys stood directly behind the bride, supporting between them the Lady Alice Hylton, looking glorious in cream silk, but who was trembling both from the bitter cold and from the weakness of her legs. Francis, heir to the Earldom of Hylton, braced himself behind Doric, beaming with unreserved pleasure.

Standing a little further back and nearly swept sideways by the gale, Isabella, her new husband Robert and their daughter Gisella stood, somewhat huddled together, Annie Smithson hanging on beside them all. The entire household of Hylton House, even the gardener, formed a virtually solid wall at the back. Gisella, who had never known the exact day of her birth, had now been informed that she would be nine years old on the second day of February the following year, since this was a day which Isabella remembered very well indeed.

Wearing the first brand new gown of her life, Gisella stood grinning at the first marriage ceremony she had ever attended and rested warm between the hugs of her newly discovered mother and father, the first parents she had ever known in her life. She hadn't washed a dish or cup in days, had not even made her own bed, but had actually slept in real bed for the first time in her life, since previously she only ever slept on a straw pallet on the floor. She was indeed one of the many experiencing an exciting new beginning which she had never before contemplated.

Since the number of enthusiastic guests was unusually large, even during such inclement weather, and being St. Stephen's Day and the first of the Christmas season, other surprisingly elegant strangers were pushing forwards through the crowd.

But Doric saw only Louisa, and Louisa saw only her husband as they gazed into each other's eyes, listening to the bishop as he announced their union. They held hands as instructed, and then Doric leaned forwards and kissed his new wife very briefly on the lips.

Then, followed by their guests, only too eager to escape from the gales, entered the abbey and approached the pulpit where the bishop would give them God's blessing and wish them the great happiness they knew they were about to experience.

The bishop raised the cross, each of the guests repeated the words, and Louisa felt a surge of excitement that flew in winged circles inside her head. She wondered if Doric was feeling anything similar and peeped sideways. Then Louisa met Doric's eyes, knowing immediately that his deep delight was exactly the same as hers.

On the other side of London and outside the city walls, two miles from the wedding taking place that day in Westminster, a young man wandered without specific direction.

Charles had been to the tanneries before but had never intended to return. The place was vile. But the threat of arrest and execution created such crazed and irreversible necessities. With the first threat, he had thought to return to the old and ugly remains of his birth home. It held wretched, even horrifying memories, but his own safety was more important than a few past events which he hoped to banish. He was well aware that such a hideaway was known now and would not keep him safe.

His own home in The Strand was even less secure, having no secret tunnel nor attic. The attics were crammed with the staff's quarters, and a secret tunnel had never been dug. His few friends would quickly desert him and expose his place if he asked any if them for assistance.

He believed the tanneries to be the foulest place within reach, and so somewhere that respectable folk did not go. It was the least likely area for a lord of the land to hide himself. With bitter regret and bubbling anger, Charles walked the back streets and had already slept many nights in the huts where the hides were scraped, the leathers were stacked, and the oozing rubbish was collected.

He did not remember the exact position of the ale house where he had come before to flush out his little brother to avoid scandal to his name, and where he had later managed to return in order to grab the girl that had seduced the boy, and haul her off to her own execution.

And yet now he faced the same himself, except that it seemed so absurd to him, that surely that unforgivable humiliation could never occur.

Charles accepted that he would have to divert eventually to the countryside. He could not imagine himself sleeping under trees or in some farm's cow sheds. His fury grew but had no opening for relief, nor tinder box to light the explosion. Instead he wandered, aimless or turbulent, but always shivering with cold.

His horse was long gone. Sold for a miserable price, but at least bringing him sufficient for food and ale, one night spent in an inn and another in the straw above the stables where now his own horse cheerfully browsed. He had eaten well for many days, had twice stolen food, and had helped himself to what he discovered in the kitchens of some old and dilapidated house on the tannery outskirts. There were tenements too, but here, disgusting as the rooms all were, the inhabitants were even more disgusting, and knowing him to be no paying inhabitant since his clothes, although in poor condition, were far too grand and far too hungry for status, Charles was almost immediately kicked down the stairs, punched and thrown back into the rain.

But the once grand old house closer to the city wall was considerably less violent and more accommodating to strangers. Although from the outside it appeared utterly ruined, within the walls there were empty bedchambers, some with beds, pillows, blankets, even chamber pots, tallow candles and old unwashed cups. This was where he found the kitchen and food, though stale, remained apparently edible.

For three days Charles stayed in the old house, choosing for himself a genuine bedchamber, unclean but sheltered. The mattress was comfortable enough and he ignored the urine stains on both the coarse linen sheet and the wedge of mattress beneath. He remained dressed at night, pulling the two blankets around himself, and using a bolster instead of the pillow which still appeared wet with dribble. At first sleeping day and night, he summoned the energy to explore the house and its grounds and found only three other occupants, although there was space for more.

One was a young woman, presumably a whore. Another, sleeping in an annex outside the great hall, was an old man who seemed permanently bad tempered, but unable to speak clearly. He had perhaps recently suffered a stroke of the heart and could not easily move.

The third was a tanner who came looking for the whore. This man stared at Charles, seeming to recognise him. But nothing was said, the tanner left the following morning, while both the girl and the old man ignored him.

After four days of the greatest comfort he had experienced since being forced to abandon his own home, Charles faced the arrival of the same tanner, who had reappeared.

His thumb pointing to the old broken staircase, Charles had said, "She's upstairs, I believe. The usual room."

But the tanner, carrying the tools of his trade, brought out a short-handled rake in one hand and a knife in the other. Charles stared.

"Who are you?" he demanded. "You are entirely unknown to me, and if this is intended as a threat, I should point out that I am a lord of the land, the Earl of – great title."

"Maybe you is and maybe you ain't," the tanner said, his forked scraper upraised. "But I surely knows yer face, mister. You is the bastard what tried to beat up Annie the brewster. And I heard as how you took Annie's lass Joletta what has never come back."

"Rubbish," Charles said, pushing past the other man. "I have no idea what on earth you're talking about. I know none of these people, nor anyone else in this foul place."

"Then wot's you doing 'ere?" the tanner demanded.

Charles once again pushed the man aside and strode to the door. "This old house," he exclaimed, hoping the lie would not be easily disproved, "was originally owned by my dear father, the earl. Now after his sad death, it is my property. I came here to see what could be done with it. To decide whether or not it is worth redeveloping."

The tanner wasn't sure, and hesitated. He gripped the handles of both scourer and knife, but raised neither. "Where's Eva? Reckon she'll know wot's the truth."

Charles reached for the door handle, escape one breath away. "I told you, fellow. Upstairs."

With one foot already out into the rain, Charles felt the horribly painful and utterly deafening crash against the back of his head, and fell forwards onto the from step. Its jagged broken tiles ripped into his cheeks and he lost coherence. His previous wounds had been healing slowly and now he felt his skull cracked and his cheek bleeding. From the puddled he stared up. Over him stood the nameless old man. He held a copper saucepan, and appeared ready to swing it again.

The man spluttered but his words were difficult to understand. "Bloody worm-shit humbaloo pig headed pickle booshickle whubbin," said the old man, tottering with the weight of the saucepan he carried. "Andrew tis, biggun lord wot he is now, Cobam tis, not yourn. Ridly-buggering liar you is, mister. So piss off."

"Seems you's a bastard liar," the tanner grinned, helping to hold the old man upright. "So I reckon you'd best do as this gent says, and bugger off. Otherwise I gonna tell me mates in the tanneries wot I done found, being the gent as tried ter do in little Annie at the ale shop, and her lass Joletta and all. Come ter fink of it, they's both gorn last time I were there. So wots you done wiv 'em?"

Charles had gone. He did not know where he was going, but he ran from the open swamp of the surrounding garden and into the shadows beyond.

Since then he had slept badly, sharing sheds with chickens, buckets of lime and once in the part sheltered gutter outside a storeroom. So three more nights frozen and miserable as he ate almost nothing, but nurtured his simmering fury. When he woke from another gutter, and heard two women singing, he realised it was the first day of Christmas, sixth of December, and yet while others celebrated, he would be sobbing inwardly with hunger, his stomach churning, and his temper exacerbated with the knowledge that his last penny was gone.

Others joined the singing women, holding hands and weaving between the soaking pits. Men looked up and clapped.

Five women now, of every age, holding out their hands for more to join. There was no music, but the women remembered words and melody and sang, while apprentices ran, grinning, joined to clasp hands, and danced around the pits, through the back lanes, past the sheds and back to the open square.

"Tis St. Stephen's day," one man called, "bless him, and Christmas is come again."

"Tis the day me wife starts the puddin'," another shouted, "wot's the best feast o' the year."

The young girl at the end of the line held out her hand to Charles. "Come join us, mister."

But he scowled and turned away. That others dared be happy when he was bitterly miserable, infuriated Charles more. An older man grabbed the girl's hand. "You got yer Pa instead, lass. Come, dance away."

Skipping, hopping, a small boy with a smile that almost split his face as he was bouncing, while the line joined other lines and the tanneries leapt from stench to glowing delight.

"Tis me daughter does the cooking in my tenement," another man shouted as he emptied two buckets into an empty pit. "Mince pies it is, every blessed year, and me lass minces the mutton wiv a proper grinder, she does, and puts in them raisins too, wot we bin saving all year. A little o' wot she calls spice, and we has the best mince pies in the country."

"Can't be better'n mine," yelled one old woman, waving her arms as she joined the dance.

Two miles away on the western side, the wedding had continued, and after the blessing within the abbey, Louisa and Doric were entwined and their guests were clapping.

Outside, although skirts and capes were slapping against their owners, against each other and against the abbey walls while the wind gathered even greater strength, everyone talked at the same moment, and the bishop held up his cross with a beaming smile, Isabella, Robert and Annie cheered, and Louisa, once released from Doric's arms, was laughing that she had not even truly married the man she loved, since it was Doric she adored, and not the unknown Matthew Attlewood, whom she imagined was a respectable goldsmith somewhere, or a scullery boy in some grand house, or perhaps even the grosser of fruit and cabbages in some far off market.

"And," she said, "I do not care who he is, for I've married a wandering minstrel with the most beautiful voice in all England, who writes the most beautiful music and is the most beautiful player of the lute, and we'll live forever with my daft little brother in his nice big house, which is sort of mine too, and make sure he doesn't fall in love himself with anyone unsuitable."

"Too late now, of course," Doric whispered to her, "but you do realise I hope, my love, that I am as unsuitable a husband for you as anyone could possibly be for Francis."

"You, my beloved," Louisa whispered back, "are as suitable as a king. I am the luckiest creature in the world. Of course, I should love to meet your family one day, if they are still alive. In the meantime, I love only this eccentric, the unsuitable and the penniless minstrel of heavenly music."

"I do believe," Tyballis interrupted them, "that all your friends are trying to catch your attention? You have the whole night to indulge your own dreams, you know. First you must sacrifice yourself to your demanding visitors."

"And your mother, my dear," Andrew added, "is entirely exhausted. There is a litter here waiting to carry her back to The Strand, but I feel she should be sitting in it at the earliest opportunity."

Louisa hugged him and ran to hug her mother. Alice virtually sank into her arms, and Doric stepped behind, taking her shoulders and helping her into the small wooden litter with its deeply cushioned interior, while watching the young mare pulling it, who was drinking from the puddles but snorted, clearly growing impatient.

The newly wedded couple thanked and paid the bishop, then turned back to their crowd of friends.

"Oh, all you lovely people," declared Louisa with a slightly tipsy delight, "the party is waiting back at The Strand. Come on, everyone, it must be past midday."

The Hylton House was lit like the Abbey of Westminster on Christmas Eve and doors now stood wide as the staff rushed in to begin preparing the feast, platters steaming and mince pies in their hundreds, with a good deal of the food set by for themselves. It was while the guests were seated at the long table, each chair pulled out by a page with mumbles of 'My lord. My lady.', that Doric looked up and saw someone talking to Andrew at the far end of the hall.

His face seemed to drain of colour, and he clutched at Louisa's hand as she moved beside him.

❦

Having just slipped past midday even on this day early in December, Charles had sunk down on the riverbank. His cape protected his hose from the wet grass and its slope towards the tide, but the mud still welled up and he was irritated, presuming his cape would be ruined. Although no doubt there were wash houses in the vicinity, he had neither money to pay, nor anything else to barter, except his father's ring. He had taken this long ago when he'd killed the old man, and knew it was valuable. Whatever it brought, should, he believed, be enough for a month or more of comfortable living, even if he received less than its true cost, being heavy gold and inset with a huge square sapphire. Not the most precious of jewels, but precious enough. Yet selling such an item in the slums of the tannery would be absurd. He could not, however, risk re-entering London or march to the goldsmiths of The Row, where he could sell at a fair price but would be seen and recognised too easily.

If, he decided, he had the time and energy to make his way north to one of the lesser cities, there would be a market for such valuable items, and a fair price offered. Walking north might take weeks, however, and in the meantime, he had nothing to eat. Charles wondered, with acute pain and even greater anger, if he might find paid work. But what he might be capable of doing was not easy to comprehend. The thought of working disgusted him, but the thought of starvation seemed still worse.

And then he looked up. A crowd of men was approaching and every one of them was armed with a knife, a hammer or a tool of some kind. They came from the tanneries.

It was as Charles, alarmed, stepped backwards, that two miles west, Doric stepped forwards, unsure. A tall man smiled, the soft dimples of his cheeks crinkling. But beside him a woman stretched out both arms and hurried towards him. The tall man followed, then two others, the elder so alike to Doric that no confusion remained possible. The woman wore the scarlet velvet that a mother of the bridegroom should wear, and it was the white frilled neck of her shift which scratched against Doric's hands as she hugged him.

"We were becoming worried," she whispered.

"Years of accepted seclusion," the tall man said, "so, yes. But not a silent order. Yet when we contacted the monastery they refused to explain."

Excited at his side, Louisa was kissing every cheek she could reach, while Doric's smile was slow as it crept from the corners of his mouth and up to his eyes.

CHAPTER FORTY-FOUR

The blackness was star sprigged and beneath a tester of dark silk, embroidered with stars, Louisa and Doric lay in each other's arms.

"An amazing surprise to me," Louisa murmured. "And an even greater surprise to you, my love."

"Twelve years since I escaped the monastery," Doric sighed, his fingers in his bride's loose curls. "But I hadn't seen a single member of my family for years before that. Four years in the monastery so sixteen years – I expect they thought me dead. Almost, during those first years, I was."

Louisa had never seen a man naked since her little brother grew too old for nethercloths. The fire had been lit in the bedchamber, flaring up into huge golden fingers, spirals of pale smoke and the spit of the heat over the scatter of coke. The whole room was warm and neither Doric nor Louisa pulled up the eiderdown, lying openly on the covers.

"Your mother," Louisa said, "was so delightful. She didn't want to let you go. And I loved your oldest brother."

"James. Yes." Doric gazed into the red glint of the fire dancing in her eyes. "It was father who sent me to the monastery of course. The third son, always meant for the church."

"But they could never have known what happened in that monastery. And now you can see them all whenever you wish. Often, I hope."

"When I'm not lying in bed and singing to you."

Louisa's arms were both around his waist and her hands tingled where they slipped across the warmth of his bare skin. "You're not a wandering minstrel anymore my darling. You're Matthew, third son of a great lord. Baron Frampton."

"That doesn't give me a title, my love. I'm still a nobody." For a moment he gazed over her shoulder and into the fire where the movement of flame and the scarlet playing in the clumped black coke below, seemed to tell stories, and the old predictions he had once seen for others, now appeared suddenly for himself. "Can I tell you," he asked softly, "that in a year we'll have a baby daughter."

Louisa blinked. "My mother will adore that, almost as much as I will."

He pulled her closer, discovering the pressure of her breasts against his chest, the heat of skin to his and the sensation of her hardening nipples like tiny buds in spring. He kissed her and tasted the excitement, his hands on her belly, the exploration of the soft rise and the dip of her navel, and then the slight tickle where tight curls snuggled down between her thighs.

In the tanneries, the sky blew off its clouds and the first crescent of the Christmas moon shone silver over the eastern horizon. Being Saturday evening, the tanners had gathered up their tools, closing ready for the Sunday service at the Church of St. Osman. But an older man had brought news and reported that something of great importance needed to be done before anyone went home to supper and bed.

The bitter night wind was squealing up the river from the ocean, but the gulls had settled for the night, the crows and ravens were back in the warmth of the roost and the first owl swept from the thatch over the long shed sheltering the partly cleaned hides, and disappeared into the moonshine like a silent silver ghost returning to its silver mother.

From the belfry tower of St. Osman's, the bats flew together like one massive chittering shadow, black on black. One of the tanners ducked, fearing a bad omen. But his companion mumbled back, "It ain't them little creatures we gotta fear, Ned. Tis this fellow we's staring at here, for he's the killer and a right wicked omen and all. And I reckon this time the bugger won't get away."

"This is the one wot took the lass Joletta?" the other asked.

Someone else muttered, "Not just took away, I reckon. fer I seen Annie in tears wot she couldn't control, poor lass. Dripped them tears into the ale, she did. Were told her girl bin hung on the gibbet outta town and left to die."

"By this bastard here?"

"This be him," one of the tanners yelled. "I seen him beat Annie, and I seen him grab the girl an' all."

"Then we grab him," another shouted, pushing forwards.

Louisa hadn't yet dared to explore her husband. Her arms were around his back, her mouth to his, drinking in the smothering heat and the rich wine flavoured intoxication of his breath. His lips were hard, and his tongue was dancing with her own, as though he wanted to absorb her into himself. She wondered if that was possible, and if that was how people made love.

Having thrilled to his story of them creating a daughter between them, she could now imagine herself merging into him, and, gasping as Doric released her, tried to kiss him back. He swung to face her again and kissed first her eyes, her ears, and once more her mouth. The glorious swell of her breasts against him was a delight that sprang straight to his groin, and his fingers followed the road to delight, sliding from her waist to her hips and down to her thighs. Very gently he pulled her legs apart.

⋈

Charles glared at the crowd standing, hesitating before him. At his back the road wound between the stinking stone pits but offered a possible escape. He waited. One of the men roared, "He's a killer. Get him."

They moved forwards, first tentative, then raising the tools they carried, and strode faster. Immediately Charles turned and ran. He dodged between the pits and raced back towards the city wall. For the first time the stench did not make him vomit, nor even enter his thoughts. But he quickly realised that the city gates would be locked, and he might be cornered and trapped with the vast Roman stones solid at his back.

He veered, dodging back south towards the great curve of the river where the docks would also be closed, but offer places to hide where the stampeding tanners would be reluctant to go. Charles had never before been to the docks, disinterested in trade or ships, travel or fishing. St. Katherine's Docks were upstream beside the Tower menagerie, but there were others, Charles knew, and even the possibility of grabbing a rowing boat, not that he had ever rowed anything in his life. But the thundering echo of boots and clogs was close, deafening in the greater silence of the night beyond, and Charles saw the riverbank, no docks as yet, not even a warehouse to hide him,

For a moment he was hidden as he ducked behind the machine which hauled crates from the ships' decks, and flattened himself on the mud beyond then slipping into the wet slush beneath the legs of the pier. Two wherries were roped there, and Charles saw his triumph waiting silently and close.

He heard the tramping and shouting, saw the booted feet of one man rush past. He did not dare move, although he breathed in water. South of the tanneries now, the stench was faint, but the smell of the river seemed nearly as rancid. He inched backwards, sufficient simply to recover breath, but someone whooped.

"The bastard's hiding under there. Haul him out by the feet."

"Or push him in further."

"No, reckon I got a better idea."

❧❧

Doric's palm held to the silk of Louisa's inner thigh, touching where her skin felt so smooth he knew it as virginal as a baby's cheek. And as his fingers moved, he kissed her nipple, his mouth surrounding it, his teeth closing gently and pulling, as if discovering a sweetness he had never known before.

She whispered, "What you do makes me sing inside. So you're still making music."

He laughed, looking up. "You are my music, little one."

"So make me sing again."

The fire crackled, burning low. The shutters were closed, but they heard the rattle of the window outside. Doric swept one hand down her back from shoulders to waist. "You're cold. Just a little, I think."

She had no time to deny it, and he rolled over, stood beside the bed and burying his hands beneath her, he carried her up, kissed the very tip of her nose, smiling, and brought her to the thick rug which covered the floorboards before the hearth. Then, as he bent, he pulled off the eiderdown from the bed and laid it beneath her.

She shivered, then smiled, delighted at the warmth of the fire so much closer. So she laid back as she had done on the bed, watching while he gathered up two of the pillows, pushing one beneath her head. And kneeling beside her, he once again separated her legs and kissed her belly, one hand exploring downwards, the fingers twisting into the thick curls almost beneath his face.

Once she had expected to be embarrassed seeing his nakedness while naked herself. Yet now, with the loving so slow and so sweet, she felt part of him, and relished whatever he did. She told him, "You smell like excitement. It's not the fire. It's really you."

336

"It's the smell of sex," he told her. "It's the glorious preparation as your body swears it wants me, and my body proves that it wants you."

"How do you prove it?" she whispered. "Just that special smell?"

"No," he murmured back, "there's a greater proof than that. Give me your hand, my beloved. Now, here."

⨳

Charles felt the grasp of two hard palmed hands on each of his ankles. Too strongly held to twist or pull away, he tried to lift himself onto his knees, but was suddenly dragged and could do nothing but shriek. At first his nose, hoisted backwards through the mud, was filled with dark wet suction. He could not breathe, then turned his head to the side and spat out the sludge from his mouth. Attempting to raise his hands and clear his nose, he found that instead his arms were incapable of control and foundered, knuckles on the cobbles and bleeding, the mud still smothering his face, Snorting, he cleared some, then screamed again, shrill and fervent.

The men had him and did not let him go. Holding his ankles firm, they laughed, trudging back into the heart of the tanneries, dragging Charles along the ground behind them. The ground, hard beaten earth, was wet and filthy but now not mud, instead the nauseating shit of dead animals, the growing stench of piss, lime, the fats and skins of stacked corpses, and the smell of the men themselves. As his skull bounced his hair collected the muck through which he was pulled. His head cracked against the side of one of the pits and Charles knew exactly where they had brought him.

"Release me," he shouted, his voice ragged, but the men were talking and laughing together and heard nothing except each other. They did release him, dumping him in a heap beside one of the pits, when he thought himself near death. Scrambling to his knees and then falling backwards in pain, he finally managed to sit. Entirely surrounded, he saw no avenue of escape but shouted up at the man standing closest.

"I am a lord of great fame," he stuttered, now unable to speak clearly unless keeping his voice low. He sounded more as though he whined, and the tanners laughed at him, raucous and insulting.

"You's a bloody killer, and I reckon a coward at that," the man cackled. "You kills females, doesn't you, no fighting wiv no man as strong nor stronger. But grabs them women wot can't bash you back."

"I – I was a hero in the Buckingham rebellion," Charles insisted. "I was knighted for my – heroism as I fought beside the king."

"I doesn't believe a word of it," someone else strode over, leaned down, and shouted as loud as a falling tree directly into his ear. Charles fell back again, his head against the wall of a lime pit. The stench seemed to pierce him, and he heaved, holding his stomach.

"Thirsty is you, poor fellow?" asked another of the tanners, and leaned over the side of the pit, pulling up a great metal spoonful of the liquid within. "Now, lad," the tanner roared at him, belly laughing, "this be the best drink you ever had. Tis a little stale and needs a wash-out, I reckon, and will be emptied maybe as the working week starts on Monday. For them first skins of them old cows what can't give milk no more, they bin soaking here for a week past. First we pours in the lime, then the water from the nearest well, and then four buckets of piss. Then wop, in goes them hides of the cattle, but they already bin scraped wiv shit, wot gets off the worst o' the fatty grease, it do, though there be some left like always. Brains an' all, being o' the sheep gone fer mutton and then fer sheepskin, And brains is good fer scrubbin'. Well, them skins is gone out now, ready fer a mighty good wash. But this pit be ready fer a tasty drink, I reckon, and better than any wine you velvety buggers likes to bizzle."

And he held the vast spoonful close under Charles' nose, His head swam and he thought he would faint. He hoped it would be his escape, temporary if not permanent.

Another of the tanners came behind him, sitting him forward, form and straight. Then, looking over, the tanner grabbed Charles' chin and forced open his mouth, fingers rigid on the lips now wrenched apart.

The other man with the spoon, spilling trickles down Charles' doublet, rammed the front of the spoon down his throat. Charles coughed, spluttered, but without escape, he drank. The cold swill slithered across his tongue as if it searched for its own path, the slime, so thick in ribbons it felt like swallowing worms, coated his tongue, his teeth and the inside of his mouth, gums and throat, as if carefully leaving the agony of its taste from his lips to his stomach.

Charles vomited down his own chin and chest, but he could still taste what he had drunk.

❋

Doric lay beside Louisa in front of the fire, the pillows and the feather softness of the eiderdown beneath them, the dying flames reflected not only in their eyes but in the glisten of their skin, naked in each other's embrace.

He whispered words she had never heard before as he told her, smiling and kissing her between words, what he would do, and what she would feel and how he would feel as he did it.

"They say, my beloved, that a virgin feels pain – here – when it is the very first time. I've never made love to a virgin before. But I swear I will be as careful and as gentle and as understanding as I can be. For I won't feel pain of any kind. Does that seem unfair? I will feel a miracle unknown to me before, because I've made love but never to a woman I truly loved. But if I hurt you too much, tell me, and I'll stop."

"Nothing hurts at all," she whispered back. "I feel wonderful."

He kissed her ear lobe, but his fingers were tracing the flesh at the top of her thighs. "Soon, my beautiful beloved." And then he paused, kissed her and finally touching her more intimately as she gasped and clung to him. Then, discovering courage, she pushed her own fingers down, touching him and wondering, not sure what she held.

Doric rolled her over so that her face was cradled by the billows of the eiderdown, and he caressed her hair back from her eyes as he moved his hand lightly down her back, across the tiny bumps of her spine, and over the double swell of her buttocks. Peeping up, Louisa watched him, his eyes now on her body and his lids lowered, heavy with something that seemed like hunger. Then she felt him lean over her more fully, and his mouth traced her from the back of her neck, which made her tingle, down her shoulder blade to the dip beneath her arm, then to the back of her ribs and waist until finally he kissed her hard across each of her buttocks, his hands keeping her still, until he released her, rolling her back to face him.

"My sweet beloved," he murmured. "I cannot wait any longer. If I hurt you, tell me and I will try to stop. But now you are utterly irresistible."

And he moved on top of her, while she loved the weight of him pressing across her.

※◇※

Charles cried, staring down at the muck spreading from his own mouth across his clothes below. The stench of the tanneries swilled around his head, mixing with the stench of his vomit and of the unbelievable filth still remaining in his throat and between his teeth.

Unable to stand, surrounded by the men as furious as he was, but them with the freedom to attack, and he with the lack of it. He tried again to clear his throat.

"Alright," he spat. "I'll not deny it. But I only protected my little brother. He was – innocent. The girl was a whore. She trapped him, well nigh raped him. He's a baby, never did a thing. I – rescued him – is all. The slut never loved him. Never cared for him. Tricked my boy."

One of the tanners bent down very close to Charles, almost nose to nose. "And you'll kill a lass for that. Joletta, I knew her, she worked her heart out, poor child, and tried to keep her mother fed too. What's wrong with a girl out to catch a rich husband, then? Ain't that what you folks do all the time, and don't hide it. Arranged marriages, they calls it. Well, the poor lass tried to arrange her own, and no doubt would've made a good job of it. But you, you slime-prick-bastard, you swung that poor lass up on the gibbet, without the law nor justice at your side."

Too angry to feel hopeless, Charles spat in the tanner's eye, but the tanner wiped the spit from his face and with one finger, smeared it over Charles' wide forehead. "You angry, is you, lad?" he laughed. "Well, you'll have no energy for that soon enough." And he nodded at the other man still standing behind Charles, both arms beneath his, but avoiding the thick stains of vomit.

Between them, the two tanners hauled Charles up and sat him on the edge of the great stinking pit from which he had been forced to drink. Again Charles screamed. The other tanners crowded around, waving their arms and shouting as to whether Charles had ever experienced such a bath, whether he had recently bathed at all, and whether he wanted first to piss in the pit of lime and piss. Charles was still screaming.

"I reckons the water'll be a mite chilly, but I doesn't wager you'll be feelin' cold fer too long," one of the men called.

"But don't you go sucking on them bits o' skin and fat left from them hides," another grinned. "Not a right good supper, I reckon."

"Does you swim, lad?" asked a third. "Be good fun, I'd say."

With his arms once more wrapped around her, Doric carried Louisa to the bed, and swept the eiderdown over her nakedness. Piling the pillows behind her, he kissed her again, and slipping down beneath the blankets, he laid his head across her breasts.

"Not tired, my little one? Did I hurt you? That will never happen again. Oh indeed, the loving, yes. But not the pain."

She smiled down at him. "It wasn't pain. Just a tiny shock. Sore now, but only a little. The pleasure – was – amazing."

"I promise to make it even more beautiful for you."

"And teach me how to make it better for you."

He kissed her eyes. "There is no better. Some parts of your body are velvet and some are silk. I have no words to imagine – better."

"Like playing the lute?" she asked him.

Doric said exactly what she had expected him to say. "Oh no, far better than that."

CHAPTER FORTY-FIVE

With his feet suddenly hoisted high, Charles was flung backwards and hurtled into the pit, where he struggled and flailed, his arms above the surface but the remainder of his body below. The weight of his boots pulled him down and the liquid that held him was thick and dense with its filth.

Moments later, he forced his head upwards, gasping for air. His feet could find no base for the pit was far deeper than it had seemed, having been dug far into the ground below.

Desperate, arm over arm, Charles swam to the far side, grabbing at the low rocky wall. Within sight and then within reach, he stretched out to the stone. He had drunk a great deal more of the liquid contained there, but desperation had overcome disgust. The last kick brought him safety of a sort and he rolled from the pit to its surrounding wall, toppled over it and back to the ground, and stood, shivering. He stared back over the width of his near death, and glared at the tanners smirking now at some distance.

His seething anger turned to bilious horror and then back to fury. He coughed up mouthfuls of vomit and filth, mud and many different gulps of slime, still glowering back across the flat dark waters.

"Fools," he yelled, "as stupid as your jobs, always allotted to the stupid and the ignorant," and he spun around and immediately ran.

He ran into the next crowd of tanners. With a sudden punch to the nose from two of the men, Charles stumbled back. "Nasty little bugger," one man called, staring down from his great height. "Wot you doing, jumping in them pits. It ain't healthy."

'We slung the bastard in there," the original leader of the tanners called across the pit. "That fellow is filth, so we tossed him into the filth what fits him."

"He's the cruel shit wot tried to beat poor Annie from the ale shop. And then he strung up her daughter."

"Ah," said the virtual giant, looming over him, "you's a cruel gent, right? And a cruel bustard should get a cruel death, don't you reckon?"

Not knowing how to answer, Charles backed. His nose was bleeding, and his body reeked, wracked with bruises and pain. He simply shook his head. His hair was sodden with lime and piss, and it poured from his head over his shoulders. Not daring to antagonise, he could only plead, although he had never himself released any creature who had pleaded with him. Finally he said, "Please."

"Please, no, fellow," chortled the giant, "none o' them. I reckon tis 'seize' wot's the better word right now." And with huge hands and the strength of an ox, he lifted Charles beneath the arms and threw him once more into the pit.

Weaker now, and desperate, Charles found that his clothes, being soaked already with the muck of the pit, held him down. Their weight doubled his own and he sank. The battle for air was beyond him and instead he breathed piss and lime, and was poisoned. Twisting below the surface, Charles spread only bubbles and sluggish waves, as both hands, protruding upwards, grasped for the nothingness floating in the cold night above.

He sank further. His hands disappeared, now just a faint shadow unmoving in the depths. The thick cold slapped against his eyes, leaking through the lid to the pupil within. Charles saw nothing but felt everything as his lungs closed, squeezing against the muck that oozed into them.

Twice there was a murmur of reawakening, as though the dying man's lungs discovered air. But there was neither air nor the hope of it and the body sank out of sight to the bottom of the pit.

It was the following Monday when the tanneries buzzed back to work and the lime pits were emptied and refilled ready with clean water. The slump of dead flesh lying on the stone base of one pit, was discovered with shock and surprise by other workers, setting to clean and scrub. Horrified, several men dragged the body onto dry ground, and although the many hours amongst such debris had left the face and hands eaten by lime and left unrecognisable, the value of the clothes, even though now ruined, and above all the ring on his left hand, told their own story.

The sheriff was called. Charles was now unrecognisable, and the ring had suddenly disappeared, but sufficient description of the clothes enabled identification, and the family were informed.

Hearing the details, Annie smiled secretly to herself.

It was only Alice who cried.

EPILOGUE

The Lords, sitting beneath the spangled ceiling of the great Star Chamber, and the Commons equally studious at the Chapter House, were called to the first official Parliament of his majesty's reign. The king, with the co-operation of his personal council, presented the bills nearest to his heart, which he had been preparing for some months. So the royal wishes gradually became statute, and statute gradually became accepted. The first concept of blind justice was introduced, where, as Richard had sworn in his coronation oath, every man, regardless of wealth or status, should have an equal right to the law under the law. The anomaly, much used and abused in the past, whereby a man could sell land or property to several different buyers each in ignorance of the other, was outlawed. The means for the ready corruption of judges, magistrates and jurors was blocked, and the manner of a jury's election was strictly redefined. The allowance of bail was outlined and enforced for those crimes considered either insignificant or maliciously cited. The manner by which in the past the Woodvilles had seized the property of those accused, indeed often accused by themselves, not to be returned even after the litigation was proved false and the prisoner discovered innocent, was utterly banned, with no confiscation of any goods to be permitted under any circumstances until after a guilty verdict was honestly reached by the courts. Finally, the system of benevolences, so popular with the late king by which he had readily taxed his people beyond their means, was labelled iniquitous and abolished. So justice spread and the common people, the new burgeoning middle classes and the merchants, grew to respect and were grateful to their magnanimous king. But those many who had benefited from previous corruption and easily manipulated regulations, deeply resented the them.

Since the Buckingham rebellion and his temporary distrust of the lords of the south, Richard now gave greater power and position to the northern lords whom he had previously befriended, so further southern resentments simmered like fritters in hot oil.

Now re-instigating previously abandoned negotiations, the king wrote personally to his late brother's wife, still in sanctuary within the large house beside Westminster Abbey with her daughters. He promised to forgive and protect the woman who had plotted so tirelessly against him. He promised to supply her with a reasonable pension, a comfortable home away from London in the care of one of his personal and most trusted servants, and to ensure her daughter's dowries, seeking decent husbands for them all, and treating them respectfully as his own kinswomen. The lady finally accepted.

"Well now," said Francis, "the harridan has admitted defeat at last. So how much is our beloved majesty throwing into her ample lap as a bribe?"

"He's promised her a yearly pension of seven hundred marks," nodded Doric. "That's a fairly generous sum, but for a woman who was known as the greediest, most avaricious in the land, it's a pittance. She must have finally realised she had nothing left to bargain with."

"Who cares," Louisa grinned. "I couldn't care less about money. I'm as happy as a spider in her own cobweb."

"Not sure I want to be married to a spider," said Doric, patting her knee. "Think of something else, my love."

"Alright. As happy as a frog in a pond."

"I surrender," Doric told her.

But Francis, feet up on the grate that ringed the hearth, and in danger of burning the soles as the flames spluttered and coughed, was clapping his hands. "You can all be frogs as far as I care," He said. "I'm a lord. Me! Little baby me who never even saw what a golden sovereign looked like before. I have a house and lots of money. Isn't that crazy? I'm richer than the old harridan Elizabeth Woodville. And I'd wager I'm a lot nicer too."

"We have certainly all started new lives," murmured Louisa, snuggling against her husband's velvet wedding doublet, which she encouraged him to wear as often as possible.

"I mean, Beatrice," Francis exclaimed. "Rather unexpected. Isabella and that girl of hers. And her husband or brother or lover or whoever he is, he's a nice fellow and he's been repairing the wine cellar. And Mamma, that's the best. It's amazing, isn't it. I liked living with Andrew and Tyballis, but I suppose they're glad to get rid of us all and get their house back for themselves. Meanwhile my house is actually mine and I'm a real Lord. I'm actually a proper earl."

"New lives for us all," Louisa giggled.

"Even the king," Doric said, wrapping his arm around his wife's curled embrace. "His brother died, he was all ready to arrange his nephew's coronation, when up jumps the whole family of Dame Eleanor claiming she was the first and legal wife of the old king. Now the Earl of Shrewsbury wasn't going to stand there in front of the court and clergy and lie about his daughter, was he? I've no idea how some folk argue it was all a fabrication."

"People believe whatever they find more convenient." Louisa was still laughing. "Now I, for instance, believe that my husband is the strongest and finest and most beautiful man in England."

"As a frog," Doric replied, "you may rightly believe so, But meanwhile I am glad that King Richard's wretched summer and autumn are over. What a way to start your sovereignty. But life is calm now, Christmas is here, and blessings on our king. Long may he reign."

ABOUT THE AUTHOR

My passion is for both late English medieval history and Norse legend. These form the background for much of my historical fiction. I also have a love of fantasy and the wild freedom of the imagination, with its haunting threads of sadness and the exploration of evil. Although most of my books have romantic undertones, I would not class them as romances. We all wish to enjoy some romance in our lives, there is also a yearning for adventure, mystery, suspense, friendship and spontaneous experience. My books include all of this and more, but my greatest loves are the beauty of the written word, and the utter fascination of good characterisation. Bringing my characters to life is my principal aim.

For more information on this and other books, or to subscribe for updates, new releases and free downloads, please visit
barbaragaskelldenvil.com

Printed in Great Britain
by Amazon

66506014R00215